Cast No Shadows

E. V. Thompson

A *Time Warner* Paperback

First published in Great Britain in 1997
by Little, Brown and Company
This edition published by Warner Books in 1998
Reprinted 1999
Reprinted by Time Warner Paperbacks in 2002

Copyright © 1997 by E. V. Thompson

The moral right of the author has been asserted.

*All characters in this publication are fictitious
and any resemblance to real persons, living or dead,
is purely coincidental.*

A CIP catalogue record for this book
is available from the British Library

ISBN 0 7515 2243 0

Typeset in Palatino by
Palimpsest Book Production Limited,
Polmont, Stirlingshire
Printed and bound in Great Britain by
Clays Ltd, St Ives plc

Time Warner Paperbacks
An imprint of
Time Warner Books UK
Brettenham House
Lancaster Place
London WC2E 7EN

www.TimeWarnerBooks.co.uk

Cast No Shadows

1

Menacing grey cloud lowered over Dartmoor. It rolled down the rock-strewn slopes of the Beardown tors in a silent, diaphanous avalanche of mist. As it advanced it swallowed giant towers of balancing rocks, filled hollows excavated by long-forgotten generations of grubbing tin miners and spread a cloak of damp anonymity over the moor.

Tacy Elford was acutely aware that the mist was travelling faster than she could walk.

Accompanied by her nine-year-old sister and aided by two dogs, she drove three heavily pregnant ewes ahead of her and could travel no faster. One of the ewes was lame and found it difficult to keep up with the others at their present speed.

'Look over there.' Johanna, unconcerned about the advancing mist, pointed southwestwards. 'It looks as though the prison is an island.'

Tacy looked in the direction indicated by her sister and could see what Johanna meant. The mist was spreading in an uneven pattern over the moor. From the tor behind Dartmoor prison it laid siege to the circular perimeter wall. Gaunt granite prison buildings rose from it, for all the world like grim, man-made islands, protruding from a restless grey sea of mist.

'I'm glad I'm not in there,' said Johanna. Her shiver was due in part to her thoughts, partly as a result of the mist, which had lowered the moorland temperature dramatically. 'Billy said they hang most of the people who are sent to prison. Those who aren't hung are left there to rot.'

'You should know better than to take notice of anything Billy Yates tells you,' retorted Tacy scornfully. 'You start paying attention to what he says and you'll finish up as simple as he is.'

Billy lived with his mother in a cottage on an old mine workings at Whiteworks, in a remote part of the moor. He helped the Elfords on their farm for most of the year, taking peat, farm produce and cooked foods from the farm kitchen in lieu of payment.

'His mother's told him all about prisons. She says he'll likely end up inside one of 'em if he doesn't behave himself.'

'Tillie Yates is almost as simple as Billy,' declared Tacy. 'She probably said it when she was angry with him. If she had more sense she'd realise how much something like that plays on Billy's mind. He'd have had nightmares about it. Poor Billy.'

Urging on the lame ewe, she said, 'Anyway, Dartmoor isn't *that* sort of prison. There are only French soldiers and sailors in there, not criminals. Some of them don't speak English very well, but they're no different to us, really. I should know, I meet them every time I go to the prison market.'

'That doesn't mean you know what they're *really* like,' retorted Johanna. She shivered again, but this time it was due entirely to the mist, which had now caught up with them.

'I want to pee,' she said suddenly.

'We'll be home in half an hour,' said Tacy unsympathetically. 'Wait until then.'

'I can't hold it that long,' wailed Johanna. 'I want to go now.'

Tacy was anxious to get the ewes back to Roundtor Farm before the mist became any more dense. Dartmoor was a dangerous place at such times . . . but Johanna had always been troubled with a weak bladder.

'Hurry up and go then. Over there, among those rocks if you feel shy about going here.'

She pointed to a spot where great granite rocks were scattered about the hillside, their outlines softened by the mist, 'Be quick!'

Johanna needed no urging. She hurried to the rocks and disappeared from view.

Tacy signalled to the dogs, instructing them to hold the sheep where they were. She needed to be firm with the youngest dog, Rip. It was still under training and it was Rosie who brought the sheep to a halt. Crouching low to the ground, the experienced sheepdog dared them to move.

Suddenly there was a scream from the direction of the rocks – and Tacy heard a man's voice. There was another scream and this time it continued for some seconds.

Abandoning the sheep, Tacy ran towards the rocks. As she reached them she bumped into Johanna who was shaking with fright.

Clinging to Tacy, she said, 'There's a man here. A wild man. He's . . . frightening. He spoke to me using strange words that didn't make sense!'

Tacy had a sudden glimmer of understanding. 'How is he dressed?'

'What difference does that make? I think . . . I think it might have been the Devil. Let's go, Tacy. Quickly!'

'What sort of clothes is he wearing?' repeated Tacy.

'He's dressed all in yellow. Do you think it's the Devil, Tacy?' Johanna was still trembling.

'No, I think he's an escaped French prisoner.'

Tacy occasionally took produce to the daily market held inside Dartmoor prison. She knew that prisoners-of-war unable to pay to have new uniforms made, were issued by the prison authorities with uniforms made from yellow material.

At that moment both girls heard a cry, muffled by the thickening mist.

'Which way did he go?' asked Tacy.

'I'm not sure. He ran off that way, I think,' said Johanna, pointing.

'Mudilake Marsh is over there!'

Mudilake Marsh was a large expanse of dangerous marshland. More than one moorland animal had lost its life here.

The cry came again and now it was almost as shrill as Johanna's scream had been.

'He's in the marsh. Come on, Johanna. Stay close behind me.'

'What if he's *not* an escaped prisoner, Tacy? What if it's the Devil, dressed up to look like a prisoner?'

'Don't be so stupid!' Tacy called the words back to her sister who, despite her doubts, was hurrying along behind her.

Tacy's instinct was to run, but that would be fool-hardy. That was what the unknown man had done and Tacy feared he was now trapped in the marsh. If this were so, he would be very lucky to escape with his life.

'Au secours! Au secours!'

The cry came from much closer now and slightly to one side of them.

'What's he saying, Tacy?' Johanna put the question in a fearful voice.

'I don't know . . . shh!'

Tacy stopped. The ground was spongy underfoot. They needed to be careful.

'*Au secours!*' The plea was accompanied by a whole spate of unintelligible words now and it sounded as though the unseen man was sobbing.

The sisters were advancing with the utmost caution when suddenly the swirling mist thinned – and they both saw the man in yellow. Despite being spattered with mud, the attire was clearly that of a prisoner-of-war.

The trapped Frenchman saw them at the same time and his relief was touching. He had sunk up to his ribcage in the mire. Now he held out his arms towards them imploringly, at the same time appealing to them in his own language.

He made an attempt to flounder towards them, but the mud held him fast. His struggles only served to cause him to sink farther into the marsh.

'Stay still!' Tacy called. 'Don't move. Keep your arms spread out on the marsh . . . No! Don't try to reach us!'

It was quite apparent the Frenchman did not understand her. He appealed to her once more, all the time struggling futilely to escape from the unrelenting grip of the marsh.

When she realised he could not understand what she was saying, Tacy turned to Johanna. Eyes wide with fright, the younger girl was still uncertain whether the man caught in the marsh was human or demon.

'Go back to where we left the ewes. Take the dogs and

follow the path down to Two Bridges. If you lose it, send the dogs on and follow where they tread. There'll be someone at the inn. Tell them to come up here as quickly as they can – and they're to bring a rope with them. Hurry now – but don't stray from the path. *Go on!*'

She shouted the last two words as Johanna hesitated, seemingly reluctant to leave her sister alone with this strange-speaking man – if indeed man he was.

The urgency in Tacy's voice got through to Johanna at last. She turned and was quickly swallowed up by the mist.

'Be careful . . . you hear?' Tacy called after her sister before returning her attention to the Frenchman. Despite her warning he was still struggling, snatching at coarse clumps of reedlike grass, only to have them come away in his hand.

The mud and water were enveloping his lower chest now. Tacy called to him yet again. 'Stop struggling, you'll only sink deeper. Spread your arms out and stay still. Like this.' She demonstrated what she wanted him to do. 'Help is coming.'

The Frenchman replied in his own language, clearly pleading with her to help him. He had not understood a word of what she had said. Indeed, he continued doing all she had told him *not* to do.

He was a young man of perhaps twenty-one, no more than three years older than herself. Somehow it made his plight all the more tragic. It seemed to Tacy he was sinking deeper in the mud of the marsh even as she looked at him.

She was not imagining it. No more than five minutes later he had sunk to his armpits – and suddenly he began sobbing.

Tacy found the sound unbearable. 'Please . . . please don't. Just stay still. Help is on the way.'

Her pleas had no more effect than her earlier ones. He realised he was sinking deeper into the Dartmoor marsh by the minute and his panic grew. Tacy stretched out a hand towards him to no avail.

His response was equally futile. The distance between their fingertips was more than two arms' length.

Tacy looked around her in desperation. If only there were a long pole, or the branch of a tree . . . but there was nothing.

Suddenly, she had an inspiration. She was wearing a cloak of brown, blanket-like material. Unfastening the clasp at her neck, she slipped the cloak from her shoulders. Swinging it through the air she aimed one end of it in the Frenchman's direction.

The first cast fell short and she tried again.

This time the long hem at the front of the cloak fell within reach of one of the Frenchman's outstretched hands. He grasped it eagerly.

As the cloak tautened between them, Tacy felt a great sense of achievement . . . but the Frenchman continued pulling. He was desperately trying to use the cloak as a lifeline to pull himself free from the marsh.

Thoroughly alarmed, Tacy cried, 'No! Just keep a grip on it. Use it to keep your head above the marsh. *Don't try to pull yourself out* . . . the cloak's not strong enough . . .'

Unable to understand her, the young Frenchman pulled even harder and Tacy was in danger of tumbling in the marsh herself.

But the cloak was old. It had been handed down to Tacy by her grandmother. Suddenly the strands of the cloth could take the strain no more. They parted. There was no sound of rending cloth. No warning of what was about to happen.

Tacy fell backwards and when she scrambled to her feet she was holding less than half of her cloak. The remainder was still grasped by the Frenchman.

He too had slipped backwards and Tacy saw to her horror that the mire was now above his shoulders.

He opened his mouth and his lips formed the shape of a scream, but only a low, despairing moan escaped. Tacy found this even harder to bear than his earlier cries of terror.

'Don't give up. Stay still. Help is on the way,' she pleaded, even though she knew he could not understand her words. Just saying them made her feel better.

The Frenchman continued moaning, all the time fixing her with a terror-stricken stare that seemed to contain an accusation.

At that moment Tacy thought she heard voices somewhere in the mist.

'Hello! Hello! I'm over here.'

There was no answering call and Tacy believed she must have been mistaken. Then she heard them again. There could be no doubt about it now, but the mist made it difficult to make out the distance or the direction of the voices. She realised it would be equally difficult for them to locate her.

'Hello . . . I'm here.'

She turned to the Frenchman who was now being forced to hold his chin up in order to keep it clear of the mud. 'Do you hear that? Someone's coming. Hold on. I'll just go a little way towards them, otherwise they won't find us.'

She could hear the voices more clearly now and they were calling her name. She ran towards the sound, shouting at the top of her voice.

The rescuers were farther away than she had realised,

but suddenly she ran into them. There were four militia-men and Johanna was with them. One of the men carried a rope.

'Where is he?' said a militiaman who wore sergeant's stripes on his arm.

'He's over here. Come quickly. There's not much time.'

Tacy hurried ahead of them. To her dismay, when she came to the marshy ground she realised it was not the right spot.

'Hello! Where are you?' She called out to the trapped Frenchman. There was no reply.

Frantically, Tacy ran first this way and that, until commonsense told her to stop and think.

After a moment she headed slightly down the slope. When she had taken no more than a dozen paces, she stopped and frowned.

'I thought it was about here . . . Perhaps I'm wrong . . .'

Suddenly, she looked down at her feet. She was almost standing on half of her torn cloak. Looking into the mist that swirled about the marsh, she saw the other half lying on top of the muddy ground.

There was no sign of the French prisoner-of-war.

2

'Prisoners . . . Halt!'

The shouted command from the Somerset Militia
captain prompted a surprised and ragged response
from the two hundred and fifty men marching along
the narrow Devon lane.

'Prisoners . . . Fall out! All right, you can take your
food and rest for a while now.'

'How the hell are we supposed to cook our rations?
Breathe on it?'

The grumbled question came from a giant black
man. Towering head and shoulders above his fellow
prisoners, he wore trousers, a ragged, sleeveless coat
and nothing else.

Barefooted, he left a group of other black men, padded
to the side of the lane and sank down heavily on a
rain-sodden grass bank, along the length of which were
numerous pockets of pale yellow primroses.

'You don't have to worry about cooking anything,'
said one of the militiamen. 'As usual, we've done the
thinking for you. Cooks were sent on ahead. Your

grub's ready and waiting through the gate in the field there. All you have to do is fall into line to collect it, then sit down and enjoy it, courtesy of the English Government.'

The strong, south-westerly wind had been behind the men as they marched. It dropped momentarily now and the pungent aroma of cooking fish reached the nostrils of the prisoners.

'If I wasn't so damned hungry I'd leave it where it is and let you English think how to get rid of a quarter of a ton of stinking fish stew.'

The arms of the speaker bulged with muscle and they also carried an interesting variety of scars, etched by sword and bullet.

'Eat what you can, while you can, Ephraim.'

The suggestion came from Lieutenant Pilgrim Penn. Reaching out, he picked a primrose and examined it closely. The flower reminded him of a garden in Ohio. Of his mother's flower beds. The plants had been nurtured from seeds carried with her in covered wagons on the trek westwards, as his father sought new frontiers.

'You never know, the next meal might be even worse.'

Pilgrim was probably half the age of Ephraim, but his shabby United States Marines uniform bore the insignia of a lieutenant. Ephraim's missing sleeves had carried a corporal's stripes.

'You're right there, Pilgrim. The things these English do with food would choke a hog.'

Captain Virgil Howard sat down heavily on the grass beside the muscled corporal and eased his left leg out in front of him.

'How's the leg standing up to the march?' Pilgrim asked the question anxiously. Although only seven years older than the lieutenant, Virgil was the senior commissioned officer among the American prisoners-of-war. Not only were the two men good friends but, if anything happened to Virgil, responsibility for the well-being of the men would fall upon Pilgrim's shoulders. The authority was more than a nineteen-year-old junior officer should have to assume.

The three men, Pilgrim, Virgil and Ephraim were the only members of the United States fighting forces among the prisoners. The remainder were men of the United States merchant service. All had been taken at sea by the British navy.

The three men had not been the only marines captured when the United States frigate *Delaware* was defeated in battle by two British men-of-war off the coast of Bermuda. However, during numerous changes of ship the Americans had become split up.

The three men had become separated from the last of their colleagues when, despite Virgil's barely healed wound, they escaped from a British man-of-war off one of the West Indian islands.

They were at liberty for only thirty-six hours before being recaptured by a party of British plantation owners.

The escape was the reason why the two officers had been lodged with Ephraim on board the prison hulk *Le Brave* in the Hamoaze, off Plymouth Dock.

It was usual for captured French officers to be offered parole in a small town, at a suitable distance from the coast. But American prisoners-of-war were still a novelty. The British authorities did not seem to know what to do with them.

'You stay here and rest your leg, Virgil. I'll go and fetch your food.'

Pilgrim made his way to the head of the line of men which stretched along the lane and through an open gateway into a nearby field.

Standing at intervals on either side of the lane were armed men of the Somerset Militia. They maintained a close watch on the American prisoners. One of the part-time soldiers moved to challenge Pilgrim, but a sergeant, recognising his rank, intervened and walked with him to ensure he had no more problems.

'Thank you.' Pilgrim acknowledged the militiaman's help. 'I'm fetching two meals. One for my captain. He has a leg wound that's barely healed. This march is hard on him. Do we have much farther to go?'

'About seven miles,' said the sergeant. 'But you'll notice a difference in the countryside from here on. It's moorland, and pretty bleak.'

'This prison we're going to – what's it like?' It was Pilgrim's first opportunity to talk to anyone about their destination.

'Dartmoor?' The militia sergeant shrugged. 'I'd rather be a guard than a prisoner there. They only finished building it about four years ago and I reckon the builders were glad to get away. I doubt if you'll find a bleaker place anywhere. The only time it stops raining is when it snows. Most times you won't know the difference because you can't see anything for mist.'

'It can't be as bad as that, surely?' said Pilgrim, his spirits sinking.

'No? You ask the French prisoners when you reach Dartmoor. There are about nine thousand of 'em. Some have been there since it opened.'

'Nine thousand?' Pilgrim looked at the militia sergeant in disbelief. 'How big is this place?'

'Not big enough for the number of men in there right now,' declared the sergeant. 'But you shouldn't be too badly off. You and your captain will be put in the Petty Officers' Block, I daresay. There's a bit more room there – though not too much.'

Collecting two bowls of fish stew, Pilgrim returned to where Virgil was now sitting alone. He repeated what the militia sergeant had told him.

'Whatever it's like, it can't be worse than life on that stinking hulk,' declared the American marine captain. Taking a spoonful of the soup, he pulled a wry face. 'Ephraim's right about the food. Salt haddock doesn't make a good stew.'

'It's an uppity nigger who'd dare complain about his food,' commented a merchant navy officer sitting nearby. 'Most of those we have down south are only too happy to be given anything at all to eat.'

'We're not "down south" now,' retorted Pilgrim. 'And Ephraim's not an "uppity nigger". He's a corporal of marines, who's earned his rank in battle. He's entitled to good food, same as the rest of us. I, for one, will make damn sure he gets it.'

'I don't care what he's done,' persisted the merchant seaman. 'A spoiled nigger is a dangerous nigger. You'll learn that, one day.'

With this warning, the merchant navy officer rose to his feet and walked away.

Angry by now, Pilgrim would have gone after him but Virgil put a restraining hand on his arm. He inclined his head to where the subject of their exchange was walking towards them.

Ephraim had only just sat down with his bowl of food when the militia officer began shouting for the prisoners-of-war to fall in again to resume the march.

There was much grumbling from the Americans, but the guards moved among them, threatening to use musket butts to add weight to the militia officer's orders.

'You all right?' Pilgrim's anxiety showed once more as Virgil struggled to his feet.

'I'll last another seven miles,' said the captain, gritting his teeth. 'Come on, let's fall in with the others.'

The militia sergeant had been right about the nature of the countryside through which they were soon marching. The narrow lane climbed steadily and less than an hour after their meal stop they were on Dartmoor.

For as far as could be seen there was a bleak, rolling landscape, dotted here and there with tors surmounted by bare, grey, tumbled rocks.

The rain was heavier now, preventing the prisoners from seeing for much more than a mile. However, the impression they had already gained was that the moorland went on for ever.

The moor was not entirely deserted. They were nearing their destination when a young girl of perhaps seventeen or eighteen came into view. Accompanied by two dogs, she was driving sheep inside a large paddock enclosed by freestone walls.

The sight of the lone girl brought a noisy outburst from the Americans. Few had even glimpsed a woman during many months of internment on board the prison hulk. They ignored the attempts of the militiamen to bring them to order.

The girl tried to ignore the calls of the men, as did the older and more experienced of the two dogs. The other was younger and not yet fully trained. For some moments it seemed undecided whether the sheep or the marching men were of more interest.

The men won the day. The dog ran towards them, barking noisily, ignoring the shouted command of the young shepherdess for it to return to her.

The dog's disobedience was compounded by the prisoners-of-war who whistled and shouted encouragement to the errant animal.

For some of the men it was a genuine wish to commune with the dog. After months spent in the dehumanising confines of a prison hulk, it was a link with life as they had once known it.

To others it was merely a mischievous and not-too-serious diversion.

Eventually, the captain in charge of the militiamen rode back along the line of men from the head of the column, to ascertain the reason for the noisy disorder.

Captain Henry Pollit was the only mounted member of the escort. The young dog immediately began barking at the horse. Running around it excitedly, it was urged on by the prisoners.

'Get away! Go on. Off with you!'

The officer's unsuccessful attempts to drive away the dog brought howls of glee from the American prisoners.

Henry Pollit possessed no military experience whatsoever, and was unused to commanding men. The only reason he had been granted a militia commission was because he had influential family connections in his own county.

He also possessed an exaggerated view of the importance of his command. Angered by the derision of the American prisoners-of-war and the antics of the disobedient dog, he called to one of the militiamen.

'Corporal! I'll not allow a blasted dog to threaten discipline in such a manner. Shoot it!'

The militiaman looked at the officer uncertainly. 'It's not really doing any harm, sir. It'll leave us in a few minutes.'

'Damn you, Corporal! Did you hear what I said? I gave you an order. Shoot it, or I'll take your gun and do it myself.'

Reluctantly, the corporal put the musket he carried to his shoulder and took aim.

The move brought a howl of protest from the marching men. At the same time, Pilgrim saw the girl begin to run towards the column, aware of what was about to happen to her young and disobedient dog.

He was among the men closest to the corporal. As the militiaman thumbed back the hammer on his musket, Pilgrim jumped at him without pausing to think of the consequences of his action.

He knocked the barrel of the weapon up at the very moment the militiaman pulled the trigger. A thick cloud of white smoke enveloped both men, but the musket ball sped harmlessly away, to fall to earth far away on the open moorland.

The noise of the shot succeeded where all else had failed. The dog turned and fled towards the running girl.

'Seize that man!' Furious, Captain Pollit pointed to Pilgrim. Before he could return to the column of prisoners, he was secured by two of the militiamen.

The move brought an angry response from the other American prisoners, all of whom had come to a halt. But the sound of the shot had brought other militiamen to the spot. Their muskets and bayonets were sufficient deterrent to any attempt to help Pilgrim.

'Put manacles on him. When we reach Dartmoor he'll be dealt with for assaulting a militiaman.'

One of the part-time soldiers produced a pair of heavy manacles. As they were secured to Pilgrim's wrists, Virgil limped forward and addressed the militia captain.

'I must protest, sir. Lieutenant Pilgrim Penn is an officer of the United States Marines and a prisoner-of-war. He is not a common criminal.'

'He's lucky he wasn't shot,' retorted Captain Pollit. 'He's under escort and he assaulted one of my men.'

'All he did was stop you from shooting my dog.' The girl was close enough to hear the captain's words.

Brushing long, dark hair back from her face, she spoke angrily and breathlessly. 'You should be grateful to him. The dog belongs to Sir Thomas Tyrwhitt, Lord Warden of the Stannaries. He gave it to my father for training. It's to be a present for the Prince Regent. If it had been shot you'd be in serious trouble now.'

The militia captain was startled by her disclosure. Although he had never met Sir Thomas Tyrwhitt, he certainly knew *of* him. Personal secretary and a close friend to England's future monarch, he was a man who wielded great power. There was no doubting the truth of the girl's words. But Henry Pollit was not prepared to admit he might have acted hastily.

'Your father should keep the dog at home until it's learned obedience, not send it out with a slip of a girl to stir up trouble among prisoners-of-war.'

Tacy bit back an angry retort. Instead, she looked to where Pilgrim stood between the two militiamen, his wrists manacled in front of him. 'Are you going to release him now?'

'No. He'll be taken to Dartmoor prison and punished for assaulting one of my men.'

'Then I'll have my father tell Sir Thomas you ordered one of your men to shoot his dog. You'll be hearing from him, have no doubt about that!'

Turning her back on the stubborn militia captain she spoke to Pilgrim for the first time. 'Thank you for saving the dog. I'm sorry it got you in trouble, but I'll tell Sir Thomas what happened. What's your name?'

The rowdier element among the prisoners had resumed their whistling and catcalling and Captain Pollit called to the girl. 'Stop talking to the prisoners or I'll have you arrested too.'

Pilgrim just had time to call out his name to the girl before he was pushed back among the others and the prisoners-of-war were prodded into movement once more. He would have liked to ask her name too, but they had moved away from her now. He was not even certain she had heard his words.

He thought it made little difference. He would probably never see her again – and he had other matters to worry about. In manacles now, he wondered what would happen to him when he and his fellow prisoners-of-war reached their destination.

He was certainly in trouble. What came of it would depend on how determined the militia captain was to press charges against him.

3

When the high granite walls of Dartmoor prison came into view, the American prisoners-of-war fell strangely silent. To Pilgrim, the prison resembled the drawings of grim medieval castles he had seen in books on the shelves of his grandfather's library in Washington, before Pilgrim's father took his family westwards, to Ohio.

But the pictures had lacked reality. The prison did not. The sheer size of it was awesome. It had been built on land which sloped gently away from the road. Because of this, despite its eighteen-feet-high circular perimeter wall, it was possible for a while to see something of the tall grey granite buildings rising inside the walls.

However, as the Americans drew closer, the walls themselves towered above them and nothing more could be seen of the prison buildings.

'Here we are, Pilgrim. This is likely to be our home until the war's over.'

Virgil spoke to the manacled young lieutenant, but it was Ephraim who replied. He had joined them to check whether Virgil had any orders for him when they entered the prison.

'It don't look a lot like the cabin back home on the plantation,' he said laconically.

Despite his predicament, Pilgrim smiled at the marine corporal's dry humour. He was aware that Ephraim had been born a slave. How he had escaped from his environment was something Pilgrim had never queried.

Probably the only coloured recruit in the United States Marine Corps, Ephraim had originally joined them as a blacksmith. However, he had proved himself to be a superb fighting man. Enlisted into their ranks, he had quickly earned both promotion and the respect of his fellow marines.

'With any luck the war will soon be over and we'll go home before we grow to like it here,' said Virgil.

'I'll be happy for now just to get inside and have these things taken off.' Pilgrim held his manacled wrists out in front of him. 'I swear their weight has increased tenfold since they were put on.'

'Well, if you will go around siding with some dumb dog against a puffed-up English militia officer you've got to learn to take the consequences, Lieutenant.'

The look Ephraim gave Pilgrim was more sympathetic than his words. 'Mind you, you're the first Yankee among us to have an English girl speak to him. Would you say she was pretty, Lieutenant?'

'Yes, she was.' Pilgrim thought of the girl with her black hair, and eyes that had seemed incredibly blue when she expressed her anger with the militia captain. He gave a mental shrug. After almost a year without any feminine company whatsoever, most girls were likely to appear to be attractive.

At that moment the sergeant of militia, John Straw, came back to where the three men walked together.

Addressing Virgil, he said, 'We'll be entering the prison in a few minutes, sir. There are nine thousand Frenchmen in there to watch your arrival. I thought you might want to be at the head of the men. Make some sort of impression, if you know what I mean.'

'Thank you, Sergeant. It's very thoughtful of you.'

Speaking to Pilgrim, he said, 'You ought to be up there with me.'

Pilgrim shook his head and held out his hands. 'Not with these on. You're the captain. Go on ahead. We'll march in behind you as smart as we're able.'

Virgil was stopped by one of the militiamen when he reached the head of the column of prisoners. When he insisted he be allowed to take his place at the head of the men, the militia captain was called to the scene.

Virgil told Captain Pollit the reason he wished to enter the prison at the head of his fellow Americans. He also asked for a few minutes to address the men before they reached the prison gate.

'As I see it, the French prisoners-of-war will outnumber us by about thirty-six to one. If we're to avoid trouble inside the prison, we need to establish ourselves immediately as a separate, disciplined entity and enter the prison in good order. It's equally important for my men to know what's expected of them.'

The militia captain thought about Virgil's words for a few moments, then he shrugged. 'Governor Cotgrave is quite capable of maintaining discipline, but I can't see it will do any harm. I'll call a halt for you to say your piece – but keep it brief. Governor Cotgrave will already have been informed of our approach. I don't intend keeping him waiting.'

Captain Pollit believed it would do no harm to have the senior American officer kindly disposed towards him. He was convinced his action in respect of the dog had been correct, but it might be misrepresented to the Warden of the Stannaries.

Virgil's next words dented this plan.

'There's also the matter of my second-in-command. I'd like his manacles taken off before we go in.'

'I haven't decided yet what measures will be taken against him. Until I do, the manacles remain.'

Virgil realised it would be futile to argue. He had gained one concession. He did not want to lose the opportunity to talk to the other prisoners-of-war.

The men were brought to a halt beneath the walls of the forbidding prison. Meanwhile, Captain Pollit sent a militiaman ahead to give the governor official notification of their imminent arrival. Forewarning the governor of their presence was a more acceptable reason for halting the prisoners-of-war than acceding to a request by Captain Howard.

Calling his countrymen about him, Virgil told them all he had learned about their future home. They gasped when they learned the prison was already occupied by nine thousand Frenchmen. He impressed upon them his determination that the Americans should keep their identity and remain together as a single unit.

He warned them of likely language difficulties with their fellow prisoners-of-war. It would no doubt lead to many misunderstandings between them at first. Virgil stressed that they should not try to settle their own differences. Any problems were to be brought to him, or to the committee he intended setting up to take care of the interests of American prisoners-of-war.

Looking at the faces of the men, Virgil could see he had their general agreement. Then Ephraim voiced the concern of the slaves and ex-slaves.

'Are we all going to be represented on this committee,

you're setting up, Cap'n? Will it look after *our* interests too?'

It sounded very much as though Ephraim was questioning Virgil's authority and there were angry mutterings among the southern-based merchant seamen.

Pilgrim said nothing. He, Virgil and Ephraim had already discussed what was likely to happen when they reached Dartmoor prison. Ephraim had told the officers that it was the intention of the black prisoners to break off all relations with their white countrymen if it were possible. The black prisoners had also agreed that Ephraim should assume leadership of their group.

Ephraim was by far the largest man among the American prisoners-of-war. He was a natural leader too – but he was also a marine. It was necessary to show the others he was capable of questioning white authority.

'You're all United States citizens, Ephraim. You have the same rights as everyone else.'

'They're fine words, Captain Howard – and I know you mean what you say. All the same, there are men here who've yet to meet a white man who'd take the word of a black man against one of his own kind, whether he be American, French, or English.'

He raised his voice so he could be heard by all the prisoners-of-war. 'I hope this committee is going to be fair to *everyone*. If it isn't, and any of our people have trouble, they should come to me. To Ephraim. *I'll* see they get justice. Black man's justice. You hear me?'

There were some fifty black sailors among the prisoners-of-war and Ephraim's words had the desired effect. One or two of them cheered. The others nodded their heads vigorously.

They would accept Ephraim as their leader.

'That's enough talking, Captain Howard. Get your

men fallen in. We're going inside the prison now.' The militia captain had been listening and he feared there might be trouble.

Ephraim winked at Pilgrim before he returned to the black seamen who formed a group at the rear of the column. Meanwhile, Virgil took his place at the head of the prisoners-of-war.

Virgil trusted Ephraim to maintain control over his fellow black Americans. He hoped he might have equal success with those white Americans who were not subject to military or naval discipline.

'Prisoners, quick march!'

At the order, the prisoners-of-war squared their shoulders and attempted some semblance of a disciplined, if ragged, force.

Black and white Americans marched towards the prison with at least an outward semblance of unity.

4

Led by Captain Virgil Howard and surrounded by a strong escort of Somerset Militiamen, the United States prisoners-of-war marched in through the high, arched gate of Dartmoor prison.

Over the gates was the Latin inscription, *Parcere Subjectis*.

Pilgrim had dropped back until he was marching just ahead of Ephraim. As they passed through the gates, Ephraim said, 'Look at them words. What are they supposed to mean?'

'It's Latin and means "Spare the Vanquished",' explained Pilgrim. 'The Romans used to kill their prisoners. It's what one of their poets said when he pleaded for them to change their ways and spare their captives.'

'Why have they put it up there in Latin?' asked Ephraim, clearly puzzled. 'I thought the people in this country spoke American.'

Pilgrim smiled. 'It's considered clever to inscribe Latin quotations on buildings and tombstones, things like that.'

'What's clever about carving words that nobody understands? They might as well have carved a picture.'

'You're quite right, they might as well have, Ephraim. They probably never thought of it.'

Passing beneath the archway, they marched through a small courtyard to a second rectangular yard, surrounded by a high wall. At the far end was a gate, guarded by half a dozen militiamen.

Waiting here for them was a reception committee headed by a man wearing the uniform of a Captain in the British Royal Navy. This was Captain Isaac Cotgrave, RN, the prison governor. His appointment had been made by the Transport Board, a department of the Admiralty, the body responsible for prisoners-of-war.

The Americans were brought to a halt and told to form three ranks against one of the walls.

Marching smartly up to the prison governor, the militia captain reported his arrival. Waving forward a corporal, Captain Pollit took a satchel from him and handed it to an official who stood beside the prison governor. Inside the satchel was a list of the prisoners being transferred from the hulks to Dartmoor prison.

The two officers talked for a few minutes, during which time the prison governor frequently cast glances in the direction of the latest arrivals in his prison.

Suddenly, he pointed to Pilgrim. 'Why is that man wearing manacles?'

Pilgrim was not close enough to hear the militia captain's reply – but Virgil was.

Before the men of the militia guard could prevent him, he confronted the governor and the officials about him. 'That's not true! Lieutenant Penn assaulted no one. He merely prevented your corporal from killing a young sheepdog.'

'Who are you?' the prison governor demanded angrily.

Virgil came to attention. 'Captain of Marines Virgil Howard, sir. Senior United States officer present.'

'I recognise no ranks among the inmates of my prison, *Mister* Howard. You are all prisoners. If one of your countrymen has assaulted a militiaman he can expect to be punished.'

Turning to one of the prison officials, he said, 'Have that manacled man thrown into the *cachot*, Mr Williams. We'll let him reflect upon his folly for a week or two.'

'I object most strongly, sir,' said Virgil. 'Lieutenant Penn is being punished arbitrarily, without being afforded an opportunity to defend himself.'

'Object as much as you like,' snapped the governor. 'When I've looked into the matter I'll likely have him flogged. Now, go back to the ranks, or you'll join your countryman in the *cachot*. It's not an experience I would recommend.'

Virgil would have continued to argue, but the governor turned his back on him and two of the militiamen came forward to drive Virgil back to the other prisoners-of-war.

One of the two was Sergeant Straw. As Virgil was driven back towards the others, the sergeant said quietly, 'Don't argue with Captain Cotgrave, sir. He'll do as he says. He had the reputation of being a hard captain when he was at sea. Having a shore post's done nothing to improve his temper.'

Virgil allowed himself to be pushed back to the other prisoners-of-war but instead of taking his place at their head, he found a place in their ranks beside Ephraim. With the other Americans, the marine corporal booed loudly as Pilgrim was led away.

Scowling in their direction, Captain Cotgrave told

the militia commanding officer to take the prisoners to Number Four Prison Block, where they were to be housed.

Hurrying back to his men, Captain Pollit passed the order on to Sergeant Straw. The order to fall in and turn right to march to their prison block was given, but there was no response.

Sergeant Straw repeated his order, louder this time. The result was the same. Nobody made any attempt to obey him.

The sergeant looked towards his commanding officer uncertainly. Captain Pollit stalked towards the prisoners and shouted a command for them to prepare to move off. The Americans ignored him.

His face scarlet with anger and humiliation, the officer shouted, 'What do you think you're playing at? Come to attention and prepare to move off.'

Yet again nothing happened.

The prison governor had been watching with growing anger. Now he called to the militiaman, 'What's going on, Captain Pollit?'

'The prisoners are refusing to obey orders, sir. They won't march off.'

'Won't they, indeed? We'll see about that. Order your men to fix bayonets. A jab or two should soon bring them to their senses.'

The militia sergeant looked uncertainly at his commanding officer.

'You heard what Governor Cotgrave said. Order the men to fix bayonets, Sergeant.'

When Sergeant Straw gave the order, Captain Pollit brought his men into line and gave them the order to advance upon the American prisoners.

Before the militiamen reached them, the nearest prisoners sat down. They were quickly followed by the others. Within a few minutes, all the Americans were seated upon the ground.

The militiamen halted uncertainly but Captain Pollit ordered, 'Get them on their feet. They're to go inside the gate to Block Four . . .'

One of the militiamen prodded a prisoner hesitantly. A cry went up immediately from some of the Americans that he had drawn blood.

Among the staff surrounding Governor Cotgrave was George Dykar, the prison surgeon. Now he said to the governor, 'I must protest, sir. These are unarmed men . . .'

'They are prisoners-of-war and in a state of mutiny, Mr Dykar.'

'It's a passive mutiny, sir. They pose no threat to anyone. Should serious wounds be inflicted, requiring my attention, the facts will have to be registered in my report.'

Governor Cotgrave glared at the surgeon. Neither of the men liked the other and Cotgrave was aware the surgeon would do as he said.

'Where's that captain of marines?' Seeking him out, he approached until he stood no more than seven or eight paces away from Virgil.

'You! Tell these men to stand up and march to their quarters.'

Without rising to his feet, Virgil said, 'Are you acknowledging that as senior United States officer here I have a responsibility for the well-being of the American prisoners-of-war, sir?'

'I am acknowledging nothing,' snapped Governor Cotgrave, furious at Virgil's opportunism. 'But if you are as concerned for their well-being as you claim to be, you'll persuade them to take up their quarters immediately.'

'I *am* concerned, Governor. However, I am not prepared to help you. As you told me a while ago, I am just another prisoner-of-war. Nevertheless, I can assure you that any report I forward to my Government on their behalf will be taken very seriously indeed.'

'Your country is a long way from Dartmoor,' snapped Governor Cotgrave. 'A single Dartmoor night should be sufficient to make you change your mind – and those of your countrymen.'

Turning back to Captain Pollit, the prison governor said, 'You and your men seem particularly inept at soldiering, perhaps you might prove better at guarding the prisoners. I'll have the yard lit by lanterns. You will arrange for a strong guard to be placed on the prisoners all night. They will be ready to listen to reason by morning.'

5

The confrontation between the American prisoners-of-war and the governor had been witnessed by a great many French officers, all of whom seemed to have freedom to wander about the prison at will.

There were also a number of French prisoners watching from viewpoints in the upper-storey windows of one of the nearby prison blocks.

As the governor and his entourage walked away from the seated Americans, the watching Frenchmen cheered and jeered loudly, adding to the anger of Governor Cotgrave.

When darkness fell over the prison, lamps were lit and placed upon poles around the defiant American prisoners. With the darkness, the drizzle that had been with them intermittently throughout the day, turned to sleet.

Sitting shivering with the others, Virgil called out to his countrymen, 'Move back until you're tight against the wall. Huddle together as close as you can to keep warm.'

The men were seated in the lee of a high interior wall. It afforded them some degree of protection from the bitterly cold wind. Now they edged even closer, huddling tightly together to share what scant body heat they were generating.

Ephraim was squatting on the ground close to Virgil and he said quietly, 'I know you and I can last out, Captain, but how about the others? After all, they're not marines.'

'This was their idea, remember? Besides, it doesn't matter now whether they last out or not. We've let the governor know we Americans stick together. He'll need to take that into account when dealing with us during the time we're here.'

'Do you think it might persuade him to turn Lieutenant Penn loose?'

'That would be too much of a blow to his pride, but I intend lodging an official complaint about it as soon as we can . . .'

He was interrupted by a sudden upsurge of sound from nearby. Something had been thrown over the wall behind them. It was quickly followed by many more items.

The word went around quickly and excitedly. They were being bombarded with rolled-up blankets by the Frenchmen who occupied the compound on the far side of the wall. They had been locked up for the night but, as the Americans would learn, their allies were adept at obtaining and duplicating keys. Indeed, they had the capabilities to manufacture all manner of objects.

Soon dozens of blankets had landed among the seated men. The American prisoners quickly discovered that many of the bundles also contained bottles of spirits!

Before long most of the newly arrived prisoners-of-war were huddled beneath blankets while bottles containing rum, brandy or wine were circulating among them.

The morale of the American prisoners soared enormously. Someone declared loudly that if this treatment continued they should remain seated in the prison's market square for the whole of their internment.

'What do you think we ought to do about it?' One of the militiamen guarding the American prisoners-of-war put the question to Sergeant Straw.

'Nothing.' The reply was immediate and positive. 'We were told to guard them and make sure no one escapes. That's what we're doing. Nobody said they shouldn't be allowed any scrap of comfort that comes their way. I only wish someone would throw a bottle of something warming in our direction, that's all.'

Outside the punishment cell known by the French word *cachot*, meaning 'dungeon', Pilgrim had his manacles removed by one of the prison turnkeys.

'You won't be lonely in there,' said the guard unfeelingly. 'You'll be with someone who's been locked up long enough to find his way around – not that there's much in there to be found.'

A moment later a hand was placed against Pilgrim's back and he was shoved through a low doorway and sent stumbling inside the gloomy, rough concrete *cachot*. The heavy iron door slammed shut behind him.

'Who is that?'

The question was in French, a language Pilgrim had learned as a boy from the French trappers who had passed through the hills close to his home in Ohio, heading northwestwards.

'My name's Pilgrim. What's yours?'

'You are English?' There was disbelief in the Frenchman's voice.

'No, American.'

'Ah! We heard you had entered the war against England. But so many rumours circulate in a prison. I am Henri Joffre. I will not insult you by bidding you welcome.'

The Frenchman spoke in English now, in a flat, emotionless voice. He slurred his words in the manner of a man who had grown unaccustomed to conversation. Seated on the cold, concreted floor he made no attempt to rise to his feet.

'How long have you been in here?' Pilgrim asked.

'It is difficult to measure time in the *cachot*, m'sieur, especially in winter. Some days are little lighter than night. If the gaoler forgets to bring a meal, as is frequently the case, it is impossible to tell night from day. I think perhaps it is five or six weeks?'

'Five or six weeks? In this place . . . ?'

It was dark inside the *cachot*. The only light entering the dungeon-like structure filtered through two tiny holes. No larger than a man's hand, each was set high in the wall beneath the eaves. What light there was showed the *cachot* to be perhaps six paces square, with rough concrete floor and walls. Apart from a large wooden slop bucket in one corner, it was totally devoid of furniture. There was not even straw on the floor.

Pilgrim was aghast at the Frenchman's words. He had expected to be incarcerated here for a day or two, at the most.

An uncomfortable thought suddenly occurred to him. It was possible the other man was guilty of some particularly heinous crime . . .

Hesitantly, he asked him the reason he had been cast in the *cachot*.

'I tried to escape, m'sieur. We have a market in the large square inside the gates. I became friendly with a young girl who sets up a stall there every day. We would talk long together. She became very fond of me – and I of her too, of course. One day she brought some clothes to the prison for me. Women's clothes. Night comes early to the moor in winter. By the time the market ended it was dark. When the traders left the prison I went with them, dressed as a woman.'

The Frenchman was silent for a while and Pilgrim prompted, 'What went wrong?'

In the gloom of the *cachot* the Frenchman made a sound that might have been an attempt at a laugh. 'Nothing – at first. I walked through the gate without being challenged. Then, on the way through Princetown we encountered a large party of off-duty militiamen. They had been drinking heavily. I think it was to celebrate a victory in battle by their county regiment over my countrymen, in the Spanish Peninsular.'

When the Frenchman fell silent yet again, Pilgrim asked, 'Did their celebrations make you angry? Is that how you came to be recaptured?'

'Angry? No, m'sieur. In war there are defeats and victories in battle for both sides. Only the final battle is of importance. I did not resent their celebrations. Unfortunately, the drink they had consumed had also made them amorous – and I was dressed as a woman, you understand?'

Pilgrim thought he *did* understand, but the French officer was talking once more.

'. . . One of the militiamen was especially persistent. When he began taking liberties I hit him. Not as a woman might, with the flat of my hand on his cheek, but with my fist, on his chin. Then the other militiamen and the traders joined in. During the mêlée I lost my bonnet and one of the militiamen recognised me.'

Pilgrim could just make out the Frenchman's shrug as

he added, 'For escaping I expected to be punished, but when I was brought before the governor charged with assaulting a militiaman I protested most strongly. I was defending my honour, you understand. But it was to no avail. Now I have been left to rot here in the *cachot*.'

Pilgrim was dismayed, not only at the length of the Frenchman's stay in this primitive cell, but at the thought that he too was here for assaulting a militiaman! He wondered whether he would also be kept for weeks in the semi-darkness of this dungeon-like punishment cell?

6

The rain that had been falling across the high ground of the moor turned briefly to snow before ceasing altogether. However, once the snow ceased the temperature plummeted.

In the market square, the American prisoners-of-war huddled together as closely as was possible. By sharing the blankets thrown to them by the Frenchmen, a pair of men could enjoy the protection of two blankets and whatever warmth was generated by their bodies. But it could not keep the chill of the night away altogether.

In the *cachot*, Pilgrim was spending one of the most uncomfortable nights of his young life. He consoled himself with the thought that the accommodation for his companions was probably only marginally better than his own.

As yet, he was unaware they were still outside, enduring the bitter cold of the prison's market square.

Pilgrim and Henri sat on opposite sides of the bare, concrete room. Neither was talking now. Conversation had ceased when the cold, seeping in through the small apertures in the outside wall, began to numb the facial muscles of both men.

Slumped against a rough wall in the small building, Pilgrim was deep in thought when he became aware of a sound that had been increasingly impinging upon his thoughts. He suddenly realised he was listening to the chattering teeth and ragged breathing of his companion.

The sounds were alarming. 'Henri . . . ?'

'It's . . . it's all right. This . . . isn't the first . . . cold night . . . I've spent in here.'

Talking brought on a violent fit of coughing. When it ended Henri fought hard in an effort to breathe normally once more.

Pilgrim also felt desperately cold, but he knew he was in much better health than the Frenchman. Weeks spent in the comfortless *cachot* after years of imprisonment were finally taking their toll.

Climbing stiffly to his feet, Pilgrim shrugged off his coat. 'Here, take this. I can probably withstand the cold better than you . . . for one night, at least.'

When the Frenchman protested, albeit weakly, he said, 'Well, take it just for a while. Until you feel warmer. Then we'll take turns with it.'

As he wrapped the coat about the Frenchmen he could feel the man's whole, thin body shaking.

He was about to sit down on the floor once more when there was a sound at the door and the small hatch was opened. A voice which Pilgrim recognised as belonging to John Straw, the friendly militia sergeant, whispered, 'Here, take these. They'll help warm up the night.'

Something was pushed through the hatch and dropped to the floor of the *cachot*. Feeling around, Pilgrim located a bundle. It comprised two rolled-up blankets – and inside was a bottle.

Pulling the cork, Pilgrim breathed in the pungent fumes of what promised to be a cheap and fiery, but nonetheless welcome brandy.

When Henri took a first swig from the bottle he choked for so long Pilgrim thought he might expire. Then, his voice hoarse and strained, the Frenchman gasped, 'My family . . . have distilled Cognac for very many years. It is renowned throughout France . . . throughout *Europe*, but never have they produced anything that tastes better than this. I feel the heat from it exploring every part of my body.'

'There are blankets here too. They'll help keep the heat in once it's made its way around your veins.'

'My friend! Have you been sent by the gods to work miracles in this most grim of all prisons? Companionship, compassion, Cognac – and a blanket too! Will I wake in the morning to find it all gone – and you with it?'

Despite his surroundings and the predicament he was in, Pilgrim grinned. 'Well, *I'll* still be here, I don't know about the blankets – or the bottle. They're both likely to be taken away if a turnkey sees them. I suggest we do something about the contents of the bottle, at least.'

'It would be rare indeed for a gaoler to actually come inside the *cachot*, but it is not impossible. However, do not worry, there is a space above the door, between roof and wall, where we can hide them. A hole has been carefully made over the years by those who have been here before us. There are messages hidden inside, written to their families by men with no expectation of leaving Dartmoor alive. You must read them when there is sufficient light entering through the rat-hole that passes for a window. They make touching reading.'

Huddled in their blankets and with the chill of the night held at bay, albeit temporarily, the two men talked far into the early hours of the Dartmoor morning.

The brandy had put new life into the Frenchman. At times it seemed to Pilgrim he was trying to make up for all the conversation he had lacked during his lonely sojourn in the primitive punishment cell.

Yet Pilgrim was grateful for the company of Henri Joffre. From him he learned a great deal about the prison that was likely to be his home until the conclusion of the war between Great Britain and the United States of America.

Built of grey, moorland granite, the whole prison complex was contained within a mile-long, circular wall, constantly patrolled by militiamen. Within this was a second, lower wall.

The actual gaol blocks were built inside one half of the circle and the *cachot* was located within this area. There were seven prison blocks in all, arranged in a half-circle like the spokes of a gigantic wheel. One end of each block pointed to the centre of the circle.

The blocks were numbered one to seven and Pilgrim learned that Block Four contained the worst elements of the French prisoners-of-war. So desperate were they considered to be that a wall had been built about this particular block to separate them from the other prisoners.

In the remaining half of the circle was the hospital and a block known as *Le Petit Cautionnement*, or Petty Officers' Block. It contained French officers who, for one reason or another, had not taken parole, or had had it refused or taken away.

The market square was within this half of the prison area. Farmers and traders from the surrounding countryside were allowed to bring goods here for sale to those prisoners with sufficient money to purchase them.

Built into the high prison wall on either side of the main gate were the houses occupied by the governor, and the prison surgeon.

After a while, Pilgrim found his concentration wandering as the Frenchman chattered on. He began thinking of the forests and fertile plains of Ohio, so unlike the bleak moorland wastes on which the prison stood; of the home and family he had left behind in America.

His father, once a marines officer himself, was now a Congressman, representing the newly established State of Ohio, able to bring pressure to bear in the seat of government in Washington. Pilgrim wondered whether his father would use this influence in an attempt to have his only son freed.

He decided his father would probably not yet be aware that he was a prisoner-of-war. All he would know was that the ship on which Pilgrim had been serving was missing.

It had been impossible to write and have letters taken for delivery from the prison hulk on which the American prisoners-of-war had been held until now. He hoped it might be possible to send a letter from Dartmoor prison, giving his whereabouts to the family.

But first he needed to obtain his release from the *cachot*. He was younger than Henri Joffre and probably far fitter, but he hoped his fitness would not be put to the test of spending months locked away in the semi-darkness of this grim punishment cell.

7

Tacy Elford was working in the yard of Roundtor Farm. The small moorland holding was rented by her father from the Duchy of Cornwall.

The Dukedom of Cornwall was one of many titles held by George, the Prince Regent, currently ruling England on behalf of his deranged father, King George the Third.

The Duchy would remain in his possession until he took formal possession of the Crown of England. Then the title and all income from Duchy lands would pass to the next male heir to the throne. If there were not one, the income would be retained by the king and his successors, until one was born.

Included in the Duchy lands was most of Dartmoor and the surrounding countryside.

Roundtor farmhouse had been thoughtfully sited beside a narrow river, in a valley at the foot of the tor from which it took its name. The tor afforded the farmhouse protection from the prevailing westerly winds.

Dartmoor was a beautiful but unrelenting environment. Everything on and about the small isolated farm was designed to counter the effects of the harsh moorland winter weather.

The house and outbuildings formed a square, with the doors of the farm buildings opening into a central courtyard. Many of the domestic animals were brought in during the severest weather. They and the householders needed to be able to survive being cut off from the rest of the world for days – or even weeks in a particularly severe winter.

This had been no more than an average winter. Much of the snow had already come and gone, although some still lingered in pockets among the rocks of the surrounding tors.

Tacy's father, Tom, was not a well man. He had suffered for years from a chest complaint that restricted the amount of work he was able to do. At this moment he was checking on the sheep in a pen not far from the house. Pregnant ewes were gathered here, in anticipation of the lambing that would soon take place.

Tacy was throwing hay down into the courtyard from a hayloft, helped somewhat indifferently by her sister, Johanna, and Billy Yates.

Suddenly, the gate to the yard creaked open noisily on ungreased hinges, and Billy sucked in his breath.

Tacy looked up to see Sir Thomas Tyrwhitt ride his horse in through the yard gateway. The friend of the Prince Regent waved a hand before dismounting. As he tethered his horse, the young sheepdog ran across the yard to give him a warm greeting.

Tacy waved her hand in return and stopped working, but she remained in the open doorway of the hayloft.

Sir Thomas Tyrwhitt was a very important man in his own right and his close friendship with the Prince

Regent commanded additional respect. He was a local landowner and, as Lord Warden of the Stannaries, he wielded a great deal of influence in south-west England.

The appointment had lost much of the vast power it had once carried when the Stannaries – the tin-mining areas – had produced great wealth for the Crown, but it was still important enough to make him a very influential man.

He was also a generous man. Yet Tacy had always been somewhat in awe of him. She felt happier remaining on the upper floor of the hayloft.

Ignoring Billy, Sir Thomas raised his hat to Tacy and pointed to the dog. 'How is Rip coming along? Will he make as fine a sheepdog as his mother?'

'He shows great promise, Sir Thomas, but he still has a lot to learn. Mind you, we're lucky to still have him with us. He was almost shot by a militiaman yesterday.'

'It's a shame to want to shoot a dog like Rip.' Billy was indignant. 'It's not right. I wish I'd been there. I'd have showed him what I thought of him.'

Continuing to ignore the simple young man, Sir Thomas frowned. He advanced until he was standing directly beneath the open hayloft door. '*Almost* shot . . . ? Tell me about it.'

Tacy described the incident involving the American prisoners-of-war and their militia escort. By the time she ended her story, the landowner was having difficulty controlling his anger.

'That militia captain may not be aware of it but he has good reason to thank the American. Had he shot Rip I'd have had him stripped of his commission and sent back to his home in disgrace. The trouble with these part-time soldiers is that a little power goes to their head. It's something I was discussing with the Prince Regent only the other day . . .'

The conversation he repeated to Tacy, although un- doubtedly true, was intended to impress her. Sir Thomas never missed an opportunity to remind a pretty young woman what an important man he was.

Nevertheless, he *was* a kindly man and Tacy genu- inely liked him.

'I suppose you didn't happen to get the name of the American? I'll send him a little something to show my appreciation of his actions. It might make his life a little easier if it's known I'm taking an interest in him. The Good Lord knows, a man needs something to make things more bearable if he's locked up inside Dartmoor prison. But you won't have been in there, Tacy?'

'She has, Sir Thomas,' said Billy, eager to be noticed by the landowner. 'She goes in there sometimes to sell things from the farm. I've been in there with her. I went along to see that none of them prisoners hurt her.'

'And I was very pleased to have your protection, Billy. Now, will you go to the house and tell my ma that Sir Thomas has come calling?'

When Billy had gone, beaming happily to have been given praise from Tacy, she said, 'I go to the prison quite often, Sir Thomas. Pa sends me there to sell peat and sometimes eggs and chickens. Vegetables too when we have some to spare – and I did manage to learn something of the American who saved Rip's life. He's a lieutenant. Lieutenant Pilgrim something-or-other. But I don't know if they'd allow you to send anything to him. After he'd knocked the militiaman's gun up, they put manacles on him before marching him off with the others. Pa says he'd have no doubt been thrown in a punishment cell as soon as they got to the prison.'

'Your father is probably right.' Sir Thomas looked

thoughtful. 'The governor might also order him to be flogged – and that would be most unfair. This happened only yesterday, you say?'

'Yesterday afternoon. He doesn't deserve to be flogged. All he did was stop the militiaman from shooting Rip.'

'You're quite right, of course.' The Lord Warden of the Stannaries arrived at a sudden decision. 'Do you think you would recognise this American again if you saw him?'

'I'm certain of it.' Tacy hoped she had not sounded *too* positive, but the American had been young and good-looking. Quite unlike any of the young men she had met about the moor.

'Then why don't we take a ride to the prison and find out what's happening to him, Tacy?'

'You want *me* to come with *you* . . . now? To the prison?'

'That's right.'

The suggestion took Tacy by surprise.

'I'll need to ask my pa. He's up at the sheep pen, on the tor.'

'I'll come with you,' said Billy eagerly, as he returned from the house.

'That won't be necessary, Billy, but thank you all the same. You stay here and help Johanna. She'd like that.'

Behind Billy's back, and unseen by the simple young man, Johanna put out her tongue at her sister, but Sir Thomas was talking once more.

'Come on down, Tacy. We'll stop and speak to your father along the way. We shouldn't waste any time if we're to save this American from the lash.'

Tom Elford was no more enthusiastic about having his daughter go off with Sir Thomas across the moor than she was. But he knew how upset she had been the previous

day, when she was telling him of the incident. Especially
when she described how the American prisoner-of-war
had been manacled before being marched away by the
militiamen. It had brought back the memory of the helplessness she had felt when the escaped French prisoner
had died in Mudilake Marsh.

'Of course she must go, if it will help the man who
saved Rip. But the governor will want to entertain you
afterwards, Sir Thomas, and Tacy's not dressed for such
company. You go on together now. As soon as I've fed
these ewes I'll make my way to the prison and wait
outside the gate for Tacy. When she's found this young
man for you, she and I can return home together.'

'There's really no need . . . but that's up to you, Tom.
It's your own time, to spend as you wish. Come along,
Tacy. Give me your hand and climb up behind me. It's
all right, girl, I won't bite you. We'll be there a sight
more quickly than if you walk and I have to keep the
horse moving at your pace.'

Tacy climbed up behind Sir Thomas and was forced
to wrap her arms about him when he put the horse to
a trot. She was relieved her father had said he would
come to the prison and wait for her.

None of them saw Billy.

Naturally clumsy, he had dropped his hay fork from
the hayloft, into the yard. When he went down to
retrieve it, he could see through the gate to the sheep
pen.

He saw Tacy climb upon the horse behind Sir Thomas,
and he stood and watched them ride away.

It made him unhappy. Not because he questioned Sir
Thomas's motives. Such a thought would never have
occurred to Billy. Sir Thomas was a *gentleman*. As such,
his motives were beyond reproach.

Billy was unhappy because *he* would never own a

horse. He would never know what it was to have Tacy riding behind him, her arms about *his* waist.

He watched the horse and its two riders until Johanna called to him crossly, 'Are you supposed to be helping me, Billy, or are you going to spend all your time down there leaning on that old fork, day-dreaming?'

'I'm coming, Johanna.'

Billy hurried to the ladder which led to the hayloft. He did not want to upset Johanna. He loved her almost as much as he did her older sister.

8

A penetrating, cold wind was blowing across the expanse of open moorland between Roundtor Farm and the prison and Sir Thomas Tyrwhitt showed little inclination to dally along the way.

The prison governor's house had been built into the high perimeter wall, to the right of the main prison gate. When they reached it Tacy slid to the ground before Sir Thomas dismounted. After he had tethered his horse, they walked together to the house.

The servant who opened the door informed them that the prison governor was inside the prison.

'He'll be in the market square,' she explained, 'only there's no market there today, on account of them troublesome Americans.'

'Troublesome?' queried Sir Thomas.

'Yes, Sir Thomas. When they arrived yesterday they refused to leave the market square and go to their prison block. They've been sitting out there in the cold ever since. They're still there. You can just see them from a window upstairs in the servants' quarters, if you've a mind.'

'And Captain Cotgrave is with them?' queried Sir Thomas.

'That's right, Sir Thomas. He's been out there for about half an hour now.'

'Then we'll go inside the prison and speak to him. You have a back door that leads inside the prison, I presume?'

'Yes, Sir Thomas, but . . .'

'Good!' Sir Thomas brusquely interrupted her. 'You can show us the way. Come along, Tacy. Let's find out what's happened to your young American.'

Sir Thomas's positive manner precluded further argument. The young servant girl had strict instructions that the door leading to the prison yard was to be kept locked at all times, but she could not refuse Sir Thomas permission to use it. She hoped her employer would understand . . .

'Cap'n, isn't that the girl whose dog got Lieutenant Penn into trouble?'

A blanket wrapped tightly about him, Ephraim nudged Virgil and inclined his head to where Tacy and Sir Thomas were walking from the direction of the governor's house.

Virgil looked up, bleary-eyed. There had been little sleep for any of the Americans during the night. The blankets donated by the French had afforded only a degree of protection against the cold night wind. The prisoners-of-war had been numbed by an insidious chill which seeped inside a man's bones and remained there.

'It certainly looks like her . . .' mused Virgil. 'But what would she be doing in here – and who's that with her? By the way everyone's jumping one of the two must be pretty important – and I don't think it's the girl.'

'What was the name of the man she said owned the
dog Lieutenant Penn saved?'

'It was a Sir something-or-the-other.' Virgil took a
renewed interest in the couple who were approaching
the prison governor and his party.

'Look at the way everyone's scuttling his butt off to
meet him.' The deference accorded to Sir Thomas was
making a big impression upon Ephraim.

When Virgil struggled stiffly to his feet his muscles
were cold and unresponsive, his wounded leg giving
him particular trouble.

'Where you going, Cap'n?' demanded the big marine
corporal.

'If it's who we think it is and he's brought the girl
with him, he must be here to help Pilgrim. I want to
make sure no one puts him off.'

Picking his way between the other American prisoners-
of-war, Virgil limped towards Sir Thomas Tyrwhitt, Tacy
and the prison officials.

The militiamen forming a half-circle around the seated
prisoners were looking towards the new arrival. Virgil
almost made it through their line before he was stopped.
Then two of the militiamen reacted swiftly.

One seized him by the arm as the other confronted
him. The bayonet attached to the second militiaman's
musket puckered the material of Virgil's uniform coat,
in the vicinity of his navel.

'Where do you think you're going?' The question
came from the militiaman wielding the bayonet.

'I want to talk to the gentleman who has just arrived
with the girl.'

'If Sir Thomas Tyrwhitt wants to talk to you he'll send
for you. Get back with the others.'

Virgil held his ground. 'I'll stay here until I can attract
Sir Thomas's attention.'

The militiaman increased the pressure on the bayonet pressing against Virgil's midriff and it pricked his skin through the cloth. 'The longer you stand here, the more of my bayonet you're likely to taste. Stay here long enough and you'll know how a pig on a spit feels.'

'I've faced bayonets held in the hands of *real* soldiers,' said Virgil contemptuously. 'They didn't frighten me any more than yours does. I'll stay here until I'm noticed.'

Governor Cotgrave had seen Sir Thomas the moment he left the house and entered the prison yard. He hurried to meet him, closely followed by many of the senior prison officials with whom he had been speaking.

The governor and his staff had been discussing the best course of action to take against the American prisoners-of-war.

Cotgrave favoured calling in all off-duty militiamen and forcibly removing the stubborn Americans from the yard. Most of his officials felt perhaps a day without food, followed by one more night in the open would be sufficient to break their will.

George Dykar, the prison surgeon, was opposed to both these solutions. Called from his bed, there had been no time to consume his usual morning intake of brandy. Uncharacteristically sober, he argued that moving the men forcibly would provoke violence, resulting in casualties. There might even be fatalities – on both sides.

He also pointed out that refusing food to the men and leaving them in the open for another cold night would have equally serious consequences. The Americans had spent many months in the unhealthy confines of a rat-infested convict hulk. Already weakened, they would not have the constitution to withstand another bitterly cold night.

Either way, there would certainly be more work for the surgeon and his assistants.

Dykar favoured reasoning with them. If it proved necessary, he believed they should release the young marine lieutenant.

Such a solution was strongly opposed by Governor Cotgrave. The differences between governor and surgeon had still to be resolved.

When Sir Thomas had shaken hands with the governor and the senior members of his party, he said, 'I came here to see you concerning one of your prisoners, but I seem to have arrived at a somewhat inopportune moment.'

'We are having trouble with the American prisoners-of-war who arrived yesterday,' explained Governor Cotgrave apologetically. 'The supervisor of the hulk at Plymouth warned me they were likely to prove troublesome. He was happy to be rid of them.'

At that moment, Tacy said excitedly, 'That's the American who was with the lieutenant who saved Rip.'

As Sir Thomas turned away from Governor Cotgrave, she pointed in Virgil's direction.

Aware of the governor's questioning frown, Sir Thomas explained, 'This young lady is Tacy Elford. Her father farms below Roundtor. She's training one of my dogs for me – an animal with a first-class pedigree. Going to be a champion one day. I intend presenting it to the Prince Regent. It's the reason I'm here today. A damn-fool militiaman was about to shoot the dog when one of these Americans knocked his gun up. I came here to thank him and to see if there was something I could do for him while he's here. I knew the late American ambassador to London very well. It distresses me that we should be at war with his country. After all, we share the same language and have a great deal in common. I can't for the life of me see why they've allied themselves with the French. Expediency, I suppose. Do you mind if I have a few words with the American recognised by Tacy? By his dress he would appear to be an officer.'

Even as he asked the question, Sir Thomas was walking briskly towards Virgil. Hard put to keep up with him, Governor Cotgrave was given no opportunity to interrupt his flow of words before the Prince Regent's friend reached his objective.

Frowning at the militiaman who had brought Virgil to a halt, Sir Thomas pushed the man's musket and bayonet to one side, using only a forefinger of his right hand. 'I really don't think that is necessary. This officer poses no threat to anyone.'

To Virgil, he said, 'Good morning, sir. I'm Sir Thomas Tyrwhitt. Unless I'm mistaken you're wearing a captain's insignia. I'm seeking one of your lieutenants, Pilgrim something-or-other. According to Tacy here, he prevented one of my dogs from being shot.'

'That's right, Sir Thomas.' Virgil spoke quickly, aware that the prison governor wanted to speak. 'Lieutenant Pilgrim Penn saved the life of your dog. He's been thrown in a punishment cell as a result.'

'He has been placed in a punishment cell for assaulting a militiaman.'

The prison governor was angered that the American marine captain had been allowed to put his version of the incident before he had been able to give Sir Thomas the official explanation. 'Striking a guard, or an escort, is a very serious offence. There are more than nine thousand prisoners in this prison. Discipline is of paramount importance . . .'

'Lieutenant Penn struck no one,' declared Virgil firmly. 'He knocked up the militiaman's musket so that the shot went wide of the dog. No more than that.'

'That's *exactly* what he did,' agreed Tacy heatedly. 'When the gun went off it frightened Rip and he ran back to me. Then the lieutenant stepped back among the others again. That was when the militia officer had the manacles put on him.'

'You will have spoken to everyone involved in this unfortunate incident, of course?' Sir Thomas's question was directed at the prison governor.

Captain Cotgrave was an autocratic governor, unused to either seeking or accepting the views of others. It galled him to have his actions queried by anyone. Nevertheless, he was aware of the enormous power wielded by Sir Thomas Tyrwhitt.

'The actions of the prisoner's countrymen forced me to defer my inquiries into the matter until today, Sir Thomas. They defied orders given to them upon their arrival and refused to take up their quarters.'

Sir Thomas had already been given this information by Cotgrave's servant girl, but he pretended to be shocked. 'These men have been here all night? Out in the open?'

'The night air has undoubtedly chilled them through. Hopefully, it will also have given them time to reflect upon their actions. Had I called upon the militia to move them there would have been considerable bloodshed. Deaths too, I have no doubt. I took the humane course.'

'Why would they not go to their quarters? Is there something wrong with them?'

Before the governor could reply, Virgil said, 'It was a spontaneous protest at the unfair arrest of Lieutenant Penn. The men saw what happened out there on the moor. He'd done nothing to deserve being arrested. If anyone deserves punishment it's the militia officer. The order to shoot the dog was neither necessary nor reasonable.'

'No one asked your opinion, Captain. You may rejoin the other prisoners.'

Governor Cotgrave reacted angrily to Virgil's comments, but Sir Thomas countermanded his order.

'I would like him to remain here – with your permission of course, Governor.'

The rider was added as a sop to Governor Cotgrave's pride. Nevertheless, it was a command.

'I would also like to meet the young officer who saved my dog. I have no doubt you will wish to release him in view of what we have both heard?'

Inwardly seething with anger, Governor Cotgrave carefully controlled his feelings. 'I will arrange his release immediately. Perhaps you would like to return to my house while the order is carried out?'

'I will be delighted to accept your offer, Governor Cotgrave, but shall we see this matter resolved first? I presume it won't take long once you have issued the necessary order . . . ?'

9

When the inner prison gate opened and Pilgrim appeared, flanked by two militiamen, a great cheer went up from the American prisoners-of-war. They immediately began climbing stiffly to their feet.

Pilgrim was escorted to the small group of people which included Virgil, Tacy, Sir Thomas Tyrwhitt and the prison governor.

Aware of the part Tacy must have played in his release, Pilgrim nodded his head to her in grateful acknowledgement. Sir Thomas looked from one to the other with interest. The young American could only be a year or two older than Tacy . . .

He dismissed such an idea as preposterous. They had met only briefly the day before.

Governor Cotgrave was the first to speak. 'Lieutenant Penn, Sir Thomas Tyrwhitt has come to the prison to intercede on your behalf. In view of what he, this young lady, and your senior officer have said about the incident for which you were placed in the punishment cell, I feel justice will best be served by releasing you. I will, of course, conduct an inquiry into the circumstances of your arrest.'

Inclining his head to the prison governor, Pilgrim said, 'Thank you, sir.'

Turning to Sir Thomas and Tacy, he said, 'I would like to thank both of you, too. I am very grateful.'

'It is I who should be thanking *you*,' said Sir Thomas warmly. 'According to Tacy you saved the life of the dog I intend presenting to His Royal Highness the Prince Regent.'

'It's a spirited young animal and should please His Royal Highness,' replied Pilgrim.

'As I have just said to the governor, I find it distressing that our two countries should be at war with each other. Before hostilities began I made many friends at the United States Embassy in London. As a matter of fact a namesake of yours was ambassador there. We became good friends.'

'That would be my Uncle Richard, Sir Thomas. He too is unhappy that our countries are at war.'

'Your uncle, you say! Well, I'm damned . . . begging your pardon, Tacy. Now I am doubly glad to have been able to sort out this misunderstanding, young man. I feel I have done something to repay your uncle for the many hours I spent in the embassy enjoying his warm hospitality.'

The prison governor had been following the conversation in tight-lipped silence. Now Sir Thomas turned to him. 'I would like to stand as a guarantor for this young man if parole can be arranged, Governor Cotgrave.'

The prison governor shook his head. 'I'm sorry, Sir Thomas. No decision has yet been reached by the Admiralty about parole for American officers. Much will depend upon their conduct, as you will appreciate. I regret, they have not impressed the authorities so far.'

With a gesture, he indicated the Americans who were still noisily acclaiming the release of Pilgrim. 'I doubt very much whether this demonstration will make it any easier for us to relax the conditions under which they are detained.'

'No doubt the situation will improve before too long,' declared Sir Thomas meaningfully.

Addressing Pilgrim once more, he said, 'We will talk more of parole in due course, young man. In the meantime, if there is anything you need, you have only to send word to me. I live very close to the prison and Tacy comes here occasionally to sell produce from her father's farm. She will carry any messages you might have.'

Sir Thomas smiled in Tacy's direction, but she was looking at Pilgrim.

'Thank you, Sir Thomas,' said Pilgrim. 'You're very kind. In fact, there's something you might do right now that would make me feel much happier.'

Sir Thomas frowned, but he said, 'Of course. What is it?'

'I shared a punishment cell – the "*cachot*", I believe it is called – with a French officer. He has been there for about six weeks. He could not be more precise himself, having lost all sense of time. He's a very sick man and should be seen by a doctor as a matter of some urgency.'

'Six weeks in a punishment cell? What was his offence? It must have been extremely serious.' Sir Thomas put the question to the governor who promptly turned to one of his staff for an answer.

The man in question appeared embarrassed at being singled out for attention. 'It's the Frenchman who escaped and assaulted a militiaman. It was quite a serious assault, I believe. It was feared at first the militiaman's jaw had been broken.'

'I see.' The governor looked maliciously at Pilgrim. 'You are not suggesting the Frenchman is also innocent of the offence for which he was committed to the *cachot*?'

Pilgrim smiled. 'No, he certainly hit the militiaman, but . . .' Pilgrim related the story of the Frenchman's escape, and the circumstances of his recapture.

By the time his story came to an end only the governor was unsmiling. Undeterred, Pilgrim said, 'I'm sure you'll agree, sir, he had a great deal of justification for the action he took?'

'It occurred in the course of an escape attempt,' snapped the governor. 'He was fortunate not to have been shot.'

'Perhaps,' agreed Pilgrim enigmatically. 'One thing's certain, he'll die just as surely – but more miserably – if he's left to rot in the *cachot* for very much longer.'

The governor looked from Pilgrim to the Lord Warden of the Stannaries. He could see that Sir Thomas's sympathies were with the Frenchman.

To the prison doctor, he said, 'Surgeon Dykar, will you have a look at the man in the *cachot*? If you think it advisable, have him transferred to the hospital. When he's well he may return to the petty officers' mess.'

Expressionless, he said to Pilgrim, 'I suggest you rejoin the other prisoners-of-war now.'

He next addressed Virgil. 'I presume your country-men will now agree to take up your quarters and cause me and my staff no further problems?'

Virgil inclined his head to the governor. 'You'll have no more trouble now, sir. We'll go wherever you wish. Come on, Pilgrim. Let's get the men moving.'

As Pilgrim walked off with Virgil, heading towards their fellow American prisoners, he looked back.

Sir Thomas and the governor were talking, surrounded

by the prison officials. Only Tacy was looking in his direction. Pilgrim smiled at her and she waved a hand in return. Then she and the prison party began to move slowly towards the governor's house.

Pilgrim felt he had found an unexpected friend in Sir Thomas Tyrwhitt. He also looked forward to meeting Tacy again in the not-too-distant future.

10

'I'm not sure we weren't better off outside in the yard!'

The comment came from Ephraim as he and the others surveyed the interior of Number Four prison block. The building was likely to house the American prisoners-of-war until the war between Britain and the United States came to an end.

Although completed only a few years before, the prison accommodation left a great deal to be desired. Constructed from blocks of moorland grantie, the building had the comfortless feel of a fortress. This impression was heightened by windows which, although fitted with stout iron bars, had no glass to keep out the chill winds blowing across Dartmoor.

It had been built of Dartmoor granite. The porous qualities of the material was no doubt a contributory cause of the glistening damp which accumulated and ran down the inside of the bleak, grey walls.

Long tables and bench stools ran almost the whole length of the communal rooms, with crude lift-up lockers located at either end of each prison 'dormitory'.

Beside the lockers were stowage racks to house the hammock beds of the prisoners during the daylight hours.

'The Frenchman who shared the *cachot* with me said Number Four is the worst of all the prison blocks,' Pilgrim told Virgil and Ephraim. 'Apparently this is where the prison authorities place all the French thieves, thugs and misfits.'

'Then we'll need to establish ourselves as a separate entity right away,' declared Virgil. 'We'll begin by taking over this section of the ground floor. The Frenchmen can move elsewhere.'

The high-ceilinged room, or dormitory, that Virgil intended taking over occupied one half of the ground floor of Number Four cell block. It was divided from the other half by a wooden partition which reached from floor to ceiling. Above it was one more floor, reached by a series of concrete steps, plus a narrow 'attic' located immediately beneath the roof.

Henri Joffre had told Pilgrim the attic was occupied by prisoners considered bad even by the very worst elements among the French prisoners-of-war. They were degraded men who had lost all sense of decency. Many went about completely naked. Having gambled away even their clothes and blankets, they were ready to steal anything moveable and rob their more industrious countrymen.

The men interned here were so violent that prison guards never ventured into the 'attic' of Number Four cell block.

The announcement by the Americans that they intended to take exclusive control of half the ground floor of the building was greeted with derision by the Frenchmen already occupying the room.

At first, Virgil tried reasoning with them, suggesting that he meet with the senior Frenchmen who represented the men occupying the block.

'You're wasting your time,' declared Pilgrim. 'The other blocks have committees of prisoners to see that things run smoothly but, according to Henri Joffre, anarchy reigns here.'

'Well, it's not going to reign in this part of the building,' said Virgil firmly. 'If they won't be persuaded by reason there's nothing for it but to throw their things out and take it over for ourselves.'

Moments later the Americans were removing every article of personal belongings from the section of the building they had decided to make their own.

The move provoked howls of protest from the French and brought men hurrying from other parts of the building to see what was going on.

Pilgrim believed they would have trouble, but the uninvolved occupants of the building seemed to find the proceedings highly amusing. There *were* fights, but they were between Frenchmen from different parts of the building. No one attempted to make a physical assault on the Americans at this stage.

'That went easier than I imagined,' grinned Virgil when the last of the French belongings were heaved out through the door. 'Now we'll see if we can get hold of some soap and water and scrub this place out from end to end. The French must have been here for at least four years and I doubt if it's been properly cleaned in all of that time.'

It was two days before the prison authorities provided soap and scrubbing brushes for the Americans to clean up their quarters. By this time their scant belongings had arrived from the prison hulk.

On the second day the previous occupiers of the quarters made an attempt to return by force, but Ephraim led the resistance and the Frenchmen were quickly routed.

It was not long before the Americans settled down to a routine in their new life at Dartmoor prison. Cooks were detailed to prepare their daily rations and orderlies rostered for the various chores that needed to be undertaken.

It quickly became apparent that the greatest threat to their existence here would be boredom. Apart from a daily muster at nine o'clock every morning, there was nothing for the men to do.

The same problem had been present on the prison hulks anchored off Plymouth, but conditions there had been so cramped it had proved impossible to relieve the tedium. Here it was different.

The militia sergeant, John Straw, came to see how they were settling in. Through him, Pilgrim and Virgil were able to arrange for various writing materials to be made available to them.

With these, they began classes in as many subjects as it was possible to find tutors. Many men were unable to read or write and it was easy to find others to teach them these skills.

Virgil taught them mathematics while Pilgrim and one of the more respectable Frenchmen from another block began classes in French. If the Americans were going to share a gaol with their allies for very long it seemed to Pilgrim a sensible thing to do.

There was also a choir that became surprisingly popular. Most of the singers were black Americans. Included in their repertoire were many of the soulful songs learned during years of working on plantations in the southern states of America.

Large numbers of the Frenchmen would come along in the evenings to listen silently to the music of the black

Americans. John Straw told Pilgrim it was also popular with the guards. They made a habit of gathering on the walls close to the prison block. Here they listened to music which had its origins a long, long way from the bleak hills of Dartmoor.

But this was a prisoner-of-war establishment and tensions were never far below the surface. Soon they were to explode in a fashion that would rock the inmates and the prison authorities to the core.

11

A fortnight after the American prisoners-of-war had taken up residence in Number Four prison block, Henri Joffre paid them a visit.

Pilgrim did not immediately recognise him. In the semi-darkness of the *cachot* the Frenchman had been no more than a small, emaciated figure, his face hidden by weeks of dark beard.

Standing before him now was a trim, clean-shaven man dressed in the tight-fitting, green walking-out uniform of a captain of Napoleon's 9th Dragoons.

Shaking hands with the Frenchman, Pilgrim offered his apologies for failing to recognise his visitor before he had introduced himself.

'You need not apologise, my friend,' said Henri. 'Even had there been light in the *cachot* my face was buried in hair, and I was not dressed like this . . .'

A movement of his hand indicated his smart uniform. 'Fortunately, some of our men have become skilled tailors during the years we have spent here. You must take advantage of their talents. In fact, we have all become very industrious. No matter what is required, it can be made . . . even English money.'

'It's good to see you looking so well,' said Pilgrim. 'I was concerned about you.'

'The prison surgeon told me of your insistence that he must attend to me. I am deeply grateful. I do not think I would have survived many more nights in the *cachot*, especially after I lost the pleasure of your company. I had to spend ten days in the hospital before I was fit enough to return to the *Petit Cautionnement* – or, as the English call it, the "Petty Officers' Block". It is where they place those officers who refuse parole, or who have tried to escape.'

Henri used his hands in an expressive gesture once more, this time registering distaste for the large damp room in which they were standing. 'This is not a place for gentlemen. Those of our men who have been put in this building are not even wanted by other Frenchmen. This is why we insisted that a wall be built about them. It is not right for *any* of your countrymen to be here. For an *officer* . . . it is unthinkable!'

'It's better than the *cachot*,' Pilgrim pointed out.

'Every place is better than the *cachot*,' agreed Henri. 'But that makes no difference. This is not satisfactory accommodation for a gentleman.'

Virgil had been listening to the conversation between the two men. Now he said, 'No one's given us any choice in the matter. Even if they had, we couldn't go off and leave the others to the mercy of the riff-raff in here. To do so would be failing in our duties.'

Pilgrim had already introduced his companion to the Frenchman and Henri shrugged. 'You have been here for only two weeks. By the time the weeks have become months and the months years, you will have learned that personal survival is all that matters in Dartmoor prison. It becomes one's only duty. It is a sad lesson to have to learn. Yet, even if you feel obliged to remain here, why do you not take advantage of the market that is held in the prison square every day?'

To Pilgrim, he said, 'I told you of the woman who helped me to escape?' Without waiting for a reply, he said, 'Yes, I did. She came to the market yesterday. With her was a young girl. A very pretty young girl who asked after you. I was told it was she who arranged for you to be released from the *cachot*. I think she is perhaps unhappy you have not tried to see her.'

'It isn't that I haven't tried,' explained Pilgrim. 'We've requested the same privileges as your countrymen, but the governor refuses to discuss the matter. According to one of the turnkeys we've been branded as trouble-makers and are to be kept under close supervision.'

'Do you consider yourselves troublemakers, M'sieur Pilgrim?'

'Some of us have tried to escape once or twice in the past,' admitted Pilgrim guardedly. 'But then, so have you. Yet you and your fellow officers seem to be able to go wherever you wish inside the prison.'

'That is so,' agreed Henri. 'Of course, there are more than nine thousand Frenchmen here. The governor would find it very difficult to control so many without our co-operation. You are few. He does not feel it is necessary to make concessions to you. However, one of the turnkeys has told me another two hundred and fifty Americans are on their way. They will arrive very soon. The governor might be more inclined to listen to you when you have greater numbers. Perhaps he will allow the officers, at least, to attend the market.'

'Being given such permission will be a moral victory only,' said Virgil. 'Unfortunately, we have no money.

Representations have been made to our Government, but we've heard nothing from them yet.'

'Your lack of money need present no problem, Captain Howard. My father arranged for a considerable sum to be deposited in a London bank for my use. I will loan you all you need. Please . . . !'

He held up a hand to halt Virgil's immediate protest. 'France and America are allies, are they not? And M'sieur Pilgrim and I are friends. Had he not been able to secure my release from the *cachot* all the money in the world would not have been able to help me. You will repay me when your money arrives – as I am quite certain it will. Your Government takes good care of its own people, I know. Two of my uncles fought with your countrymen to gain your independence. One was killed. The other fell in love with your land – and with an American girl. He remained in your country.'

Returning his attention to Pilgrim once more, Henri said, 'Tomorrow I will no doubt be seeing the young lady who is so anxious about you. Would you like me to give her any message?'

Aware that others were listening and that Virgil in particular seemed highly interested in his reply, Pilgrim felt tongue-tied. 'Tell her . . . tell her I'm grateful for her concern . . . I'll come and speak to her as soon as I'm able. Perhaps you'll explain that we aren't allowed to leave the compound and visit the market.'

'I will tell her this, M'sieur Pilgrim. I will also discuss your problems with my senior officers. We have a committee to deal with French problems. Once a month they meet with Governor Cotgrave. He was at first reluctant to agree to any recommendations made by those who are his prisoners. However, experience has taught him to pay attention to what we suggest. If he does not, there is likely to occur an unexpected outbreak of trouble. This

upsets him greatly. He much prefers to enjoy a quiet life.
I think he will agree to allow you and Captain Howard
to attend the market. When there are more of you here,
we will make arrangements for the officers to come and
join us in the *Petit Cautionnement*.'

'Thank you, Henri. When we feel there are enough
Americans here to protect themselves against the unruly
element in Block Four we'll be delighted to come and
share your quarters. I'm sure they're much better than
these.'

'But of course! We have servants there. At table we
eat like gentlemen – not like the pigs with whom you
share this building.'

As Henri made this comment there was a sudden din
from the far end of the Americans' quarters. A party
of brawling, ragged French prisoners spilled from the
hallway beyond the doorway to the yard outside.

'We're getting used to them now,' said Virgil with a
gesture of resignation. 'They're about all the entertain-
ment we can enjoy in Block Four.'

'I will have some playing cards sent here for you,'
said Henri. 'But be on guard against the men with whom
you share this block. They fought for France, but I refuse
to regard them as true Frenchmen. They are animals.
Unfortunately, like animals, they are also dangerous.
You must take care. It is rumoured they are planning
to take revenge upon you for evicting them from a part
of the building they regard as their own. I have heard
nothing specific, you understand. At the moment it is
no more than a rumour, yet it is one that should be
taken seriously. If I hear more I will inform you.'

Bowing to each man in turn, Henri Joffre took his
leave, his smart attire in marked contrast to the rags of
his countrymen as he pushed between them on his way
to the gateway that led to the remainder of the prison.

'Do you believe there's any truth in what he says about the French planning to take revenge on us?' asked Virgil.

'I think we have to take his words seriously,' warned Pilgrim. 'There's not very much happening in here that Henri doesn't know something about. Besides, he feels he owes me something. We should begin by placing guards on the doors to our part of the building – and keeping them there, day and night.'

12

When the second batch of American prisoners-of-war arrived at Dartmoor prison, Pilgrim and Virgil were reunited with many of the surviving marines and sailors from the United States frigate *Delaware*.

It was an emotional reunion – the marines had believed the two officers and Ephraim to be dead. Rumours to this effect had circulated soon after the escape of the three men from custody in the West Indies.

Also included among the new arrivals were a hundred battle-hardened soldiers from the regular United States army, with their own experienced non-commissioned officers. They had been captured at Queenston, when the Americans launched an abortive invasion into Canada.

The soldiers had been sent to England for internment because it was feared that holding them in a prisoner-of-war camp closer to their homeland would tempt them to escape.

The arrival of so many disciplined fighting men came as a great relief to Virgil. Still the senior officer present, he now felt confident that if Henri Joffre's fears were justified, the Americans would be able to hold their own against the French prisoners in Block Four.

The Americans now took over the whole of the ground floor of the building. This time, the eviction of the remaining Frenchmen was carried out by the militia guard force on duty at the prison.

Governor Cotgrave had reluctantly accepted that the French and Americans in this block did not get along with each other. Although the two nationalities were allied in their war against Great Britain, they required separate quarters if there was not to be constant friction between them.

However, the disciplinarian governor was unable to forestall violence when it eventually erupted.

The turnkey arrived early one morning to carry out his usual duty of unlocking the iron grille doors that opened from the prison block to the exercise yard.

It promised to be a fine and warm early summer day and the prisoners, both French and American, took the opportunity to get out of the overcrowded and evil-smelling dormitories as quickly as possible.

The intention of the Americans was to enjoy the fresh morning air before mustering for the nine o'clock roll call.

It was Ephraim who commented to Virgil on the uncharacteristic silence of the French prisoners as they filed out to the yard. Usually, they spilled from the building in a torrent of loud-voiced humanity.

Today they left the prison block in near silence and began forming up in an irregular line, some ten or twelve deep, facing the doors through which the Americans were leaving the building.

'They're definitely up to something,' agreed Virgil.

'I'll get our marines and the soldiers out there as quickly as I can. Meanwhile, go outside and warn the others to stay close to the building, Pilgrim. Better still, get them back inside. You go with him, Ephraim.'

Pilgrim hurried outside with the giant marine corporal close behind him – but they had left it too late to forestall a fight.

The American prisoners who had already left the building were belatedly aware that all was not as it should be. Previously warned by Pilgrim and Virgil that the French were planning revenge on them for taking over the ground floor of the prison block, they now realised the time had arrived.

They began pushing back against those still leaving the building. For a few moments there was total confusion. This was when the Frenchmen waded in to the attack.

The French prisoners-of-war had somehow managed to accumulate a wide variety of makeshift weapons. Among these were pieces of timber torn up from the attic floor, and large stones prised from the wall around Block Four.

The more vicious of the Frenchmen had armed themselves with scissors, taken apart to make crude but highly effective daggers.

Outside the prison building, Pilgrim and Ephraim battled against the tide of Americans desperately trying to regain the uncertain sanctuary of the prison block. The majority were merchant seamen, not fighting men. They were no match for soldiers who had seen active service with Napoleon's army on many successful campaigns.

The Frenchmen who occupied Dartmoor prison's Block Four were undoubtedly the very dregs of their country's army – but they were no strangers to fighting.

For many of them, brought up during the bloody years of the revolution, violence had always been part of their way of life.

As Pilgrim and Ephraim drew closer to the vengeful Frenchmen other marines and soldiers of the United States army struggled to join them. Many were more prepared for trouble than was Pilgrim.

Quite as resourceful as the Frenchmen, they too had acquired and secreted a wide variety of weapons during their internment both in Dartmoor and on the prison hulks.

They had stout sticks and stones and some had managed to acquire a variety of iron bars. When they clashed with the French attackers, their makeshift weapons were put to effective use.

Suddenly finding himself in the front line, facing the Frenchmen, Pilgrim was about to be struck with a half-scissor dagger tied to a broom-handle when a large stone struck his would-be attacker between the eyes.

Pilgrim's rescuer was Ephraim. Pushing Pilgrim to one side he picked up the makeshift pike of the fallen Frenchman and wielded it to devastating effect. He was a formidable warrior and his great size commanded respect. Within moments there was a space about him that extended for as far as his long arms and the scissor-pike could reach.

The battle was brief, but savage. Although heavily outnumbered, the Americans held their own and were soon able to check the onslaught of the Frenchmen.

Suddenly, the gate to the prison yard was flung open and armed militiamen poured inside the Block Four exercise yard. With bayonets fixed and muskets extended menacingly, they advanced upon the fighting prisoners-of-war.

The French belligerents held their line for only a few

minutes before they broke and ran. The savage battle was over, but when they fled from the compound they left a great many men lying on the ground.

Most were Americans – and among their number was Pilgrim.

The American marines and soldiers had rallied around him to form the nucleus of the American resistance. Then, at the very moment when the Frenchmen fled the field, a half-naked ruffian lunged forward with a stick that had been sharpened to a dangerous point. With this makeshift weapon he succeeded in stabbing the American lieutenant in the stomach.

Pilgrim sank slowly to the ground, both hands clutching the wound and blood oozing out between his fingers.

Even as he protested to the men bending over him that he was not seriously hurt the world began to spin about him. In mid-sentence he drifted off into a state where pain disappeared and he hovered between lethargy and unconsciousness.

Then faces and sounds drifted away and he knew no more.

13

Pilgrim recovered consciousness slowly. It was very many minutes before it registered that he was lying in a bed in the Dartmoor prison hospital.

He became aware of groaning. When he turned his head he could see other men in nearby beds, some heavily bandaged, others wearing crude splints.

As Pilgrim moved his head an English hospital orderly came along and stopped at the foot of his bed. 'Well! I'm surprised to see you back in the world of the living, dearie. The surgeon had given you up for dead – and so had I.'

'I'd like . . . a drink.' Pilgrim's tongue seemed to fill his mouth and felt as though it was made of old leather.

The orderly went to a nearby table and transferred some water from a jug to a heavy mug. As he returned, Pilgrim tried to sit up. He let out a gasp of pain. It felt as though his stomach was on fire. Then he remembered the fight . . . and the stabbing.

The orderly helped him raise his head and held the

mug to his lips. When Pilgrim lay back on the pillow once more, he was gasping, as though he had done something strenuous.

'The fight . . . ?' he spoke breathlessly. 'Were many of our men seriously hurt?'

'More Americans than Frenchmen – but only just. We've got forty of you in here. If you ask me, it's a miracle no one was killed. You came as close to it as anyone, yet here you are talking away better than some of them. Him over there, for instance.' The orderly pointed vaguely in the direction of the far side of the ward. 'He's lost half his teeth and has a broken jaw.'

The orderly straightened the blanket on Pilgrim's bed. 'Call me again if you need anything. I'll go and tell Surgeon Dykar you've come round. He'll be pleased. He doesn't like losing patients; it upsets him. Trouble is, it means he's unhappy for most of the time in this place. In the last few months we've lost more than ever before, what with gaol fever, measles and fights. Still, I'm sure it's a blessed release for some of 'em. Especially those in the block where they've put you Americans. We're supposed to be here to save lives, but there's some of them I wouldn't work very hard to keep alive.'

Having made this stark and harsh observation, the orderly went on his way, pausing here and there along the ward to speak to some of the patients.

The surgeon did not come to the hospital until the morning after Pilgrim had regained consciousness. Watching him as he made his way along the ward, inspecting the wounds of those involved in the fight between Frenchmen and Americans, Pilgrim grimaced at his rough methods. He thought he probably owed his own recovery to the fact that the surgeon had believed him to be dying and had done little to treat his wound.

The surgeon's method of removing Pilgrim's dressing could only be described as brutal, but he ignored his patient's cry of pain. Looking at the wound for a minute or two, he prodded around it none-too-gently and sniffed it. Then, breathing wine fumes over his patient, he said, 'It appears to be healing well enough by itself, so we'll leave it to take its course. You're lucky, young man. Whatever it was you were stabbed with seems to have missed your vital organs. With any luck you'll be back on your feet in a week or so.'

That afternoon Pilgrim had two unexpected visitors. One was Captain Henri Joffre. The other was Tacy. She walked self-consciously along the ward beside the Frenchman, her progress marked by appreciative cat-calls and whistles from the injured and sick men.

'Good afternoon, Pilgrim.' Henri smiled down at him. 'I met a hospital orderly at the market this afternoon and asked after you. He told me you had regained consciousness. I passed the information on to Tacy and she asked if she might come and speak to you.'

'I'm very pleased to see you,' said Pilgrim, feeling ridiculously elated. 'It's good to see you both,' he added belatedly, realising he had been looking only at Tacy when he spoke. 'But I'm surprised the governor gave permission for Tacy to come in here.'

'Ah! Governor Cotgrave does not know. He is away in Plymouth and the surgeon is having his usual afternoon "rest". It was the orderly who proved obliging – and for no more than a couple of guineas.'

When Pilgrim began thanking him, Henri cut him short. 'We do not have much time. Do not waste it. I will leave you and Tacy alone for a few minutes. One of the men in my regiment was also injured in the fight. He is in the next ward. The man is a rogue,

but he was a good soldier. I will visit him for a few
minutes.'

When Henri had gone there was an awkward silence
between Tacy and Pilgrim for a few moments. It was
broken by Tacy.

'I've brought a couple of things from the stall for
you. A few eggs. A piece of cheese. It's not much,
but we'd almost sold out of things by the time Captain
Joffre found me and said I might be able to come and
see you.'

'It's very kind of you . . . Tacy. I like that name. I
know a woman back home in Ohio named Tacy. She
and her family are Quakers.'

'It's a Quaker name,' explained Tacy. 'It was my
grandmother's name. She was a Quaker until she married my grandfather.'

'My mother was a Quaker!' Pilgrim seized on the
common ground they had discovered. 'She was made
to leave the Society when she married my pa.'

For a few minutes they talked about Quakers in
America and in Devon, then they both fell silent once
more.

'It really is nice of you to come here to see me,' said
Pilgrim sincerely, 'but it's not the nicest of places for a
girl to visit.'

'It's the least I could do,' said Tacy. 'Especially after
what you did for Rip. I'd been hoping you would come
to see me at the market. I've been here almost every
day since you arrived at the prison. But Captain Joffre
explained that the governor won't allow the Americans
to come and buy things.'

'I thought you only came to the prison market very
occasionally?' said Pilgrim.

Tacy coloured up. 'I do as a rule, but we seem to have
had a few more things than usual to sell just lately.'

'I'm glad,' said Pilgrim, a little more enthusiastically than he had intended it to sound. 'Your coming here today has cheered everyone else in the hospital too.'

The fact that Pilgrim was happy to see her pleased Tacy, but she tried not to allow it to show too much.

'Do you think you'll be able to come to the market when you get out of here? Captain Joffre says he's trying to arrange for you and your Captain to be allowed to come to the market and buy things for the others.'

'If Henri says that's what he's trying to do then he'll probably succeed,' said Pilgrim. 'He's pretty good at arranging things – except perhaps his own escape.'

Tacy giggled and it was a pleasant sound. 'He very nearly succeeded. Mary – that's the girl who brought the clothes in for him – is a friend of mine. She'd do anything to get him out of here. She hopes that if she helps him to escape he'll take her to France with him. She hasn't got a very happy life here.'

Before Pilgrim could question her about her friend, she said, 'Here's Captain Joffre coming back. He seems to be in a hurry.'

When Henri reached them, he said breathlessly, 'I've just seen the orderly. Governor Cotgrave has returned sooner than was expected. Tacy and I must leave immediately.'

Tacy's expression of disappointment matched Pilgrim's own.

'I'll try to see you again – as soon as I can,' he said to her.

'I look forward to that . . . Do you think they'll let you out on parole?'

'Come. We must leave.' Captain Joffre took Tacy by the arm.

'I don't know . . . can you write?'

Tacy nodded.

'Write to me. I'll write too. Send the letters through Henri and Mary . . .'

The orderly put in an agitated appearance at the entrance to the ward and Henri began hurrying Tacy away. She turned at the end of the ward to give him a brief wave, then she was gone.

Behind her, Pilgrim lay back on his pillow and closed his eyes. He was tired after talking to her, even though it had been for a relatively short time, but he felt incredibly happy that she had come to the hospital to see him.

It seemed unbelievable that he, a prisoner-of-war in the grim, moorland prison of Dartmoor, should have been fortunate enough to meet up with someone like Tacy . . .

14

Pilgrim remained in the prison hospital for two weeks. He was the last of the American casualties involved in the fight with the Frenchmen to be released.

During this time, Virgil was able to visit him only twice. The visits were sanctioned by the governor, but for some reason he insisted that Virgil be accompanied on each occasion by two militiamen.

Despite this petty restriction, Virgil was able to report that conditions seemed to be improving for the Americans, at last. Notification had been received that the United States Government would soon deposit a large sum of money with a certain Reuben G. Beasley, an American citizen currently resident in London. He had been appointed as the United States agent in London.

Once the money had been received, the agent had been instructed to make a regular allowance to American prisoners-of-war. He had also been instructed to visit Dartmoor and listen to any grievances the American inmates might have about the conditions of their internment.

There was also talk of transferring the two Marines
officers and some of the more senior ship's captains to
the *Petit Cautionnement*.

This news was particularly welcomed by Pilgrim.
Such a move would enable him to visit the daily market
and meet with Tacy there.

With nothing else to occupy his time in the hospital,
he had thought a great deal about the young Devon girl.
He had spoken of her to Virgil, but the Marines captain
did not share Pilgrim's enthusiasm for the blossoming
relationship.

'Be careful, Pilgrim,' he had warned. 'In your present
condition you'd find any young girl attractive. If one is
kind to you as well, you'll be in over your head before
you even know you're in there swimming.'

Pilgrim realised this was a matter over which they
were unlikely to agree and he changed the subject.

'The last time a move to the petty officers' block
was mentioned you said you wouldn't even consider
it. What's happened to make you change your mind?'

'A number of things. With the arrival of our marines
and the army, we now have some good NCOs capable
of taking care of things in Block Four. That reminds me,
I've promoted Ephraim to sergeant. An official letter
to Marines headquarters to confirm his promotion is
on its way right now. I did this because some of the
army NCOs from the southern states have been making
things difficult for him – for the other coloured men
too. We'll have trouble if we're not careful. Ephraim's
now one of the most senior men in the Block. I trust
him to keep things the way they ought to be, particularly among his own people. He'll no doubt welcome an opportunity to run things his way, without
having us around breathing down his neck the whole
of the time.'

A more frequent visitor to the prison hospital was Henri. Each time he came he carried a small gift from Tacy. Most often it was some item of farm produce or fresh bread, but once he brought a cake she had baked especially for him.

On two occasions he also brought letters from her, but Pilgrim found them disappointingly short and formal. She politely expressed the hope that his health was improving then went on to tell him domestic news of everyday happenings on the farm where she lived.

The letters gave him a glimpse of the hard-working yet apparently happy way of life she and her young sister shared on Roundtor Farm. They also indicated she had caring and loving parents, although a constant theme in the letters was the concern she felt for the health of her father.

With paper and a pencil supplied by Henri, Pilgrim was able to reply to her letters. He tried to inject something of the way he felt into the writing. Yet, despite all his efforts, he found they contained little more than a 'thank you' for her gifts and the hope that he would soon leave the hospital block and be able to attend the prison market and see her once more.

Looking through the latest letter he had written, Pilgrim realised it was every bit as formal as those he had received from her.

When Pilgrim was eventually discharged from the hospital and escorted back to Block Four, he found there had been a number of changes. Only the day before, the black Americans had moved out, *en masse*, from the ground floor of Number Four block. They had taken over part of the 'attic', where the toughest and most dangerous of the Frenchmen were housed.

The move had come about after a recently arrived American prisoner-of-war, a ship's mate from Georgia, claimed to have recognised Ephraim.

The sailor declared Ephraim was an escaped slave. Moreover, he swore that Ephraim had murdered an overseer during his flight from the plantation to which he belonged.

It was a rumour Pilgrim and Virgil had heard before, but it had never been substantiated and had not affected Ephraim's service in the United States Marine Corps.

The mate's denunciation of the runaway slave provoked anger against Ephraim among the mate's fellow American seamen, many of whom came from slave-owning southern states.

Virgil and Ephraim's fellow marines had prevented any serious trouble from erupting, but it remained a volatile situation.

A temporary solution was found by Ephraim himself. He had formed a friendship with the self-styled leader of the *Romains*, the name by which the French occupants of the Block Four attic liked to be known.

Evicting a number of his own men, the French *Romain* leader invited Ephraim and his fellow black Americans to occupy part of the 'attic' with him.

Virgil did not like the idea of splitting the American prisoners-of-war into separate racial groups. Yet he was aware the move offered at least a short-term solution to the animosity that existed between black and white Americans.

It also meant Ephraim would be able to maintain his control over his fellow black Americans even though they were separated from the other American prisoners-of-war.

Virgil was forced to accept that the problem which divided the United States of America could not be solved here on Dartmoor, amidst the added pressures that existed in a prisoner-of-war gaol.

It would take a war, and the loss of millions of lives in a divided country, to lay the foundations of a truly united nation. Meanwhile, he trusted Ephraim to maintain control over those who had gone to the Block Four attic with him.

15

'I wish we all knew a little more about this young man of yours, Tacy. It worries me, you being sweet on someone who's locked up in a prison. It doesn't seem right, somehow.'

Joan Elford voiced her concern to her daughter as they kneaded dough for bread in the kitchen of Roundtor Farm.

'I'm not sweet on him, Ma – and he's not my "young man". As for him being in prison . . . He's not there because he's done anything wrong. He's locked away because he was captured while he was fighting for his country. There's nothing wrong with that.'

'If you're not sweet on him, why wouldn't you let me read the letters he sent to you – or the ones you wrote to him?' The interruption came from Johanna.

'Because they're none of your business, that's why.' Tacy threw a glance at her younger sister that was intended to silence her. Instead, it provoked a mischievous grin.

'Billy thinks you're sweet on the American. He's unhappy about it. He told me so.'

'Billy doesn't know any better. *You* should.'

Silencing her younger daughter with a stern glance, Joan Elford returned her attention to Tacy. 'You've never written letters *or* baked a cake for any man before.'

'I've never written to a man because I've never known one who's locked away in prison, and I made the cake because Lieutenant Penn was stabbed in a fight and put in the prison hospital. There's no one else to do anything for him – and he almost died.'

'Stabbed? You never told me *that*! How did he get himself stabbed? What was the fight about?' Joan Elford was genuinely alarmed. 'If he's the sort who gets himself involved in fights, then he's *definitely* not a young man you should be getting mixed up with. I don't know what your father's doing encouraging you . . .'

'Ma!' Tacy placed flour-dusted hands on her hips and glared in exasperation, first at her highly amused young sister, then at her disapproving mother. 'Lieutenant Penn is an officer. There was a fight between American and French prisoners-of-war. Hundreds of them were involved. It was his duty to try to stop the fight. *That's* how he came to be stabbed. He wasn't *fighting* anyone. It was a French officer told me that. He'd hardly be likely to take Lieutenant Penn's side if it wasn't true, would he?'

'I don't know about that. From what I hear it's a mistake to trust these French officers. You look at young Polly Pearce, over at Sheepstor Farm – and Carol Williams, whose father is churchwarden at Ashburton. They trusted French officers. Now they're both expecting.'

Joan Elford wiped a flour-streaked hand across her nose. 'If this young man of yours is as trustworthy as you say he is, then why hasn't the prison governor given him parole, same as has been given to the French officers?'

'Nobody knows, really. The French officer that Mary Gurney's friendly with thinks it's because the Americans speak English so they could easily pass themselves off as Englishmen and escape. I expect they'll be allowed out on parole soon, though. When they do, Sir Thomas Tyrwhitt says he'll stand surety for Lieutenant Penn, so he must think he's all right.'

'What sort of a recommendation is that supposed to be? The likes of Sir Thomas don't have the same standards as ordinary people. Mind you, them as rule over all of us aren't very much better. The Prince Regent, who ought to have important things to do in London, has been spending more time on Dartmoor than he should – and it's not for the good of his estates, either. They say that between 'em, Sir Thomas Tyrwhitt and the Prince Regent have worn a path between Tor Royal and Dolly French's cottage that's easier to follow than the main road to Plymouth! It's an affront to decent folk, that's what it is.'

'Well, while Sir Thomas is spending his time with Dolly French he's leaving others alone,' said Tacy enigmatically. 'If he wants to stand surety for Lieutenant Penn I can't imagine anyone suggesting he's not a suitable person.'

'Perhaps they'll let Tacy's young man come and stay here,' said Johanna. With an air of exaggerated innocence, she added, 'Then, if Tacy has a baby I could help her look after it.'

'That's quite enough from you, young lady,' said her mother firmly. 'I should know better by now than to talk of such things in front of you. Go out and collect the eggs. While you're there – and since you're so interested in babies – go and see how the old sow is. According to my reckoning she should have had her litter a day or two ago.'

Johanna left the kitchen without argument, although she paused at the door to turn and put out her tongue at her sister. Everyone in the household of four had their own responsibilities on the farm. Johanna's was taking care of the chickens.

When the door closed behind the young girl, Tacy spoke hesitantly to her mother. 'Do you think Lieutenant Penn might possibly be given parole here?'

Seeing her mother's expression of amazement at the unexpected suggestion, she added hurriedly, 'With Pa being ill most of the time we could do with help on the farm this summer, what with the haymaking, and everything.'

'We could use extra help for perhaps two or three months of the year, girl. What would we find for him to do for the rest of the time? Besides, Billy's on hand to give us help during the busy months. Are you saying we should stop him from coming here?'

'No, of course not,' said Tacy. 'That wouldn't be fair. Billy's simple, but he's never done an unkind thing to anyone in his life. He loves coming here. It makes him feel useful. I couldn't hurt him.'

Joan Elford was aware that the young American had assumed considerable importance to her eldest daughter. She also knew the reason why. Roundtor Farm was in an isolated situation. There was not a young man of Tacy's own age living within miles. Nevertheless, it was tragic that the first young man to attract her attention should be a prisoner-of-war, incarcerated in Dartmoor prison.

When Tacy lapsed into an unhappy silence, her mother said gently, 'Don't get carried away with your dreams, Tacy. This young American is a prisoner, far from home – and he's been hurt. It's right you should show him Christian kindness, but don't get too sweet on him. I heard you telling your pa the other day his uncle had been the American ambassador in London and a friend of Sir Thomas's. With such a background he's hardly likely to want to live or work on a small farm like ours, even if we did ask him to come here. He's a gentleman. I expect he'll be paroled to somewhere like Ashburton. That's where most of the French officers go.'

'I suppose so,' conceded Tacy unhappily. 'But he doesn't behave a bit like Sir Thomas. Until he gets parole I'll still take one or two things into the prison for him.'

'Of course. It's a very kind thing to do. All I'm saying is that it would be foolish to grow too fond of him. You'll only end up being hurt if you do. If he's given parole he'll be mixing with the fine friends of Sir Thomas, not with the likes of us. Remember, too, that one day he'll be going home to America and out of your life.'

Tacy had still not replied to this observation when Johanna burst in through the kitchen door. 'Ma, Tacy! Come quick. The sow's having her babies – there's six already and more are coming. They're dropping out like maggots from a dead sheep!'

Joan Elford was not sure she approved of the simile, but she allowed it to pass.

'It's cold out there and that old sow won't let any of 'em feed until she's had them all. Start bringing them in, Johanna. You help her, Tacy, while I finish the bread. Bring them in and lay them in front of the fire.'

Piglets were a source of quick profit. Joan Elford knew from past experience that this particular sow became very agitated when giving birth. Unless the piglets were taken away from her until the last one had arrived, she was likely to roll on those already born and kill or injure some of them.

While the girls were out of the kitchen she found a piece of cloth and laid it in front of the fire. The piglets would be placed upon it to keep warm until the last of them was born. Then they would be returned to their mother.

An hour later there were thirteen tiny piglets laid in a row before the fire. The two girls were pleading that they be allowed to remain in the house for 'just a minute or two more'.

Watching the two girls crouched before the fire with the piglets, Joan Elford wished they might both remain innocent young girls for a few more years, but she realised it was not to be. Tacy was already a young woman. She would marry and leave the farm as soon as the right young man came along.

She wished Tacy could have found him before meeting the young American. Joan could see Lieutenant Pilgrim Penn bringing nothing but unhappiness into the life of her elder daughter.

16

Another two hundred Americans arrived at Dartmoor during the next few days. Among their number was a ship's captain named Steiger. He was also the owner of a small fleet of ships which sailed out of Savannah, in Georgia.

Steiger was a difficult man and furious to have been taken prisoner while he was sailing in a merchantman. He also seemed to think he should have been allocated a whole prison block to himself, but he was lodged in the other half of the block occupied by Virgil and Pilgrim.

One of the men who had been taken prisoner with him was Steiger's slave. The shipowner would not have him sharing the same section of prison building, but still expected the man to carry out all the duties of a slave.

Ephraim had other ideas.

Soon after the arrival of the newcomers, the slave abruptly ceased serving his master and disappeared from view.

It was discovered he had taken up residence in the attic with the other black Americans. It was strongly rumoured that the parting of master and slave had been engineered by Ephraim.

Steiger was furious. He and Ephraim had a fierce argument. Violence was averted only by the intervention of Virgil.

Not to be thwarted, Steiger and his crew, accompanied by a number of seamen from the southern states, laid in wait for their black countrymen, hoping to lay hands on the missing slave.

A fight ensued but this too was quickly broken up by the marines before anyone was seriously hurt. Virgil realised it was merely postponing a showdown. Trouble between the two groups of men would remain, constantly simmering beneath the surface of prison life, as would the enmity between the Americans and the Frenchmen of Block Four.

Virgil discussed the problem with Pilgrim soon after the latest incident, and spoke with irritation of the newly arrived Captain Steiger.

'Would you know whether this shipowner's name is *Conrad* Steiger?' asked Pilgrim.

'That's his name. You know him?'

'No, but I certainly know *of* him. He lived in Washington for a while after making his money as a privateer. Then he moved west and stood for Congress against my father, in Ohio. He was a bad loser. It didn't help him gain votes when it was rumoured he was involved with a slave girl. Steiger took the girl as his mistress, and after he'd had her husband sold off and shipped elsewhere, he moved back to Washington. When his wife left him he moved the girl into his house, as a so-called "servant". Apparently, it caused one of Washington's biggest scandals for years. That's the reason he moved south and went back to sea. There have been other rumours about him since. Trouble seems to follow him around. We could do without him here.'

'Well, he won't be upsetting Block Four for very much longer, but you and I aren't going to lose him. The governor's finally agreed to move you, me, and the ships' captains to the 'Petty Officers' Block'. It'll give us more freedom of movement. Once our money arrives we're to be allowed to attend the market and buy provisions for those of our men who are left here. Ephraim will be the senior American in the block, although he'll never be accepted by the southerners. However, Governor Cotgrave has agreed to give him access to us at all reasonable times and he'll be able to tell us what's going on here.'

Pilgrim was impressed. 'Things really are looking up! What persuaded the governor to change his mind? I get the distinct impression he doesn't like Americans.'

'I doubt if he's changed his mind about us, but he likes a quiet life. There are more of us now and the French officers have been agitating for some time for the transfer of our officers. I think your friend from the *cachot* had a great deal to do with it.'

Two days later nine Americans were transferred to the Petty Officers' Block. Among their number were Pilgrim, Virgil and Conrad Steiger.

Despite the prospect of greatly improved living conditions in their new block, Steiger complained bitterly because he had been refused permission to locate and bring his slave with him from Block Four.

Henri Joffre headed the party of French officers waiting to greet the Americans upon their arrival in their new quarters. Walking inside the Petty Officers' Block with the others, it seemed to Pilgrim they had been transported to a different world.

Most of the Frenchmen had been in Dartmoor prison for four years. They had used the time to make their quarters as comfortable as money and ingenuity would allow.

Each man had been allotted a carefully measured space. It was not large, but within its chalked lines were a bed and a slim wooden wardrobe. Some men had also managed to fit a stool and small table within their allotted area. In addition, many small rugs were strewn about the concrete floor.

Everything in the block had been made by craftsmen among the French prisoners-of-war and paid for from the private funds which seemed to be freely available to all the Frenchmen here.

Upon their arrival, Henri introduced Pilgrim and Virgil to fellow members of the Petty Officers' Block's 'committee'. All were either officers of high rank, or belonged to influential families in their home country.

The French officers had instigated a disciplined regime throughout the prison for prisoners of a lower rank than themselves. Only the men of Block Four contemptuously refused to acknowledge their authority, going about in their own degraded way.

Pilgrim learned that the wall around Block Four had actually been erected at the suggestion of the French officers' committee. Once completed, the dissidents inside had been largely ignored by their more law-abiding and industrious countrymen.

Henri listened patiently and politely to Conrad Steiger's complaint about the loss of his slave, before saying, 'We have a number of men in the prison who were slaves before being taken prisoner, m'sieur. However, we are all here because we were captured while serving our country. It has been decided there will be no slaves in Dartmoor prison. Only prisoners-of-war. It makes sense, if you think about it, M'sieur Steiger. Rather than acknowledge themselves as slaves, many would offer their services to the British navy – as free men. We would therefore be helping the enemy, would we not?'

Henri smiled amiably at the disgruntled American shipowner. 'If you find it essential to have a servant, you will find many excellent Frenchmen willing to oblige you – for a fair wage, of course.'

'I have no money to pay a servant,' complained Steiger bitterly. 'All the money I had with me was stolen when my ship was taken by the British.'

'I understand that arrangements are being made for you to receive an allowance from your Government,' said Henri with continuing patience. 'It should also not be too difficult to have private money transferred to an English bank, as many of us have done. In the meantime, we have established a fund to provide a temporary solution for such problems. You may repay the fund when your own money is received.'

Turning away from the complaining American, Henri returned his attention to the two Marines officers. 'Your friends will be attended to by other officers, but I have had space made for you next to me. You will be comfortable enough, I assure you. All we lack here is privacy. For the rest, I can offer you a wide choice of drinks. Would you like a Cognac . . . ? Wine . . . ? Or champagne, perhaps, to celebrate your improved status within the prison?'

17

Tacy and her father were among the vendors selling goods when Pilgrim and Virgil paid their first visit to the market the following day, accompanied by Henri Joffre.

Tacy held a basket containing cakes and eggs for sale. Her father had brought a cart loaded with blocks of peat, dried and ready for burning. It was a commodity that was always in demand within the prison.

Wealthy French officers had purchased stoves during their first winter in the cold and damp prison. Much of the moorland fuel would go to them in the Petty Officers' Block. The remainder would be burned in the kitchens, where food for the prisoners was cooked.

Tacy's face lit up with surprised delight when she saw Pilgrim. 'You're better – and they've allowed you to come to the market! I'm very happy for you. But you're far too thin. You need to put on some weight . . .'

Placing her basket on the back of the open cart, she rummaged inside and pulled out a cake. 'Here, this is full of good things. I've got some eggs here too . . .'

'Wait a minute, Tacy. I don't have any money yet.'

Tacy looked offended. 'I'm not asking you for money. They're presents.'

'I thought we'd come here to sell things, not give them away!' Tom Elford walked towards them from the front of the cart where he had been removing a nosebag from the pony. The moorland farmer looked every bit as frail as Pilgrim was himself. His smile was intended to wipe away any criticism implied in the words.

Despite the moorland farmer's smile, Pilgrim was uncertain how Tacy's father viewed her friendship with an enemy of their country.

'That's just what I was telling Tacy . . .'

Tom Elford waved Pilgrim's explanation aside. 'I was only joking.'

Extending a hand, he said, 'You'll be the young man who saved Rip – and who seems to have been the subject of more talk on Roundtor Farm than anything else I can remember for years past.'

'Pa!'

The word came out as a rebuke from Tacy, her cheeks fiery with embarrassment.

'I'm sorry . . . !' Pilgrim apologised hesitantly, still not quite certain whether or not Tacy's father was expressing disapproval.

'There's nothing to apologise for,' said Tom Elford. 'I should be thanking you. Before Tacy met up with you we'd only sent things here for sale when we had too much of something or another. Now, because we've been here so often, we have customers for all the cake and eggs we can carry, as well as all the peat we can cut. We'll be bringing crops here too, later on in the year. It will save us carrying them all the way to town.'

'Tacy's been very kind and very generous,' said Pilgrim. 'I do appreciate it. There's one thing of which you can be certain. When money starts coming through from our agents, we'll buy all the cakes you can bake to pass on to our men. It'll be a taste of home for them.'

'You don't need to wait for any money,' said Tom Elford generously. 'Have the cakes now. We'll settle up when your money arrives.'

'That won't be necessary,' said Henri. 'We have a fund in the Petty Officers' Block. It will provide money for all that Pilgrim and Virgil wish to buy.

'It makes good sense,' he added when it appeared Tom Elford would protest. 'There are many Americans here and more are coming all the time. If you are not paid immediately for what you sell to them, they will very soon run up such a debt it will not be possible for you to buy ingredients for so many cakes. Accept the money I can provide and your earnings will be limited only by the hours your family is able to spend baking.'

Tom Elford conceded that Henri's words made sense. Making and selling cakes would provide a good income. It was probable that by baking for the Americans held in the prison, the women of Roundtor Farm might make more money than he could earn from farming!

Speaking to Pilgrim once again, he said, 'I realise our countries are at war, but it won't last for ever. We none of us know what's likely to happen in the future, but if you ever have the opportunity to step outside this place you can be sure of a warm welcome at Roundtor Farm. Remember that.'

On the way home to Roundtor Farm that evening, Tacy took her father gently to task for embarrassing both Pilgrim and herself.

When he protested that he had meant no harm, she conceded it had not been a serious embarrassment and thanked him for the invitation he had issued to Pilgrim.

'It took me by surprise,' she admitted. 'The last time we spoke about it you seemed to disapprove of me even knowing him. You said I should get to meet some of the local young men and not waste my time on someone locked up in a prison.'

'I'd still like you to find a decent young man . . . All right!'

He held up a hand in a weary gesture intended to pre-empt the protest he knew she was about to make. 'I realise they're few and far between on the moor, but you'll find the right man one day. In the meantime, I meant what I said to your young American. He's very likeable. It's not his fault he's inside a prison. All he's done is fight for his country. I admire him for that. If I'd been a fit young man with no responsibilities when the war with France began, I'd have done the same.'

Tacy knew her father had always been envious of one of his younger brothers who had left the family farm on the far side of Dartmoor to enlist. Serving with Wellington's army in Spain, he had taken part in many of the battles fought there.

The occasional letters home told of a life far removed from that he had known as the younger son of a tenant farmer on a moorland farm in Devon.

'I wonder how long he'll be here?' mused Tacy, half to herself.

'As a prisoner-of-war, you mean?'

Tom Elford cast a glance at his daughter and saw she was daydreaming. It was something she had always done, since she was a small girl.

'For as long as the war lasts – and that's likely to be quite a while. Wars don't usually start and end within a few months, or even a few years. I suspect he'll be lodging in Dartmoor prison for much longer than he would care to think about.'

Smiling sympathetically at his daughter, he added, 'Time enough for you to become an old maid, if you're not careful.'

Tacy said nothing. Being able to continue to meet Pilgrim for the foreseeable future was a pleasant thought – although she hoped it might not always be inside the high walls of Dartmoor prison.

She believed that if he had to remain a prisoner-of-war for some years the authorities might relent and allow him out on parole, on similar terms to those offered to French officers. Some had been paroled for many years. A few had succeeded in bringing wives and families to England to be with them. She had also heard of one in Ashburton, who had courted and married a local girl during his years of parole.

On the other hand, if Pilgrim was not offered parole and the authorities forced him to remain inside the prison, she could always consider doing what Mary Gurney had done with Henri, Pilgrim's friend . . .

Tacy smiled at the thought of Pilgrim dressed up in some of her clothes. Nevertheless, the idea of helping him to escape from the prison and thoughts of what they might do once he was free, excited her.

Roundtor Farm was in a remote part of the moor. It might be possible for Pilgrim to remain there undetected for as long as the war between Britain and the United States lasted.

It was something that would fire her imagination for a great many hours during the weeks and months ahead.

18

The occupants of the Petty Officers' Block were awakened by the sound of an uproar. A disturbance was taking place somewhere beyond the wall that separated them from the main prison blocks.

Pilgrim and Virgil were immediately concerned that another fight might be taking place in Block Four. Suddenly, a jubilant French officer came hurrying towards them. With a delighted expression, he beckoned excitedly.

'Come. Come quickly!'

They ran close behind him up the stairs that led to the upper storey of the Petty Officers' Block. Despite their repeated questioning along the way, he either did not understand or was deliberately refusing to expand on his brief command.

The windows of the upper floor were crowded with Frenchmen. Grinning widely, those men at one of the windows moved to one side to allow room for the two marines officers.

A Frenchman pointed to where the grey bulk of Block

Four rose above its surrounding wall. Looking in that direction, Pilgrim gave voice to a cheer which was taken up by Frenchmen and Americans alike.

Flying from the roof of Block Four was not one, but *two* United States flags.

'Of course! It's Independence Day!'

Pilgrim's delight was shared by Virgil, but the senior officer sounded a note of warning. 'There's going to be hell to pay over this. We'd better get across there and try to prevent bloodshed when the militia go in to take down the flags.'

Pilgrim and Virgil hurried from the first-floor window to the ground floor, but the doors of the building were securely locked. They were unable even to leave the Petty Officers' Block.

The usual daily routine was that the doors of every block, including that which housed the officers, were locked each evening and unlocked the following morning. Today, because of the troubles in Block Four, the turnkeys had not gone the rounds to carry out their duties.

Despite loud protests from the officer inmates, the doors remained securely locked until mid-afternoon. By this time the two flags had disappeared from the roof of Block Four. Nobody knew whether they had been removed by the militia or by the prisoners themselves.

During the hours their doors were secured, the Frenchmen and Americans in the Petty Officers' Block and the other buildings continued to crowd the windows overlooking Block Four, shouting encouragement to their defiant fellow-prisoners.

When the doors were eventually opened, the noise within the prison was deafening. Hungry prisoners were banging metal plates, wooden tables and anything else capable of making a noise.

'It's about time someone let us out,' complained Virgil to the turnkey who opened the Petty Officers' Block door. 'We'll be lucky if there's time for even one meal today.'

The turnkey shrugged his indifference. 'You can blame your men in Block Four, not me.'

'Can I go over there and speak to them?'

'No,' said the turnkey. 'A couple of hundred militiamen are searching the block. They've found one flag, but are still looking for the other. I'd say there are likely to be more Americans in the *cachot* tonight than in Block Four.'

'Has anyone been hurt?' asked Pilgrim.

'One or two, but no one on either side has suffered any serious injury. The surgeon's still over there, but he hasn't taken anyone to the hospital as far as I know.'

'I'd still like to speak to the Americans who've been involved,' repeated Virgil.

'You'll need to wait 'til tomorrow,' said the turnkey. 'When the militia come out I'm to lock all the doors in the block. Governor Cotgrave's said they can all go without a meal today, as a punishment.'

'The Frenchmen are being punished too?' The question was put by Henri. 'That is not fair. The committee will complain to the governor.'

'Complain as much as you like,' said the turnkey. 'Perhaps next time your people will do something to stop the Americans getting up to their antics, instead of cheering them on.'

Henri and his fellow committee members would complain, but it was intended to be no more than an irritating thorn in the flesh of the harassed governor. Cotgrave represented the common enemy of Frenchmen and Americans, someone to be harangued whenever possible. However, he still possessed ultimate power over the prisoners. It would not do to push him too hard.

'May we go to the market now?' asked Pilgrim.

'There's no market today. The gates weren't opened because of the troubles, so your countrymen will have made no friends there, either.'

The turnkey left the Petty Officers' Block with the clamorous protests of Americans and Frenchmen ringing in his ears.

Not until the following morning was a deputation of American and French officers allowed to enter Block Four to learn what had happened during the previous day's rioting.

Ephraim came down from the attic to speak to them. In answer to Virgil's question, he admitted, 'They gave us a good going over, but there'll be a great many Englishmen this morning with a bruise or two to show for their efforts.'

'Did they eventually find both flags?' Pilgrim put the question to the sergeant of marines.

'No. They searched just about everywhere they thought it might be hidden but we managed to save the one. We'll raise it again as soon as we find something else to celebrate. Thanksgiving, perhaps.'

'Where did you hide it?' asked Pilgrim. He was aware there were few places in the prison block where a flag might be concealed.

'Where it'll stay until it's needed again,' said Ephraim. 'Wrapped around my body. Mind you, I wish I knew what the Frenchmen put into some of the dye we used to make it. When it gets really warm it stinks worse than a skunk. I'll have no friends left, come the end of summer.'

*   *   *

The events of Independence Day angered Governor Cotgrave. He called Virgil to his office to express his disapproval of the activities of the American prisoners-of-war.

'I was warned by the Superintendent of Hulks that you and your men would cause trouble,' fumed Cotgrave, glaring across his large desk at Virgil. 'I had hoped he was exaggerating. It's now quite apparent he was not.'

'I think we need to keep this matter in perspective, sir,' replied Virgil amiably. 'Yesterday was American Independence Day. The American prisoners-of-war wanted to celebrate the occasion. No doubt they would have asked your permission to fly the United States flag had they thought it would be granted.'

'Must I remind you that you are prisoners-of-war, Captain Howard? You are under British jurisdiction. Would your country have allowed *our* prisoners to fly the Union flag to celebrate a victory against America?'

'No,' conceded Virgil, 'but I look upon this as no more than a very minor disciplinary matter. You'll find my men will behave themselves every bit as well as the Frenchmen while they are here. If this is the most serious incident that occurs during your governorship you can consider yourself very lucky.'

'That remark is insolent, Captain Howard. I regret I must take it into consideration when I reply to the letter I have just received, suggesting you and your fellow officers be considered for parole. My recommendation will be that parole should be refused.'

Viewing Virgil's surprised expression with satisfaction, he said, 'Thank you, Captain Howard. You may return to the Petty Officers' Block now.'

19

'. . . But why would you *want* to consider parole? Do you think it would be so much more enjoyable to live with the English?'

Henri Joffre made a deprecating gesture with his hands. 'Their manners leave much to be desired. English food is terrible, and even their smugglers cannot obtain such Cognac as this.'

Henri held up his brandy goblet and the liquid amber of its contents reflected the light from the lamps hanging about the cell block walls. 'Even in France such Cognac is enjoyed by only a favoured few.'

'It's very fine Cognac indeed,' agreed Pilgrim, 'but there's more to life than satisfying one's stomach.'

'Ah yes!' Henri swirled the contents of the goblet he held in his hand and smiled down at it. 'I forget. You are talking, of course, of the young women who are to be found outside the prison. *English* women. Be careful, my friend. They walk in a manner deliberately intended to arouse a man's passions, but should he respond . . . !'

Again there was an expressive gesture from the

Frenchman. 'She will recoil in mock horror and protest that her honour is being threatened. Many of my countrymen in this very building have stories to tell of this. Some have lost their parole because of these women. Others have been flogged. Only last year two Frenchmen were hanged, solely on the evidence of an Englishwoman. They protested their innocence to the scaffold.'

Henri took another sip from his goblet. 'Forget all ideas of parole, M'sieur Pilgrim. Remain in the *Petit Cautionnement*. You must admit, life here is not altogether unpleasant.'

'Yet you've tried to escape,' pointed out Pilgrim.

'Of course! I am a patriot.'

Henri appeared offended that Pilgrim had thought it necessary to question his actions. 'I wished to escape not to enjoy the English way of life, but to return to France, in order to usefully serve my country once more.'

'Is Mary Gurney aware that was the reason she was loaning you her clothes?'

Pilgrim put the question casually and Henri had the grace to look at least mildly embarrassed.

'It is not something we have discussed, but she knows I am anxious to return to my country as soon as possible. My father is not a well man.'

'Perhaps Mary hopes that if she helps you to escape from here you'll take her to France with you?'

Henri shrugged. 'It is not impossible, of course, but, as I have said, it is a matter we have not discussed. Now, let us forget about English women and enjoy some more Cognac . . .'

The following day the market was allowed to take place in the prison once more. Tacy was among those offering goods for sale.

She expressed her relief at learning no harm had come to Pilgrim. 'When we arrived here yesterday I saw strange flags flying on one of the buildings. Someone said they were American flags and I knew there was trouble. When we were not allowed to come inside the prison I thought there must have been a riot and that you might have been hurt again.'

'I suppose it was a riot, of sorts – but only a very minor one. It was more high spirits, really.' He explained the significance of Independence Day to her.

'I'm glad you weren't involved,' she said, with some relief. 'But Governor Cotgrave must have been livid.'

'He wasn't pleased,' agreed Pilgrim. 'He called Virgil to his office and told him we Americans are a troublesome lot who can't expect to be granted any extra privileges while we're here. It doesn't mean very much. Our men aren't treated as leniently as the French as it is. They're not allowed to come to the market, for instance, even though money from our Government is beginning to trickle through now.'

'Perhaps all that might change very soon . . . for you, at least.'

'I don't understand . . . In what way might it change for *me*?'

Tacy had spoken without thinking. Now she seemed embarrassed. 'Perhaps I shouldn't be saying anything to you just yet, but Sir Thomas Tyrwhitt returned from London yesterday evening. His carriage happened to be coming along the road by Two Bridges when Pa was bringing sheep from over that way with Rip helping him. Sir Thomas stopped to talk about how Rip's training was coming along. Before he went on his way he said Pa was to tell me he had some good news for you. He felt it would repay you for what you did to save Rip.'

'I wonder what that could be – and when I'll hear about it?'

'Perhaps they're going to let you out of the prison on parole, like the French officers who're staying over at Ashburton.'

'It could be something like that, I suppose.' Pilgrim recalled the conversation with Henri the evening before. He also remembered the comments Governor Cotgrave had made to Virgil on the subject. 'I doubt it, though. Cotgrave has already said he's against giving parole to Americans.'

'He won't be able to do very much about it if Sir Thomas says he's to give it to you,' Tacy spoke with great confidence. 'He'll know that whatever Sir Thomas does has the approval of the Prince Regent.'

At that moment one of the French prisoners-of-war came along to buy a dozen eggs from Tacy. Before handing over his money he inspected each one carefully, insisting that she change two of them because he considered them smaller than the others.

When the Frenchman was eventually satisfied with his purchase and parted with his money, Tacy said to Pilgrim, 'Would you take parole if it was offered to you?'

He had a feeling his reply was of importance to her, but his words were guarded. 'I don't know. I would have to think about it carefully before making up my mind.'

Tacy seemed upset by his lack of enthusiasm. 'Why? Why do you say that? Surely you don't want to remain in here one minute longer than you have to? It's an *awful* place. I wouldn't wish to put my worst enemy in here!'

Pilgrim smiled, he could not imagine Tacy having a 'worst enemy'. 'Don't get the wrong idea. I'd *love* to be out of here, but not if it smacked of favouritism and all the others were left behind. I'd want Virgil to be given parole too. Anyway, even if it were offered we'd need to stay close enough to the prison to remain in touch with the soldiers and marines left behind. As officers we're responsible for them, even though we're now all prisoners-of-war.'

'Sir Thomas's house at Tor Royal is no more than a mile from here. If you were offered parole to stay there you'd take it?'

Tacy did not feel it necessary to add that Tor Royal was little more than the same distance from Roundtor Farm.

'If Virgil were offered parole at the same time and we were able to keep in touch with our men, I'd be delighted to accept parole. To be honest, Tacy, I think it's only the fact I can meet and talk with you a few times a week that's keeping me sane. It's a whole lot better than the prison hulk, certainly, but it's never possible to forget I'm a prisoner. We're shut up inside walls and the doors are locked as soon as it gets dark. Perhaps being an American makes it worse. I come from Ohio, where there are miles and miles of empty, open space. There's a sense of freedom there like you'll never have known . . .'

The way he spoke of his home was the way *she* felt about Dartmoor. If he took parole it would not be very long before he came to share her love of it.

20

Pilgrim and Virgil were summoned to Governor Cotgrave's office three days after Sir Thomas Tyrwhitt's return to Dartmoor from London.

On the desk in front of the governor was a letter bearing an impressive seal. It sat amidst a variety of other documents which he shuffled about in an apparently aimless fashion before speaking to the two prisoners-of-war.

'I have had a letter from the Transport Board, in London. It authorises me to offer parole to you and the other Americans held in the *Petit Cautionnement*.'

Pilgrim and Virgil exchanged glances in which were mingled surprise, delight and faint amusement. It was as though the conversation between Governor Cotgrave and Virgil resulting from the Independence Day troubles had never taken place.

Choosing to ignore their expressions, the governor continued, 'As you are both mentioned by name and are to be offered parole on special terms, I have decided to speak to you before I call in your countrymen.'

'Special terms?' queried Virgil. 'Are they less favourable than those offered to the others?'

Governor Cotgrave did not reply to the question with a direct answer. 'Sir Thomas Tyrwhitt has offered you parole accommodation in his own home, at Tor Royal. It's no more than a mile from the prison. He will stand as guarantor for your behaviour – on condition you give your word of honour to him personally that you will not attempt to escape. As the Prince Regent is known to visit Tor Royal from time to time, Sir Thomas will no doubt require additional assurances from you in respect of your conduct during your parole there. In return, you will be granted a number of concessions not usually enjoyed by paroled officers. Do I take it you both agree to this rather exceptional offer?'

Pilgrim held his breath. He wanted parole and knew Virgil did too, but the captain of marines would not accept it unless he were satisfied the American prisoners-of-war remaining in the prison would not suffer as a result of their absence.

His heart sank when Virgil said, 'There are one or two matters I would like to clarify before I reply to your offer, Governor.'

'What sort of "matters"?' Cotgrave snapped the question at Virgil. He was not at all pleased for prisoners-of-war to be given any special privileges – especially American prisoners.

'I am the senior United States officer in the prison. If I accept parole I would need to know I will have regular access to my men and the other Americans. I accept that it must be at a reasonable hour, and will require your permission, of course – but I need your assurance that such permission will not be unreasonably withheld. I also insist that I be informed should any serious incident occur involving any of the United States citizens in your care . . .'

Banging the desk in front of him with his clenched fist, Cotgrave cried, 'Insist? You . . . *insist*? You are being offered parole on quite exceptional terms – far better than you deserve, yet you have the gall to try to set conditions? Not only are you ungrateful, Captain Howard, you are impertinent too!'

'Gratitude has nothing at all to do with this matter, Governor Cotgrave. I am pointing out my duty as a United States officer of marines. I have no doubt that were our roles reversed, you would act in a similar manner.'

Governor Cotgrave wished he could have sent both men back to the *Petit Cautionnement* and forgotten them – and any question of parole for American prisoners-of-war – but he did not dare.

The letter instructing him to arrange parole made it clear the suggestion had originated in the office of the Prime Minister. It also made it plain the order had the support of the Prince Regent himself.

Captain Cotgrave's seagoing service had not proved sufficiently illustrious to bring a peerage to the Cotgrave family. It was his hope that in his present post a combination of unbending discipline and rigid application of regulations would succeed where valour had failed. The instructions contained in the letter before him on the desk stuck in his craw, but he did not intend allowing an enemy of his country – until recently a colonial – to thwart his ambitions.

'Your devotion to duty is both understandable and admirable, Captain Howard. Under the terms of your parole you will present yourself at this prison once a fortnight. You may visit your men then.'

Pilgrim hoped Virgil might agree, but the captain now

insisted that one of the marines, possibly Ephraim, be given permission to visit him at Tor Royal. He also had a number of other points to raise with the prison governor.

Governor Cotgrave had agreed to Ephraim acting as a messenger between prison and Tor Royal only when Virgil reminded him that such a procedure had been granted to the French for much of their time in Dartmoor. He also raised the question of granting the American rank-and-file prisoners the same privileges as their French counterparts. Included in this would be the right to attend the market and be generally granted greater freedom of movement within the prison.

Aware that he was on stronger ground than he had been over the question of parole for the officers, Governor Cotgrave pointed out that the French had been in Dartmoor prison since it opened, four years before. Many had been captured some years before this. There had been ample time for the British authorities to assess their behaviour.

The Americans, on the other hand, had been in Dartmoor prison for a matter of months only. During this short time their behaviour had already left much to be desired.

This argument was countered by Virgil with details of Frenchmen who had escaped, attempted to escape, or broken their parole. The figures had been given to him by Henri Joffre and were quite staggering. The number of French officers who had tried to escape, or seriously broken the conditions of their parole ran into hundreds.

After much argument back and forth, Cotgrave had finally agreed to allow Ephraim, or a named substitute, a bi-weekly visit to Tor Royal, but he had refused to concede anything more.

While his friend was negotiating with the prison governor, Pilgrim maintained a discreet silence. Filled with admiration for the tough stand Virgil was making on the issue of the terms of their parole, he was fearful lest the captain of marines push the governor too hard and so lose the opportunity of parole for both of them.

Eventually, Governor Cotgrave brought the acrimonious interview to an end.

'Prisoners-of-war are defeated men, Captain Howard – and defeated men do not dictate terms to their victors. Should it be necessary, you will both be allowed reasonable access in addition to your fortnightly visit and, yes, your sergeant will be allowed out to report to you. Now, do you or do you not accept the terms of the parole you have been offered?'

Pilgrim held his breath until Virgil said, 'I do, Governor. But before I leave the prison I would like to visit Block Four and tell my countrymen all that has been agreed between us.'

Relieved to have finally resolved the matter, Governor Cotgrave said, 'Very well. Both of you sign the parole agreement now, then you may pay a visit to Block Four. In the meantime I will send word to Sir Thomas Tyrwhitt that you will be released tomorrow. I understand he wishes to see you settled in at Tor Royal before he returns to London.'

There were grumbles of discontent from the assembled American prisoners-of-war when Virgil broke the news of the impending parole of American officers.

Pilgrim felt sorry for them. He, Virgil and the other officers were already enjoying the comparative comfort of the Petty Officers' Block. Now they were being paroled. Meanwhile, the men here were forced to endure conditions worse than in any other block of the prison.

Furthermore, they were in constant fear of those French prisoners who had been virtually disowned by their own countrymen.

'There is no question of deserting you,' Virgil sought to reassure the Americans. 'Lieutenant Penn and I will be reporting to the prison once every two weeks and are to be allowed to visit you, to make sure you're all keeping well. In addition, Sergeant Ephraim is to be granted permission to leave the prison to report to me at Tor Royal on the weeks I don't come here. If he is unable to come to me, another named deputy will take his place.'

The news that Ephraim was to be given freedom to leave the prison did not please many of the merchant seamen. They protested noisily.

When Virgil had quietened them, he said impassively, 'I suggest you choose the substitute for my approval. The governor has also agreed I will be notified immediately if you have any serious problems.'

When Virgil's talk to the American prisoners-of-war came to an end, there were grudging good wishes from some of those who would be remaining behind, but silence from many more.

They were particularly aggrieved because many of them had been captured whilst serving on United States merchant vessels. They believed, with certain justification, that they should not be held in Dartmoor at all. They were civilians, caught up in a war in which they had taken no active part. Yet in captivity they were being treated as though they too were combatants.

However, they conceded that Virgil and Pilgrim would be able to do more to help them from Tor Royal than from the Petty Officers' Block in prison. They would elect one of their number to visit Tor Royal should Ephraim not be able to go on any particular occasion.

Despite their grumbling, there was not one man among them who did not envy Virgil and Pilgrim their imminent departure from the grim confines of Dartmoor prison.

21

Pilgrim and Virgil's release from Dartmoor prison on parole was devoid of all ceremony.

Issued with parole documents, each carried a small bundle in which was wrapped what few personal belongings he had succeeded in gathering during his imprisonment. Thus frugally equipped, they passed through the high archway and the heavy wooden prison gates slammed shut behind them.

There was no one outside to meet them and they had only sketchy directions of how they would find Tor Royal. Standing hesitantly in the lane outside the prison, beneath a watery early morning sun, they found it difficult to take in their changed circumstances. To all intents and purposes, they were now free men, albeit in the country of an enemy.

Pilgrim was surprised that Sir Thomas Tyrwhitt had sent no one to escort them to Tor Royal, but there was no one in view for as far as they could see.

To their right, the lane wound around the high tor that overlooked the prison. To the left they could see the small cluster of buildings that comprised the small prison hamlet of Princetown.

Behind the prison, hidden from view for the moment by the high, granite perimeter wall, was open moorland, stretching away for as far as the human eye could see.

The instructions Pilgrim and Virgil had been given would take them through Princetown and they set off in that direction. They expected to find the house of the Lord Warden of the Stannaries in a valley on the far side of the hamlet that had sprung up about the prison.

'Do you notice anything in particular, Pilgrim?'

The question from Virgil came when they had left the prison behind them and had an uninterrupted view of rolling moorland to their left.

'Yes. Space,' replied Pilgrim. 'I feel I can breathe freely again.'

'That's it, Pilgrim . . . the *air*. It's fresh. We've left the stench of prison behind. I've only just realised how bad it was.'

Virgil was right. Pilgrim filled his lungs once more. The air carried on it the aroma of grass and furze. It was a sweet, clean smell.

'How will you spend your time in our new surroundings?' Pilgrim put the question to his companion as they walked together.

'Sir Thomas might have some ideas on that,' replied Virgil. 'But I intend addressing a barrage of letters to our Government. I want to tell them of the conditions endured by our men on the hulks and in the prison here. I'll see if I can get them to do something about it. How about you, how do you intend occupying your time?'

'I became very unfit in the prison, especially after I came out of the hospital. I'd like to do some physical work. On a farm, perhaps.'

Virgil gave Pilgrim a knowing smile. 'Would you have any particular farm in mind? One where the farmer has a pretty young, dark-haired daughter who goes by the name of Tacy, perhaps?'

'I don't know where her farm is,' said Pilgrim truthfully, but evasively. He had already decided he would locate Roundtor Farm at the earliest opportunity.

Once Princetown was reached, they came to a large building set back on the right of the road. Beside it, a number of militiamen were being drilled under the supervision of an officer.

These were not the Somerset militiamen who had brought the Americans to Dartmoor prison from the hulks at Plymouth. The Somerset men had been replaced a few weeks before by a Welsh militia regiment.

Pilgrim and Virgil were wearing new uniforms, tailored for them by a Frenchman who worked in Cell Block Five. Made from good-quality blue cloth, the money to pay the tailor had been provided by Henri Joffre.

Both men had protested that the Frenchman should not spend his money on them. He had countered that they owed it to the United States Marine Corps to which they belonged, as well as to their country, to look their best when they left the prison and went out to live among the English.

The bright colours of the American uniform attracted the attention of an officer sitting astride his horse and watching the militiamen being drilled. Assuming the two men to be French prisoners-of-war, he sent one of his non-commissioned officers to stop them and bring them to him.

With the officer who had brought them from Plymouth in mind, Pilgrim and Virgil approached the militia officer with some apprehension.

But this was a very different man to Captain Henry Pollit of the Somerset Militia.

Mounted on a superb horse, Lieutenant Colonel Cecil Hawke was a man of aristocratic bearing. He sat upright in his saddle, watching the approaching prisoners-of-war with great interest.

As the two men drew closer, Pilgrim could see the empty right sleeve of the militiaman's coat folded neatly and pinned to the shoulder.

When they reached him, Lieutenant Colonel Hawke spoke to them in passable French to enquire what they were doing.

'We're Americans, not French,' replied Virgil. 'We've just been granted parole and are on our way to the house where we'll be staying. Here are our parole documents.'

He handed the papers to the one-armed colonel. He did not even look at them.

'Americans, eh? No wonder I didn't recognise the uniforms.'

His glance shifted to Pilgrim for only a moment before returning to Virgil. 'You were limping as you approached me. Have you been wounded?'

'I was shot in the leg during the battle in which I was made a prisoner. Fortunately I was treated by an American surgeon. He was less drastic than the man who attended you, sir.'

Virgil correctly assumed the other man to have been a regular soldier who had been retired as a result of losing his arm. He wore the insignia of a lieutenant colonel. It was a far more senior rank than was normal for an officer commanding a militia unit responsible for guarding prisoners-of-war.

Lieutenant Colonel Hawke glanced briefly down at the empty sleeve. 'The best surgeon in the world couldn't have saved my arm, Captain. I am afraid that in the wars of today mounted men are no match for the weapons of the artillery – especially when a cavalryman meets an enemy with as many guns as his squadron has horses. But I can still serve my country, albeit in a somewhat frustrating capacity.'

He nodded his head to where the militiamen were making fumbling attempts to attach bayonets to muskets.

'I despair of ever making soldiers of such material. Few have seen life outside a farmyard . . . Make them do that again!'

He bellowed the order at the sergeant who was drilling the militiamen, adding, 'This time tell them to put some life into it. An enemy's not going to stand back and wait while they fiddle around fixing bayonets!'

Shaking his head in exasperation, Lieutenant Colonel Hawke said, 'I swear that when they're given an order they check on what the weather's going to do before they decide whether or not to obey!'

Momentarily dismissing the clumsy militiamen from his thoughts, he said, 'Where will you be staying during your parole . . . Ashburton? That's where most of the French officers are.'

Virgil shook his head. 'We're to live at Tor Royal.'

The reply took the militia lieutenant colonel by surprise. 'At Sir Thomas Tyrwhitt's home? You'll be keeping illustrious company there, Captain.'

He looked at the two men speculatively. 'Is there a reason why Sir Thomas should be taking a special interest in you?'

'Yes, sir.' Virgil nodded his head in Pilgrim's direction. 'Lieutenant Pilgrim Penn was able to perform a service for Sir Thomas recently. As a result Sir Thomas learned that Pilgrim's uncle was United States ambassador in London. It seems he and Sir Thomas were good friends.'

Virgil had decided it would do them no harm to impress this colonel of militia – and he was right.

'My father fought against your people when you rebelled against us,' said Lieutenant Colonel Hawke. 'He has retained a great admiration for Americans as soldiers. He's also of the opinion we should not be at war with you now. Indeed, he firmly believes we should both be fighting Napoleon Bonaparte together.'

Waving a hand in the direction of the large building beside the makeshift parade ground, he said, 'I'm senior officer of the militia mess. You must come there as my guests before I return home. It'll make a refreshing change to talk to soldiers who know what it is to go into battle. Whose idea of "wounded in action" is more serious than tripping over their sword on parade – or dropping a bayonet and piercing their foot.'

He added the last remark as one of the militiamen pulled a bayonet free from his boot and limped from the ranks.

'All right, Sergeant, get someone to go with him to find the surgeon . . .'

Returning his attention to Virgil, he said sympathetically, 'If your leg is bothering you I would be pleased to loan you horses to carry you both to Tor Royal.'

'It's a very kind offer, sir, but we're in no hurry. It's a delight to be able to savour newfound freedom after spending months in prison.'

'Of course. I quite understand,' said Lieutenant Colonel Hawke. I am very pleased to have met up with you both. If you find you need anything – anything at all – don't hesitate to call on me.'

Unexpectedly, Pilgrim said, 'You mentioned your

father had fought against us in our war of independence. Would he be *General* Hawke?'

With an expression of delight, Lieutenant Colonel Hawke said, 'Yes . . . You've heard of him?'

'Of course. He is held up as an example of all that was fine with the British. Had there been more like him we might never have broken our ties with your country. I believe my father met him at the end of the war. He'll be thrilled to know I've made the acquaintance of the son of such a distinguished soldier, sir.'

Virgil and Pilgrim walked away from the militia parade ground in the knowledge that they had made a friend of yet another man who might possibly have an influence upon their future.

22

Pilgrim and Virgil were still discussing the militia lieutenant colonel when they reached the lane which led
to Tor Royal. Here, much to Pilgrim's delight, they
found Tacy and her young sister Johanna waiting for
them.

'I was beginning to think you weren't coming,' said
Tacy brightly.

'You knew we were being released today?' Pilgrim
found it difficult to hide his pleasure at seeing her.

'Yes, Sir Thomas told father last night you'd be coming
to Tor Royal this morning.'

'And you decided to come and meet us?'

'Well . . . there wasn't much happening at the farm.
It was something to do . . .'

'That isn't true!' exclaimed Johanna indignantly.
'There's a whole lot to do at the farm. You told Pa
you'd work late tonight to get it done if he'd let you
come here and meet him.'

She jabbed a finger in Pilgrim's direction.

Tacy tried hard not to look discomfited by her young

sister's impish revelation. 'I thought you might have trouble finding Tor Royal. Lots of people miss the turn-off from the road. They think this is just some old track because you can't see the house until you're almost up to it.'

'Then it's a good thing you've come to show us the way,' lied Pilgrim. 'We'd have probably walked right past without even noticing it.'

'You can hardly miss it,' snorted Johanna derisively. 'Tor Royal is bigger than our farmhouse and all the buildings put together.'

'Have you been to Tor Royal often?' Virgil put the question to Johanna as they began to draw ahead of Tacy and Pilgrim.

'Lots of times,' replied the young girl positively.

'She *hasn't*,' said Tacy to Pilgrim. She spoke quietly, lowering her voice so it would not carry to her sister. 'She's got a vivid imagination.'

'Is that why she said you *did* have work to do on the farm, when you'd said you hadn't?'

Tacy's glance went to his face quickly, before dropping away. 'I *do* have work to do, but it's nothing that won't keep. I thought it would be nice for you to have someone to meet you when you left the prison. A familiar face. Had Sir Thomas been with you, Johanna and I would have gone home again and you'd never have known we'd been waiting.'

Pilgrim was taken aback. 'You mean . . . you wouldn't even have come to say "Hello"? Why not? You know Virgil and me – and you know Sir Thomas.'

'I know him, but I wouldn't dare speak to him unless he spoke to me first. He's a rich and important man. I'm only the daughter of a moorland farmer – a *tenant* farmer.'

'Such things don't matter very much in my country,'

said Pilgrim. 'A man with nothing can head westwards, find a place he likes and settle there on as much land as he can manage. It doesn't matter who he is, or where he's from. He's accepted for what he is, and what he can achieve.'

'But you're from an important family. I heard you and Sir Thomas talking.'

'My pa's respected because he fought for the independence of our country and proved himself a good leader. My uncle became an ambassador because he's a clever man and was an adviser to General Washington in the early days. But that's because it's what they *wanted* to be. I've another uncle who's a trapper somewhere up Canada way, one who's working down in Mexico, and another who, the last we heard of him, had taken a Cherokee wife and was living with her and her tribe up in the Blue Mountains. He went there after almost getting himself hung for shooting someone.'

Tacy did not know who, or what, a 'Cherokee' was, but it sounded exciting.

'Tell me about America.' Tacy was happy just to be with Pilgrim, but she wanted to learn as much as possible about him and the country from which he came. She also liked listening to his voice.

'It's a great big country, Tacy. A huge country, with land for the taking. Nobody even knows quite how much there is.'

'Doesn't anyone live there at all?'

'Only the Indians and they don't do anything with the land. They just hunt over it and fight each other whenever they meet up.'

'But . . . what do the Indians do when you take their land from them?'

Pilgrim frowned. 'They just move on westwards.

There's so much land in America there's plenty for everyone.'

'What will happen when there's no more land for them to move on to?'

'That'll never happen, Tacy. There's more than enough land for everyone to do just what they want and still leave some for everyone else.'

'How much land does your family own?'

'If you stood on one of these hills and looked around, it would be just about as much as you could see in every direction.'

It was a bald statement of fact, not made in an attempt to impress her. Yet it was altogether too much for Tacy to take in. At that moment they came to a gap in the high-banked hedge and Pilgrim stopped.

The view from here was across a wide valley. Beyond it the moor stretched for as far as could be seen, dotted here and there with tors of varying heights.

Many of the tors were dominated by tumbled heaps of rock. A light sprinkling of ponies and sheep grazed in scattered groups across the landscape. There was not a dwelling, or any sign of human habitation to be seen anywhere.

Pilgrim drew in his breath sharply. 'This could almost be Ohio,' he said. 'When we were making our way westward we passed through country just like this.'

'Then you'll feel at home here.'

'I think I might,' agreed Pilgrim. 'I think I could feel very much at home.'

When he spoke he was looking not at the countryside but at Tacy.

They looked at each other for a few seconds and felt themselves drawing closer. The moment was broken by Johanna. She and Virgil had stopped and the young girl called back, 'You can see Tor Royal from here.'

When Tacy and Pilgrim caught up with the others, Johanna pointed to the rooftops of a substantial house, just visible through a line of trees.

'That's Tor Royal.'

'Yes,' said Tacy. 'We'll leave you here.'

Her statement took Pilgrim by surprise. 'Won't you at least come to the house with us?'

'No.'

'Why not?' Pilgrim was puzzled. 'You've met us and showed us the way here. I'm sure Sir Thomas will be delighted to see you both.'

For a moment Tacy thought he was teasing her. When she realised he was not, she said, 'As I said just now, Sir Thomas is a titled man who mixes with royalty. My pa is only a tenant farmer. He needs to work as hard as he's able, in order to pay the rent for his farm and make a living.'

Tacy felt very unhappy in a way she could not entirely explain. 'We live in a very different world to that of Sir Thomas.'

She thought of what Pilgrim had just told her about his life in America and the land owned by his family there. Even allowing for a degree of boastfulness it seemed his family owned more land than Sir Thomas Tyrwhitt.

Unconsciously or otherwise, Pilgrim had told her that his family were on a par with the Lord Warden of the Stannaries. Perhaps he had not intended that his words should be interpreted in such a way, but she now realised, beyond all possible doubt, that Pilgrim belonged in the world of the Dartmoor knight.

'Come on, Johanna, we've a lot of work to do back at the farm. We've showed Lieutenant Penn the way. We must go home now.'

23

'Well, did you meet up with your young American?'

Joan Elford put the question to Tacy as both her daughters entered the kitchen. Behind them, Billy staggered in through the open doorway, his arms laden with more peat than could comfortably be carried.

Her attention momentarily diverted, Joan said crossly, 'Billy! I've told you before, don't try to bring it all in at once. You'll strain something. Make two journeys, as any sensible young man would.'

'It's all right, Mrs Elford, it's not too heavy for me. I'm really strong, you know I am.'

Billy looked at Tacy before lowering his heavy load with some difficulty to the stone floor beside the kitchen fireplace.

He had hoped to impress Tacy with his strength. Much to his disappointment, she did not appear to have even noticed him enter the room bearing his heavy load.

Joan returned her attention to her daughter. 'You haven't answered me, Tacy. Was your young lieutenant released from the prison?'

'Yes, he was.' Johanna answered on behalf of her sister. 'We met him at Princetown. Tacy walked all the way to Tor Royal with him, but it doesn't seem to have made her very happy. She's hardly said a single word to me all the way home.'

'Why don't you just mind your own business, Johanna? Nobody was speaking to you. Anyway, I've said before, he's not *my* young lieutenant and there's nothing to talk about. I'm going upstairs to change my clothes. Then I'll clean out the cow's shed before I milk her.'

Tacy hurried from the kitchen leaving everyone there looking at each other in surprise. It was rare for her to give way to such a bad-tempered outburst. After a few moments, Joan wiped her hands on her apron and set off after her daughter.

'Who's made Tacy unhappy?' asked Billy, unable to comprehend what was happening. 'I'll go and speak to him if it'll make her happy again.'

'I don't think it'd do any good, Billy,' said Johanna. 'It's that American who saved Rip when the militiaman was going to shoot him. Our Tacy's sweet on him. Perhaps he doesn't feel the same way about her. I don't really know. Anyway, I'm going outside to clean out the henhouse. You can come and help me, if you like.'

Billy knew that if he went to help Johanna he would end up doing all the work, but he did not really mind. It would help to take his mind off Tacy for a while. He did not like to think of her being unhappy, whatever the reason.

'Do you want to tell me about it, Tacy?'

Joan stood in the doorway of the room shared by both her daughters. Tacy had not begun to change into her working clothes yet. She was sitting in a chair looking out of the window, her back to her mother.

'Not really.'

'You can do better than that, my girl. When you left here this morning you could hardly stand still for more than two moments at a time, you were so excited about the release of this young American of yours. What happened to change your mood like this? What did he say to upset you? Was he nasty to you?'

'Like I told Johanna, he's not *my* American – and no, he wasn't nasty. In fact he was as nice as I could have wished him to be. Perhaps that's the trouble, he was *too* nice.'

Joan frowned. 'I'm sorry, I don't understand . . .'

Tacy shrugged miserably. 'It's what you've been telling me all along, really. About Pilgrim and Sir Thomas being two of a kind.'

Suddenly alarmed, Joan tried to remember the conversations between Tacy and herself in which she had compared the unknown American with the Lord Warden of the Stannaries.

She could remember nothing of what she had said about the American – but she *had* warned her daughter on many occasions about Sir Thomas.

'What is it you're trying to say, Tacy? Did this American try to do something to you?'

'Of course not!' Tacy was indignant. 'I don't mean that he's like Sir Thomas in *that* way. No, it's what you told me about him being rich. We spoke about his family today. From what he said to me, it seems they're even richer than Sir Thomas.'

She shrugged in a dejected manner. 'When we were looking out across the moor, up by Tor Royal, he said it reminded him of where he lived in America. I asked him how much land his family owned. He said if you stood on a high hill and looked around, all the land for as far as could be seen belonged to them.'

Owning so much land was a difficult concept for Joan to accept. 'Perhaps that wasn't exactly what he meant. It could be that, like us with the moor, they have grazing rights over that much land.'

Tacy shook her head miserably, 'No, Ma. He said they own it – and that's exactly what he meant. His family must be rich, Ma. Very rich.'

Joan looked in silence at her daughter for some minutes. Then she said, 'You really have been smitten by this young man, haven't you?'

Tacy nodded her head unhappily. 'I like him an awful lot, Ma.'

Joan held out her arms and Tacy rose from the chair and came to her, much as she had done as a child whenever things were going wrong in her young life.

Stroking her daughter's hair gently, Joan said, 'I *am* sorry, Tacy. Had I known the way you felt about him I would never have let you go up to that old prison so often.'

Pulling away from her, Tacy managed a weak smile. 'It's not your fault, Ma. You did warn me.'

She managed a shaky laugh. 'It's funny, isn't it? So many girls are made miserable because their men pretend to be far richer than they really are. Yet here's me unhappy because Pilgrim's probably told me the truth!'

'You mustn't feel too bad about it, Tacy. He's not the only man in the world. There'll be another nice young man come along for you before too long, you just wait and see.'

'Thanks, Ma,' Tacy grimaced, 'but I think perhaps I'll forget about men for a while. Right now I'll go out to the yard and sort out that old cow of ours.'

24

Pilgrim found it strange to be inside a house once more, with the routine of everyday life going on about him.

There were many servants employed at Tor Royal. Each of them behaved politely enough, but he had the impression they believed he or Virgil were likely to explode at any moment! However, Pilgrim and Virgil were received warmly by Sir Thomas Tyrwhitt.

Also staying at Tor Royal were Sir Thomas's sister, Winifrith Cudmore, and her daughter, Sophie. Making the introductions, Sir Thomas explained that because he remained unmarried, various members of his family were in the habit of paying him extended visits.

They came, he said, to enjoy the tranquillity of Tor Royal and the moor on which it was built. Then they spent much of their time suggesting the names of suitable women who might enjoy sharing such an idyllic lifestyle with him.

Sophie seemed somewhat subdued, although she was polite enough when she was introduced to the two Americans.

By way of contrast, Winifrith Cudmore acknowledged them with undisguised disapproval. After an almost discourteously brief period of time, she ushered her daughter from the presence of the two men.

The newly paroled officers could not fail to notice her attitude, but it was left to Virgil to put it into words.

'Mrs Cudmore would appear not to approve of our presence in your house, Sir Thomas. I sincerely hope we won't prove an embarrassment to you.'

'Embarrassment? Dear me, no, Captain. The trouble is, Winifrith *will* try to run my life for me. No, that's not strictly true. She tries to run the lives of *everyone* she meets. She has tried to find a wife for me on more than one occasion. She's peeved because I never consulted her about bringing you to Tor Royal on parole, that is all. Take no notice. I will not have her, or any other woman, running my life for me.'

He looked meaningfully at Virgil before adding, 'She's also had problems with young Sophie, I understand. The situation came very close to a scandal. She became involved with some young army officer working in the War Office. He's being packed off to his regiment in the Spanish Peninsular and Winifrith's brought Sophie here. They'll stay until the scandal has died down. No doubt Winifrith is still a little wary of young men who wear a uniform.'

Sir Thomas smiled disarmingly. 'But you must not allow my family and their problems to spoil your day. I've arranged a small dinner party this evening. We'll celebrate your release from that dreadful prison. I was responsible for having it built on Dartmoor, you know? But I never intended that *gentlemen* should be locked up there.'

The dinner party was a small affair. Only nine people

sat around the dining table, including those who were staying at Tor Royal.

One of the dinner guests was the militia officer, Lieutenant Colonel Hawke. He had been invited because Virgil had told Sir Thomas of the conversation the soldier had held with the two paroled prisoners-of-war earlier in the day.

Cecil Hawke was delighted to be at Tor Royal and he was a bluff and lively guest.

The remaining three around the dinner table were the Reverend Alfred Cotterell, vicar of the moorland parish of Sheepstor, his wife Agatha and their daughter.

Jemima Cotterell was a very pleasant young girl, about two or three years older than Sophie.

Sophie and the vicar's daughter seemed to know each other, but Pilgrim observed a look cast in Jemima's direction by Winifrith during a conversation between the girls. He drew the conclusion that Sir Thomas's sister considered the vicar's daughter hardly more suitable as a companion for Sophie than were the two Americans.

However, it became increasingly apparent during the course of the evening that Winifrith Cudmore's love for alcohol was as much of an embarrassment as Sophie's love for the army officer who was being despatched to the war in the Peninsula.

By the end of the meal she had consumed twice as much champagne as anyone else at the table and her voice had grown in volume.

The company was not large enough for the men and women to go their separate ways after dinner. Instead, they all adjourned to the drawing room – losing Winifrith somewhere along the way.

No one commented upon her absence, but after she had been missing for a while, Sophie left the party, murmuring something to Sir Thomas on her way from the room.

When she returned, Sophie sat down on the settee, alongside Virgil. She seemed more relaxed now her mother was not with her and engaged Virgil in polite conversation. She asked the circumstances of his capture and questioned him about the conditions for captured soldiers and sailors inside the Dartmoor prison.

She shuddered at his description of life there and then turned the conversation towards more personal details about his family and their home in the United States of America.

Pilgrim was being equally assiduously questioned by the wife and daughter of the clergyman, but he did not seem to be enjoying the experience as much as the captain of marines.

The party did not break up until almost midnight when the clergyman reluctantly placed his empty glass upon the small table beside his comfortable armchair and said it was time he took his family home. He had a funeral to conduct in the morning.

The militia colonel reluctantly decided he too should return to his barracks in Princetown. The remaining members of the party went out into the night to see them off.

The clergyman's carriage rumbled away from the house with a hand waving a white handkerchief from one of the windows. Pilgrim commented to Sophie that it was an almost forgotten luxury to be free to walk in the night air.

Sophie glanced towards Virgil before replying, 'I don't suppose you saw many horses inside the prison either?'

'No . . . except those which drew carts to and from the prison.'

'Uncle, may I take Pilgrim and go and check on your favourite hunting mare? Virgil might like to come too.'

Sophie put the question to Sir Thomas, adding, 'She looked as though she was close to foaling earlier this evening.'

'If you don't mind, I think I'll go on to bed,' said Virgil. 'It's been an exciting day.' In truth, his wounded leg was bothering him. He needed to rest it.

Sir Thomas hesitated. 'I'm not certain your mother would approve, Sophie . . .'

'She wouldn't, but you don't have to tell her – and it's not as though we'll be alone. One of the grooms is staying in the stable, just in case the mare foals during the night.'

'Well . . . all right,' agreed Sir Thomas reluctantly, 'but don't be long. There's quite a bite to the wind. I don't want you coming down with a chill, or your mother *will* take me to task.'

Afraid he might change his mind, Sophie startled Pilgrim by reaching out and taking his hand, whispering, 'Come along, before Uncle has second thoughts about it.'

Once out of Sir Thomas's hearing, she said, 'Uncle Thomas has very old-fashioned ideas of how I should behave. I suppose that's because he's never married and had children of his own.'

'His caution is quite understandable,' said Pilgrim. 'After all, I've only arrived in his house today. He doesn't really know very much about me.'

'Nonsense!' declared Sophie. 'He was friends with *your* uncle for years. Besides, I *can* trust you, can I not? I feel I shall go quite mad if I'm not able to talk to someone my own age for a while. You can tell me about yourself – and about Captain Howard.'

'You *can* trust me, but you don't really know any more about me than does Sir Thomas.'

'You're beginning to sound just like him!' retorted Sophie. 'Anyway, we're at the stable now. Look! There's a light on in the mare's stall.'

There was not *one* groom, but two in the stall and the mare was in the throes of labour.

She was not having an easy time. Although the night was growing cold, one of the grooms was stripped to the waist and perspiring profusely. He was also bloody from fingertips to shoulder.

He looked up as they entered the loosebox and glanced from Pilgrim to Sir Thomas's niece.

'This is no place for you right now, Miss Sophie. The mare's in trouble.'

'Don't be ridiculous,' snapped Sophie haughtily. 'What's wrong with her?'

'The foal is the wrong way round and won't come out. I've tried to turn it, but the mare's too far on. She needs help bad, but she's so highly strung we can't do things for her the way we should. She needs someone to hold her head still while we get on with things at this end.'

'Can I hold her?' Pilgrim volunteered his help.

'It might be better if I were to do that,' said the other groom. 'She feels safe with me. Do you know anything about horses?'

'We've got quite a few at home,' replied Pilgrim. 'I've helped with more than one difficult birth – and I've never lost a foal yet.'

'Then see if you can help Alfie. I'll hold her head and try to keep her still – but you'd better take that fancy coat off if you don't want to get it bloodied.'

Pilgrim stripped off his French-made Marines coat and rolled up his sleeves.

The birth of the foal was difficult. Very difficult. It

was eventually pulled from the body of its mother by sheer brute force. By this time Sophie too was helping.

While this was going on Sir Thomas had come from the house, concerned about Sophie's continuing absence. He was accompanied by Virgil. Despite his troublesome leg, Virgil was anxious that his country-man should not find trouble on his first night of freedom.

'Is it alive?' Sir Thomas asked the question as the foal slithered to the ground.

The foal supplied an answer by spasmodic move-ments of its legs that grew in strength.

'It's a fine young stallion foal,' said Pilgrim proudly. 'It needed to be strong to survive all it's been through. He'll prove a good stayer.'

'He wouldn't have survived at all had Pilgrim not been on hand to help,' declared Sophie. 'He's worked hard.'

'Everyone's worked hard,' said Pilgrim, 'including you, Sophie. But the little fellow's going to be worth all our efforts.'

'We've a great many fine horses at Tor Royal,' said Sir Thomas. 'You're welcome to ride any of them whenever you wish. They'll enjoy the exercise.'

'So would I,' declared Pilgrim, 'but I'm not certain the terms of my parole allow me to ride horses . . .'

'Nonsense, dear boy! But if you're in any doubt, take out the big grey from the stable across the yard. It belongs to the Prince Regent. Say you're exercising it on his behalf and it'll be a brave man who takes you to task for it.'

'Yes, take Henry out,' said Sophie eagerly. 'I'll come with you. Captain Howard can come too. There are some wonderful rides on the moor around Tor Royal. I'll show them to you.'

'We'll discuss it another time,' said Sir Thomas hurriedly. He took a large watch from his pocket. 'It's nigh on two o'clock. It has been a very exciting day for everyone, now I think it is time we all went to our beds. If we remain here very much longer we'll see the sun rise and I have much to do tomorrow, or, more properly, I should say *today*.'

'It's been a wonderful day, Sir Thomas,' declared Pilgrim. 'One I shall remember for the rest of my days.'

'There will be many more,' promised Sophie eagerly. Glancing at Virgil, she added, 'We'll all work very hard to make your stay in that prison seem no more than a bad dream.'

'I do hope so,' declared Sir Thomas fervently. 'I think this war between our two countries is the height of foolishness. I have said as much to the Prince Regent on many occasions . . .'

Shortly afterwards, Virgil and Pilgrim wished each other goodnight as they entered their adjacent rooms.

'It's wonderful to be leading civilised lives again,' declared Pilgrim. 'I think I'm going to enjoy my stay here.'

'I trust so,' said Virgil cautiously. 'It's certainly better than life inside the walls of the prison. I like Sir Thomas's niece, too . . . She's a good-looking girl – yet she's desperately unhappy and lonely. As for her mother . . . well, she's trouble if ever I saw it!'

25

Although it had been very late when he retired to bed, Pilgrim woke soon after the household came to life. When he remembered where he was, he lay in bed for a while, just listening to the sounds in and about the house.

He tried to identify the various activities that had been absent from his life for such a long time.

There were the muted voices of servants; the sound of a hard brush sweeping on stone and the squeaking of a pump as water was drawn for use in the house. Somewhere farther away in the yard it sounded as though a carpet was being vigorously beaten.

In addition to all the household noises, birdsong in the gardens provided a constant background to all the other sounds. He was able to identify the soft, pleasant murmuring of a dove but the songs of most other birds were unfamiliar to him.

There had been no birdsong within the bleak confines of the Dartmoor prison.

Pilgrim lay listening for perhaps twenty minutes

before deciding he wanted to be a part of the world he could hear. Rising from his bed he first of all washed in a bowl, using water from a jug placed on a marble-topped table in a corner of his room.

When he went downstairs he was surprised to find Sir Thomas already seated at the dining table, taking breakfast alone.

The landowner invited Pilgrim to join him, explaining he was riding to Cornwall to attend a Stannary meeting. It was possible, he added, he would not be returning that night.

During breakfast, Sir Thomas tried to explain to Pilgrim what his duties as Lord Warden of the Stannaries entailed.

As he talked, it became apparent to Pilgrim that the title had meant a great deal in years gone by. When mining operations dwindled, so too did the authority wielded by the Lord Warden.

When he finished eating, Sir Thomas dabbed his mouth with a napkin. 'It's a grand morning. Why don't you take one of the horses and go for a ride?'

'It's a very kind offer,' replied Pilgrim, 'but today I think I would rather go for a walk. I want to savour the feeling of being part of the world once more.'

'Of course.' Pulling out his watch, Sir Thomas peered at it and said, 'I must leave now. I need to be at my destination by lunchtime. Enjoy your freedom, Pilgrim, and please treat Tor Royal as though it were your home.'

For almost an hour after he had finished his breakfast, Pilgrim wandered about the grounds, watching gardeners, estate workers and the house servants going about their various duties. Then he went to the stables and for a while watched the foal he had helped bring into the world.

When he returned to the house and asked after the others, Pilgrim was told by the butler that he was still the only guest up and about.

Pilgrim decided he would not wait about the house until the others woke.

'When Captain Howard rises, will you please tell him I've gone for a walk on the moor?'

'Yes, sir . . .' The butler hesitated before asking, 'Do you mind if I ask which direction you intend taking, sir?'

Mindful of the terms of his parole, Pilgrim replied resentfully, 'Why? Are you concerned the prison authorities will inquire after me?'

'I don't think they are likely to do that, sir, but you are new to the moor. Mists often come down here without any warning. It's very easy to get lost. If you're caught in mist your best plan is to stay exactly where you are and wait for someone to come out and find you. That's why I would like to know the direction you intend taking.'

Sheepishly, Pilgrim said, 'Of course. Even in the prison we were aware of how suddenly the weather here could change. Thank you for thinking of it.'

He hesitated a moment before saying, 'I shall head northeastwards. I believe the farm of the Elford family is that way?'

'That's right, sir. Drop down into the valley and you'll find it a comparatively easy walk. I know the farm – and the Elfords too. They're one of the nicest families on the moor. Enjoy your day. I hope the weather stays as fine for you as it is now.'

Pilgrim set off with the rising sun in his eyes. As he walked, he thought wryly that the weather seemed to crop up in conversation with every Englishman he had met on the moor. He decided it was because it dominated every activity that went on here and so was vitally important in their daily lives.

However, the weather could hardly have been better than it was right now. He walked along relishing his freedom.

Following the curve of the tor, he became aware from the position of the sun that he was gradually heading farther northwards. Then, as he dropped down towards the valley floor, he could hear the sound of tumbling water.

A clear, fast-flowing stream ran along the valley. Picturesque and shallow, the tumbling water divided around numerous polished granite rocks.

For a few minutes Pilgrim stopped to watch a small, black and white bird as it darted about the stream, spending as much time beneath the surface of the water as it did above. It seemed to be searching for food as it darted here and there with incredibly fast movements.

He had been walking for perhaps half an hour when he came upon a young man cutting oblong slabs of peat and stacking them with exaggerated precision nearby.

At the same time, Pilgrim could see the roofs of a house and outbuildings farther along the valley.

Billy had seen Pilgrim approaching in the distance, but he did not cease working until Pilgrim was no more than a few paces away. Leaning on his long-handled peat cutter, he looked at the American uncertainly.

'Hello.' Pilgrim was the first to speak. Indicating the partly visible farm with a nod of his head, he said, 'Is that the Elfords' farm?'

'That's right.' Billy's face wore a puzzled expression when he spoke again. 'Why do you talk so funny?'

Pilgrim realised he was talking to a simple young man and he smiled. 'I expect I sound funny to you because I'm an American. You've probably not met one before.'

Billy's puzzlement became a frown. Looking at Pilgrim reproachfully, he asked, 'Are you the American who upset Tacy? The one they let out of the prison yesterday?'

Pilgrim was taken aback by the accusation. 'I didn't even know Tacy *was* upset! What am I supposed to have done?'

Billy shrugged. 'How should I know? All I can tell you is that she was in a funny mood when she came back from seeing you. She went straight up to her room and didn't speak a word to me for the rest of the day.'

'I'm sorry to hear that. I don't think it can have had anything to do with me, but I'll try to find out.'

'You won't upset her again? I don't like to see her upset.'

Pilgrim smiled sympathetically at the earnest young man. 'I promise to try very hard not to upset her. What's your name?'

'Billy. I live over there . . .' He nodded his head vaguely in a southerly direction '. . . but I like coming to help on the farm. Mr Elford lets me take all the peat we need and Mrs Elford gives me eggs and milk. Bread and cakes too when she bakes 'em.'

'Then you're a fortunate man, Billy. I've tasted some of Mrs Elford's cakes. You'll not find better anywhere. My name's Pilgrim. I'll be on my way now, but I've no doubt we'll meet up with each other again.'

Pilgrim extended his hand and, after a moment's surprised hesitation, Billy took it and the two shook hands.

When Pilgrim had gone on his way, Billy looked from the departing American to his hand. He beamed happily. No one had ever shaken his hand before. It made him feel very important.

26

Coming from the dairy, Joan Elford saw the tall, rather thin, uniformed young man as he turned to secure the gate after entering the farmyard. She realised immediately who he was, but was uncertain what her attitude would, or should, be.

She stood in the kitchen doorway, undecided, as he approached.

Crossing the yard, Pilgrim removed his hat and tucked it beneath his arm as he neared the waiting woman. He slowed down when she remained silent.

'Mrs Elford . . . ?' Pilgrim spoke hesitantly, remembering the conversation he had just had with Billy. He felt sure this woman must be Tacy's mother. It was possible she too believed he had said or done something to upset Tacy.

'You'll be one of the American officers who's staying up at Tor Royal.'

'That's right, ma'am. Lieutenant Penn. Pilgrim Penn.'

There was an awkward lull in the conversation. It was broken, hesitantly, by Pilgrim. 'I came to thank Tacy and

Johanna for showing me and Captain Howard the way to Tor Royal yesterday.'

'I'm the only one at home at the moment. My husband and Johanna have gone to the prison market. Tacy's out with the two dogs. She's rounding up sheep to have them ready for Tavistock market later this week.'

Although Pilgrim believed he was hiding his disappointment well, it was evident to the farmer's wife.

'May I go and look for her?'

'You'd be wasting your time. I couldn't even tell you in which direction to begin looking,' said Joan, untruthfully. 'But she'll be bringing the sheep into the home pen soon. We'll be able to see her from the house. Won't you come in and have a cup of tea while you wait?'

Pilgrim would much rather have gone off on his own, seeking Tacy, but he said, 'That's very kind of you. It's been a long time since I tasted tea.'

Pilgrim needed to duck his head in order to enter through the kitchen doorway. As he did so the smell of baking hit him. For a moment he could almost have been in the kitchen of his own home, far away in Ohio.

When he expressed his thoughts to Joan, she said, 'Were you in the habit of visiting the kitchen in your house . . . in America?'

'Of course. Aren't all children?' Pilgrim was puzzled by her question.

'They certainly are in *this* house, but the kitchen's where we all eat, as well as being where the cooking's done.'

'It must be very cosy during the cold winter months.' Pilgrim continued the polite small talk.

Joan shrugged. 'It's as cosy as anywhere else. Mind you, like just about every moorland house, you can't get rid of all the draughts – nor the damp. You can see

where the wet's coming in over by that window.' She
pointed to the offending spot of dampness. 'It comes
straight through the wall.'

Pilgrim smiled. 'You'll never know what damp and
draught are until you've lived in a log cabin. When the
mud between the logs is new a heavy rainstorm will
wash it out quicker than you can fill it in. When it gets
old and dry the mud shrinks and lets in the wind.'

Joan looked at the visitor quizzically. 'You've lived
in a place like that?'

'Pilgrim nodded. 'That's right, ma'am, but it was
sheer luxury after living for months in the back of a
wagon.'

Joan looked confused. 'But . . . Tacy said your family
owns a great deal of land.'

Delighted that Tacy should have spoken of him to
her mother, Pilgrim explained, 'We do, but so do
a great many folk in Ohio. Land is there for the
taking.'

The concept of simply taking over vast tracts of land
without paying rent to anyone was beyond the compre-
hension of the Dartmoor farmer's wife. She was certain
that *ordinary* people did not have such vast landholdings
– and it did not seem compatible with the type of home
he had just described to her.

'Are you telling me your family owns all this land and
yet you live in a wooden cabin?'

Pilgrim smiled. 'No, ma'am. Not any more. We lived
in it for more than a year, though, while a proper house
was being built for us. Now we've got one of the finest
houses in Ohio.'

Listening to Pilgrim talk, Joan was undecided whether
or not Tacy was right about this very likeable young
American. She had believed he was probably exaggerating the wealth of his family in order to impress

Tacy. Now she realised her daughter had probably been right. Pilgrim's family had a substantial landholding.

'Does your father farm the land himself?'

'When he's home, but that's not so often these days. We were the first settlers in our part of Ohio so folk got used to asking him about things. When it was decided to send someone to Congress it seemed natural for them to elect my father.'

Observing Joan's frown, Pilgrim explained, 'Congress is very much like your Parliament, I guess.'

'Oh, I see.'

If confirmation was needed about his place in society, this was it.

Sir Thomas Tyrwhitt had also been a Member of Parliament until only a few years ago and she told Pilgrim so.

'Sir Thomas seems to have a finger in a great many pies around here.'

'He's a very important man. So, too, I suspect, is your father.'

Pilgrim smiled once more. 'I'm not sure Pa would agree with you about that. He says he's just a natural-born fighter. He's had to fight for everything he's ever wanted. Now *he's* got it he's fighting so that other folk can have what *they* want . . .'

Pilgrim's voice trailed away. While he was speaking he had glanced through the window. He could see one of the dogs and some sheep.

'Would that be Tacy arrived back?'

Joan also looked through the window. 'Yes. At least, I can see Rip, so she won't be far away.'

'Would you mind if I went out to meet her?'

After what Pilgrim had just told her about his family background, Joan was not pleased that he should be taking such an interest in her elder daughter. Wealthy men

– and the sons of wealthy men – did not interest themselves in working girls with a view to *marrying* them. However, if he went out to meet Tacy now the two of them would hardly be out of sight from the farmhouse.

'Tell Tacy not to be too long. With Johanna away she'll need to clean out the pigs, as well as tending to the cow.'

Rip saw the approach of Pilgrim before Tacy did. It was not until the dog began barking that she looked in Pilgrim's direction, shielding her eyes with her hand against the sun.

Pilgrim waved to her. Tacy's return greeting was a decidedly perfunctory gesture and he remembered Billy's words.

'Hello! It's such a fine morning I thought I'd take a walk over here to see you and your farm.'

'You've chosen a bad day,' replied Tacy. There was little enthusiasm in her voice. 'Pa and Johanna are at the prison market and I have a lot to do.'

'Then I've probably chosen a *good* day. I can make myself useful and help you.'

Pilgrim was puzzled by Tacy's attitude towards him. She had always seemed to be prepared to go out of her way in order to see him. Only yesterday she had waited for him upon his release from the prison.

Yet today she was behaving in a decidedly off-hand manner. He suddenly remembered her mother's message and passed it on.

'In that case, if you're serious about helping me you could make a start on cleaning out the pigs.'

It was not what Pilgrim had in mind when making his offer of help. He had expected they would be working together, but he said, 'All right. Where will I find all the things I need?'

Now it was Tacy's turn to be taken by surprise.

After she had explained where everything was kept, she watched him walking back to the farm and felt increasingly guilty. She had thought he would object to carrying out such a menial task, yet he had raised no objections whatsoever.

As she had done so many times during the past twenty-four hours, she wished he was an ordinary man and not a gentleman . . .

27

Pilgrim hardly had the appearance of a gentleman when Tacy returned to the farm, half an hour later. His smart uniform coat was now hanging behind the kitchen door in the farmhouse. In its place he was wearing an old smock, over a pair of well-patched corduroy breeches. Both items of clothing belonged to her father.

He was also perspiring heavily, but the pigsty was cleaner than Tacy had ever seen it.

'You've got some fine hogs here,' Pilgrim said, gesturing towards the old sow and her piglets. 'They're as strong and healthy as any I've seen at home.'

'I didn't mean for you to clean out the sty on your own,' said Tacy guiltily. 'I was on my way to give you a hand when the sheep broke out of the pen. I had to gather them up again.'

'It's all right, I enjoyed the work,' said Pilgrim truthfully. 'Once the old sow realised I wasn't going to hurt her family, we got along fine. Mind you, it took a while to convince your mother I was serious about cleaning them out.'

Tacy knew her mother would have something to say to her about it later, but Pilgrim was talking again.

'I've just about finished here. What needs doing next?'

'There's a whole lot of junk to be cleaned out of the old cowshed,' said Tacy. 'Your people up at the prison have asked if we can supply them with more milk, so we've two more cows and a calf being brought over here this afternoon . . . But it's something I can do any old time. You've done enough work for one day. More than enough.'

'We can do it together,' declared Pilgrim. 'And we can talk while we work. That's really why I've come over here today. So I can talk to you.'

The idea appealed to Tacy and they walked across the farmyard together, watched by Joan Elford through the kitchen window.

The farmer's wife had taken an instant liking to Pilgrim. He had a ready smile and possessed none of the 'airs and graces' she associated with gentlemen. He had been perfectly ready to wear old clothes that even her husband objected to wearing. Nevertheless, she still had deep reservations about his friendship with Tacy. The girl was more fond of him than was good for her. Joan was firmly convinced it was a friendship that would bring nothing but heartache for her daughter.

If Tacy still nurtured any doubts about Pilgrim's ability to sustain hard, physical work because he was a 'gentleman', they were quickly dispelled when they began clearing out the old cowshed together.

She was used to working hard on the moorland farm, but she found it difficult to maintain the pace he set.

As they worked, Pilgrim chattered away happily and Tacy discovered she was enjoying his company even more than she had imagined.

Yet again she found herself wishing his family circumstances were more similar to her own.

Such thoughts made her quieter and more withdrawn than she would otherwise have been. After they had been working together for some time, Pilgrim suddenly stopped work.

'Have I done something to upset you, Tacy?'

Startled, Tacy replied, 'You're helping me with my work. Why should that upset me?'

'I don't necessarily mean today – although you haven't said very much to me . . . not that we've spent enough time together for me to know how you usually behave! But on my way to the farm today I met someone named Billy. He wasn't pleased when he learned I was coming here. He seemed to think I'd made you unhappy yesterday. He warned me not to do the same again.'

Tacy managed a self-conscious laugh. 'You don't want to take any notice of anything Billy says, but he's quite harmless. He wouldn't hurt a fly, really.'

'He thinks the world of you.'

'Billy's grateful to anyone who's kind to him,' said Tacy.

'So nothing I said or did yesterday made you unhappy,' Pilgrim persisted.

'Of course not!' Tacy lied. 'We weren't together for very long, were we?'

'I couldn't think of anything, but it had me worried for a while. As you say, Billy's a little simple. He probably imagined it.'

Setting to work again he said, 'Right, let's get this finished off then we'll see what else needs to be done.'

Pilgrim continued chatting quite freely to Tacy and they worked together happily until soon after noon. At this time Joan came to the cowshed to fetch them both back to the farmhouse.

As they entered the kitchen together, Billy came into the farmyard. Tacy's mother called to him, 'You're just in time, Billy. We're going in for something to eat.'

For a moment it seemed Billy had not heard her; he was staring at Pilgrim in disbelief. 'You . . . you're the American! You been working?'

'That's right, Billy,' Pilgrim smiled at him. 'I've been cleaning out the hogs and helping Tacy get the cowshed ready for the new cows the Elfords are buying.'

When Billy looked from Pilgrim to Tacy and her mother there was a bewildered and hurt expression on his face. 'But . . . *I* was going to help you clear the cowshed, Tacy. You said I could.'

'Did I? I'm sorry, Billy. I forgot.'

'You *promised*, Tacy. You know I like helping you do things.'

'There'll be lots of other things for you to do, Billy,' said Joan, in an attempt to soothe Billy's hurt feelings. 'More than you can manage, no doubt. Come inside and have something to eat now.'

'No! She promised . . .'

Suddenly and unexpectedly, Billy turned about and ran from the farmyard, ignoring the calls of Joan and Tacy to come back.

'Oh dear! Poor Billy. I've never seen him so upset,' said Joan, deeply concerned. 'It isn't like him to behave this way.'

'I'll go and bring him back,' said Tacy.

'You'll never catch him,' said Pilgrim, looking after the running figure of Billy.

'Yes I will.'

Tacy pointed to the top of the rock-strewn tor behind the sheep pen. 'He'll be up there. Ever since he was a young boy he's gone there when something's happened to make him unhappy.'

'Then let me go and find him,' said Pilgrim. 'I'll bring him back.'

'He won't come for you,' declared Tacy.

'I think he will,' said Pilgrim confidently. 'Anyway, I'd like to try.'

As he hurried towards the farmyard gate, Tacy went to follow him, but her mother reached out and gripped her shoulder. 'Let him go, Tacy. I think he understands what's upsetting Billy. It's right for him to go.'

28

Pilgrim soon discovered that the smock he wore was more suited to working in a farmyard than climbing a Dartmoor tor. However, he persevered and was soon approaching the summit of the hill.

The granite boulders here were much larger than they had appeared to be from the farmyard.

He thought he might have difficulty locating the unhappy young man. Then he rounded a piece of broken granite more than twice his own height and here he found Billy. He was seated with his back to another giant rock and was desperately unhappy, as was evident by the tears running down his cheeks.

He made a feeble attempt to cuff them away as Pilgrim approached. Billy was aware of Pilgrim's presence but, without looking up, he drew up his knees, rested his forehead upon them and wrapped his arms about his head.

Pilgrim sat down beside him and felt the coarse granite rock warm against his back.

'I seem to be making a habit of upsetting people just

lately, Billy. Tacy yesterday and now you today. I'm
sorry, I truly am.'

'Go away.'

Billy did not raise his head from his knees and the
words were muffled.

'I'll go away in a few minutes, Billy, but there are a
couple of things I want to say first in a man-to-man talk,
with just the two of us here.'

Billy made no reply, but Pilgrim knew he was listening.

'First of all, why do you work for the Elfords? Do they
pay you well?'

The question was so unexpected, Billy raised his head
and gave Pilgrim a puffy-eyed glare.

'I wouldn't take money from them,' he declared indignantly. 'They feed me and let me take as much peat
home as we need. I work for them because they're kind
to me, and I like them. I like Tacy, especially.'

'I can't think of any better reason for working for anyone, Billy. They appreciate your help too, they've told
me so. With Mr Elford not being so well they've come
to rely on you. You're very important to them. I couldn't
take your place – and I certainly don't want to.'

'Then why did you help Tacy clear out the cowshed
today, when she said I could do it?'

Billy's question was still resentful, but the belligerence
had gone.

'For the same reasons you help them, Billy. Because
Tacy's been kind to me. She brought Sir Thomas to the
prison and had me released from the punishment cell.
She brought cakes to the prison when I had no money
to pay for them, and she came to see me in the prison
hospital when I'd been hurt.'

Pilgrim had Billy's full attention now. 'I want to repay
Tacy for her kindness – just as you do. Like you, the only

way I can think of to do that is to help her and the Elford family on the farm.'

Pilgrim eased his back off the hard rock. 'There'll never be any question of me taking your place, Billy. You'll be here long after this war is over and I've gone back to America. Tacy and her family *need* you. I don't want to do anything to upset them, or you either, but I'd like to do as much as I can to help during the time I'm here. Far from taking over what you do about the farm, I believe that together we can do a whole lot more to help them. You'll know of some of the things they might have always wanted to do, but couldn't because there was neither the time nor enough hands to do it. Is there anything particular you can think of right now?'

Billy had been concentrating very hard on what Pilgrim was saying. He frowned now as he tried to think.

Suddenly his expression lightened. 'They could do with having the wall built up properly around the big sheep pen. They can't put sheep in there any more because they keep getting out. Then there's that old tumbledown barn in the corner of the yard. Tacy's always said if it was rebuilt they could keep more calves – or perhaps a lot more chickens.'

'There you are, Billy. If you and me work hard during the time I'm here we could do all those things and make Tacy and her family *really* happy. It'd make me happy too. When the time comes for me to go home to America I'd leave with the knowledge that I'd been able to do something lasting to repay their kindness. Not only that, whenever you looked at what we'd done together you could feel proud because it was your idea and resulted from us working together.'

Pilgrim could see by Billy's expression that he had won, but he added, 'What do you say, Billy? Shall we work together and do all we can to make this the best farm on the moor for the Elfords? We can do it, you and I.'

Fired with Pilgrim's enthusiasm, Billy climbed to his feet and nodded his head vigorously, his earlier unhappiness dispelled. 'Yes . . . and we could dam up that old stream and make a pond for them . . . and repair the roof on the long barn. I'd have time to cut more turf too. They could sell it all at the prison and make a lot more money.'

'There you are, Billy. With all the ideas you have, there's no end to the things we can do together for the Elfords. That's if you don't mind having me around to work with you, of course.'

'I'd like it. I expect I can think of a lot more things too.'

'I don't doubt it, Billy.' Pilgrim smiled at his companion and there was a genuine warmth in the expression. 'Shall we go back to the farm together now?'

Billy hesitated and Pilgrim realised he probably felt embarrassed because of the manner in which he had left the farm.

'I . . . I don't know if I'll have time to have anything to eat today. I promised I'd go and fetch the two cows and a calf from Mr Pearce's farm. It's quite a way from here.'

'I'll tell you what then, Billy. You go and fetch the cows while I go back to the farm and ask Mrs Elford to keep something for when you get back. But won't you need one of the dogs to help you?'

Billy grinned happily. 'You don't need to worry about that. I just have to give my special whistle and old Rosie'll come running to me. Rip'll come too, I expect.'

'Then I'll get on back to the farm and tell them what you're doing. They'll be worrying about you. I'm glad we've had our talk, Billy. I look forward to working with you and doing as much as can be done for Tacy and her family. They're good folk.'

'I'm glad too, Mr Pilgrim. Nobody's ever spoken to me about things the way you have – except Tacy, sometimes. We'll make it the best farm anywhere. Tacy'll be happy then.'

The two young men shook hands for the second time that day.

As Pilgrim walked back to the house, he heard a shrill whistle, repeated three or four times. Then he saw the two farm dogs running along the valley, making for the now unseen, but very happy, Billy.

29

Tacy and her mother were concerned when they saw Pilgrim returning from the tor alone and he had difficulty assuring them that Billy was no longer unhappy.

'He was very upset when he ran off,' said Joan.

'Well, he's perfectly happy now,' said Pilgrim. 'He's taken the dogs with him and gone to fetch the cows and the calf you've bought.'

Joan was still dubious. 'Billy usually takes days – weeks even – to recover from the sort of upset he's had today.'

'Not this time,' said Pilgrim confidently. 'He's gone off thinking of all the things he's always wanted to do for you and will be able to do now he's got some help.'

'That's all very well for now,' said the farmer's wife. 'But what happens when he realises there's going to be no miracle – that Roundtor Farm won't change overnight to being a gentleman's farm? We need to work hard here to survive. There isn't the time, or money, to do all the things that need doing, and you won't be around for ever. The war between our countries could end any day. When it does you'll go home and that'll be the end of all these plans you have for Roundtor.'

Joan was being deliberately blunt and pessimistic. She had seen Tacy's barely concealed delight when Pilgrim was talking of spending time working with Billy at Roundtor Farm. It was not only Billy who seemed to think this young American was the saviour for whom the farm had been waiting.

'Billy realises I might not be around to see all our plans made good. But he and I agreed that together we'd do all we could in the time I have here. Somehow I think that's likely to be a year or two, at the very least.'

'That's as maybe,' retorted Joan, unreasonably disturbed by his words. 'All the same, you'll not be working every day of the week, month in and month out at Roundtor. Sir Thomas will expect you to spend some time with him and his friends, at Tor Royal.'

'I certainly owe it to Sir Thomas to fall in with his wishes,' agreed Pilgrim patiently. 'But I understand he spends much of his time in London. Working here will help keep me out of mischief while he's away. I might even be able to persuade Captain Howard to come and give a hand occasionally.'

Pilgrim was a little puzzled by Joan Elford's lack of enthusiasm for the suggestion that he and Billy should work to improve Roundtor Farm. 'Perhaps I'm being a little presumptuous. You might not want me to come here quite so often?'

Joan realised she had been less than gracious in her response to Pilgrim's offer of help. She felt suddenly guilty. 'It isn't that . . . You can come to Roundtor as often as you like.' The words were accompanied by an apologetic smile. 'But you mustn't think you have to work whenever you come calling. We get by, especially now we have a market for our cakes up at the prison.

Whatever happens on the farm, we'll still have money coming in. All the same, we're glad of any help we can get. If you actually *enjoy* farm work we'll be grateful to you for helping out.'

Tacy was relieved at her mother's conciliatory words. She had listened with increasing alarm to her apparent determination to put Pilgrim off coming to Roundtor and helping on the farm.

Further discussion was brought to an unexpected halt by a woman's voice. It came from somewhere beyond the farmyard gate and was calling Pilgrim's name.

Peering through the kitchen window, Pilgrim said, 'That's Sir Thomas's niece, Sophie. What can she want? I'd better go and find out.'

He hurried from the kitchen, leaving Tacy and her mother standing in the doorway, looking after him. The two Roundtor women were witness to Sophie's peal of laughter when she saw him.

'Pilgrim! What on earth are you doing in that ridiculous garb?'

Sophie spoke loudly, apparently unaware that the two women were standing in the farmhouse doorway and able to hear all she was saying.

'Are you taking part in a masquerade?'

'I'm wearing clothes that are eminently practical for farm work,' retorted Pilgrim. 'But I don't imagine you've ridden all the way here from Tor Royal to discuss how I'm dressed.'

'No – although those clothes are certainly worthy of comment. A message arrived at Tor Royal from the prison. An agent has arrived there to talk about aid from the American Government for your countrymen. Virgil thought you should both be there to hear what he has to say. He's already gone on ahead.'

'I'll go straight there,' said Pilgrim.

'Will you please wear your smock back to Tor Royal afterwards – and those breeches, of course. It would cause great merriment.'

Ignoring her taunts, Pilgrim said, 'I'll go to the farm-house to change, before going to the prison.'

'We'll go there together. Then I'll ride back to Tor Royal and tell them you won't be back for lunch. But I still think you should remain in those clothes. They must be in need of some amusement at the prison.'

When Pilgrim returned to the farm kitchen, he told Tacy and her mother that he had to leave.

'Oh?' said Tacy icily. 'Has Sir Thomas's niece come to tell you that you shouldn't be spending the day on a farm and must return home now like an obedient boy?'

Pilgrim looked at Tacy sharply. Her earlier iciness had thawed while they were working together in the cowshed. It seemed to have returned with increased intensity.

'Sophie's called to say Virgil and I are needed at the prison. The United States agent has arrived to tell the men of our Government's plans to help us while we're here.'

'Then you'd better go, and not keep her waiting, hadn't you? No doubt *she'll* go with you, to keep you company.'

'Possibly, but I doubt if she'll be allowed inside the prison, as you are.'

Puzzled by Tacy's sudden swings of temperament, Pilgrim asked, 'Will it still be all right for me to come here again, when I can?'

Tacy shrugged her shoulders. 'That's up to you, I'm sure. No doubt you have lots of other things to occupy your time.'

'Of course it will be all right,' said Joan Elford unexpectedly, her sympathy suddenly going out to the perplexed young man standing before her. 'Come as often as you wish.'

As Pilgrim set off for Tor Royal, walking beside Sophie's horse, Tacy's unhappiness was so apparent that her mother put an arm about her shoulders and squeezed affectionately.

'I think this has brought the situation home to you far more clearly than any words of mine might. He's a nice young man, Tacy. A rather special young man who's very far from home. But don't allow yourself to care too much for him. He belongs with the likes of Sir Thomas Tyrwhitt and those who visit Tor Royal, not here, at Roundtor.'

When Tacy made no reply, she added, 'I don't doubt he means well, but helping on a farm is no more than an amusing pastime for him. He's no need to work anywhere. One day he'll tire of it and we'll see no more of him.'

30

On the way to Dartmoor prison, Sophie questioned Pilgrim closely about the family at Roundtor Farm. She was particularly interested in Tacy and the manner in which they had first met. He added that had it not been for her he would probably never have met with Sir Thomas and been paroled to Tor Royal.

'It's a very good reason to be grateful, certainly,' agreed Sophie. 'But her family has gained from it too. It would seem they now have a very lucrative business selling their wares at the prison market. There's no reason at all for you to spend time on their farm, dressed as a peasant and performing menial tasks for them. It's demeaning, Pilgrim. What would your family think?'

'I don't think the Elford family see farm work as demeaning. Neither do I. There's nothing wrong with physical work. My father is a congressman now, but when we first settled in Ohio he cleared the land and built our first cabin with just me to help him.'

'That was different. He wasn't just building a cabin,

he was helping to build a whole new country. Now he's a leader of that country.'

Pilgrim realised he would be wasting his time if he tried to explain the American way of life to Sophie. She would not understand. She had been brought up to accept without question that birth and not ability dictated the place of a man in society.

He led the conversation away from Roundtor Farm and they spoke of less controversial subjects for the remainder of the journey to Dartmoor prison.

Virgil was waiting for Pilgrim in the governor's office. Together they were escorted to Block Four, where they met up with the United States agent.

Both men found Reuben G. Beasley a disappointment. He was already talking to the American prisoners-of-war, including those from the Petty Officers' Block, when they arrived there – and he was being given a difficult time.

As they entered the building an angry howl had just escaped from the throats of the assembled men. The noise increased when the Americans saw the two marines officers.

'What's going on?' Virgil shouted the question to Ephraim above the din. The marines sergeant had come across the room to meet them.

'Beasley's come to Dartmoor with nothing more than talk to offer the men right now – and very little more in the future, if you ask me.'

'Then why *is* he here?' Pilgrim asked.

Ephraim shrugged. 'Probably to justify the fat fee our Government's paying him to take care of our interests. Whatever the reason, it seems there's nothing coming our way just yet.'

'Well, we're not going to get anywhere in here with

this din going on. I'll see if the governor will let Lieutenant Penn and me use his office to have a chat with Beasley. We might be able to get some sense out of him there.'

Calming the men with difficulty, Virgil told them what he intended doing. He promised he would let them know the result of his talks. Then, much to the perspiring agent's relief, the three men were escorted from the block, followed by a number of the frustrated prisoners-of-war and the jeers of the remainder.

Before they left the yard, Ephraim caught up with them and spoke to the frightened agent. 'This money that's supposed to be coming to American prisoners-of-war . . . is it just for the army and navy men?'

'No,' replied Beasley, 'it's to be granted to every United States citizen who's been taken prisoner by the British.'

'Whether they're black or white?'

As the agent hesitated, Virgil said firmly, 'It will go to everyone who is being kept in here because he's an American citizen, Ephraim. I'll make out a list of names and have it sent to Mr Beasley. No one will be left out.'

'That wasn't what was being argued before you arrived, Cap'n. Steiger was in there saying none of the Government money should go to anyone who's believed to be a slave. He said it would make them "uppity". Them's his words, Cap'n Howard, not mine.'

'And I stand by them . . .'

Virgil had not realised that Conrad Steiger had walked from the Block Four building behind him. '. . . Give a nigger money to make him independent and he'll think he's as good as us. It's a bad precedent. It might mean nothing to you men from the north, but those of us who are from the south will one day have to deal with the trouble you stir up.'

'I'll make a note of that, Mr Steiger,' said Agent Beasley.

'No you won't,' said Virgil firmly. '*I'll* make out the list of who is to receive our Government's money. Every American in this prison will receive an equal share, whether he's black or white.'

Ephraim acknowledged Virgil's words, but said, 'The men trust you, Cap'n Howard, but Mr Steiger won't take this lying down. If we're to stay clear of trouble in here you're going to have to do something about him. If you don't, some of us surely will.'

'You heard that, Howard! That was an out-and-out threat. The governor should be told about this . . .'

'It's quite likely he will, Steiger. Unfortunately, if he does you're likely to be the loser. I hear you're applying for parole? You won't get it if word reaches the governor's ears that you're a troublemaker. I suggest you make your way back to the Petty Officers' Block right now and leave me to deal with what needs doing here.'

Surrounded by some of his southern friends, Conrad Steiger made his way to the gate leading from the Block Four compound. He was not a happy man, but he *had* applied for parole. He did not want anything to spoil his chances of leaving the prison. He would say nothing more – for now.

'Steiger's the worst of the southern men here, but there's a great many men who feel the same way as he does, Cap'n. They're beginning to push us just a little too hard.'

'Keep things under control, Ephraim. Trouble will help no one, least of all you and your people.'

Ephraim shrugged. 'We were born to trouble, Cap'n. If we don't find it, as sure as there's a heaven and a hell it'll find us.'

'You can handle it, Ephraim. Just don't go looking for it, that's all I ask.'

'I hear you, Cap'n. For all our sakes I hope you'll say the same thing to Steiger.'

In the governor's office, Reuben G. Beasley showed Virgil and Pilgrim the correspondence he had received from the United States Government. They had promised to make an allowance to the prisoners-of-war of one and a half pence a day.

'So far, promises are all I have,' complained the unhappy agent. 'I tried to explain this to your men, but they wouldn't listen. They blame me for not coming up with money for them.'

'I can understand their point of view,' said Virgil. 'They're desperate for money. They have no comforts whatsoever. Can't you use these letters to borrow money for them?'

Reuben Beasley spread his hands wide in a gesture of helplessness. 'No one's likely to loan money without charging interest.'

'How much interest do you think they would want?' asked Virgil.

'I haven't asked anyone,' admitted the agent. 'After all, who would want to loan money to the men of an enemy country?'

'This war won't last for ever,' retorted Virgil. 'The written authority of the United States Government should be enough for any bank, or wherever else you go to borrow the money.'

Reuben Beasley looked unhappy, 'I'm sorry but I can't commit the United States Government to repaying a loan.'

'Of course you can. You can. You've been appointed our agent here – and you're in possession of letters showing our Government's intent to pay money to the prisoners.'

'Yes . . . but not to pay interest on a loan.'

'Dammit, man! The men you're supposed to be taking care of don't have a cent between them. To pay every American in here a month's allowance wouldn't take much more than a hundred English pounds. If you feel you can't stand security for such an amount then let me do it. Our Government's not going to quibble over a few pounds of interest.'

'If they do then *I'll* pay it,' said Pilgrim. 'As Captain Howard says, stop making excuses and get some money for the men.'

Turning to the prison governor who had been seated at his desk listening to the discussion without saying anything, Pilgrim said, 'You'll witness my agreement to this, Governor Cotgrave?'

Governor Cotgrave nodded his head, still without speaking. This was something he wanted no part of. Possession of money by prisoners was a two-edged sword. Some would use it to buy a few small luxuries and be more content with their lot. Others would become involved in the type of gambling which had reduced some of the French prisoners to the level of animals.

The men confined to the upper levels of Block Four were reduced to scavenging for their very existence. Those who proved less successful than their fellows at such means of survival quickly became so emaciated they succumbed to the first minor ailment that came their way.

'Well . . . as long as you're prepared to accept full responsibility for any interest charged . . .' Beasley was still reluctant to support the idea.

'Governor Cotgrave, do you have pen and paper, please?'

When the governor pushed the items across his desk, Pilgrim picked up the pen and acknowledged in writing his responsibility for whatever interest would be charged on a loan up to the amount of two hundred pounds.

When it was written, he passed the paper to the American agent, saying, 'There! Now you have no excuse whatsoever for not providing at least a single month's allowance to the prisoners here. I expect you to produce the payment within days, Mr Beasley, you understand?'

Looking pained, Reuben G. Beasley said, 'I'll do my best, Lieutenant Penn, but our Government has been extremely tardy, to say the least. I have even been forced to pay my own fare from London.'

31

That night it began to rain. It rained with a ferocity unimaginable to anyone who did not live on Dartmoor. All across the moor an intricate skein of streams carried the water to a hundred small rivers and the rivers became raging torrents.

To Pilgrim, looking out from a sitting room window at Tor Royal, it seemed as though God must have decided to send another unheralded deluge to cover the face of the earth.

'Have you ever experienced rain like this in America?'

Sophie had entered the room silently and she came to stand beside Pilgrim at the window.

He shook his head. 'I once saw rain like it during a hurricane in Florida, but it didn't last all that long. Is it often like this here?'

'I've never known rain quite like this before, but Dartmoor weather is often more extreme than it is anywhere else, whether it's rain, wind or snow.'

She gave him a sidelong glance. 'You won't be able to visit your farmer's daughter in this.'

'No . . . and it looks as though it will continue for a month!'

'I sincerely hope not,' Sophie spoke with considerable feeling. 'I want it to be fine by this weekend.'

Something in her voice caused Pilgrim to turn and look at her. 'Is something special happening then?'

'No! No, nothing's happening. Nothing at all. It's just . . . well, weekends are special somehow, aren't they?' Sophie seemed inexplicably flustered, but she was saved from further embarrassment by Virgil.

Putting in an appearance at the doorway, he called, 'Sir Thomas has suggested we have a game or two of cards as the weather precludes anything else.'

'You go,' Sophie said to Pilgrim. 'I'm not fond of cards. I shall take one of Uncle's books to my room and read for a while.'

When Pilgrim explained Sophie's absence to her mother and Sir Thomas, it brought a comment from the landowner that he thought she had looked somewhat pale and drawn that morning. He hoped the sudden change in the weather had not brought on a chill.

'It's more likely to be the letter she received yesterday evening from one of her London friends,' replied his sister. 'I expect it told her all that is going on in the capital and she is wishing herself back there.'

'That's a fairly healthy state of mind,' said Sir Thomas. 'She's a high-spirited girl and there's not a great deal of social life here.'

'Sophie is twenty-one years of age. It's high time she found herself a suitable husband and settled down,' retorted Winifrith. 'But where marriage is concerned she is not set a very good example by *some* members of her own family.' She glared pointedly at Sir Thomas.

'Quite! Shall we cut the cards for who is going to deal? I think you and I should be partners, Winifrith, against

Virgil and Pilgrim. We will make it an international contest . . .'

By the end of the second day of rain, everyone in the house was beginning to get on each other's nerves. Sophie, especially, appeared to find being confined to the house particularly irksome. She was irritable with everyone.

On the third morning the household awoke to discover the rain had ceased. However, it had been replaced by a dense mist. On the moor it was impossible to see anyone at a distance of more than three paces.

Despite this, Pilgrim found it a welcome relief to be able to get out of the house, even though a visit to Roundtor Farm was out of the question until the mist thinned considerably.

While Virgil wrote letters and Sir Thomas was out with the Tor Royal head gardener, assessing the extent of the damage caused by the rain, Pilgrim made his way to the stables. He thought he might check on the progress of the foal.

To his surprise, he found Sophie there, grooming her own horse.

'It's something to do,' she explained. 'Another day in the house with my mother would drive me mad.'

Pilgrim smiled sympathetically. 'I must admit, the house seems somewhat smaller after being inside for a couple of days.'

Sophie was silent for a few moments. Thinking she probably wanted to be on her own for a while, Pilgrim begain to walk towards the stall where the foal was kept.

'Don't go, Pilgrim. Stay here and talk to me for a while.'

When Pilgrim returned, Sophie was silent for a few

more moments, then she said, 'Do parents in America control the lives of their children to the same extent as they do in England?'

'I'm not sure I know just how much control they have here. In America it depends pretty much on the family, I guess – and whether you're a son or a daughter. Were you thinking of anything specific?'

'Oh, you know,' said Sophie vaguely. 'Deciding who you can, or cannot marry. That sort of thing.'

'In some American families it still matters, I suppose,' replied Pilgrim thoughtfully, 'but that's among the more wealthy families in the east. Virgil will know more about that than I do. Further west folk tend to grow up more quickly and make up their own minds about most things, including marriage.'

Pilgrim thought he knew why she was asking the question and he sympathised with her. 'But I guess things are different here?'

'I don't see why they should be!' said Sophie angrily. 'I don't see why anyone should decide about something that's going to affect the whole of someone else's life.'

When Pilgrim made no reply, she said with slightly less passion, 'Would your parents try to stop you if you wanted to marry someone they thought was not suitable? That young girl at Roundtor Farm, for instance?'

Her question took Pilgrim by surprise. 'Tacy? I hardly know her well enough to have thoughts about anything as serious as marriage!'

'Well, suppose you had, would they object?'

Pilgrim thought seriously about the possible implications of his reply. He decided to give her a truthful answer – but only as it applied to him.

'I think my pa would say I'm as much of a man as I'm ever likely to be and can make up my own mind. Ma would probably say I'm too young to marry anyway. But if she felt it was to the girl I really wanted she wouldn't stand in my way.'

He looked at her apologetically. 'That doesn't help you a lot, does it?'

Sophie seemed about to say something, but changed her mind. She shrugged. 'I suppose it confirms what I've known all along, really. The only person who can make up my mind about it all – is me.'

'You're not thinking of doing something silly, are you, Sophie?'

'Silly? Silly for whom, Pilgrim? For me? My mother – or for everyone else?'

At that moment there was the sound of the door being opened and Winifrith entered the stables. She looked from Pilgrim to her daughter suspiciously.

'One of the servants told me I would find you here, Sophie. Had I realised Lieutenant Penn was with you I would have come here earlier.'

Addressing Pilgrim, she said icily, 'Such things probably don't matter in your country, Lieutenant Penn, but in England a young woman is at grave risk of being compromised if she is taken off by a man, away from the company of others. It's something no *gentleman* would think of doing.'

'Mother! You really have surpassed yourself this time. Pilgrim took me nowhere. I was here grooming my horse when he came to check on the foal.'

Unabashed, Winifrith said, 'It doesn't matter how you both arrived here. You are in the stables together. An *English* gentleman would have apologised and left immediately.'

'Had he been an *observant* English gentleman, Mrs Cudmore, he would no doubt have noticed the stable-hand just two stalls along from here, as I did.'

The stablehand had been mucking out a nearby stall

and had heard every word of the exchange. He stood up now and grinned in Pilgrim's direction.

'I think you owe Pilgrim an apology,' said Sophie to her mother.

Carefully avoiding looking at Pilgrim, Winifrith said, 'No mother need apologise for trying to protect the good name of her daughter – and I'm sure I don't know why it is necessary for you to groom your own horse. Sir Thomas employs stablehands to do that – and not to skulk around eavesdropping.'

The stablehand hastily ducked from view and Winifrith said, 'I shall expect to see you back in the house within fifteen minutes, Sophie. If you have not returned by then I shall come looking for you once more.'

With this, she turned about and made her way to the stable door. Opening it, she stepped outside into the mist which swirled in around her.

'Since my mother refuses to apologise then I must do it for her,' said Sophie unhappily. 'It's the second time it has happened. She did the same thing when I took a walk with Virgil. I am truly sorry, Pilgrim.'

'You can't take the blame for your mother's behaviour,' said Pilgrim. 'Anyway, as she said, no mother can be blamed for trying to protect her daughter.'

'Protect? No, Pilgrim, *humiliate* is a more accurate word. She *enjoys* humiliating me.'

Sophie began vigorously brushing the startled horse. 'God! I shall be glad to be rid of her!'

They were words Pilgrim would remember.

32

Not until Sunday morning did the heavy mist disappear from Dartmoor. But Pilgrim was unable to visit Roundtor Farm. He, Virgil, Sir Thomas, Winifrith and Sophie were to attend a service at Sheepstor church. They would then spend the remainder of the day at the vicarage with the Reverend Cotterell and his family.

At the very last moment, Sophie complained of a headache. She announced she would remain at Tor Royal and not go with the others to Sheepstor.

'This is very tiresome of you, Sophie,' complained her mother. 'Could you not have mentioned it earlier?'

'Mother, I do not choose when to have a headache. It just happens. I think I shall go to my room and remain there for a while.'

'Then I'll stay home with you,' declared her mother.

'That's the very *last* thing I want!' said Sophie heatedly. 'You would be coming up to my room every five minutes, demanding to know how I was. I would have no rest at all. If you go to Sheepstor with the others I have no doubt I will recover in half the time.'

'Well! That's all the thanks I'm given for caring about my daughter,' said Winifrith, to everyone in general. 'But I realised long ago that the young people of today do not recognise the values we were taught as being important. So be it. Come, Thomas, we must not keep Reverend Cotterell waiting.'

As Winifrith led the way from the room, Pilgrim spoke quietly to Sophie. 'Are you really going to be all right?'

She nodded. 'Yes – but thank you for caring, Pilgrim. You and Virgil. Thank you for everything.'

Her words disturbed Pilgrim. They sounded somehow as though they were a farewell. He thought about it for a long time. However, by the time the party reached Sheepstor, he had convinced himself he was worrying unnecessarily. Everyone had been closeted in Tor Royal for far too long during the period of rain and mist.

Sophie and her mother, in particular, had found it difficult. Both were basically city dwellers. They found the limitations of country life irksome. A day spent apart from each other would be good for both of them.

The visit to Sheepstor lasted much longer than anyone could have anticipated.

After the morning service and a very pleasant day at the vicarage, the party attended Evensong. When this service was over they intended returning to Tor Royal.

However, when they left the church, the mist had descended once again. It was extremely dense and they discussed whether or not it would be safe to undertake the journey across the moor.

Even as they talked, the mist was becoming thicker. It was hardly possible to see one's hand when held at arm's length.

Eventually, it was decided the Tor Royal party would have to spend the night at the vicarage.

Winifrith expressed her concern for Sophie, but Sir Thomas assured her she would be all right at Tor Royal with the servants to take care of her.

Winifrith looked squarely at Pilgrim when she said, 'Yes, of course she will. There is no one there to take advantage of her.'

Pilgrim thought it would be a relief for Sophie to be free of her mother for a few more hours.

The mist had not entirely dispersed when the party left the Sheepstor vicarage the next morning, but it had thinned to such an extent it no longer posed a danger to moorland travellers.

It was a happy party that travelled home. Only Winifreth was particularly quiet. Pilgrim believed, somewhat ungenerously, that her lack of conversation was due in part to the large quantity of port she had consumed during the previous evening.

When the carriage came to a halt before the main entrance to Tor Royal, the party was helped to the ground by a footman and greeted at the door by the butler.

'Good morning, Sir Thomas, Mrs Cudmore; gentlemen. We are all happy to see you safely back at Tor Royal. The staff were concerned last night that you might have tried to journey back though the mist. I assured them you would decide to remain at Sheepstor.'

The butler looked past them before adding, 'Will Miss Sophie be returning later, Sir Thomas?'

Winifrith looked at him sharply. 'What do you mean, "returning later"? Isn't she in the house?'

The butler seemed confused by the question. 'No, madam. She left the house soon after you, yesterday.

She said her headache was better and she had decided to go to Sheepstor after all. She went on her horse – and took two saddlebags of clothes with her. She said they were for Miss Jemima to distribute to the poor women of Sheepstor village.'

'Took clothes . . . ? Let me through!'

Winifrith pushed past the others and hurried through the hallway to the stairs.

'What do you think can have happened to Sophie?' Virgil put the question to Pilgrim, as Sir Thomas hurried after his sister.

'I believe she's probably had as much of her mother as she can take. It's my opinion she's gone off to make a life for herself.'

Pilgrim told Virgil of the conversations he had held with Sir Thomas's niece.

'She's spoken to me in a similar vein,' admitted Virgil. 'Do you think we ought to tell her mother?'

'No,' said Pilgrim firmly. 'Whatever she's doing, Sophie has thought it all out and made her plans accordingly. We'd be wrong to interfere in any way.'

A few minutes later, Sir Thomas came down the stairs. He was mopping his brow and appeared harassed.

'The girl's gone,' he said. 'Packed her personal belongings and a few clothes, and taken off bound for God-knows-where. Her mother's having a fit of hysterics in her room.'

Tucking the handkerchief inside his sleeve, a fleeting smile crossed his face. 'Who'd have thought young Sophie had the nerve to do such a thing? Mind you, I don't really blame the girl. I can't imagine anything worse than the thought of spending the foreseeable future in the company of Winifrith.'

'What will Mrs Cudmore do now?'

'She seems to think Sophie has run off to London to

stay with one of her friends there. We'll be taking the carriage and setting off after her this afternoon. It will mean leaving you both on your own, of course, but no doubt you'll be able to find plenty to keep you occupied.'

Sir Thomas gave them a benevolent smile. 'You both seemed to get along well with the Cotterells and their charming daughter. You're welcome to take one of the horses whenever you feel like paying a call on them.'

Sir Thomas waved Virgil's protest aside before it was even uttered. 'Yes, I know all about the terms of your parole. I'll write a letter stating you are travelling beyond the limits of your parole area with my express permission. That should be sufficient to keep you out of trouble, I think.'

The handkerchief came into play once more. 'Now, if you will excuse me, I must arrange to have the carriage made ready and my clothes packed.'

He shook his head. 'The more I see of other people's children, the happier I am that I never married. I hope you two young gentlemen will take note!'

When Sir Thomas had gone from the room, Virgil said, 'I wish Sophie well. Now, do you have anything planned for the remainder of the day, Pilgrim?'

'I thought I might take a walk to Roundtor this afternoon. Why don't you come with me?'

'I don't think you need my company. I'll keep myself amused here. Go off and meet your young country girl – but remember Sir Thomas's warning. Don't get too serious about her.'

33

As he approached Roundtor, Pilgrim saw Tacy working in the hillside sheep pen with Johanna. The sisters were building up one of the walls.

Tacy saw him approaching. For a moment she seemed pleased to see him, then the expression became one that was less easily read.

'I thought I'd come across to see how you made out during the bad weather,' he said when he was within calling distance.

'We had a flood come down the slope behind the pen,' said Johanna before her sister could reply. 'It washed part of the wall away. We're building it up again now.'

'You're making a very good job of it,' said Pilgrim. 'I'm surprised Billy isn't here to help you.'

'So am I,' said Tacy, 'but perhaps the streams between here and his cottage have risen too high for him to get here. If he doesn't come tomorrow I'll go and find out whether anything is wrong.'

Looking about him across the still sodden moor, Pilgrim asked, 'What happened to your sheep?'

'All the ewes escaped,' said Tacy. 'Ma and Pa are out looking for them. They've found a few and shut them up in the yard, but Pa's not very well, so they can't cover as much ground as they ought to.'

'We've got a leak in the roof of the house too,' said Johanna. 'Water poured into the room where Tacy and me sleep. We've had to move in with Ma and Pa.'

'That's right.' When Tacy spoke, Pilgrim thought she looked tired.

She brushed a long lock of hair back from in front of her face and said, 'The roof's going to have to wait until we've caught all the ewes and can get someone in to work on it. Pa's not fit enough to go clambering around up there.'

Picking up another stone and adding it to those on the freestone wall, Tacy said, 'No doubt you, Sir Thomas's niece and the others have been comfortable enough up at Tor Royal.'

'Well, life hasn't been without incident,' replied Pilgrim, 'but I'll tell you about that some other time. More to the point right now is that I've done a little bit of work on roofs in my time. Do you have anything I can use for new thatch?'

'Loads of it,' replied Tacy. 'But . . . are you sure?' Although she expressed doubt, Tacy was secretly delighted. 'You fix the roof and you'll be Ma's friend for life. She wept when it happened and water poured in.'

'Tell me where I can find the thatch, then you carry on here. I'll borrow the ladder from the barn and make a start. Who knows, I might even have it finished by the time your ma and pa return home.'

The repairs to the thatch were not completely finished

by the time Tom and Joan Elford returned home, but they were well on the way.

In fact, Pilgrim did not fully complete his work until it was almost too dark to see what he was doing.

Climbing down to the ground, he expressed the opinion that the roof was now as good as new. He explained that, in addition to repairing the storm-damaged section of the roof, he had checked out the remainder. He was confident it would withstand any future severe weather.

'God bless you, Pilgrim!' said Joan fervently, calling him by his Christian name for the first time. 'I've been dreading the thought of it raining again and ruining more of the precious things Tom and I have managed to get together over the years. Now, let me cook something for you. It's a meal well-earned, I'd say!'

'Thanks all the same, but I have to be getting back to Tor Royal. The terms of my parole are that I should be indoors an hour before sunset. Not all the servants at the house are happy about us being there. If one decided to report me to Governor Cotgrave at the prison, I would be in trouble.'

'It's very nearly dark now. By the time you reach Tor Royal it's going to be too dark to see your way – and you don't know the moor.' Joan expressed her concern.

'I'll walk back with him.'

Tacy saw the fleeting expression of disapproval on her mother's face and she added, 'I know the moor better than anyone. I'll have Pilgrim at Tor Royal more quickly than anyone else could.'

'It's all right, I'm sure I can find my way,' Pilgrim protested.

'And I'm equally certain you can't,' said Tacy firmly.

'Take Johanna with you,' suggested her mother.

'Oh, Ma! I'm tired. I've been heaving stones all day up in the sheep pen.'

'Come on, Pilgrim, we're wasting time and you're right. A couple of the servants up at Tor Royal have brothers in the navy who might be fighting Americans right now. They wouldn't think twice about reporting you for being out late.'

Tacy's manner brooked no further argument. A few minutes later she and Pilgrim were striding out together across the moor.

There were many stars out, but no moon. They had not gone far before Pilgrim admitted to Tacy that, had she not insisted she come with him, he would probably have become hopelessly lost.

'I know that, and so does Ma. That's why she didn't make any real fuss about me coming with you.'

They walked on in silence for a few moments, then Tacy said, 'Is anyone likely to come out looking for you from Tor Royal?'

'No, but Virgil will be worried.'

'How about Sir Thomas's niece?'

It seemed a casual question, but Pilgrim remembered Tacy's reaction to Sophie when she had come to Roundtor Farm.

'She's not at Tor Royal.'

Pilgrim told Tacy the manner of Sophie's leaving and her mother's belief that she had run off to London.

'Do you believe she's gone to London?' Tacy had detected doubt in Pilgrim's voice when he talked of Sophie's disappearance.

'I'm not at all sure. There was a man in her life before she came to Devon. Someone she really cared about. I think she might be with him – but that's a wild guess. I could be hopelessly wrong.'

'Are you sweet on her?'

The question took Pilgrim by surprise. After a moment's thought, he said, 'I hadn't known her long enough to think how I felt about her. I liked her, yes, although sometimes I felt that she and I came from different worlds. I guess I sometimes find your social distinctions difficult to understand.'

'Do they *really* not matter so much in America?'

'If they do, then I've certainly never noticed them in the same way I have here.'

Pilgrim's words gave Tacy much to think about. The main barrier between Pilgrim and herself was their vastly differing backgrounds. His family was rich. Hers, although not poor by Dartmoor standards, needed to work very hard to make a living.

If such things *really* did not matter in America it might change everything between them.

They were close enough to see the lights of Tor Royal now and Tacy came to a halt. 'There's the house. I'll leave you here.'

'Thanks very much for walking me home, Tacy.' They both stood close in the darkness, seemingly trying to find words to say.

'I'd better go now – and you shouldn't leave it any later going inside.'

'No, you're right.'

'Goodnight then.'

As she started off, he called, 'Tacy!'

'Yes.' She stopped only a couple of paces away.

'Wait for me in the morning. I'd like to walk to Billy's house with you.'

Tacy disappeared into the darkness and Pilgrim wished he could have found some excuse to persuade her to stay with him for a while longer.

Then her voice came back to him.

'Pilgrim?'

'I'm here.'

'Goodnight. See you in the morning.'

34

The next morning Pilgrim was on his way to Roundtor Farm when, in the distance, he saw someone hurrying towards Sir Thomas Tyrwhitt's house. The figure was coming from the direction of Princetown.

Pilgrim's attention was drawn to the figure by the bright yellow of his clothes. It was the colour of the uniform issued to many of the Dartmoor prisoners-of-war.

Turning back, Pilgrim reached Tor Royal only a minute before Ephraim.

'What's wrong? Has there been more trouble at the prison?'

Out of breath from hurrying, Ephraim nodded his head vigorously.

'Come inside. I'll call Captain Howard.'

As Pilgrim led the way to the sitting room, the breathless Ephraim eyed the luxuriously furnished interior of Sir Thomas Tyrwhitt's house.

'Come in here and sit down.'

Pilgrim waved Ephraim to an armchair but the giant marines sergeant perched himself gingerly on the edge of a wooden chair which seemed hardly stout enough to take his large bulk.

Pouring a brandy despite the early hour, Pilgrim handed it to Ephraim. 'This might help you get your breath back while I go and find the captain.'

Ephraim took the drink gratefully and Pilgrim hurried away.

When Pilgrim returned with Virgil, the glass was empty and Ephraim was standing at the window looking out at the neatly trimmed lawns and the colourful flower beds.

Turning to greet them, Ephraim said, 'This is a better view than the one from Block Four, Cap'n.'

'There's no disputing that, Ephraim, but what's brought you here this morning? Lieutenant Penn says there's trouble at the prison.'

'That's right, Cap'n, and it's likely to get worse. Little Mo's been given a bad flogging. At least fifty lashes, I'd say. It's taken all the skin and most of the flesh off his back.'

'Little Mo? Should I know him?' The name meant nothing to Virgil.

'He was Steiger's slave. They were captured together.'

Pilgrim and Virgil both remembered the man now. Much lighter-skinned than most of his fellow Negroes, he was a small, rather frail man. Pilgrim winced at the thought of him taking a flogging.

'Who had him flogged? Cotgrave?'

'No, it wasn't the governor, Cap'n. It wasn't even an official flogging. It was Steiger.' Ephraim spoke angrily. 'He's not admitting it, but it was him who ordered it.'

'How do you know?' Pilgrim put the question to Ephraim.

'We were mustered in the Block Four yard yesterday

morning. The captains and shipowners from the Petty
Officers' Block were there too. Some money had finally
arrived from the agent. Each man was given three
shillings and nine pence, English money. A month's
allowance. Steiger objected to money being given to
Little Mo. He said it should come to him. That he's
the one who should decide if and when any money
was going to be handed out to Little Mo. When it was
given over anyway, Little Mo was told by Steiger that he
was still a slave and should remember what happened
to slaves when they didn't obey their masters.'

Ephraim's fists clenching and unclenching rapidly
were the only outward sign of his anger.

'Sometime during the night, or this morning, Steiger's
men got him. It wouldn't have been difficult. Little Mo
has problems with his breathing so he slept out on the
attic landing, close to the window. He was found this
morning lying at the bottom of the steps on the ground
floor. He'd been tied to a railing and gagged. Then he'd
been flogged until he passed out – and after that too,
I suspect. He's in the prison hospital now, more dead
than alive.'

Virgil's expression was grim when he asked, 'What's
the mood among your people?'

'They're angry, Cap'n. For a while it's not going to be
safe for a white man – any white man – to be caught by
them on his own anywhere in the block.'

'You can't be absolutely sure this is Steiger's doing.'

Virgil was clutching at straws. Pilgrim was aware of
it, and so was Ephraim.

'We don't have a signed confession, Cap'n, but we
don't need one. Anyway, nothing is a secret for ever
inside Dartmoor. Sooner or later we'll know the names
of the men who carried out the flogging. When we do,
they'll be killed. I couldn't stop it, even if I wanted to.'

Virgil nodded acknowledgement of Ephraim's statement before speaking to Pilgrim. 'I think we'd better
pay the prison a visit right away. Governor Cotgrave
is going to have to make a few decisions before the
day's out.'

'I've got something else for you to think about along
the way, Cap'n – and this concerns Steiger too.'

Pilgrim pulled a wry face. 'I told you Conrad Steiger
was trouble, Virgil. What else has he done, Ephraim?'

'You've both heard the story of Steiger taking a
slave girl as his mistress, I suppose, and of having
her husband sold off and shipped away?'

'We've heard it,' agreed Virgil. 'But it's only an
unsubstantiated rumour, as far as I'm concerned.' Virgil
did not want to provide more fuel for the hatred against
Steiger that had already taken hold in the attic floor of
Dartmoor Prison's Block Four.

'It's more than a rumour, Cap'n, that's for sure now.
The woman's husband was among the latest batch
of prisoners-of-war to be brought to Dartmoor. He's
vowed to get Steiger before this war's over. I, for one,
believe him.'

Listening to Ephraim's revelations, Pilgrim resigned
himself to the fact that he would not be visiting Roundtor
Farm today. Tacy would need to go in search of Billy
without him.

35

Tacy waited for Pilgrim until mid-morning. When he had not arrived she told her mother she would go to Billy's home without him.

'Well, you just be careful,' said Joan. 'I'd send Johanna with you, but with your pa the way he is at the moment you can't both be away from the farm. If it wasn't that I was so worried about Billy I wouldn't let you go there, either.'

'I'll be all right. If . . . if Pilgrim *does* arrive, don't let him come after me. The moor isn't very safe at the moment. He'd probably get lost anyway.'

'He'll be all right here until you return.' Joan looked at her daughter quizzically. 'You two didn't have an argument last night on your way to Tor Royal?'

Tacy shook her head. 'We were the best of friends when I left him. I expect he's had to go to the prison or something. He'll get here if he can.'

On the way from the farmhouse, Tacy thought of the walk in the darkness with Pilgrim. She felt it had some-how brought them closer. So close, she had expected him to try to kiss her when they parted. She had been disappointed when he did not. Tacy was aware she was deeply in love with Pilgrim. To try to convince herself otherwise would be self-deceit. She shrugged off the uncomfortable thought that Pilgrim's failure to come to the farm might be because he realised how she felt about him and did not reciprocate her feelings.

It was easy to believe that all was well with the world when walking the moor on a day like this. There was very little wind and only a few small white clouds in the blue sky. The ground was spongy underfoot, but Tacy knew the moor well and kept clear of the dangerous places.

The streams contained more water than usual, as a result of the recent heavy rains. When she came to the first, the water was flowing so fast and high over the stepping-stones it would have been dangerous to attempt a crossing. There was a stout clapper bridge upstream where she was able to cross in safety, but it meant an extra half-mile on her journey.

The second stream she met with was much shallower and she was able to wade across safely, the water coming no higher than her knees.

Soon she came within sight of the ruined mine buildings that surrounded the home of Billy and his mother.

Billy came to the door in response to her persistent knocking. He seemed surprised and strangely ill-at-ease to find her there.

'Everyone at Roundtor Farm's been worried about you, Billy. We didn't expect you during the rain, or the mist, of course, but we thought you might have come to us when the weather improved.'

Billy spoke without looking directly at her. 'I tried to get there on the first day, but the streams were too high. The water was pouring over that old clapper bridge, upstream from the crossing. I . . . I haven't tried these last couple of days because Ma's not very well. I didn't like leaving her.'

'What's wrong with her, Billy? Can I come in and see?' At any other time she would not have needed to pose such a question. It was unusual for Billy not to have invited her inside the cottage.

'She's upstairs in her bedroom. She hasn't moved from there for two days. I'm worried about her, Tacy.'

'Let me have a look at her. You should have come to the farm and told us.'

'I was going to . . . There hasn't been time, that's all.'

There was something in Billy's manner that puzzled Tacy. Something she could not fathom. He was pleased to see her, she did not doubt that, but there was an evasiveness in his manner that was out of character.

'Is your ma's illness the only reason why you've stayed away, Billy? There's no other reason you haven't been to Roundtor? None of us have offended you in any way?'

'No, Tacy. There's nothing like that. It's just . . . well, I just haven't been able to come there, that's all.'

They had reached the upstairs bedroom where Billy's mother was lying. Tacy entered the room and wrinkled her nose. The room smelled foul.

'Open the window, Billy. It could do with some fresh air in here.'

'Ma don't like having the air in her room.'

'Your ma's probably too ill to know what's good for her. Open it.'

While Billy struggled with the stiff window, Tacy went over to the bed. She pulled back the bedclothes, the better to look at Tillie Yates, and two dark, bright eyes looked back at her fiercely.

'What you doing here, Tacy Elford? Can't a woman have some peace when she's not feeling very well?'

'It's because you're not feeling well that I'm here. What's wrong with you?'

'I told you. I'm ill – but I'm better than I was. For days I couldn't eat a thing without bringing it up again. Now I reckon I could – that's if we had any food in the house.'

'I'll bring some across to you in the morning – unless Billy comes back with me to collect it now.'

'Why haven't you brought any with you before this? When you was here yesterday – and the day before?'

Tacy was puzzled. 'I haven't been here before. Today's the first time I've tried to get here, what with the storm and the mist.'

'Don't you lie to me, Tacy Elford. I've heard you downstairs talking to my Billy. Laughing too. At me being up here and not able to get up and about to see what you was up to, no doubt.'

Tacy would have argued with the woman, but she changed her mind. Tillie Yates had never been altogether sensible. The illness seemed to have made her more unbalanced than usual.

'Well, it doesn't matter. I'll see you have some food. Will you come back to Roundtor Farm with me to collect it, Billy?'

'I . . . I don't know.' Billy was definitely not happy about something. 'I don't really like to leave her when she's like this.'

'Liar!' Tillie spat out the word. 'You haven't bothered about leaving me before, when you've wanted to go downstairs to speak to *her*.'

'It's all right, Billy.' Tacy put out a hand to stop the protest Billy was about to make. 'We'll go now and talk about it downstairs.'

'Don't you keep him talking half the night again, either. I'm a sick woman, I need my rest . . .'

Tillie could still be heard complaining when Billy and Tacy reached the bottom of the stairs.

'I'm sorry, Tacy . . .'

'It's all right, Billy. Do you have anything to eat for tonight?'

'I caught a rabbit yesterday. It's cooking in a pot now.'

'Good! I think your ma needs something to build her strength up. Give her some of the rabbit stew and I'll see what I can bring from home. I doubt if it'll be today, though. There's a lot to be done at Roundtor and only me and Johanna to do it. My pa isn't too well either.'

'What about Lieutenant Pilgrim? Hasn't he been helping?'

'He should have been there today, but I think something must have happened at the prison. Anyway, never you mind about it. You just do what you can to help your ma get better and I'll get some food across to you as soon as I can.'

'Thanks, Tacy. You're very good to us.'

Billy seemed far more upset than the situation warranted and Tacy said, 'Are you sure there's nothing else worrying you, Billy? We're friends, remember?'

Once again Billy seemed desperately unhappy, but he shook his head. 'No, I'm all right.'

'Then just take care of things here and we'll get some food to you as soon as possible. If you need anything in the meantime, just call on us. You can cross the stream at the clapper bridge now, and the water level's still dropping. Goodbye, Billy.'

On the way home to Roundtor Farm, Tacy tried to put behind her the thought that Billy was keeping something back. Yet she could not help thinking he was worried about something more than his mother's illness. She determined that on her next visit she would question him more closely. She would discover what it was that was troubling him.

36

Pilgrim reached Roundtor Farm the following morning as Tacy was preparing a heavily laden basket of food to take to Billy and his sick mother.

After briefly explaining the reason why he had not come to the farm the previous day, Pilgrim said he would accompany her to the Yates's home today.

Tacy desperately wanted Pilgrim to come with her, but there were many things to be done about the farm. Due to the recent bad weather and the state of her father's health, they were falling behind with the work.

Reluctantly, she suggested it would help her more if he remained at Roundtor and helped with some of the chores.

Her mother's relief at Tacy's suggestion was short-lived. Tom Elford, looking decidedly frail, was seated in the kitchen. He said, 'There's no need for Pilgrim to spend every day he's here working at something or the other. I'm feeling a lot better today. The pair of you go off to Billy's. What doesn't get done here will wait for another day.'

'Now, Tom. I don't want you working outside yet. You're not well enough . . .'

'I'm well enough to use my tongue and tell Johanna what needs doing. Go on, Pilgrim. Get on your way to Billy's with Tacy, before her ma changes my mind for me.'

'Are you quite sure?' I don't mind working here to help out.'

'Of course I'm sure. If you can come again tomorrow and help out I'll be very grateful to you – but don't get thinking you *have* to work every time you come to Roundtor. You and our Tacy are still young. Life will force work upon you both soon enough. Learn to take the opportunity for a day off when it comes your way now. Off you go.'

Tacy gave her father a hug, then she and Pilgrim went out of the house together.

'I wish I was as happy as you are about sending the two of them out together for a day on the moor.' Joan voiced the concern she felt to her husband. 'That young man has no reason at all to show a sense of responsibility while he's in this country.'

'But he will,' said her husband. 'He's that sort of man – and I believe he's genuinely fond of our Tacy.'

'She feels far more strongly than that about *him*,' declared Joan unhappily. 'I would have thought that reason enough not to send them off alone.'

'Does that mean Tacy *might* have a baby soon?' asked Johanna brightly. 'Can I look after it instead of working out on the farm?'

'I've told you before about talking such nonsense,' said her mother sharply. 'I've no doubt I'll have far more trouble with you than I've ever had with Tacy when you're of an age. Now, if any of us are to get any work done today you can both get out of my kitchen for an hour. I can't work with you cluttering up the place.'

It was a glorious day for walking on the moor, even though Pilgrim was burdened with the heavy basket of provisions destined for Billy and his mother.

When they reached the stream which had been dangerously swollen the previous day, they discovered the water level had dropped considerably. Even so, the fast-running water was lapping the top of most of the unevenly spaced stepping-stones.

Despite Tacy's protest that she could cross perfectly well by herself, Pilgrim went first. After depositing the basket on the far bank, he came back to help her.

She had crossed this stream many times before, but she allowed him to help her and to retain a hold on her hand when they were both on the same side as the basket.

As they set off together once more, Pilgrim looked about him and said, 'This really is beautiful country, Tacy.'

'I think so,' she agreed.

'You'd like Ohio too. Sometimes you wake up there in the mornings and feel that if you reach up far enough you could touch the sky. You'd love it.'

'Perhaps I'll go there some day and see it for myself.'

'I'd like to think you will, Tacy.'

She looked at him uncertainly, hoping there might be a hidden meaning in his words, but he was not looking at her.

Tacy wondered whether he was aware his statement might have been misconstrued and was wishing he had not made it.

She shrugged off the thought. 'Pa often says that when he was young he used to dream of one day going off to see the world. Poor Pa. With all his dreams, he's never gone farther than a mile or two off the moor. I don't think he ever will now.'

'You never know,' replied Pilgrim sympathetically.

After a moment's hesitation, he asked, 'What will happen if he ever becomes too ill to run the farm? Will you, Johanna and your ma carry on, or will you move somewhere else?'

'Where could we go?' asked Tacy. 'We'd still need to keep ourselves. But if anything happens to Pa I suppose we'll have to find somewhere else to live. It's always been Pa's hope that Johanna and I would be married before anything happened to him and that one of his sons-in-law would want to carry on farming at Roundtor.'

When Pilgrim made no immediate reply, they walked on in silence.

Deciding it was time they spoke of something else, Tacy told Pilgrim about her visit to Billy's home the day before, and of his peculiar manner towards her.

'It might just be that he's particularly worried about his mother being ill,' suggested Pilgrim. 'Or perhaps he's feeling guilty because he hasn't been to Roundtor to do any work, even though your pa is ill too.'

Tacy shook her head. 'That's what I told myself, first of all. But the more I thought about it the more convinced I became that Billy was lying to me and didn't feel comfortable about doing it.'

'Why should he lie? You saw his mother. If she really is sick there was no need for him to be embarrassed about it. You don't think you were imagining it?'

'No, I've known Billy too long. He was hiding something from me, and that's not like him.'

'Well, perhaps we'll find out today what it is that's bothering him.'

Walking along beside Tacy, their arms and hands touching frequently, Pilgrim was determined not to allow anything to spoil the happy mood he was in today.

37

For the remainder of the walk from Roundtor, Tacy and Pilgrim spoke of generalities, enjoying the warmth of the day and each other's company.

Eventually they came within view of a small jumble of derelict buildings and spoil heaps. Tacy stopped and pointed. 'That's where Billy lives. In the cottage on the left.'

The cottage was almost as derelict as the other mine buildings but, unlike the others, the roof of the cottage was intact.

As they walked along together, Pilgrim had occasionally shifted the basket from one arm to the other. Now he stopped and placed it on the ground, flexing both his arms.

'Go on ahead and knock at the door. Tell Billy I'm here with you and give him time to get used to it. He still doesn't know me all that well. It might not be a good idea to spring surprises on him, especially if he has something on his mind.'

'That's a good idea.' She smiled and inclined her head in the direction of the basket. 'Has it grown heavier since we left Roundtor?'

'I'm probably not as fit as I should be. Go on, I'll catch up with you.'

Pilgrim's gaze followed Tacy as she walked away from him, towards the house. She wore a thin summer frock which showed off her slim figure. She really was a very lovely young woman. His affection for her was growing stronger with every day that passed. He had never felt this way about anyone before.

Had he met her in the United States he would have been able to tell her how he felt and their relationship would have progressed rapidly. He had much to offer her there. But here in England . . . ? He was a paroled prisoner-of-war, liable to be recalled to prison at the whim of the British Government. It was a wonder her parents allowed her to spend so much time in his company.

Pilgrim watched as Tacy walked up to the front door. She paused for a moment before knocking. Then she walked inside the cottage without waiting for a reply.

Suddenly someone ran from behind the house. He was able to catch only a glimpse before the running figure disappeared behind a spoil heap. It was sufficient for him to see that it was a young girl.

Pilgrim was puzzled. No one had ever mentioned that a young girl lived in Billy's house – and why had she run away in such a manner?

He was intrigued. Billy must know of the girl's presence. She must be the reason there had been such a puzzling change in his attitude towards Tacy.

Picking up the basket, Pilgrim carried it the remaining distance to the cottage.

Entering through the front door he was met by Tacy. He followed her to the kitchen which was situated at the back of the house. Here he noticed there was an outside door that might have been used by someone fleeing from the house.

Billy was here, but he seemed ill-at-ease and there was no warmth in his greeting. Pilgrim understood immediately why Tacy was concerned about him. Something was making the simple young man decidedly unhappy.

'Hello, Billy. It seems a long time since we last met. How's your mother?'

'She's getting better,' replied Billy. His words were devoid of the enthusiasm he had shown when he and Pilgrim had last spoken.

'Billy says she should be up and about again in a couple of days.' Tacy spoke to fill the uncomfortable gap that widened after Billy's words. 'That's good news, isn't it?'

'Very good,' agreed Pilgrim. 'It must be very lonely out here when you don't have your mother to talk to. Is it only the two of you living here?'

'Yes.'

If there had been any doubt in Pilgrim's mind that Billy was hiding something, it was dispelled now. Billy did not enjoy telling lies. Pilgrim wondered why he felt it necessary to do so.

'I was just telling Billy that I'm really impressed by his housekeeping,' said Tacy. 'I've never seen the house so neat and tidy.'

Looking about him, Pilgrim was in full agreement with her comments. There was not a dirty plate or dish in sight and everything was stowed away neatly. The hard dirt floor too had been brushed clean.

'Will you take me up to see your ma, Billy? I'd like

to ask her if there's anything she needs. There might be things she wouldn't tell you about.'

Billy nodded, but once again, he seemed less than enthusiastic and Pilgrim determined he would get to the bottom of this particular mystery.

'You go on upstairs with Billy, Tacy. I'll stay down here. Mrs Yates won't want a stranger paying her a visit when she's not feeling well.'

When the others had left the kitchen, Pilgrim opened the door quietly and slipped outside. He made his way to where he had seen the young girl disappear.

There was no one behind the spoil heap, but a roofless and doorless building stood nearby. It had probably once been a small storehouse.

Treading lightly, Pilgrim made his way towards it. He reached the doorway and was about to pass inside when a young girl fled from the building and tried to slip past him.

Pilgrim caught her by the arm and the girl immediately bit him. Instead of releasing his grip, he wrapped both his arms about her in such a way that she could neither bite, nor strike him. She could still kick, but as she wore no shoes it proved quite ineffectual.

'Let me go.' She had a shrill, young voice, but as she struggled violently he realised she was not quite as young as he had first thought. She was probably fifteen years old, or thereabouts.

'Stop your struggling. No one intends hurting you, but you're not going to get away.'

Eventually, when Pilgrim's words got through to her, the struggling grew weaker, then stopped altogether.

'Let me go, then.'

'Sure – but remember I can probably run faster than you. Just tell me what this is all about. Who are you and what are you doing here?'

'Who are *you*?' she countered. 'And what's that uniform you're wearing?'

Pilgrim released his hold on her and for a few
moments they stood warily facing each other.

'My name's Pilgrim Penn. What's yours?'

'That's only answered one of my questions. Why are
you wearing that uniform?'

'I suggest we go to the house. There are quite a lot
of things that need clearing up – but I still don't know
your name.'

It was Billy who provided the answer. He had heard
the commotion from the house and he came running,
with Tacy close behind him.

'Are you all right, Emma?' His concern for the girl
was such that Tacy and Pilgrim exchanged surprised
glances.

'I think you ought to tell us what this is all about,
Billy.' Pilgrim made the suggestion.

'It doesn't matter what they say, Billy. I'm not going
back to Charlie and Bella. I'll top myself first. I swear I
will.'

'As far as I know there's no one with the slightest
interest in taking you anywhere, but who are Charlie
and Bella?'

Pilgrim's question was directed at Emma, but it was
Tacy who broke in with the answer.

'I know! It's that pair of tinkers who were passing
through the moor a week or two ago. They came to the
door with a grindstone, offering to sharpen scissors, or
anything else needing a good sharp edge. When they'd
gone I found two of our chickens were missing. There
weren't as many eggs as there should have been, either. I
thought then they must have had someone else working
with them. Was that you?' Tacy put the accusation to
Emma.

Scared but defiant, the young girl said, 'You can't prove nuffing – and if he tries to take me in for it I'll bite him a sight harder than I did just now.'

'Why do you keep suggesting I'm going to take you somewhere or the other, Emma?'

Pilgrim's question was asked quietly. He had been looking more closely at the girl and his sympathy went out to her. Her clothes were old, frayed and ill-fitting. She was pinched-faced, barefooted and under-nourished, but she and her clothes were clean. He was of the opinion she had not always been a tinker's girl.

'Why do you think Pilgrim might take you back to the tinkers?' Tacy prompted her.

'Well, he's wearing a uniform, ain't he? And I belong to Charlie and Bella. At least, they've always said I do. Charlie said he paid for me all kosher-like.'

Pilgrim frowned. 'People aren't animals, Emma. They can't be bought and sold.'

Even as he was speaking, Pilgrim thought uncomfortably of the men who occupied the attic floor of Block Four, inside Dartmoor prison.

Brushing such thoughts aside, he said, 'Anyway, what do you think this uniform means?'

'I dunno! Militiaman, soldier or constable, I suppose. Whichever it is, it means you're not going to be taking my side.'

'It's a Marines uniform, Emma. An American Marine – and America is at war with England. I'm a prisoner from Dartmoor prison. They've let me live outside the prison only for as long as I behave myself. I'm hardly likely to want to get anyone else in trouble, am I?'

'You've been locked up inside Dartmoor gaol?' Emma looked at Pilgrim with an expression of awesome respect for a few moments. Then her expression hardened. 'That don't make no difference. Charlie's been put away more'n once but it hasn't made him any better. It hasn't stopped him trying to get me in trouble, neither. He tries it on every time Bella's back's turned.'

The look exchanged between Pilgrim and Tacy was a mixture of pity, anger and disgust, but it was Billy who spoke now.

'I won't let him get you into trouble any more, Emma, and neither will Pilgrim. You can trust him.'

'I don't trust no one,' she replied fiercely. When she saw the hurt expression that came to Billy's face, she added hurriedly, 'Except you, Billy. You're the first one I've ever trusted.'

When she was satisfied she had placated his hurt feelings, she returned her attention to Pilgrim. 'Well, now you've found me here, what you going to do about it?'

'Pilgrim's already told you he doesn't intend doing anything,' said Tacy. 'But we'll need to decide what's going to happen to you now.'

'Why? I'm all right here. If ever Billy gets fed up with having me around, I'll just move on to some-where else.'

'I won't get fed up with you, Emma. You can stay here for as long as you like.'

As though suddenly afraid he was being disloyal to Tacy, Billy explained, 'Emma's helped me a lot while Ma's been ill. She's made food and cleaned up the place. She's even done some washing.'

'I thought the place was looking especially clean,' said Tacy approvingly. 'But it's not me you need to convince. You know what your ma is like about having strangers around.'

Billy did know. When his mother had been ill a few years before, Tacy had brought some food for her. She had stayed to carry out some much-needed tidying, only to be chased from the cottage by a nightdress-clad Mrs Yates.

Standing in the doorway wielding the broom hastily dropped by Tacy, Tillie Yates had triumphantly declared that if ever Tacy returned she would teach her such a lesson she would never dare come snooping around the house again.

She had come to accept Tacy as a visitor since then, but would tolerate no one else.

Billy looked unhappily from Tacy to Emma and back again. 'Where can she go? She doesn't know anyone except me.'

It was apparent to both Tacy and Pilgrim that Billy was seriously smitten with the young tinker girl.

'Let's not worry too much about it just yet, Billy. It's no problem while your ma's upstairs ill. In the meantime I'll talk to my ma. Perhaps she'll let Emma come to stay with us. Then you can see her whenever you come to work at Roundtor.'

Tacy's suggested solution seemed to cheer up Billy somewhat, but he was still not entirely reassured. Realising this, Tacy added, 'She could come over to see you whenever she wished. Then perhaps one day your ma will let her come back here to live.'

'Don't I have no say in what's going to happen to me?' The question was put to Tacy by a scowling Emma.

'I'm just making suggestions,' said Tacy, taking offence. 'I don't even know whether my ma will let you stay at Roundtor Farm – but I'm quite certain Billy's ma won't have you here once she's up and about.'

Tacy looked at Emma. 'Where will you go if she sends you away?'

Reality took the place of belligerence and Emma said, 'I don't have any place to go. All right, if your ma says I can come to your place I'll come there – but you don't own me. None of you own me. If I don't like it, I'll leave. I mean it.'

'You're quite free to do exactly as you want, Emma,' said Tacy gently. 'But I think you'll be happy at Roundtor, and I believe Billy will be relieved to know you're somewhere safe, too.'

38

'I'm sorry for not telling you about Emma before you found her at the house, Tacy. But she was so frightened about being caught and taken back to the tinkers, she made me promise to tell *no* one. No one at all – and it was you who told me a promise must never be broken . . .'

'Billy! You don't have to keep apologising to me about it. I *do* understand.'

Tacy and Billy were cleaning out the cowshed together and it was at least the sixth time that day Billy had apologised to Tacy for not telling her about Emma. She was trying very hard not to become exasperated with him.

When Joan Elford had heard the story of Emma, and Tacy had suggested she come to stay at Roundtor Farm, she had been dubious about having a self-confessed thief living in the house.

However, when Emma arrived, scrubbed and as tidy as was possible in view of the threadbare frock she wore, the farmer's wife had weakened.

She quickly realised the young girl was trying desperately hard not to show that what the Elford family thought of her really mattered. Joan had relented and given Emma a warm and impulsive hug. The tinkers' girl had a new home.

Emma had settled in well, proving to be as hard-working as she was clean. She was also very, very kind to Billy.

He, in his turn, was so besotted with her that Johanna would have been quite jealous had Emma not made a fuss of her too.

While Tacy and Billy cleaned out the cowshed together, Pilgrim was helping Tom Elford fit a new axle to the small farm wagon. In the house, Emma, Johanna and Joan were baking cakes in the farm kitchen.

'I was a bit upset at first because you hadn't told me about Emma right away,' admitted Tacy to Billy, 'but once I knew the full story I was proud of you. I don't think I would have been able to keep such a secret to myself.'

Billy's cheeks glowed with pleasure at her words. He had been desperately concerned that his secretiveness would cost him his friendship with Tacy. His relationship with her still meant a great deal to him.

'I *wanted* to tell you about her. I would have too, soon.' He gave her a look that revealed the affection he had for her. 'Had it happened a while ago I would have been even more unhappy about finding someone else I like so much, but it's easier now you have Pilgrim. Do you love him, Tacy?'

Billy's unexpected and direct question took Tacy by surprise. 'What . . . ? I . . . That's not the sort of question you ask someone, Billy.'

'Why not?'

'I . . . Well, it just isn't, that's all.'

Billy was puzzled by her evasiveness. 'I think he loves you.'

'What makes you think that? Has he said anything to you?' Tacy asked eagerly.

'He doesn't have to, does he? He wouldn't come here and work like he does if he didn't. I mean, he doesn't need to work. I like Pilgrim. He's been kind to me, and to Emma.'

'It's time I started on the milking,' said Tacy abruptly. 'Hurry up and finish off in here, Billy. Then you can go and turn some of the peat on the stack down by the big rock.'

A few minutes later Tacy sat on the low stool milking the cow, her cheek resting against its warm body, thinking of Billy's words.

She tried not to dwell upon her feelings for Pilgrim, nor his for her. They spent a great deal of time together, but more and more often recently it seemed they were always accompanied by someone else – usually by Johanna.

When they *were* alone Tacy often felt Pilgrim was on the verge of saying something of importance to her, but it never came to anything.

She wondered whether it was because he did not care as passionately for her as she did for him?

'Have you fallen asleep against that old cow? You'll certainly get no milk unless you work at it.' The voice of Joan broke in on her daughter's thoughts. 'I've just come out here to get some fresh milk because I want to do some baking. What were you up to, girl?'

'Oh, just thinking, that's all.'

'What about?'

'Nothing in particular,' Tacy lied as she set to work to draw milk from the cow. 'We seem to have had a lot of new people come to the farm this year. First Pilgrim, sometimes Virgil and Ephraim, and now Emma. What do you make of her, Ma?'

'It'll take more than a day or two to get to know that one,' her mother replied, 'but if first impressions are anything to go by, I quite like her.'

'Billy's absolutely head-over-heels in love with her,' said Tacy.

'Of course he is. Billy doesn't expect much from life. If someone shows him anything approaching affection he'll do anything for them. You should know that. Now, I'll take the milk you've got and put it in this jug. Then I'll go back to see what's happening in the kitchen.'

When she had gone, Tacy carried on with the milking and thought of what her mother had said about Billy. She wondered whether he and she were very different. Tacy decided not to dwell on how she might react if Pilgrim ever displayed more than a gentle affection for her. It was an exciting thought.

She only just succeeded in saving the wooden bucket as the cow kicked out at it. She decided it was not a good thing to have exciting thoughts when she was milking a cow.

'How long do you think this foolish war between our countries is likely to last, Pilgrim?'

Tom Elford put the question to Pilgrim as they began bolting the new axle into place on the cart, prior to attaching the wheels.

'Not too long, I hope.'

Pilgrim was perspiring heavily. Tacy's father was as well as he would ever be, but he was not a strong man. Most of the hard work involved in replacing the axle had been performed by Pilgrim.

'. . . From all accounts the French are being driven back into France by your General Wellington. Once that war comes to an end there should be no quarrel between our two countries. There'd be none now if British ships hadn't taken to stopping ours on the high seas and impressing seamen with British backgrounds for your navy.'

Not wanting to enter a discussion about the rights, or wrongs of the British actions, Tom Elford said, 'I suppose you'll be off home as soon as the war's over.'

'It'll no doubt take a while before they get around to returning prisoners.'

'Our Tacy will miss you.'

'Do you really think so?'

There had been a time when Pilgrim would not have felt it necessary to question such a statement. In the days when he had still been in prison he had imagined how things would be between himself and Tacy if only he was outside the prison walls. When he had been granted parole he thought his dreams were about to come true.

There were still times when he thought so, but somehow there always seemed to be an invisible barrier raised between them. He had never been able to decide whether it was placed there by Tacy or by himself. Perhaps it was there because he was reluctant to do anything that might upset her and so destroy the very easy relationship they enjoyed at the moment.

He had come close to it on more than one occasion when they were alone, but always backed off. He was constantly aware of being a prisoner-of-war. There was little of any substance he could offer her until this war was over.

'I know so, lad. One of her mother's biggest worries has always been that one of these days you'll go off back to America, leaving our Tacy behind with a broken heart.'

Tom Elford smiled wryly. 'I shouldn't be talking to you like this, should I? A father's duty is supposed to be to warn off young men, not encourage 'em.'

'I wouldn't do anything to hurt Tacy, Mr Elford. I think far too much of her for that.'

Tom Elford lifted a wheel clear of the ground with difficulty and eased it on to the greased end of the new axle. 'That's what I keep telling her mother – and it's what I believe, or I wouldn't be talking to you like this right now. Tacy's a good girl, Pilgrim. All the same, I'd like her to have more from life than I've been able to give her mother. There's more drudgery to a woman's life on a moorland farm than most.'

'I'm not sure Mrs Elford would agree with you. She's one of the most contented women I've ever met.'

'It's nice of you to say so, boy, but it's not because of what I've been able to give her. I've just been lucky to find her, I suppose. I don't know why, but she loves me enough to take up a tinker's life if that's all I had to offer.'

Seeming to concentrate on what he was doing, Tom Elford said, 'Our Tacy takes after her mother in that way. She'll make a man a good wife some day. I only hope I live long enough to see her settled with him.'

Straightening up, Tom Elford stood back from the wheel with satisfaction. 'There, that's one of them done. If the other one goes on as easily I'll say it's the best job I've ever seen done.'

He suddenly grinned. 'If only we could sort folk's lives out as easily as mending a farm wagon. Come on, let's get that other wheel on then we'll go inside the house and have a drop of something. I was given some cider the other day in exchange for a few chickens. I've been waiting for the right opportunity to sample some of it . . .'

39

Sir Thomas Tyrwhitt returned to Tor Royal, accompanied by his sister Winifrith, in the autumn of the year. They had discovered no trace of Sophie in London. It seemed her whereabouts was as much of a mystery to her friends as it remained to her mother.

Winifrith suspected the two Americans of knowing more about Sophie's disappearance than they had disclosed. She made no secret of her suspicions, especially after she had been drinking heavily.

Pilgrim, in particular, became a target for her sharp tongue. He began to dread the evenings when Winifrith dined in at Tor Royal.

A couple of weeks after his return, Sir Thomas Tyrwhitt held a farewell party for Lieutenant Colonel Hawke. The duties of the one-armed army officer and his militiamen had been taken over by a contingent of Irish militiamen.

Lieutenant Colonel Hawke and his men were due to march away from Dartmoor the following day.

'I won't be sorry to see the last of Dartmoor,' Cecil

Hawke confided to Virgil and Pilgrim as they stood in a corner of the crowded Tor Royal room. 'All the same, I wish I were leaving you in better company. On my brief acquaintance with them, I find the discipline of these Irishmen leaves much to be desired. I had intended holding this party at the mess, but I think Sir Thomas was wise in persuading me it might be better to hold it here.'

He did not add that he had suggested to the land-owner that the presence of the two American paroled prisoners-of-war might prove too provocative to the indisciplined Irish militiamen.

Pilgrim believed the militiaman's assessment of the men who were assuming responsibility for the secur-ity of the prisoners-of-war in Dartmoor was probably accurate. The party had been in progress for little more than an hour, yet already some of the younger officers were becoming rowdy.

At that moment the Reverend Cotterell entered the room, accompanied by his wife and their daughter.

The glance of Jemima went around the room quickly. When she saw the two Americans her face lit up with an expression of pleasure.

Pilgrim was taken by surprise. Then he realised the smile must have been for Virgil. He had visited the Sheepstor vicarage almost as often as Pilgrim had been to Roundtor. Virgil and Jemima must know each other quite well.

For a moment, he felt a twinge of jealousy that they were able to meet each other on occasions such as this and he and Tacy could not.

The feeling soon passed. He remembered the look Winifrith had given to Jemima on the first occasion they had visited Tor Royal. She did not consider the vicar and his family socially acceptable at Tor Royal.

She would be outraged by the presence of the daughter of a tenant farmer at such a function. Pilgrim would not want Tacy to be the subject of her acid tongue.

Reverend Cotterell waved in the direction of the two Americans and the vicar and his family made their way towards them.

'I was not expecting there to be quite such a crowd here,' said the Sheepstor vicar as he accepted a drink from a servant. 'But you have been a popular commanding officer, Colonel Hawke.'

Cecil Hawke snorted loudly as a loud shout went up from the far end of the room. 'I fear some of the young men here this evening would accept an invitation from the Devil himself if free drinks were on offer.'

It rapidly became a very noisy evening. At the height of the party, Pilgrim glanced across the room to see Jemima looking uncomfortable as she stood talking to an Irish militia officer. He was swaying ever closer to her as he talked, the drink in his glass coming perilously close to spilling over her as he leaned forward.

'Excuse me a moment.' Pilgrim broke off his conversation with one of Cecil Hawke's officers and hurried across the room. Seeing where he was headed, Virgil put down his drink and followed him quickly.

'Hello, Jemima. Is everything all right? Perhaps you would like another drink?'

Jemima's relief at his intervention was evident, but the Irish militiaman was less pleased. He was not prepared to relinquish her so easily.

Focusing upon Pilgrim with some difficulty, he said haughtily, 'I don't know how you behave in the colonies, sir, but it's not done here to interrupt a gentleman when he's talking to a lady.'

'I'm not aware how the men in your colonies behave,

either, sir, but I certainly wouldn't dream of interrupting a *gentleman* anywhere in the world.'

Controlling his anger, he offered his arm to Jemima, and said, 'Shall we find that drink for you?'

It was a moment or two before the implication of Pilgrim's words sunk in to the befuddled mind of the militiaman. When it did, he flushed angrily.

'I think you intended that remark to be insulting, sir.'

'I really don't give a damn *what* you think,' said Pilgrim quietly. 'But I *do* care when a man who has had more drink than he can hold makes a nuisance of himself in the presence of a lady.'

'I agree wholeheartedly,' said Virgil, moving quickly to place himself between Pilgrim and the Irish officer. 'Indeed, were I not on parole in this country I would call you out, sir. Regrettably, were I to do so you would die and I would no doubt be charged with your murder.'

Some of the militiaman's fellow officers had become aware that their drunken colleague was in danger of provoking a major incident. Three of them crossed the room hastily. While one paused to murmur apologies to Jemima, the other two hurried the protesting militia officer away.

When they had passed beyond hearing, Pilgrim turned to apologise to Jemima.

'I'm sorry, Jemima, but his attitude was quite unacceptable . . .'

He broke off when he saw the expression on her face.

'You were wonderful, Pilgrim. I am truly grateful to you.'

Suddenly aware that her praise was a little too gushing, she turned to Virgil. 'You too, Virgil. It was

most gallant of you. Indeed, I feel you gave the militiaman a much-needed lesson in manners, but . . . would
you really have fought a duel on my behalf?'

'Probably not.'

Virgil had the impression Jemima was disappointed
by his reply and he added, 'A militiaman is *not* an army
officer. He was also very drunk. Killing him would have
been closer to murder than I care to come.'

Mrs Cotterell was beckoning across the room to her
daughter, but before she moved off, Jemima said, 'It's
very difficult to talk here tonight, but please come to
the vicarage some time soon, Pilgrim. I really am *most*
grateful to you for coming to my assistance.'

40

The Irish militia officer was not the only person at Sir Thomas Tyrwhitt's party to have drunk too much. Shortly after the incident involving Jemima, Pilgrim was leaving the room when he came face-to-face with Winifrith.

Giving him a malicious look, she said, 'I saw you making up to that vicar's daughter, just as you did to poor Sophie. Were you encouraging her to run off and leave her parents too? It was a sad day when my brother allowed you to come to Tor Royal.'

'That is most unfair, Mrs Cudmore. I have no more knowledge of Sophie's whereabouts than you.'

'I don't believe you – and I never will.'

Winifrith turned to go back the way she had come, but her words had been heard by a number of guests standing nearby.

Among them was Lieutenant Colonel Hawke.

'Pardon me, ma'am, but am I to understand you are not aware of your daughter's whereabouts?'

'And what business is it of yours, pray?' replied Winifrith belligerently.

'None at all, ma'am,' said the militiaman coldly. 'I was merely trying to be helpful by telling you where your daughter is likely to be.'

'You know where Sophie is?' The shock of his words momentarily sobered Winifrith.

'I do.'

Lieutenant Colonel Hawke was being deliberately reticent. He did not like Winifrith and was beginning to wish he had said nothing.

'Then tell me, for God's sake! Don't you know that Sir Thomas and I spent weeks searching London for her?'

'You won't find her in London, ma'am. When I saw her she was on her way to the war in the Spanish Peninsular. She was in the company of a captain wearing the uniform of the Rifle Corps. I thought she was probably married to him, but it seems I could have been mistaken.'

'A captain in the Rifle Corps! Did you hear that, Thomas? It's that *dreadful* young man she met before I brought her down here.'

Returning her attention to Lieutenant Colonel Hawke, she demanded, 'When did you see her? How long ago?'

'A long time,' said the militiaman, frowning in concentration. 'It was immediately after those few days of heavy rain and fog, as I remember. I was in Plymouth seeing off a friend who was on his way to join Wellington's staff. I tried to speak to your daughter . . . Sophie, is it? But she turned away and I thought she had not recognised me. There was no time to pursue the matter, a port is a busy place when soldiers are embarking.'

Winifrith tried to gather her wits, then with a stifled howl she fled from the room.

'Oh dear! I seem to have distressed the lady,' said Lieutenant Colonel Hawke, but with little contriteness in his expression.

Turning to Pilgrim, he said in a low voice, 'I only hope I have given the poor girl ample time to carry out her intentions, whatever they are, before her mother catches up with her.'

As Lieutenant Colonel Hawke walked away, Pilgrim was left wondering why he was not really surprised by the news that Sophie had run away from her mother to be with the man she loved.

Once again Winifrith Cudmore threw the household at Tor Royal into turmoil when she made another hurried departure in search of her missing daughter.

She set off for London the day after the party. As before, she was accompanied by her patient, titled brother.

Their destination was once more London, but on this occasion Winifrith knew exactly where she was going. She intended taking the War Office by storm. She would demand that they send an immediate despatch to Lord Wellington, ordering him to have Sophie Cudmore returned to England immediately.

In the unlikely event of the War Office officials refusing to make her demand one of their top priorities, she intended setting off for the Spanish Peninsular herself. Woe betide either Wellington or Napoleon if they did anything that might thwart her plans.

Sir Thomas told all this to Pilgrim and Virgil while he was waiting for his carriage to be loaded with his sister's luggage.

'I do hope the officers at the War Office will accommodate her,' he said, displaying a rare, nervous concern. 'I believe the war on the Continent has turned in our favour. It would be most distressing if Winifrith did anything to upset Wellington at such a critical stage in his campaign.'

He saw the expressions of barely concealed amusement on the faces of the two American marines and said, 'Yes, it sounds quite ridiculous, gentlemen, but I *know* my sister. I fear the War Office and my Lord Wellington do not.'

At that moment Winifrith descended the staris. She stalked past Pilgrim and Virgil without deigning to look at either of them as she made her way to the waiting carriage.

'Goodbye, gentlemen,' said Sir Thomas. 'I have no doubt there will be many occasions during the coming days when I will envy you the peace and tranquillity of Dartmoor.'

41

Pilgrim was on his way downstairs to breakfast the morning after the departure of Sir Thomas and Winifrith, when he met with a servant on the stairs.

'I was just coming up to your room to find you, sir,' she said. 'There's a girl at the back door asking to speak to you. I told her it was too early to bother you, but she said I was to tell you it was urgent.'

Pilgrim thought immediately it must be Tacy. Something must have happened at Roundtor Farm. Possibly it had to do with her father . . .

He hurried downstairs and through the kitchen to the back door, only to discover it was not Tacy who was waiting there but Mary Gurney, the girl who had befriended Henri.

She would not say anything to Pilgrim immediately, but drew him away from the house, out of hearing of the servants. When she was certain they could not be overheard, she blurted out, 'Henri is in desperate need of your help, Pilgrim. He's escaped from the prison.'

'Again?' Pilgrim was alarmed. 'Does he have a plan this time?'

'Yes . . . Well, he *did* . . . but you must come to speak to him. It's very important.'

Mary was so agitated she was unable to stand still. 'Please come with me.'

'Of course.' Pilgrim hurried after Mary as she set off. 'Where is he now?'

'Not far away. I left him hiding behind a wall along the lane to Tor Royal. I'll show you.'

Only a very short distance from the house Pilgrim saw Henri. He was not hiding behind a wall, as Mary had stated, but was sitting upon it. He was not dressed as a French soldier, but was wearing clothes that befitted an English gentleman.

Henri greeted Pilgrim effusively, but with little outward sign of agitation. 'My friend! You are looking very well. Freedom is good for you.'

'It's *your* freedom we're concerned about right now, Henri. What are you doing here? More to the point, what do you *intend* doing?'

'Ah yes! I escaped with a very carefully laid plan in mind but, as with many plans, things have gone wrong. I should have escaped over the wall of the prison soon after dark. It was arranged with one of the prison turnkeys. A man would be waiting for me with a horse to guide me to a boat on the river – the Tamar, I believe. The boat is leaving at noon today to rendezvous with a party of French smugglers. I should have been on board by now.'

'Why aren't you? What went wrong?'

Henri spread his hands wide. 'It is the new militiamen. They have not yet settled in and keep changing their routine. I was crouching beneath the wall on the inside of the prison for much of the night. Not until it was almost light was I able to climb over the wall. Unfortunately, by this time my guide had become frightened, fearing all was not well. He had gone, taking the horse I was to ride with him. Only Mary remained – but there are no riding horses on her father's farm.'

Henri smiled at Pilgrim apologetically. 'I suggested we should come to speak to you. I felt certain you would be able to obtain the loan of a horse on my behalf.'

'You'd have it returned by tonight,' promised Mary. 'My brother's waiting for Henri at Morwelham Quay. He'll bring it back.'

Pilgrim frowned. 'How is Henri going to find his way to this Morwelham Quay without a guide?'

'I've told him how to get there. It's not hard to find – but he must be there by noon. The boat has to set off by then.'

'That is not the only reason why I must leave very soon,' said Henri. 'As you well know, there is a nine o'clock roll call in the prison. It will be discovered I am missing and they will begin searching for me. I do not wish to be caught and sent to the *cachot* once again. I doubt if I would find another friend such as you there.'

Pilgrim was thinking fast as Henri was talking. 'I think I might be able to get a horse for you, Henri, but if it isn't returned by this evening I'll be forced to give an explanation for its loss – and then it will be *me* for the *cachot*.'

'My brother will bring the horse back by this evening, I promise!' declared a very agitated Mary. She was close to tears. 'He's got to come back to tell me that Henri is safely on board the boat. If . . . if anything goes wrong I'll come to Tor Royal and say I stole the horse and gave it to Henri to help his escape. But it won't go wrong. It *won't*!'

'You would do this for me?' Henri was fully aware that by taking such a course of action, she would be inviting a sentence of death for horse stealing. He looked at her with an expression that contained both incredulity and affection.

'Of course.'

Suddenly and unexpectedly, Henri cupped Mary's face in his hands and kissed her.

When he released her, Mary's cheeks had turned scarlet, but she gazed at him happily.

'Have you ever known such devotion?' Henri said to Pilgrim.

'I'll go and get you a horse. Mary will take you to an old sheep pen, halfway between here and Roundtor Farm. Wait for me there. I'll bring the horse as quickly as I can. We must hurry if you're not to miss the boat. Go now and I'll be as quick as I can.'

When Pilgrim returned to the house his breakfast was ready, but he told the servants he had promised to make an early start at Roundtor Farm and would forego the meal.

The same reason was given by him for wanting to take a horse from the Tor Royal stables, but here he encountered an unexpected problem. He was informed by one of the grooms that a party of dignitaries would be arriving at Tor Royal by carriage later that morning. Sir Thomas Tyrwhitt had arranged for them to be provided with horses from his stable and taken out on the moor. It was intended to give them an idea of the sport they might expect when the hunting season began. It was an arrangement that had been made some weeks before.

'So you see, sir, there's not a spare horse to be had today.'

This was disastrous news. If Henri was not sent on his

way within the hour, mounted on a good horse, capture would be inevitable for him.

Then Pilgrim had a sudden brainwave. 'What about the Prince Regent's horse? Is it going out with today's party?'

'No, sir.' The groom looked doubtful. 'But he's in peak condition. He won't be satisfied with just a brief trot from here to Roundtor.'

The groom, in common with all the other Tor Royal servants, was aware that Pilgrim spent most days at the Elfords' farm.

'Then I'll make certain he has a good run. Will you saddle him up for me, please. I'll go as soon as he's ready.'

The Prince Regent's horse was saddled quickly and Pilgrim rode off. He found Henri and Mary waiting for him at the appointed place.

Henri was a cavalry officer and knew horses. He was filled with admiration for the big stallion. Walking about the animal, he said, 'My friend, you have done me proud. This is a horse fit for a king.'

Pilgrim smiled broadly, but he did not enlighten the Frenchman. One day he would tell him, but not now.

'It is indeed,' he agreed. 'Go now. Catch your boat and see that the horse is returned on time. Good luck, Henri – and find some way of letting us know you have reached France safely.'

'Of course! I will send you a keg of the finest brandy. But now I must say farewell to my Mary. Would that she were coming with me.'

Minutes later, Henri was galloping away, heading for Morwelham Quay and freedom.

Standing beside Pilgrim, tears running down her cheeks, Mary waved until Henri passed out of sight.

'You're a brave girl, Mary. It's something Henri is very aware of. You haven't seen the last of him.'

'I hope not,' sobbed Mary. 'I love him very much. But his father is ill. He had to get home quickly. Now I must get home too. Thank you for getting the horse. I'll see it's returned to you. Will you be at Roundtor?'

Pilgrim nodded.

'It'll be brought there to you.'

Pilgrim was walking away in the direction of Roundtor when Mary called to him.

When he turned, she said, 'Give my love to Tacy. You can tell her about Henri, if you like. She'll say nothing to anyone. Besides, I've done nothing she wouldn't do for you if the need arose.'

Her words gave Pilgrim much food for thought as he walked to the Elfords' farm.

42

For two hours after arriving at Roundtor Farm, Pilgrim had to keep the news of Henri's escape a secret. Tom Elford and Johanna had gone to the prison with cakes and produce from the farm, leaving Pilgrim, Tacy and Billy at work repairing the roof of the cowshed.

There had been a strong wind blowing across the moor during the night. It had caused one of the roof timbers, riddled with woodworm, to finally collapse.

Not until the roof had been shored up and three pieces of timber replaced did Billy leave the others and go off across the moor to cut peat. Winter was approaching and sales of the moorland fuel to Dartmoor prison had been so good it had left the farm short.

When the young man had gone, Pilgrim told Tacy of the morning's happenings.

She was very excited at the news of Henri's escape and Mary's part in it, but was also fearful of what would happen if the prison authorities learned of Pilgrim's involvement – as they surely would if the Prince Regent's horse was not returned to Pilgrim that day.

This was a possibility that had been niggling at Pilgrim all morning and he shared Tacy's concern. 'Is Mary's brother as reliable as she says he is?'

'He's all right – when he's not been drinking.'

Pilgrim was hammering a final nail into a wooden beam. He missed and struck his thumb. Shaking his hand in a vain bid to get rid of the pain, he asked, 'What do you mean by that? Is he a drunkard?'

'Michael could never settle down to farming and he hated the moor. He was always arguing with his father about something. Eventually he left the farm and moved to Tavistock.'

Pilgrim knew Tavistock to be a fair-sized market town on the western fringe of Dartmoor, but Tacy was still talking.

'His going away didn't make much difference to the family. There were plenty more brothers and sisters to do the work on the farm. In fact, the main problem has always been to feed them all. They were probably pleased to get rid of one. Though I believe Michael's been in trouble with the town constable in Tavistock once or twice, for being drunk.'

Pilgrim looked at Tacy aghast. 'This is the man who's been entrusted to return the Prince Regent's horse to me?'

Pilgrim began to wonder what he had done!

'It'll be all right.' Tacy hoped she sounded more confident than she felt about the outcome of Pilgrim's actions in support of his French friend. 'Mary and Michael have always been pretty close. He's not the most reliable of men, but I don't think he'd do anything to let her down. Mary can certainly he relied on. If she's said she'll take the blame if anything goes wrong, that's exactly what she'll do. She'd sacrifice anything for Henri – even her life. Anyway, I've heard that Michael hopes to marry soon. He's probably settled down a lot more than when I knew him.'

Pilgrim sincerely hoped Tacy was right. If Henri escaped safely and the horse was returned, it would be a very satisfying incident. He did not like deceiving Sir Thomas Tyrwhitt. The owner of Tor Royal had been very generous to Virgil and himself. Nevertheless, the United States and France were both at war with Britain. Helping a French prisoner to escape by using a horse belonging to the man who ruled England would make a good story once the war was over.

Henri's escape pleased Tacy for quite another reason. Pilgrim had been shown that love was capable of overcoming the vicissitudes of war and prison walls. She hoped the lesson might not be lost on him.

They were still tidying up after repairing the roof, when a fearful Emma came running across the yard to the cowshed from the house.

'Pilgrim! Tacy's ma told me to come and tell you. Some militiamen are coming towards the farm. One of 'em's riding a horse.'

Pilgrim's immediate thought was that Henri must have been captured and the militiamen were coming to arrest him, bringing the Prince Regent's captured horse as evidence of his complicity in the escape.

He ran to the door and looked out. Beyond the farm he could see half a dozen uniformed men accompanied by an officer, riding a horse. The mount had none of the breeding of the stallion from Tor Royal and Pilgrim breathed a sigh of relief. This was probably one of many search parties out scouring the moor for the escaped prisoner-of-war.

When he returned to the cowshed, he saw Emma clambering up among the rafters.

'What are you doing up there?' he demanded.

'The militiamen might be looking for me. I'll hide away up here until they're gone.'

'They'll not be interested in you, Emma. I believe a French officer has escaped from the prison. They'll be looking for him.'

Emma was not convinced. 'I'm not taking any chances. If they don't find the Frenchman they might take me instead.'

Pilgrim smiled. 'If they search the farm, as well they might, they'd find you up there and want to know the reason why you're hiding from them. The best thing you can do is come down here with us. They'll probably think you're Tacy's sister and won't even ask any questions of you.'

Emma thought carefully about his words. She was a bright girl and realised there was much sense in what he said, but she was still doubtful. 'Are you sure they're not looking for me?'

'Of course he is,' said Tacy. 'Anyway, Pilgrim knows most of the militiamen, don't you?'

Pilgrim shook his head. 'Not any more, the ones I knew have been replaced by Irish militiamen.'

Looking through the open door of the cowshed he watched the men approach the gate. He felt a sudden unease when he recognised the man on the horse. It was the officer who had been involved in the argument with him and Virgil at the Tor Royal party.

'Irish militiamen?' Emma dropped to the ground from her refuge among the beams. 'I thought all Irishmen were tinkers. All those I've met have been.'

Pilgrim smiled despite his misgivings at seeing the Irish officer. 'I wouldn't repeat that in front of the militiamen, Emma. I don't think the officer, in particular, would take it very kindly.'

Before the militiamen entered the farmyard, Pilgrim dusted himself down and put on his uniform coat. Then he walked from the cowshed accompanied by Tacy and Emma.

His sudden appearance caused considerable excitement among the militiamen and he realised it was the sight of his uniform. These men were newly arrived at Dartmoor. They could probably not distinguish between a French and an American uniform. All they would know was it was not an English one.

His suspicions were confirmed when two of the men ran towards him, muskets extended menacingly.

They stopped when they reached him and one of the militiamen waved the muzzle of his musket dangerously close to Pilgrim's face.

'You. Are you the escaped prisoner?'

Pilgrim pushed the muzzle away from his face. 'I'm not an escaped anything. I'm a United States prisoner-of-war on parole from Dartmoor prison.'

The militiaman seemed to hear only what he wished to hear. Calling to the officer, he said, 'It's a prisoner all right, sir. But he says he's not a Frenchman.'

'Bring him here,' called the officer.

'You heard the lieutenant. He wants to speak to you.' The second militiaman prodded Pilgrim.

Trying hard to control his anger, Pilgrim made his way with as much dignity as he could muster to where the militia officer sat upon his horse.

'What's your name?' The Irish lieutenant looked down at Pilgrim unsmilingly.

'Lieutenant Pilgrim Penn.' The last time Pilgrim had seen this haughty young man, he was drunk and being helped from the room.

'Are you paroled to this farm?' It was evident that Pilgrim's recognition of the other man was not mutual.

'No.' Pilgrim spoke with considerably more patience than he felt towards this arrogant young man.

'Your parole licence, if you please.'

Pilgrim reached inside a pocket and a wave of despair hit him. He had removed the licence the previous day when the coat was given to one of the Tor Royal servants to brush and clean.

He began to explain to the militia lieutenant what had happened, but his explanation was cut short.

'You are aware that you are required to carry your parole licence with you at all times?'

'Yes, but as I was explaining . . .'

'You can explain it to the governor at Dartmoor prison. Two of you take him there. If he tries to escape – shoot him! He might be telling the truth, or he might not. It doesn't matter. He's in breach of his parole regulations. No doubt the governor will take him back where he belongs. Inside the prison.'

43

The militiamen made a search of the farmhouse and outbuildings, despite the objections of Joan and Tacy Elford, before Pilgrim was led off across the farmyard by the two militiamen.

He offered no resistance. His two guards were so excited at having a prisoner, their reaction to any form of protest would have been both unpredictable and dangerous. Besides, their officer had given them *carte blanche* by telling them to shoot him if he made an attempt to escape.

Should he be shot when they were out of sight of Roundtor Farm there would be no one to dispute the militiamen's version of events.

Pilgrim believed the officer's instruction had been given in a moment of inexperienced bravado, rather than an instruction to the two men that they should dispose of their prisoner. However, he did not intend antagonising them in any way and putting it to the test.

As Tacy passed by the officer sitting importantly upon his horse, she ceased her haranguing of the militiamen to call to Pilgrim, 'Shall I go and tell Sir Thomas Tyrwhitt what's happened here?'

'Yes. Tell him I've been arrested and sent to the prison by the militia officer who insulted Jemima Cotterell at Colonel Hawke's farewell party.'

Pilgrim knew Sir Thomas was in London and not at the house, but he hoped the use of Sir Thomas's name might help his cause.

The immediate effect of his words was to prompt one of the two militiamen accompanying him into giving him a painful prod in the back with his musket.

The action was seen by Joan who was standing in the doorway of the farmhouse kitchen, wiping flour-coated hands on her apron.

She too recognised the danger Pilgrim was in from their over-enthusiasm. 'Emma, follow Pilgrim and the militiamen all the way to Dartmoor prison, while Tacy runs to Tor Royal. Keep your distance, but don't let them out of your sight. If they do anything they shouldn't, you'll bear witness against them.'

'Wait!'

The officer's shout brought Pilgrim and his escort to a halt. Peering intently at Pilgrim, he said, 'How do you know what happened at Tor Royal?'

Pilgrim looked at the Irish lieutenant impassively. 'I was at the party too. I am paroled to Sir Thomas Tyrwhitt at Tor Royal. As I recall we were introduced, Lieutenant Kennedy.'

'You're one of the Americans who is friendly with the vicar's daughter?'

The Irish lieutenant seemed suddenly to be uncertain of the action he was taking and Tacy chose this moment to say, 'Sir Thomas Tyrwhitt is a personal friend of Lieutenant Penn's family. Pilgrim knew Colonel Hawke too. He'd never have dreamed of arresting him.'

In the course of their many conversations together, Pilgrim had told Tacy of the regard in which his father had held Lieutenant Colonel Hawke's father when they had fought on opposite sides in his country's war to gain its independence.

Pilgrim was grateful for Tacy's intervention. He was caught up in a dangerous situation. There was the added complication of the Prince Regent's horse. His arrest might precipitate the discovery that the animal was not in his possession.

All these things had gone through his mind before he replied to Lieutenant Kennedy's question.

'I am – and the man who offered to call you out is my commanding officer.'

Lieutenant Kennedy was silent for some moments as he mulled the situation over in his mind. Arriving at a decision, he said to the two militiamen guarding Pilgrim, 'You can rejoin the others for now.'

'But what about the prisoner?' one of them protested.

'He's not the man we're looking for. He poses no threat to anyone. Rejoin the others.'

Grumbling because their brief prospect of glory had been brought to a premature end, the two men reluctantly rejoined their companions who were now drinking water from a bucket provided for them by Joan Elford.

Dismounting from his horse in order that he might speak more confidentially to Pilgrim, Lieutenant Kennedy had lost his bombastic manner. He was almost apologetic when he asked, 'Did I make an absolute ass of myself the other evening?'

Surprised and greatly relieved at the welcome change of attitude from the militiaman, Pilgrim replied sarcastically, 'You didn't exactly cover yourself in glory. But be thankful you're alive. Had Captain Howard not been aware how drunk you were, he might well have called you out – and he's the best shot in the United States Marine Corps.'

'I'd had a great deal to drink,' admitted the un-expectedly contrite lieutenant. 'Far more than I am used to. I had been celebrating my birthday.'

When Pilgrim offered no comment, the young Irish lieutenant asked, 'Do you think Captain Howard would accept a written apology? I would send one to the young lady too, of course.'

After a moment more's hesitation, he added, 'Perhaps I should apologise to Sir Thomas Tyrwhitt as well.'

'I think your fellow officers were able to spirit you away before Sir Thomas became aware anything was amiss,' said Pilgrim. 'It might be as well if he remained in ignorance of what went on.'

He looked to where Tacy waited uncertainly beside the farmyard gate, ready if need be, to fire a final verbal volley at Lieutenant Kennedy before hurrying off to enlist the aid of Sir Thomas Tyrwhitt.

'Am I still under arrest, or may I rejoin my friends? There's a lot to do about the farm and work has come to a halt on my account.'

Lieutenant Kennedy looked at Tacy admiringly before replying to Pilgrim. 'You seem to have found a most attractive and spirited champion, Lieutenant Penn. You must explain to me some time how you Americans manage to allure such young women. Yes, you may return to her. I am searching for an escaped French prisoner. I have no wish to disrupt the lives of local residents.'

Looking pointedly at Tacy, he added, 'Besides, I shall certainly be passing this way again.'

Mounting his horse once more, Lieutenant Alan

Kennedy inclined his head in Tacy's direction. Calling on his men to resume their search for the escaped French prisoner-of-war, he turned his mount towards the farmyard gate.

The two militiamen who had expected to convey Pilgrim to Dartmoor prison scowled as they passed him by. The others smiled sheepishly in his direction.

As they passed through the gate, the Elford family and Emma gathered around Pilgrim and he thanked them profusely for their support.

'Had it not been for you – all of you – I would be on my way to the *cachot* – the punishment cell – inside the prison right now.'

He grimaced and explained to Joan Elford, 'I've been there before, fortunately only briefly. I didn't enjoy the experience. That's where I met Henri, Mary Gurney's friend.'

'Talking of Henri, didn't I hear one of the militiamen say they were searching for a Frenchman named Henri something-or-other?'

'That's right, Ma,' replied Tacy. 'It's the same man. He's escaped again.'

The glance exchanged between Tacy and Pilgrim was not lost on the farmer's astute wife.

'I hope Mary isn't involved in his escape this time – or anyone at Roundtor, either. The militiamen we've had at Dartmoor until now have been willing to turn a blind eye to a lot of what's gone on. I don't think these Irishmen are going to be as understanding.'

44

Mary's brother, Michael, reached Roundtor, riding the Prince Regent's horse, in the early evening. Mary was walking beside him, smiling happily.

Michael was full of praise for the stamina and speed of the horse. At the same time he expressed concern at the level of militia activity on and about the moor.

'There are patrols on roads all over the place,' he said. 'It's a good thing Henri went when he did. He'd never have got off the moor now.'

'They're all over our part of the moor too,' declared Mary. 'That's why I set off to meet Michael. I was anxious about him.'

'Did any of the militiamen stop and question you?' asked Pilgrim.

'No. When Mary met me we left the roads and came across the moor. She knows it better than anyone you'll meet – with the possible exception of Billy Yates.'

Pilgrim was relieved. The Prince Regent's horse was distinctive in size and colouring. He did not want any militiaman remembering it at a later date.

'Did Henri get away safely?'

Michael grinned. 'He did. He even found time to call at an inn between Tavistock and Morwhelham on his way there.'

Pilgrim was aghast. 'What did he think he was doing? His accent could have given him away. Had he been brought back to Dartmoor we'd all have been in trouble.'

'He said he was thirsty. As a matter of fact his accent was commented on at the inn. He told them he was an Irishman, over here to buy bloodstock. Those at the inn didn't know any different. Henri said he could have wined and dined for a week at the expense of the country's horse breeders, if he'd had the time.'

In spite of his concern for what *might* have happened, Pilgrim admired Henri's effrontery.

'The boat left on time,' said Michael. 'They'll have cleared Plymouth by now. If the weather holds they'll make good time. By nightfall tomorrow Henri should be back in his own country.'

'Thanks to Mary,' said Pilgrim.

She was a short distance away, talking to Tacy. Dismounting from the Prince Regent's horse, Michael patted the animal affectionately, then, lowering his voice, he said to Pilgrim, 'I think Mary was hoping he would take her with him. As it is, I doubt if she'll ever see him again.'

Mary's hearing was more acute than her brother had realised. Rounding on him, she cried, 'I *will* see him. He told me so. Pilgrim was there.'

'That's so,' agreed Pilgrim. 'I also know that Henri is very fond of you, Mary – and so he should be after the risks you've taken for him.'

'I've done nothing that Tacy wouldn't do for you. The only difference is that she's got you here. Henri and I are going to be hundreds of miles apart until this war is over. I won't even know what he's doing.'

'He'll find some way to get word to you, don't you worry. Henri's one of the most resourceful men I've ever met.'

Pilgrim hoped he was right. Mary would be desperately unhappy if she never heard from him again – and Henri was still an officer in Napoleon's army. He was liable to be sent anywhere he was needed.

Pilgrim was also thinking about the remainder of Mary's opening statement. He thought of how Tacy had sprung to his defence when the Irish militiamen were going to take him away.

He looked to where she was taking Mary inside the farmhouse, an arm about her friend's shoulders. He wondered what *her* thoughts were at this moment.

Mary and Henri would soon be hundreds of miles apart, yet Mary seemed to have very few doubts about the way Henri felt about her.

Despite the fact he and Tacy spent almost every day in each other's company, she would be far less certain of how Pilgrim felt about her.

He told himself yet again there was a very good reason for this, but he wondered whether Tacy would agree with such reasonableness.

Pilgrim decided that when the time was right he would have a talk with Tacy. Explain honestly how he felt about her and the situation in which they found themselves.

He had very little experience with women, but Pilgrim believed she would prove understanding.

Later that evening, Pilgrim breathed a huge sigh of relief when he handed the Prince Regent's horse over to a groom. He even managed a grin when the groom commented that the animal looked as though it had been ridden harder than at any time in its life.

Virgil came to the stables to meet him and, as they walked back to the house, Pilgrim told Virgil what had occurred.

The captain of marines saw the humour in the situation. At the same time he pointed out what might have happened had things not gone according to plan.

'Sir Thomas would have been very upset. He would quite rightly have regarded it as a breach of his trust. No doubt we'd both have had our paroles revoked.'

'I'm sorry, Virgil. I never even considered you might become involved.'

Virgil was struggling with his conscience. Suddenly he put a hand across Pilgrim's shoulders. 'Ignore what I've just said, Pilgrim. Life is so comfortable here I'm forgetting who and what I am. What we both are. We're first and foremost officers of the United States Marine Corps. Our country is at war with Britain, and France is an ally. We're on parole and have given our word we'll not take advantage of our position to attempt to escape, but we've given no promises about not helping others. You were right to do what you did and you've managed it without apparently affecting anyone adversely. Well done.'

Virgil gave Pilgrim a wry smile. 'I'm sure you'll understand if I don't submit a report commending your actions until after we return to the States. Now, you're not the only one to have had an interesting and exciting day. Come inside the house and meet someone. On the way I'll try to fill in as much of the story as I can . . .'

45

Had Winifrith Cudmore delayed her departure from Tor Royal by little more than twenty-four hours, her journey would not have proved necessary. She would also have changed the destinies of a number of people, including that of her daughter.

When Pilgrim entered the house with Virgil he was flabbergasted to see Sophie seated on a settee in the drawing room. She was suntanned, but appeared very tired and looked desperately unhappy.

'But . . . your mother's gone to London looking for you! She thinks you're in Spain,' said Pilgrim, inanely.

'She's unlikely to learn very much from the War Office in London,' explained Virgil. 'Sophie has come direct from the battle front, landing at Plymouth only this morning. News of the war in Spain is unlikely to reach London for another day or two. Even then there will be nothing to indicate that Sophie's returned to England.'

Pilgrim looked from Virgil to the unhappy woman

and back again. 'I'm sorry . . . I really don't understand what's happening.'

'Sophie was married in Spain. To the army officer Winifrith was trying to keep her from.' Virgil seemed to find it difficult to carry the explanation any farther and Sophie herself completed the explanation for him.

'Harry, my husband, was in the Rifle Corps. He . . . he was killed in the fighting near San Sebastian. He and his men were surprised by a French cavalry force.'

Tears welled up in Sophie's eyes and began to roll down her cheeks, but she continued. 'I was in camp when I heard about the action. I set off to try to find him but there were only a few survivors. One was a badly wounded sergeant. He brought me Harry's signet ring. Harry had given it to him for me, before he died . . .'

As she spoke, she wound the signet ring in question around and around in a distressed manner on a finger of her right hand.

'The sergeant died before he could pass on a report to anyone else. As a result Harry has been listed only as "missing". Although I know the truth, he won't be listed among the casualties for some time . . .'

Sophie closed her eyes as though in pain, but it did not stop the tears.

'You don't need to tell me any more, Sophie. You've had a very, very unhappy time. Here, Virgil's poured a brandy for you.'

Sophie took the drink with some difficulty because her hand was shaking alarmingly. She took a couple of gulps of the fiery drink and then stood up.

'I . . . I'm sorry, but I think I'll go to my room now.'

'Of course.'

Pilgrim and Virgil stood up and watched in silent sympathy as she headed for the door.

With her hand on the door knob, she turned to look

back at them. 'Thank you both for your kindness. I am glad I found you here and not my mother.' Although she addressed her words to both of them, she looked only at Virgil. Then she opened the door and was gone.

Without speaking, Virgil poured some of Sir Thomas Tyrwhitt's brandy into two glasses and handed one of them to Pilgrim before he sat down heavily upon one of the padded leather chairs.

'She's a courageous girl. A *very* courageous girl,' he said, eventually. 'She gave up everything for the man she loved, only to have him killed within a few weeks of their wedding.'

He took a deep draught of the brandy in his glass, then sat looking down at the remainder before speaking again.

'When she first arrived back here, she told me a little more about what happened. It was almost as though she was desperate to tell someone. She cried a lot too, but it's hardly surprising.'

Finishing off the still quite considerable amount of drink left in his glass, he stood up and refilled it once more, holding out the bottle to Pilgrim, who shook his head.

'She went off looking for her husband's body, you know, but the French were advancing. She would have been taken prisoner by them had some of her husband's regiment not taken her back forcibly.'

'She certainly deserves more happiness than she's found,' agreed Pilgrim, 'especially after throwing convention to the wind in order to go off with him.'

Pilgrim looked up at Virgil. 'Will you write and let Winifrith know she's here?'

'I have no intention of writing to Winifrith,' declared Virgil firmly, 'but I do feel we owe it to Sir Thomas to let him know. However, Sophie needs a little time to put herself back together before she meets up with either of them. I'll write to Sir Thomas, perhaps tomorrow, or the day after – and send the letter off a day or two after that. I somehow feel Sir Thomas will understand.'

Virgil sat down heavily and gave Pilgrim a sad smile. 'With any luck the news might take another day or two getting from Sir Thomas to his sister. Given another week or more, Sophie might be more capable of coping with her mother.'

46

Pilgrim told Sophie's story to Tacy as he turned the handle of a butter churn for her at Roundtor Farm three days later.

He had been unable to visit the farm during the intervening period. Trouble had flared up once more between the French and American prisoners-of-war in Dartmoor prison. On this occasion the fault lay with the Americans. Pilgrim had been at the prison instigating an inquiry on behalf of Virgil.

Listening to Pilgrim now, Tacy was torn between very real sympathy for Sophie and a feeling of uneasiness because the Tor Royal owner's niece was once more living beneath the same roof as Pilgrim.

Sophie was a very attractive woman. She now had the added appeal of having travelled to Spain in romantic circumstances, becoming involved in the war there and being dealt a tragic blow by fate.

Tacy felt she had little with which to challenge the appeal of such a woman.

Sensing something of what she was thinking, Pilgrim

added, 'Sophie's been through a very unhappy and difficult time, but Virgil seems to have found a new role as her comforter. I believe it's one he's finding much to his liking.'

'Don't you mind about that?'

'Mind? Why should I?'

'Well . . . you and Sophie seemed to be very friendly before she went away. You might have expected her to turn to you for comfort.'

'She couldn't have a better man than Virgil to help her right now. He's seen far more of life than me. She'll get better advice from him than I'm capable of giving her.'

Turning the handle of the churn vigorously, Pilgrim added, 'I've had experience with my pa of opening up new lands, making a new home and of fighting both Indians and the British. I just haven't met enough girls, or women, to be of any help with their problems.'

He paused in his work and looked at Tacy. 'I know you better than any other girl I've ever met, Tacy. Yet I can't even find words to tell you some of the things I want to say.'

For a moment Tacy thought he was at last about to declare his feelings for her, but as the moments passed and he said nothing further, her optimism seeped away.

She remembered the other times she had felt the same way. As the occasions multiplied without anything being said about Pilgrim's feelings for her, she had begun to believe any idea of a romance between them was in her mind alone.

Suddenly the thought entered her head that Pilgrim might be trying to tell her something very different. That he did not want to come to Roundtor Farm any more. After all, he had no need to work. Perhaps he would be happier just enjoying life at Tor Royal with the friends of Sir Thomas Tyrwhitt. With Sophie too, despite his denial.

'Are you trying to say you'd rather not come to work at Roundtor any more?'

Her question took Pilgrim by surprise. 'Why should I say that? I *like* coming here.'

'Well, if it's not that, what is it you find so difficult to say?' Tacy decided to take the initiative and discover just what it was he found so difficult to say to her.

The tone of her voice was somewhat less belligerent, but her attitude caught Pilgrim off balance. He *had* been on the verge of saying some of the things she had been wanting to hear for so long. To open his heart and tell her how he really felt about her. At the same time he intended explaining why he had not attempted to do anything about it.

Instead, he floundered embarrassingly. 'Nothing. At least . . . nothing important. No, that isn't right, either . . .'

At that moment, Emma came to the kitchen door, across the farmyard, and called out, 'Pilgrim! Mrs Elford said to tell you a man in uniform is coming towards the farm, riding a horse. She says it looks a bit like that officer who almost arrested you.'

'What can he want?' Pilgrim had met the Irish militiaman once or twice during the past few days, but he did not feel entirely at ease in his presence.

'I expect he's come to see Tacy,' declared Johanna, mischievously. She had brought a bucket of milk from the cowshed as Emma called her message from the farmhouse. 'That's what he came here for the day before yesterday.'

'That's not true, Johanna, as well you know!'

Glaring angrily at her grinning sister, Tacy explained, 'Lieutenant Kennedy came looking for you. He said there'd been some trouble among the Americans up at the prison. He thought you ought to know.'

Pilgrim remembered meeting up with Alan Kennedy on that day as he passed through Princetown on his way to the prison. It meant the militiaman's excuse for visiting Roundtor was a deliberate lie. He must have taken advantage of Pilgrim's absence to visit Tacy.

The knowledge did nothing to endear the Irishman to Pilgrim. He found some consolation in the fact that Tacy thought it necessary to explain away Lieutenant Kennedy's visit.

But Johanna had not yet done with her mischief making. 'If he only came to speak to Pilgrim, why didn't he go away again when he found he wasn't here, instead of staying talking to you for *ages*?'

'You're just trying to cause trouble,' said Emma, who had come from the house. 'I was with Tacy the whole of the time the militiaman was here. He probably said as much to me as he did to her – not that I wanted him to. I don't much care for him.'

While they had been talking, the subject of their conversation had reached the farmyard gate. He waved to them in a friendly manner before dismounting.

Leading his horse inside the farmyard, he called cheerily to Pilgrim, 'I thought I would find you here. I called in to tell you I've just escorted twenty of your fellow Americans from the prison to Tavistock. They've been granted parole there.'

His words were for Pilgrim, but his glance rested upon Tacy for far longer than it did upon the United States marine.

'I expect Virgil or I will be given a list of their names when one of us next goes to the prison.'

Pilgrim knew it was more likely to be him than Virgil. The marines captain had been troubled by his wounded leg of late. As a result, most of the prison visits had been left to Pilgrim.

Not that Virgil was particularly upset about being restricted to the house at the moment. Sophie's concern for his comfort and well-being had been heightened by her experiences on the battlefields of Spain. She seemed to find an escape from her own deep sadness by helping Virgil in every way she could.

'There were some extremely interesting men among them,' said Kennedy. 'I was talking to one of them who owns a whole fleet of merchantmen. He was complaining bitterly about being held as a prisoner-of-war. I'm inclined to agree with him. He should never have been taken in the first place.'

'That sounds like Conrad Steiger,' commented Pilgrim. 'He'll always find something to grumble about to anyone who's prepared to listen.'

Lieutenant Kennedy frowned at Pilgrim's apparent lack of concern for his countryman. 'At least he'll be staying with a family who should appreciate his background. He's gone to live in the home of a man who owns a store as well as a small freight company. He has recently bought a share in a trading vessel, so they'll find plenty to talk about. There are also three pretty young daughters in the house.'

Pilgrim thought that Steiger was the last man who should have been billeted in a house where there were three young women, but he kept his thoughts to himself.

Lieutenant Kennedy switched his attention to Tacy. 'Would it be your sheep held in a pen about half a mile along the valley from here?'

Tacy nodded. 'Yes, some ewes and a young ram are going to market tomorrow. It'll save having to feed them through the winter. Why do you ask?'

'As I came by I noticed that some of the stones have been knocked to the ground. One sheep was actually standing on the wall. I drove it back inside, but unless the damage is repaired it won't keep them there for long.'

Tacy was alarmed. 'If they get out we'll never find them in time to take them to market. I'll need to fix the wall right away – and find any of the sheep too, if they've got out.'

'I'll come and help you,' offered Alan Kennedy immediately.

Pilgrim had been watching the militiaman. He believed he had only mentioned the broken wall in the hope that Tacy would want to deal with it immediately, thus affording him an opportunity to accompany her.

'It's all right, Tacy,' said Emma promptly. 'You and Pilgrim carry on with the butter-making. I'll go.'

Tacy hesitated. Whether it was because she did or did not want Kennedy's company, Pilgrim could not tell, but Emma was talking once more.

'You can send Billy to help when he comes back. He'll have the wall fixed in no time.'

Billy was away from the farm with the pony and cart. He was conveying peat to the house in preparation for the winter months that would soon be upon them.

Lieutenant Kennedy tried unsuccessfully to hide his disappointment. With far less enthusiasm than before, he said, 'My offer still stands. I'll come and help with the wall and the sheep.'

As Kennedy led his horse out of the farmyard behind Emma, Tacy said, 'I think Lieutenant Kennedy's rather nice, don't you?'

Pilgrim's grunted reply was decidedly non-committal and Tacy persisted, 'Don't you like him, Pilgrim?'

'Not much. He's not an officer I would want in my command.'

'Why not?' Tacy asked the question in apparent innocence.

'He's got a bit of growing up to do. He's never been in action and still believes war is fun. It isn't. Officers who think it is are a danger to the men they command.'

Tacy had hoped Pilgrim's dislike of Alan Kennedy might stem from jealousy because the young Irishman was paying her too much attention. She felt disappointed.

Tacy would have been far happier had she been able to read Pilgrim's mind. His first two meetings with the militiaman had not been propitious. Since then Lieutenant Kennedy had gone out of his way to be pleasant to him, yet he still neither liked, nor trusted the man.

Pilgrim too was wondering whether his continued dislike had its roots in Kennedy's current interest in Tacy.

47

Virgil allowed three days to pass before sending a letter to Sir Thomas Tyrwhitt, informing him of Sophie's return to Tor Royal and the true circumstances of her disappearance.

A week later a brief note was received from Sir Thomas's secretary. It said no more than that Sir Thomas had asked him to acknowledge the letter, send his love and condolences to his niece and explain that he was accompanying the Prince Regent on a visit to the north of England.

The secretary declared Sir Thomas would reply at length as soon as he returned.

Virgil revealed the contents of both letters to the Tor Royal butler, with the result that the whole household awoke to each new day wondering whether it would see the return of Sir Thomas and the formidable Winifrith Cudmore.

As the days passed and she had still not descended upon them, the household became even more apprehensive about the intentions of Sir Thomas's uncertain-tempered sister.

It was inconceivable that she would do nothing at all. The household staff sympathised wholeheartedly with Sophie, aware of all that had happened to her after she ran off from Tor Royal. They watched with undisguised approval as she slowly put the pieces of her shattered life back into place with the patient help of Virgil.

Despite the initial reservations held by some of the servants, the two Americans had settled into the household well and had gained the respect of most of those who worked there. There was particular sympathy for Virgil. His wounded leg was presenting increasing problems for him, but he bore his pain and discomfort without complaint.

Not until four weeks had elapsed did Sir Thomas return to Tor Royal. He was alone and he was able to lift, at least temporarily, the threat of the imminent arrival of Winifrith.

Genuinely fond of his niece, he greeted her warmly. Holding her to him, he murmured, 'Poor Sophie, you must have been through some absolutely dreadful experiences. Thank heavens that you, at least, have returned home to us safely. I sincerely trust your mother will do the same.'

Sophie pulled away from him. 'Mother . . . ? I am sorry, Uncle, I don't understand . . .'

Sir Thomas looked at her in astonishment, 'Do you mean you don't know? But of course not, how could you? My child, your mother left for the front, in Spain, some weeks ago. She was determined to fetch you back to England. At this very moment she is probably causing Lord Wellington more problems than Napoleon, and all because he is unable to produce you on demand.'

Sophie gazed at him in disbelief. 'You mean . . . she's gone to Spain looking for me?'

'That's exactly what I mean. When she could obtain no satisfaction at the War Office, she declared they were all totally incompetent and set off to find you for herself.'

Sophie's mouth opened twice without any words escaping, then she gave way to sudden, uncontrollable laughter.

Virgil thought it a wonderful sound. After weeks of desperate unhappiness, Sophie had begun to smile occasionally once more, but it was the first time he had heard her laugh out loud since her return from Spain.

Once she had brought her merriment under control, Sophie wiped tears from her eyes and said, 'Oh dear! I really should not find it amusing to have caused everyone so much trouble. Poor mother will absolutely *hate* the conditions she will encounter on the campaign. Lord Wellington has the scent of victory in his nostrils and is pushing the French army hard. Poor Harry always said the war would be won or lost in the course of the next few months. It's doubtful whether the British army will retire to quarters for the winter, as is usual. Mother will suffer dreadful hardships, only to eventually learn that I am already safely back in England!'

The sadness had returned when Sophie spoke of her late husband, but it disappeared once more when she said, 'I know I should be feeling terribly guilty, but if only mother didn't constantly interfere so in my life, matters would never have come to this.'

Screwing up her face in a moment of sudden anguish, she added, 'And Harry might still be alive today if she had not interfered and had him transferred to active service. She deserves to suffer a little, at least.'

'I am quite certain your mother means well, my dear,' said Sir Thomas, his arm about Sophie's shoulders. 'Although we none of us agree with the way she goes about things, she *does* have your best interests at heart.'

He cleared his throat noisily. 'However, I do agree that she has an unfortunate tendency to want to organise other people's lives for them. But you must try not to worry too much about her. I will have a letter to Lord Wellington sent off with the official despatches from the War Office. He will be informed you are safe and well, back here at Tor Royal.'

Showing little enthusiasm, Sir Thomas added, 'When the news reaches Winifrith I am quite sure she will return to Tor Royal immediately. Indeed, she may know already. If that is so, she will no doubt already be on her way home to us.'

48

'Them two are sweet on each other, ain't they?'

Emma added the question to her statement as Virgil and Sophie rode away along a curving valley, not far from Roundtor.

Sophie turned to give a final wave to Pilgrim before horses and riders passed from view behind the slopes of the tor.

Pilgrim and Emma were busily securing the roof of a low, dry-stone lean-to shelter they had built inside one of the many sheep pens scattered about this part of the moor.

Their task was being carried out at the suggestion of Tom Elford. The farmer was suffering another of his bouts of ill health. However, in common with all moorland dwellers, he could still read nature's signs. All the indications were that it was going to be an early and probably severe winter.

There was not room in the buildings about the small Roundtor farmyard for all the sheep he owned. This year he intended bringing as many sheep as possible close to the farm, in a bid to minimise his losses.

While Pilgrim and Emma worked, Tacy and Johanna were at the prison market selling bread and cakes to the prisoners-of-war. The Americans had just received some of their overdue allowance. They had money to spend on such small luxuries.

Virgil and Sophie had been out riding and decided to call at Roundtor Farm to speak to Pilgrim.

'I think they're very happy in each other's company,' agreed Pilgrim. 'It's pleasing to see. Virgil's been in a lot of pain with his leg just lately, and Sophie has been through a pretty horrific experience.'

'It's very special to find someone nice when you've been through bad times,' said Emma with feeling. 'I'm glad I've found Billy.'

'He's very happy to have you too,' said Pilgrim.

He was on the roof of the lean-to, laying squares of turf across a framework of sticks and weighing them down with stones picked up from the moor.

'If your captain and Sir Thomas Tyrwhitt's niece can go around and show they think a lot of each other, why can't you and Tacy do the same?'

'I've thought about that,' said Pilgrim. 'It's rather complicated, but I want to speak to Tacy as soon as I can, to tell her how I feel about her . . . What I think about everything.'

'I suggest you get round to it pretty quickly,' said Emma. 'And you want to keep her away from that Lieutenant Kennedy. He's no good for her. He's no good for any girl.'

'Why do you think that, Emma?'

'I don't *think* nothing,' said Emma vehemently. 'I haven't told anyone else – and I won't, either – but he tried it on with me that day when we went out to repair the sheep pen.'

Pilgrim was taken aback by her revelation, but was inclined to be sceptical.

'Was it a serious attempt to do something, or was he just making suggestions?'

'It was serious enough to give me a bruise here.' Emma touched her right breast, briefly. 'I needed to bite him good and hard before he let me go. Then he told me I was an "uppity little bitch". I won't tell you what I called him, but I'd keep an eye on him and Tacy, if I was you. I've met his sort before. They think there are two sorts of girls in the world – and Tacy and I belong to the sort that are suppposed to be here for them to do what they want with.'

She looked up at him as he squatted on the roof of the crude shelter thinking of what she had said. 'I don't want you telling any of this to Billy. He'd feel he had to say something to Lieutenant Kennedy. That would land him in serious trouble. Billy's no match for a militia officer, even though he's worth ten of that one. Yes, and most other men too.'

'You think a lot of Billy, don't you, Emma?'

'Of course I do. He may not be as clever as some, but I know a good man when I find one. I ought to, I met enough of the other sort while I was a tinkers' girl.'

'But you haven't always been a tinkers' girl, Emma. Sometimes you say or do things that no tinkers' girl would know anything about. How did you come to get mixed up with them in the first place?'

'I dunno. I can't really remember a time when I wasn't with 'em. Though sometimes, when Mrs Elford says something nice to me, I seem to remember someone just like her. Someone I feel belonged to *me*, but that's all.' Emma shrugged. 'I expect I just dreamed about it, that's all.'

With a struggle, she lifted a granite boulder above her

head and Pilgrim took it from her. She looked at him in silence for a few moments. Then, in her characteristically blunt manner, she asked, 'Do you love Tacy?'

The question took Pilgrim completely by surprise. He only just succeeded in preventing the rock he was holding falling from his arms and crashing through the turf roof.

'What sort of a question is that?' he demanded.

'A very simple one, I'd have thought. Do you love her?'

'I'm . . . I've never met anyone like her before.' He felt embarrassed and gave her an evasive reply, but it was not one that Emma was prepared to accept.

'That's not what I'm asking you.'

'I would think the way I feel about Tacy is something between me and her and no one else.'

Pilgrim felt the snub was wholly justified, but gradually curiosity got the better of him. He had known Emma for long enough to realise she must have a very good reason for asking such a question.

'Why do you want to know, Emma?' The question was asked almost reluctantly.

Emma paused in the act of handing up another boulder. She lowered it to the ground again before replying. 'I know how Tacy feels about you, but I don't know your feelings for her. I don't think she does, either. If the two of you *do* love each other, then that's all right. You won't need anyone else, will you?'

Emma sat down on the stone she had just placed on the ground and looked up at him. 'On the other hand, if Tacy's just wasting her time loving you, there's no reason why she shouldn't have a bit of fun with this Lieutenant Kennedy, I suppose.'

Resting elbows upon knees, she cupped her face in her hands and said, 'She'll know it won't mean anything, not to him, anyway, but that won't matter. I mean, look at the life she leads at Roundtor Farm. It's nothing but work from the time the sun rises, until it sets again – and beyond that too, more often than not. I ask you, what sort of life is that for *anyone*? It's all right if you're doing it because you're with someone you love, and who loves you. That makes it all worthwhile. If you're not . . . ? Well, then you've got to take what you can from life, when you can, haven't you?'

Squatting on the uncompleted turf roof, Pilgrim said, 'You're full of surprises, Emma. I'd never have thought of you as a philosopher, but that's what you are, right enough.'

'What's that mean?' asked Emma aggressively. 'Why am I a philo . . . a . . . what you said I was?'

'It's a compliment. Philosophers are clever people. They think a lot about things, Emma. They make others think about things too.'

'Well, that's all right then. I don't mind being one of them if it makes you think about Tacy. She's one of the nicest people I've ever met. I'd like her to be really happy.'

'If you mean that, then you should warn her off Lieutenant Kennedy. She'll find no happiness keeping company with him.'

'I didn't say she would,' retorted Emma. 'I said she could have some *fun* with him, if that's what she wants. But I'll make sure she goes into it with her eyes wide open, don't you worry about that.'

'I'd rather she had nothing to do with him at all, Emma.'

Giving him one of her direct looks, Emma said, 'If that's what you *really* want then I think you'd better do something about it. If I was you I wouldn't leave it too long, Pilgrim.'

Her attention suddenly shifted away from him and her expression softened.

Following the direction of her gaze, Pilgrim saw Billy had just come into view around a curve of the hill. Two dogs were driving perhaps a dozen sheep ahead of him.

Standing up and handing him the rock on which she had been seated, she said, 'Here, take this old stone. I'm going to meet Billy. Like I said, life shouldn't be all work and nothing else, should it?'

As Emma hurried off to meet Billy, she gave an occasional carefree skip. Billy was still some distance away, but Pilgrim could see his wide and happy grin as he waved to Emma.

They were an unlikely couple. The worldly-wise tinkers' girl and the simple young man who knew nothing of the world beyond Dartmoor. Yet they were ridiculously happy in each other's company.

Pilgrim smiled to himself, thinking of what Emma had said to him. She had deliberately provoked him into thinking about his relationship with Tacy.

He alone knew how much he thought of her. He had believed she was aware of his feelings. He also thought she clearly understood why he was unable to express his feelings at this time. Now he realised she had probably misinterpreted his reticence as a lack of any deep and real feeling for her.

He would need to do something about it – and do it soon if he was to nip in the bud any relationship between Tacy and Lieutenant Kennedy.

49

The hopes Pilgrim entertained of telling Tacy how he felt about her suffered a setback the following morning.

The day began early for the Tor Royal household. As a result of the pain and discomfort caused to Virgil by his leg wound, Sophie had expressed her concern to Sir Thomas Tyrwhitt.

The Dartmoor landowner had called in an eminent surgeon from Plymouth. His opinion had been that part of the musket ball which had caused the wound was still lodged in Virgil's leg. The surgeon suggested the piece of lead had possibly moved recently, causing the extra pain Virgil was suffering.

The surgeon expressed his willingness to operate in a bid to locate and remove the offending body, but he warned Virgil there was a very real danger of infection following upon such an operation. Should this occur, he declared it would prove necessary to amputate the limb.

Virgil had always held the opinion that British surgeons resorted to amputation far too readily. It was a view strongly held by his father, who had been in charge of medical services for the army of the United States during the War of Independence.

He thanked the surgeon and Sir Thomas, but declined to be operated on in England. He would wait until the operation could be performed by a United States surgeon.

Offended by Virgil's lack of faith in his ability and that of his British colleagues, the surgeon pointed out that the war might continue for many years to come. He suggested that although the presence of the musket ball was not life-threatening at present, another year might find Virgil permanently crippled by his wound.

Sir Thomas was now able to use his considerable influence once more. After a long discussion with Virgil, he arranged for him to be interviewed by the senior naval surgeon at the Plymouth naval hospital.

If the naval surgeon agreed with the prognosis of his civilian colleague, Virgil would be recommended for repatriation to the United States.

Today was the day Virgil was to travel to Plymouth for his examination. He would be riding there in Sir Thomas's own carriage, accompanied on the journey by Sophie and by Sir Thomas himself. The Dartmoor landowner had business in the busy sea port.

Two militiamen would be accompanying Virgil as an armed escort, but they would be travelling on the outside of the carriage.

The party set off early, leaving Pilgrim to prepare himself for another day at Roundtor Farm – but today was likely to be more important to him than any other.

He had lain awake for much of the night thinking about Tacy and the possibility that there might be a future for them together.

He had decided to tell her of his feelings and his hopes

and fears for the future. Once it had been said, much would depend upon her own thoughts and feelings for him.

The outcome of Virgil's medical examination was also likely to have an impact on Pilgrim's present way of life. There were a number of naval men in the prison now of equal rank to Pilgrim, but Virgil particularly wanted him to rank as the senior officer. He intended to promote him to the rank of brevet captain in the event of his own repatriation.

It was a responsibility Pilgrim did not particularly want, but he would not sidestep his duty.

All these thoughts were in his mind that morning as he finally set off for Roundtor Farm.

The house was well behind him when he glanced back and caught a glimpse of bright yellow in the lane that led from the direction of Princetown.

It was the colour of a prisoner-of-war's uniform. For a brief moment Pilgrim thought of ignoring its implications and carrying on to Roundtor.

Instead, he retraced his steps and met with Ephraim at the entrance gate to Tor Royal.

'Morning, Lieutenant. I'm on my way to the house to see Cap'n Howard. It's a matter I think you should hear about too.'

'Captain Howard isn't at the house, Ephraim. He's gone into Plymouth with Sir Thomas Tyrwhitt.'

Pilgrim told the marines sergeant the reason for Virgil's journey, and asked, 'Will your news wait until tomorrow? I'm sure the captain won't mind coming to the prison to see you.'

'For all I care about the man involved, it could wait for ever, but I reckon it's something both you and Cap'n Howard should know about right now. Things might already have gone too far.'

'What sort of "things", Ephraim?'

Pilgrim asked the question although he was already convinced he would not want to know. He could see the day at Roundtor and his planned talk with Tacy slipping farther and farther away.

'You'd better tell me all about it. Who is it who's got himself in trouble?'

'Steiger.'

Pilgrim was startled. 'But . . . he's out on parole. How is it you've heard about it and Captain Howard and I haven't?'

'He *was* on parole, Lieutenant, but he's not any more. It seems he went a bit farther than he should have with a young girl – and I'm not talking about distance from the place to which he was paroled. He and the youngest daughter of the man he was staying with were left alone in the house. Steiger plied her with drink then got her into his bed. She screamed when she realised what was happening and folk came running. Steiger was given a beating, then handed over to the town constable and returned to the prison.'

'Damn the man! His actions could undo all the goodwill that's been built up with the local people by us *and* the French. I hope the governor will keep him inside the prison now. It's the best place for him.'

'I wouldn't say that, Lieutenant.'

There was something in the way the opinion was expressed that caused Pilgrim to say sharply, 'I think you'd better explain that remark, Ephraim.'

'When he was brought back to the prison he was thrown in the *cachot*.'

'So? I can't think of a better place for him. A couple of days in there might help teach him he's not such a great man as he'd like everyone to believe.'

'It might teach him a whole lot more than that, Lieutenant. You remember me telling you that the husband of the slave girl there was so much trouble about was now a prisoner-of-war in Block Four?'

When Pilgrim nodded, Ephraim continued, 'When it was learned Steiger had been brought back to the prison and thrown in the *cachot*, the girl's husband, Steiger's whipped slave and two of the biggest ex-slaves in Block Four staged a fight. It took a whole lot of militiamen to break it up and some of them got hurt. As a result, all four were thrown in the *cachot* too.'

'With Steiger?' The very thought of it made Pilgrim's blood run cold. He had an intense dislike of Conrad Steiger, but . . .

'When did all this happen?'

Ephraim shrugged nonchalantly, 'A couple of days ago. Maybe three.'

'Good God, Ephraim! You know as well as I do what might have happened in the *cachot*. Why didn't you come to tell Captain Howard or me about this before today?'

'I don't owe Steiger any favours, Lieutenant. He's had a day of reckoning coming to him for a very long time. All the same, if the others have done to Steiger what they boasted they would do, it's probably time he was brought out now.'

'Damn you, Ephraim,' said Pilgrim angrily, 'you should have got word to us long before things reached this stage!'

Even as he reprimanded the black sergeant, Pilgrim was aware that had *he* been in his place, he would probably have behaved no differently. There was no doubt at all that Steiger deserved whatever punishment was meted out to him. Nevertheless, it could not be allowed to continue now it had been brought to Pilgrim's attention.

'We'd better go to the prison right away and speak to the governor. If Steiger's still alive he's got to be brought out of the *cachot* right away.'

50

The governor of Dartmoor prison listened with growing irritation as Pilgrim suggested that Steiger should be released from the *cachot* immediately if a violent confrontation between black and white Americans were to be averted.

'Steiger has been returned to my prison because serious allegations have been made against him by a well-respected citizen of Tavistock. Very serious allegations indeed.'

'I realise all that,' said Pilgrim patiently. 'He will no doubt go on trial to answer the allegations, in due course. If he is found guilty I expect him to be punished according to the laws of your country. That will be acceptable to the other Americans too. Unfortunately, if he remains in the *cachot* with the men who are in there with him right now I doubt if he will survive to stand trial.'

Pilgrim knew he had not yet fully convinced the governor but he felt it was very important to have Conrad Steiger released from the *cachot*.

'I'll be perfectly honest with you, Governor Cotgrave. I have no liking for Steiger. But if he dies while he's in the *cachot* the men in there with him are going to be held responsible for his death. It will provoke a bloodier riot than anything you've experienced in Dartmoor so far. It will be black American against white American and will involve some of the most violent men in your prison. It will also be on record that I warned you it was about to happen.'

'Don't threaten me, Lieutenant Penn. I will consider reasoned arguments, but not threats. Besides, what happens in the future will not concern me. I am leaving my post here at the end of next month. I would like to say I am sorry to be leaving, but that would not be honest. The authorities in London seem to believe the end of the war with France is in sight. When that happy day comes French prisoners-of-war will be repatriated. It has been suggested that *all* American prisoners will then be brought to Dartmoor prison.'

Leaning back in his chair, Captain Cotgrave said, 'I will be happy to forego the pleasure of welcoming your countrymen to Dartmoor, Lieutenant Penn. However, I have no wish to add to the problems of my successor. I will have your Mr Steiger released from the *cachot*, examined by the surgeon, and placed under house arrest in the Petty Officers' Block.'

'Thank you, Governor. You will be doing your successor a great service.'

Governor Cotgrave detailed one of the two gaolers who had been present in the room throughout the discussion to go and release Steiger. When he had gone, the governor said to Pilgrim, 'Before you leave I would like you to go through the occurrence book with me. There have been a couple of deaths. Captain Howard always took details and wrote to their relatives.

There have also been a number of new admissions. You might like to check their names and status . . .'

Pilgrim looked through the occurrence book and was copying out the names of the recent admissions to the prison when there came an urgent knocking at the door. It was repeated before the governor had time to answer and, somewhat irritably, he instructed whoever was outside to 'Come in!'

It was a medical orderly, the one who had been particularly friendly to Pilgrim during his period in the prison hospital.

Extremely agitated, the orderly addressed himself to the governor. 'Begging your pardon, sir, but Mr Dykar says would you come to the hospital right away. It's the man who's just been released from the *cachot*.'

'What is it? Is he ill? Surely Mr Dykar can deal with him. Why does he want me there?'

'It's not that he's ill, sir. It's more . . . well, it's what's been done to him while he's been in the *cachot*.'

'What's happened? Has he been attacked? Is that it?'

'Not exactly . . .' The medical orderly licked his lips, ill-at-ease. 'It's worse than that, sir . . . I think you should come to the hospital.'

'Oh . . . very well! You had better come with me, Lieutenant Penn. Why the medical orderly can't tell me what's happened, I really don't know.'

At the hospital, they found the surgeon in his office. There was a strong aroma of brandy in the air. After suggesting they should be seated, he offered his visitors a drink.

'We are not here on a social visit,' snapped a tight-lipped governor. 'Your orderly told me there was some sort of emergency. Is there, or is there not?'

'I wouldn't call it an emergency, Captain Cotgrave.

At least, it is not a medical emergency. However, it might provoke serious incidents affecting discipline in Block Four.'

'For goodness' sake, Dykar! Have all my medical staff taken to talking in riddles? If you have something to tell me then say so – and tell it to me in plain English.'

When Surgeon Dykar glanced pointedly at Pilgrim, the governor said impatiently, 'Lieutenant Penn is here on Captain Howard's behalf. He should be made aware of anything likely to affect discipline in Block Four.'

'It's Mr Steiger. The prisoner who has just been released from the *cachot*.'

'I have gathered that much, Mr Dykar. What exactly is wrong with him? Has he been attacked by the other men in the *cachot*? If so I will have them severely flogged in addition to any other punishment I might award them for the disturbance they recently caused.'

'He refuses to make any complaint against them, Governor. He also refuses to allow me to carry out a full medical examination on him.'

Governor Cotgrave expelled his breath noisily in an expression of impatience.

'I am still no wiser, Mr Dykar. Will you please come to the point and tell me why I was asked to come here. What – if anything – is wrong with Mr Steiger?'

'He has been effectively castrated, Governor. It would appear that a ligature of some description was tied around the base of his testicles so tightly it prevented the flow of blood to them. As a result they have become gangrenous and died.'

'Good God!' His impatience gone, Governor Cotgrave was genuinely shocked by the surgeon's revelation. 'Who did this to him? The other prisoners in the *cachot*?'

'He refuses to say anything.' The surgeon hesitated before saying, 'I suspect he has been abused in other ways too but, as I say, he allowed me to examine the gangrenous area but refuses to allow me to carry out a full medical examination.'

Rounding on Pilgrim angrily, Governor Cotgrave said, 'Is this the type of behaviour that goes on in your own country, Lieutenant Penn?'

'I am as shocked as you are, Governor, but not entirely surprised.' He told both men something of Conrad Steiger's background history and what he knew of two of the men who had shared the *cachot* with him.

Ending his explanation, he said, 'It by no means excuses what has been done to Steiger, but I think you now know *why* it happened.'

'Why was I not told this before?' asked the angry governor. 'Had I known, this appalling incident might have been prevented.'

'I suspect it was for the same reason I was not informed Steiger was sharing the *cachot* with the others until today. Those who might have prevented it thought he was still on parole. Those who knew had been waiting for an opportunity to take their revenge on the man. Some of them have been nursing their hatred for years.'

'Nevertheless, Steiger had a number of friends among your white countrymen, Lieutenant Penn. They will not accept what has happened without taking some form of reprisal.'

'I agree wholeheartedly, Governor. What will you do?'

'I will have the white and black Americans segregated immediately. It means there will be a degree of overcrowding for a while, but they will have to put up with that.'

He glared at Lieutenant Penn. 'In future, Lieutenant, I want to be made aware of anyone, or anything like this that is likely to create trouble in my prison, do you understand?'

'Perfectly, Governor Cotgrave. Perhaps you will reciprocate by informing me immediately a United States prisoner-of-war is accused of committing an offence and thrown in the *cachot*. I believe we both have lessons to learn from this unfortunate occurrence.'

As the men exchanged angry and defiant looks, there came an urgent knocking at the door. It was thrown open before the surgeon had time to invite the visitor inside.

It was a medical orderly and he spoke breathlessly to the surgeon. 'I think you'd better come to the ward quickly, sir. It's the man who was released from the *cachot* a short time ago.'

'Steiger? What's he done now? Has he changed his mind and agreed to a medical examination?'

'No, sir, and he'll not agree to anything now. He's just been found hanging from a beam in the blanket store. He's dead, sir.'

51

News of the suicide swept through Block Four, carried on the mysterious yet remarkably efficient information network that extended to every corner of Dartmoor prison.

At first it was generally believed he had killed himself as a consequence of the charges made against him while he was on parole in Tavistock.

Not for two days did rumours begin to circulate that his death might have been precipitated by other considerations.

By this time Block Four had been cleared of those white Americans who could be given a place in the Petty Officers' Block without upsetting the Frenchmen already there.

Pilgrim had been asked by the governor to make out the list. Working swiftly, he was satisfied he had isolated the white southerners who might otherwise have stirred up serious trouble in Block Four. By so doing, he hoped to be able to maintain peace between the two American factions.

The ploy succeeded. A number of minor incidents did take place between black and white prisoners-of-war in the Block Four compound, but hardly more than was usual in a restrictive environment, where the slightest difference was likely to be magnified tenfold.

Meanwhile, the Royal Navy doctor in Plymouth had confirmed the prognosis of the surgeon called in on Virgil's behalf by Sir Thomas Tyrwhitt.

Virgil's wound required urgent treatment. Whether it was to be by a British or American surgeon was a matter for him to choose. He chose a United States surgeon and was immediately placed at the top of the list of American prisoners-of-war due for repatriation.

As a result of all that was happening, Pilgrim spent the daylight hours of three days inside Dartmoor prison. During this time he was unable to send word to Roundtor Farm of the reasons for his prolonged absence.

On the evening of the third day, Pilgrim had gone to bed early, leaving Virgil and Sophie alone in the downstairs sitting room. Sir Thomas Tyrwhitt was attending a dinner for the tenants of the Duchy of Cornwall at the inn at Two Bridges.

Pilgrim was half-asleep when there came a soft knock at his bedroom door.

'Come in!'

Pilgrim thought it must be one of the servants with a query about his proposed movements on the following day.

To his surprise, the door opened and Virgil limped into the room. 'Hello, Pilgrim. I hoped you might still be awake. I wanted you to be the first to know.'

'Know what?'

Pilgrim sat up in bed, unable to see Virgil's face because the light from the lamp in the hall was behind him.

Virgil sat on a chair close to Pilgrim's bed. 'I've just asked Sophie to marry me. I want her to come to America with me when I'm repatriated. She's said "Yes".'

The announcement took Pilgrim by surprise. He was aware that Virgil and Sophie had become very close in recent weeks, but marriage . . . !

Leaping from his bed, Pilgrim shook his friend's hand vigorously. 'Virgil . . . I don't know what to say. I'm delighted for you. Delighted for both of you. Give me a couple of minutes to get dressed and I'll come down and congratulate Sophie too. This calls for a celebration – or should we wait for Sir Thomas to come home?'

'I've already sent a servant to the inn at Two Bridges to tell him,' said Virgil, his happy smile apparent even in the dim light within the room. 'Hurry and get dressed. I'm so glad you're pleased. I was concerned you might think I was behaving foolishly. Doing all I have told you *not* to do, in fact. Not that it would have made any difference,' he added.

Ten minutes later Pilgrim was in the sitting room, raising a glass to the health of the couple. Less than an hour later Sir Thomas returned to the house and joined in the celebration.

'I find it most difficult to decide which of you is getting the better of the bargain,' he declared. He was decidedly maudlin, a result of the drink he had consumed at the Two Bridges party. 'I hope you realise what a special and resourceful young woman you are getting for your wife, Virgil? I have no intention of finding a wife for myself but, were I to do so, I would be looking for someone just like Sophie. So, if you are willing to accept the recommendation of a confirmed bachelor, you have it.'

'Thank you, Uncle. I could not have wished for a more generous blessing.'

'I mean every word of it, Sophie – and you are getting a fine man. I have no doubt he will take care of you in a manner of which I and your mother would approve.'

'Talking of mother . . . Am I required to seek her approval before marrying?'

Sir Thomas shook his head. 'You are a widow, Sophie. Your own woman. It would have been nice to be able to inform her but, as I understand it, time is crucial to your plans. Virgil will be repatriated as soon as a ship is made available. Unless the ceremony is conducted before then, there are liable to be all sorts of complications which might well prevent you travelling to America. I presume you will wish the service to be conducted by the Reverend Cotterell, at Sheepstor?'

'Yes. We both know him and we would like to be married here, on Dartmoor.'

'Splendid. I will speak to him tomorrow morning. We must have the first banns published this Sunday and the marriage can be arranged for three weeks on Monday. Would that be satisfactory for both of you?'

'That will be wonderful, Sir Thomas. Thank you very much.'

Virgil looked towards Pilgrim. 'I seem to remember telling Pilgrim he should not contemplate marriage while he was a prisoner here, in your country, Sir Thomas. I feel I ought to eat my words now. I'm also rather surprised he has not been the one to set the precedent. I was quite sure he would announce his intended marriage long before this.'

Sir Thomas looked from Virgil to Pilgrim with a puzzled expression. 'Marriage? To whom?'

'Really, Uncle, you must be the only one at Tor Royal who isn't aware of Pilgrim's feelings for that young girl who lives over at Roundtor Farm. He's been there practically every day since he was paroled to Tor Royal. Why, he even dresses like a farmhand when he's there, in a bid to impress her.' She smiled mischievously in Pilgrim's direction as she was speaking.

'Well I'm damned! – begging your pardon, Sophie. I didn't realise you were keen on young Tacy, Pilgrim. Well, you could do far worse. She's a nice young thing.'

Sir Thomas frowned. 'But on my way to Two Bridges earlier this evening I saw her in the company of one of those young Irish militia officers. They were walking across the moor driving a couple of sheep in front of them. I thought they seemed a whole lot closer than I would like a daughter of mine to be with a young man who isn't going to be around for very much longer. It was hardly the thing for a young single woman to be doing unless she had some understanding with the young man concerned. It seems you are not the only one with designs on young Tacy, Pilgrim. You might well have left things too late.'

52

Disturbed by what Sir Thomas Tyrwhitt had told him about seeing Tacy walking on the moor with a militia officer – and Pilgrim had no doubt it was Lieutenant Kennedy – he had hoped to go to the farm the following day. But it was not to be. There was still trouble inside the prison.

The potential troublemakers had been removed from Block Four, but the men moved to the Petty Officers' Block were not finding it easy to settle in. There was no one like Henri Joffre to help them and relations between the French and Americans had sunk to a low ebb within the prison.

Things were going badly for the French on the battle-fields of Europe. The French prisoners-of-war felt the United States of America should be doing much more to relieve the pressure on their troops in the Peninsula.

In truth, there was little the United States could achieve on their behalf. Their navy was tiny in comparison to the mighty fleets of the British. It consisted of no more than a few frigates, backed up by the ships manned by privateers.

The crews of these vessels fought well when the odds of battle would allow, but single ship victories would not gain them access to the high seas and permit the movement of large numbers of troops from America to Europe, even if they were available.

For the Americans in Dartmoor prison, a cause for continuing resentment was still the meagre and irregular sums of money arriving from their Government.

As a result of long internment and close proximity to their native land, it had been possible for the French to organise an increasing flow of funds for their needs. Indeed, many of the men in the Petty Officers' Block were living almost as comfortably as they would have been in their own land.

They employed servants to wait upon them and the latest fad was to bribe the guards to allow younger American prisoners out of Block Four to become personal servants to senior French officers.

Some of the captured American merchant seamen were as young as thirteen. They were eager to escape the confines of their prison block and earn more money than their Government was paying them.

The tardiness of the United States Government was bringing other problems too. Many of the Americans were of English stock. Indeed, some were first-generation Americans.

Taking advantage of both these factors, the British authorities were offering attractive incentives to any prisoners-of-war who chose to defect and serve in the British navy.

This had increased tension within the prison. Those suspected of considering changing sides were brought before a 'court' of their fellow prisoners. If found guilty, they were severely flogged.

As a result of prison grudges, many innocent men were denounced and 'tried' by their peers. Not all were acquitted by colleagues who were themselves by no means always impartial.

Pilgrim had many meetings with black and white Americans and with the governor too, in a bid to resolve the difficulties of all involved.

Walking back to Tor Royal after a particularly tense day spent trying to sort out the problems of his countrymen, Pilgrim felt that what he wanted more than anything else was to relax in the kitchen of Roundtor Farm with Tacy and forget his responsibilities for a while.

He was sorely tempted to ignore the terms of his parole and walk on to Roundtor, even if it did mean being out after dark.

Commonsense won the day. It would be too risky. One of the kitchen servants at the house had recently lost a brother off the coast of America. He had been killed in a fierce battle between HMS *Shannon*, one of the most efficient frigates in the British Navy, and the United States frigate *Chesapeake*, manned by a virtually untrained crew.

The battle had been won by *Shannon* but at a cost of eighty-three of her crew. The Tor Royal servant's brother had been one of them.

Pilgrim had expressed his sympathy to the servant, but the words of condolence had been ignored. The other servants had also known the dead sailor. There was a tense atmosphere in the Dartmoor house right now. He felt the servants would not hesitate to report him if he broke the terms of his parole.

Thinking his own thoughts, Pilgrim had reached the lane leading from Princetown to Tor Royal when a girl rose up from the long grass of the bank just ahead of him.

For a brief illogical moment, Pilgrim thought it might be Tacy.

Instead, it was Mary Gurney.

'Mary! Have you heard from Henri?' He realised this must be the reason she was here, apparently waiting for him.

'He reached home safely! A letter came during the night and he's sent presents for you and for me.'

Mary's happiness shone from her like a light. Reaching down into the long grass, she lifted a keg by one of its two rope handles. It seemed to be very heavy.

'He sent this for you.'

Pilgrim knew without removing the bung that the keg would contain a superb Cognac. He did not doubt Henri's claim that his father produced the finest Cognac in France would be proven to be quite true.

He grinned. 'I'm surprised Henri didn't bring it himself. He certainly has the nerve.'

'I wish he had,' said Mary fervently. 'But he did the next best thing. Look.'

She wore a long gold chain about her neck. Attached to it was a locket. Snapping it open with her fingers, she held it out towards Pilgrim. Inside was a miniature portrait of Henri.

'That's exquisite, Mary. Valuable, too. It's gold and pretty old. I'd say Henri has probably sent you a family heirloom. It's a very generous gift.'

Mary beamed happily. 'I thought it might be, but I'm more pleased that he put a likeness inside for me. Now, when I'm having a bad day I can always open it up and see him looking at me.'

'I'm very pleased for you, Mary, but it's no more than you deserve. Had it not been for you Henri would still be inside the prison. What does he say in his letter?'

Mary looked mildly embarrassed. 'I'm not exactly sure. It says the brandy is for you and the locket for me, but . . . I don't read very well. One of my sisters read it for me and there were lots of words she didn't understand. I have it here. Would you read it to me, please?'

She reached inside the neck of her dress and pulled out a letter, handing it to him.

Pilgrim scanned through the letter before reading it aloud to Mary. There was nothing he felt obliged to leave out. It was a warm and affectionate letter, in which Henri praised Mary for her part in his escape. The letter explained that the locket he was sending had belonged to his mother, and her mother before her.

There was much too about Henri's feelings for Mary. He ended the letter by promising to come to England to see her when the war between their countries came to an end.

By the time Pilgrim reached the end of the letter, Mary was pink with pleasure.

'There's a lot more in it than my sister read,' she said. 'Thank you, Pilgrim.' Then, hesitantly, she asked, 'Do you think he means what he says? About coming back here after the war, I mean?'

'Henri is a man of his word, Mary. If he says he'll be back, you can be assured he will. I can see you living on a French vineyard yet.'

'I'd like that,' she said, colouring up even more. 'But how about you and Tacy? I went to Roundtor Farm looking for you earlier. It was lucky I'd hidden the keg before I went up to the house. There was a militia officer there with her. I don't know what he was doing, but I didn't like him very much. I asked Tacy about you and she said she hadn't seen you for almost a week. She said she'd heard you were spending a lot of time over at Sheepstor with Reverend Cotterell's daughter.'

Pilgrim was startled. 'That's not true, Mary! Virgil's spent some time there lately – but only because he's marrying Sir Thomas's niece at Sheepstor church in a little over two weeks' time. They're planning their wedding. Whoever told her that is just mischief making.'

'I didn't think it would be true,' declared Mary. 'I told Tacy so. But I think you should get across there as quickly as you can and tell her yourself. Perhaps she'll decide to get rid of that militiaman then. I don't like any of 'em and never have, but I could dislike this one more than most if I set my mind to it.'

53

That night Pilgrim had a serious conversation with Virgil. He explained the problems he was having at the moment finding an opportunity to tell Tacy how he felt about her, and discussing the future he envisaged for them both.

Virgil listened in silence before asking, 'Just how *do* you feel about her, Pilgrim?'

'I feel about her as you do about Sophie, Virgil – but it's been with me for a whole lot longer.'

Virgil was puzzled. 'In that case, why haven't you said anything to her before this?'

'Would you have disclosed to Sophie how you felt about her if you hadn't been told you were being returned to America on the next boat?' Pilgrim countered.

Virgil frowned. 'I don't know. Probably not.'

'You know you wouldn't, and for the same reason I've said nothing to Tacy. You can see an end to your captivity now, Virgil. I can't. What would I have to offer Tacy if I told her now that I loved her and wanted to marry her? Could we set up home and live on a penny-halfpenny a day? And *where* would we live? You and I are paroled to Tor Royal, but I couldn't ask Sir Thomas to allow me to have a wife here too.'

Pilgrim began pacing the room in his frustration. 'It might be old-fashioned, but I was brought up to believe the most important thing in life was to behave honourably – especially in dealings with women. I've had little to do with them before meeting Tacy, so I can't measure my feelings for her against anyone else I've known. I only know that I want to be with her more than I've ever wanted anything. If things were different I would ask her to marry me and I'd be the happiest man in the world if she said "yes". But I can give her nothing at all right now. Rightly or wrongly, I've thought it would be better for her if I said nothing about my feelings.'

'You're an honourable man, Pilgrim. No one can find fault with that – but being honourable is one thing. Not letting Tacy know how you feel is something very different. She *needs* to know. Keep your feelings to yourself and she'll end up thinking you don't care at all. The only person likely to gain from such a situation is this militiaman, Kennedy. I don't think he deserves to be given any advantage as far as Tacy is concerned, do you?'

Pilgrim shook his head. 'That's why I wondered whether you would go to the prison tomorrow in my place. It's not going to be an easy day. Governor Cotgrave's men have "lost" three of our men. They're in the prison somewhere, I'm certain of it, but no one knows where. If you take that problem on I can go to Roundtor Farm and try to explain to Tacy how I feel about her – and why I haven't said anything before this.'

'You go and sort out your problems, Pilgrim. Leave me to deal with things at the prison. I'll take one of Sir Thomas's horses, that will be easier on my leg. But whatever you do, don't lose Tacy to this militiaman. He's no good for her and she's a very special girl. By the way, Sophie and I have already discussed the guests we are going to invite to our wedding and we'd both like Tacy to come. Before you leave in the morning I'll write out an invitation. You can take it with you. I'll leave for the prison early and then ride on to Sheepstor. There are still a great many things to be sorted out before the wedding.'

'Will you tell Sir Thomas what we're doing?'

'He's in Cornwall for a couple of days, attending a tenants' meeting. So all you have to do is go to Roundtor Farm tomorrow, sort out things with Tacy and come back here as happy a man as I am.'

By the time Pilgrim was dressed the next morning, Virgil had already left for the prison. Pilgrim had lain awake for much of the night, going over the things he intended saying to Tacy. He now felt he would be able to find the right words to tell her how he felt and explain the reasons why he had said nothing before today.

He was leaving the house when a party of men rode in through the entrance gates. They were dressed in uniforms similar to those worn by naval officers – but these were not naval men. Pilgrim felt immediately uneasy.

Riding up to the house, a man who seemed to be in charge of the party said to Pilgrim, 'From your uniform I take it you are one of the American prisoners-of-war paroled to Tor Royal? Which one are you?'

Still apprehensive, Pilgrim replied, 'Lieutenant Penn Pilgrim Penn. And you, sir?'

'Chief Officer Cunningham of His Majesty's Revenue Service. I have reason to believe you are in possession of a keg of brandy on which no Excise duty has been paid. Will you produce the keg for us, Lieutenant Penn, or shall I order my men to search the house for it?'

'That won't be necessary. I *was* given a keg of brandy a couple of days ago. Whether duty was paid on it or not, I don't know. I'll fetch it for you.'

Pilgrim did not want Sir Thomas Tyrwhitt to suffer the embarrassment of having his home searched by Revenue men. At the same time, he realised that someone in the house, one of the servants, must have informed the Revenue men about the brandy. It was probably someone who was particularly bitter about the death of the kitchen servant's brother.

'You won't mind if two of my men accompany you, Lieutenant Penn? We don't want the contents of the keg mysteriously disappearing along the way, do we?'

The keg of brandy was in Pilgrim's room. When he showed it to them it was carried triumphantly from the house by one of the two Revenue men.

The keg was examined by the Chief Officer. His examination completed, he looked triumphantly at Pilgrim. 'There are no Excise marks on this. It's almost certainly smuggled. Would you like to tell me where it came from?'

'I told you, it was a present – from a man who was once a prisoner-of-war in Dartmoor prison.'

'A Frenchman?'

Pilgrim nodded.

'Who is the man who delivered it to you?'

'He gave no name,' lied Pilgrim. He was relieved that the Revenue officer was not aware it had been given to him by a woman. 'And I had never seen him before.

I would like to add that Sir Thomas Tyrwhitt knows nothing at all of this.'

'Sir Thomas Tyrwhitt?' It seemed the Chief Revenue Officer did not recognise the name. 'Who is he?'

'He's secretary to the Prince Regent,' said Pilgrim. 'This is his house. Weren't you aware of that when you came here?'

'I'm new to these parts,' snapped the Chief Officer. 'Where is Sir Thomas Tyrwhitt now?'

'He's visiting some of the Prince Regent's tenants in Cornwall.'

'He's a very important man in these parts,' volunteered one of the Revenue men. 'He's also the Lord Warden of the Stannaries, and was once Member of Parliament for Plymouth.'

'Then he'll no doubt be pleased to learn we've rid his house of a lawbreaker,' declared the Chief Officer. 'We've got what we came here for. Let's take him off to Plymouth.'

'Wait!' Pilgrim was dismayed by the news that he was being arrested and taken away. 'Can I write a note to my commanding officer? He's in Dartmoor prison on a duty visit. I'd like to tell him what's happening.'

'Does he know anything about the brandy?'

'Nothing at all,' replied Pilgrim hurriedly. He did not want Virgil caught up in this sorry business.

'Hm! Well, yours was the only name given to me, so we'll leave him out of this, but I don't think there's any need for you to be writing notes to anyone. I'll leave word with the house servants of your whereabouts. They can tell him. Now, let's get back to Plymouth and find out whether you know more about this brandy than you've told us.'

54

Before leaving Tor Royal, Pilgrim's wrists were shackled and he was told to walk behind the lead horse and before the remainder of the mounted Revenue men.

They had almost reached the gate when there was a shrill shout behind them. It was Sophie. The Chief Revenue Officer pulled his horse to a halt and waited uncertainly as she lifted the hem of her dress clear of the ground and ran to them.

'What on earth do you think you're doing with Pilgrim?' She directed her question at the Chief Officer. 'Where are you taking him?'

'Who are you, ma'am?' The Chief Officer asked the question, aware from the manner of her dress that she was not a house servant.

'I am Sir Thomas Tyrwhitt's niece. Lieutenant Penn is a guest in my uncle's house, paroled on the express orders of the Prince Regent. Now, reply to my questions, if you please.'

Just for a moment, Pilgrim glimpsed a touch of

Winifrith in Sophie and he hoped it might have the desired effect.

'I'm sorry, ma'am.' The Chief Revenue Officer was decidedly uncomfortable, but he had no intention of backing down. 'I received information that an American prisoner-of-war staying here was in possession of brandy smuggled in from France and on which no duty had been paid. A keg of such brandy has been recovered from Lieutenant Penn's room.'

Sophie frowned. 'Is this true, Pilgrim?'

'I was sent a keg of brandy by a French friend whom I met whilst in Dartmoor prison. I had no way of knowing whether or not duty had been paid on it.'

This at least was the truth, even though he had very strong suspicions that it had not.

'There you are then,' said Sophie ambiguously. 'Why don't you go away and sort it out, leaving Pilgrim here.'

'I'm sorry, ma'am. My duty is to take him in custody to the Customs House in Plymouth.'

'That is absolutely ridiculous,' declared Sophie. 'Sir Thomas Tyrwhitt is going to be infuriated by your inflexible attitude. It may well cost you your position in the Revenue service.'

'I'm sorry, ma'am,' said the Revenue Cfficer unhappily, 'but I must carry out my duties as I see them.'

'I have never heard of anything quite so preposterous,' said Sophie in a Winifrith-like manner once more. 'Well, if you must persist in this idiotic stance, then at least allow Pilgrim to *ride* to Plymouth. I'll have one of the grooms saddle up a horse.'

'I'm sorry, ma'am, I can't guarantee the return of a horse from Plymouth . . .'

'You don't have to,' snapped Sophie. 'The groom will accompany you to Plymouth. Another will be sent to find Sir Thomas in Cornwall. He'll have something to say about this, I can assure you.'

Sophie turned and hurried away in the direction of the stables, leaving the Chief Revenue Officer, surrounded by his silent men, wondering just what manner of hornet's nest he had stirred up.

'May I ask whether the information about the keg of Cognac was given to you by one of the house servants?' asked Pilgrim. 'One of them recently lost a brother in the war. She's particularly aggrieved at having Captain Howard and myself in the house.'

'The information was received from an officer in the militia,' replied the Revenue officer. 'Where he got it from, I don't know. But it was true enough, you can't deny that. I may be new in this part of the country, but the law is the same in any part of England.'

'I'm not denying anything,' said Pilgrim amiably. 'I was given a present. I wasn't told I needed to consult a whole lot of English law books before accepting it.'

He hoped he sounded more confident than he felt about the whole business. It was possible Henri's present would put him back inside Dartmoor prison once more – or even result in him being returned to the hulks. It was a punishment that had been meted out to more than one prisoner-of-war who had been dubbed a troublemaker.

A Tor Royal horse was supplied and the journey to Plymouth was made in comparative silence, but it was far more comfortable than if Pilgrim had been made to walk. Before leaving Tor Royal Sophie had insisted that the shackles be removed from Pilgrim's wrists. The Revenue Officer agreed, but only after Pilgrim gave his word that he would not try to escape.

The headquarters of the Revenue Service was on the waterfront at Plymouth. From his high, barred window,

Pilgrim could look across the water and see the squat, ugly shapes of the prison hulks. It was a stark reminder of what might happen to him should Sir Thomas not be able to secure his release.

Pilgrim remained in the Revenue cell for two days. During this time he was frequently questioned by the Chief Revenue Officer and others, in a bid to draw from him the name of the 'man' from whom he had received the keg of Cognac.

Pilgrim's reply never varied. He declared the keg had been brought to him by a man whom he assumed to be no more than a common carrier. He repeated what he had told the Revenue Officer earlier. He was unfamiliar with British law and had no idea he was doing wrong by accepting such a gift.

He remained unmoved at threats that the militia officer involved had been asked to ascertain whether Pilgrim was known to have had other dealings with smugglers.

By the end of the second day, Pilgrim realised that his unchanging story was beginning to worry the Chief Revenue Officer. The knowledge gave him fresh hope.

At dusk that day, when Pilgrim was eating an indifferent meal, he heard voices in the corridor outside his cell. One of them was that of a woman. With a thrill of renewed hope, he recognised it as belonging to Sophie.

A key grated in the lock, the door swung open and the next moment it seemed the small cell was filled with people.

After hugging him and murmuring words of sympathy, Sophie grimaced at the plate of food he had placed on the wooden platform, the only piece of furniture in the room.

'How utterly dreadful! Poor Pilgrim. I wouldn't feed such food to a dog!'

Behind Sophie was Sir Thomas Tyrwhitt and other men who were variously introduced to Pilgrim as the Mayor of Plymouth, the Chief Collector of Customs, a deputy lieutenant of the county and Plymouth's chief magistrate.

Minutes later, Pilgrim was being led from the building. On the way he caught a brief glimpse of the man who had arrested him. The expression on his face indicated to Pilgrim that the threats made by Sophie before he was escorted from Tor Royal had not been idle ones. For a moment he allowed himself to feel sorry for the unfortunate Chief Revenue Officer.

Then he was inside Sir Thomas Tyrwhitt's carriage. He sank back against the seat, thankful that Sophie and his host had been able to rescue him from the Revenue cell.

Before the coach moved off a Revenue officer emerged from the building carrying the keg of brandy that had been the cause of all the trouble. He handed it up to the coachman to be returned to Tor Royal and to Pilgrim.

On the way back to Dartmoor, Sir Thomas questioned him about conditions in the Revenue cells and Sophie happily informed him that she and Virgil could look forward to their wedding now there was no longer a cloud over Pilgrim's future.

55

It did not take Sir Thomas Tyrwhitt very long to learn that one of his servants had reported Pilgrim for being in possession of the keg of smuggled brandy.

It was the kitchen maid whose brother had been killed on board HMS *Shannon*.

The owner of Tor Royal dismissed the girl on the spot, but when he heard of the action taken against her, Pilgrim pleaded with Sir Thomas to keep the girl on.

'She had only recently heard of the death of her brother. Knowing he had been killed by Americans it must have been very difficult for her to have to work for two of them here in your house.'

'Her brother was a sailor on board a warship. He was aware of the dangers he faced. In fact, he died winning a notable victory. I have read the newspaper reports of the battle. Her brother was one of eighty-three British casualties. Your country's ship had a hundred and forty-six before her colours were struck.'

Pilgrim was silent for some moments while he digested

this news. He had served for a while on the USS *Chesapeake* and knew many of the crew members.

'Then we have both suffered a loss,' he said. 'Nevertheless, I understand it was her only brother. You would be granting me yet another favour were you to allow her to continue working in your house.'

After giving it some thought, Sir Thomas said, 'Very well, Pilgrim, but I will give her to understand she owes her post here to you. She will also be told she cannot expect to progress beyond the kitchen while she is here. The girl will also make a personal apology to you for all the trouble she has caused.'

The arrangement suited Pilgrim. He intended asking the girl to whom she had passed on the information concerning the brandy.

It was an embarrassing and emotional meeting. The girl came to offer her apology when Pilgrim was in the drawing room with Virgil and Sophie.

Pilgrim once again commiserated with her over the loss of her brother, keenly aware she was only a young girl. When he told her the English sailor had died in the company of some very brave men, many of them Pilgrim's own friends, she burst into tears and fled from the room. He caught up with her in the passageway outside the drawing room.

'I'm sorry to have upset you, but I'd like to ask you just one question,' he said. 'Who was it you told about the keg of brandy?'

For a moment it seemed the kitchenmaid would refuse to reply, but Pilgrim said gently, 'The answer is important to me, Katie.'

Sniffling loudly, the girl said, 'I told a man I sometimes meet in Princetown. A militiaman. I didn't really tell him to get you into trouble, sir. I was upset about my brother and was telling the militiaman that while he was getting himself killed by Americans, you was here drinking brandy brought in for you by smugglers. That's all it was. He said he would tell one of his officers, to see what could be done about it. I don't know which one it was though and I don't think I can find out. We . . . we're not friends any more.'

'Thank you, Katie.' Pilgrim thought he could guess the name of the officer. 'I'm glad we've got things sorted out between us and that you still have your work here. You can go now.'

Dropping him an awkward curtsy, the young servant girl fled in the direction of the kitchen.

'So you think it was a militia officer who reported you to the Revenue men?'

The drawing room door had been left open and Sophie put the question to Pilgrim when he returned to the room.

'I'm certain of it. The Chief Revenue Officer said so when he was questioning me.'

'Oh dear! Had I known I would never have invited the militia officers from Princetown to the wedding celebrations. It would be difficult to withdraw the invitations now.'

'Don't worry about it,' said Pilgrim casually. 'I'll probably have it sorted out before then.'

That afternoon, Pilgrim made his way to Roundtor Farm. It seemed a very long time since he was last there. Others thought the same.

Entering the kitchen, he found Joan Elford hard at work, baking. A delicious smell of pastry and cooked apples permeated the air in the spacious room.

Close to the fire, Tom Elford sat in a high-backed wooden rocking chair, eyes half closed. He looked both tired and ill.

'Well! Look who's paying us a call,' said the farmer's wife. 'We're honoured, young man. We didn't expect to see you at Roundtor again. We all thought you were moving among the county's high society now.'

'Not unless the county's society divide their time between Dartmoor prison and the Revenue gaol in Plymouth. That's where I've been.'

Brushing back a lock of hair that kept breaking free and dangling in front of her face, Joan looked at him in disbelief. 'Are you saying you've been locked up in a Plymouth cell?'

'Only for the last two days. Before then I was kept busy at the prison. There was some serious trouble involving our prisoners-of-war. Virgil is being sent back to America for treatment to his leg wound and he wants me to take over from him. It means I'm going to have to spend more time there, I'm afraid.'

'You can tell us all about that later, but what's this about you being locked up in the Revenue cells?'

Pilgrim told her of the happenings of the past couple of days and Tom Elford kept his eyes open for long enough to say, 'Well, I'll be blowed! What goings on!' at the end of the story.

'I feel sorry for young Katie up at Tor Royal,' said Joan. 'She and her brother were very close, but there was no need for her to do what she did. That was downright spiteful.'

'I'm surprised that young militia officer who's been seeing so much of Tacy never said anything about it,' said Tom Elford, pushing back on his chair and setting it rocking gently.

'I'm not,' said his wife with considerable feeling. 'Even if he knew about it he wouldn't have said anything that might make our Tacy feel any sympathy for Pilgrim. In fact, I wouldn't be at all surprised to learn he had something to do with reporting the whole business to the Revenue men.'

'Neither would I,' agreed Pilgrim. 'There was certainly a militia officer involved.'

'Then it was probably him,' declared Joan firmly. 'I wouldn't trust him an inch farther than I could throw him.'

Briskly dusting the flour from her arms, she said, 'You keep an eye on those cakes for me, Tom. Don't let 'em burn. I'm going across to the dairy to fetch in some more milk.'

'I'll go,' volunteered Pilgrim.

'I doubt if you'd find anything,' she said. 'We've shifted things around a bit since you were last here. Mind you, if you've come to help there are one or two things you could be doing. Come along, I'll show you.'

As they stepped outside the door into the farmyard, Pilgrim asked, 'Where's Tacy right now?'

'She's up at the prison market, selling cakes. Tom's having another of his bad times. We need to get some money put by for the winter in case he doesn't get any better.'

After murmuring a few words of sympathy, Pilgrim said, 'I hoped I might see Tacy at the market when I was spending so much time at the prison. I really couldn't get away, you know. It might have been different if the terms of my parole didn't mean I had to be in Tor Royal after dark. But, as was proved by the incident with the Revenue men, I need to abide by the rules. Not all the servants there are happy about having Americans staying in the house. It only needs a word in the right place to have my parole revoked. I can't expect Sir Thomas to keep getting me out of trouble.'

'When we were in the kitchen I had the impression you knew it was Lieutenant Alan Kennedy?'

'I haven't been able to prove it,' admitted Pilgrim, 'but he's the one I strongly suspect.'

'You're probably right,' agreed the farmer's wife. 'He's spending far too much time with our Tacy these days. I don't like it. I don't like it one little bit.'

They had reached the dairy now. When they entered its cool interior, Pilgrim looked about him. Everything seemed to be in the same place as when he was last here. He looked at his companion questioningly.

She did not seem in the least bit embarrassed. 'I wanted to get you away from the house to have a talk to you, out of Tom's hearing. To tell you the truth, I'm worried about this Lieutenant Kennedy and the way he's running after Tacy. He doesn't always come to the farm first, as you do. I suspect he watches the farm to see when she goes off on her own. Then he'll meet up with her, pretending it's by accident. I don't believe it is. I've taken to sending Johanna or Emma out with her whenever she leaves the house, to try to make certain she's not on her own when she meets up with him. The trouble is I can't watch her all hours of the day and night. Besides, having two people doing the work of one all the time and with Tom so ill, it means things aren't getting done about the house. To make things worse, Billy's ma is ill again. He and Emma are staying over there for a while.'

Taking a jug of milk from a wooden bucket, Joan Elford reached up on a shelf and took down a large pat of butter. 'I'll be perfectly honest with you, Pilgrim. When you first started coming to Roundtor I had my doubts about you and Tacy. I could see no future for her, but give you your due, you've always behaved like a gentleman and I've come to trust you. That's more than I can say for Kennedy. I can't bring myself to like him. I really don't know what Tacy sees in him, unless it's because she believes you're cooling off and don't *want* to come here quite as often as you once did. I probably shouldn't be telling you this, but I'm doing it because I'm worried about Kennedy, and because I trust you. Our Tacy cares very much for you. I think she's hurt because you don't seem to feel the same about her.'

'But I *do*, Mrs Elford,' said Pilgrim unhappily. 'I always have.'

Arriving at a sudden decision, he took a deep breath and said, 'You've trusted me with your thoughts, so I'll do the same with you. You tell me I've behaved like a "gentleman" and that's what I've tried to do. Now I think I've probably behaved *too* honourably. I did so because I didn't want to take Tacy into a relationship that could go nowhere. I'm a prisoner-of-war. I can't ask Tacy to marry me because I can't afford to keep her on the money my Government is allowing me and if I do anything wrong, no matter how minor, I'm liable to be thrown back into prison.'

Pilgrim shrugged. 'At least, that's the way I've *been* feeling, until lately. When I was last here Emma told me that if I wasn't careful I'd lose Tacy to Lieutenant Kennedy. That got me to thinking about things. When Virgil announced that he was going to marry Sophie, Sir Thomas's niece, and take her back to America with him I made up my mind to say something to Tacy. I don't want her to think I don't really care for her. I do. I've decided to explain to her why I haven't done anything about it before. Then she'd at least know the way I feel and we can talk about things.'

Pilgrim shrugged despairingly. 'That's what I was planning to do the morning the Revenue men arrested me. I felt that if only we could talk about it we'd be able to work out a solution. I intended speaking to her first, to see how she felt, then to you and Mr Elford. Well, now I've done things the wrong way round, but at least *you* know the way *I* feel. If you're unhappy about it I'll need to think of something else. But I *do* want to marry Tacy one day and take her back to America with me. She'd have a good life there, I promise you.'

Joan looked at Pilgrim with a strange mixture of expressions fighting for control of her face. Suddenly, she stepped forward and wrapped her arms about him to give him a fierce hug.

'You're a good man, Pilgrim. You're all I've ever hoped for as a husband for our Tacy.'

Stepping back from him, she beamed at him in tearful happiness. 'You know, when Tacy first told me about you, I thought my world was about to collapse about my ears. Yet, right now, I can't think of anyone I would rather put my trust in. You and Tacy had something very special when you first met. I realised it and it frightened me. What she felt then is still there, of that I'm certain. We just need to do something to remind *her* of it.'

56

Pilgrim saw the Elford pony and cart before he was halfway between Roundtor Farm and Dartmoor prison. Lieutenant Kennedy, leading his horse, was walking beside Tacy. Johanna was on her other side.

When she saw him, the youngest member of the Elford family waved gaily and ran towards him, throwing herself at him when they met.

'Pilgrim! Where have you been? We were beginning to think we weren't going to see you again. I've missed you.'

Swinging her off the ground, Pilgrim said, 'I've missed you too, Johanna – and I swear you've grown since I last saw you.'

As he set the young girl on the ground once more, Pilgrim was looking at Tacy and Lieutenant Kennedy as they came closer. He was unable to read Tacy's expression, but Lieutenant Kennedy's feelings were plain enough. They showed in his scowl.

With Johanna holding his hand, he advanced to meet them. Pointedly ignoring the militiaman, he said, 'Hello,

Tacy. It seems a long time since we met. I've missed you.'

'Really? I thought you would have been so busy over at the Sheepstor vicarage that you wouldn't have any time to think about us at Roundtor.'

Tacy's manner was stiff and cool. Frowning, Pilgrim asked, 'What makes you think I've spent any time at Sheepstor?'

'Are you saying you *haven't* been there?' Tacy countered.

'That's exactly what I'm saying.'

Pilgrim glanced briefly at Lieutenant Kennedy before saying, 'I don't know where your information has come from, but it seems I've been confused with Virgil. He's spent some time there, making arrangements for his marriage to Sophie.'

'Oh!' It was apparent the news came as a surprise to her.

She too glanced at Lieutenant Kennedy before asking, 'If you haven't been to Sheepstor, where *have* you been? Not that there's any reason why you should spend all your time at Roundtor,' she added hastily. 'You can please yourself what you do.'

'Unfortunately, I *can't*,' said Pilgrim. 'I'm a prisoner-of-war. When Virgil leaves I'll be the senior American officer on Dartmoor. It means I now have a lot more to do in the prison. That's where I've been for much of the time I would like to have spent at Roundtor, as Lieutenant Kennedy would no doubt have told you, had you asked him. He knows all about the trouble they've had inside the prison.'

Once again Tacy glanced at the militia officer, but he was looking at Pilgrim impassively.

'I also have a great many rules I must obey while I'm on parole,' continued Pilgrim. 'I must never forget

I'm an enemy in your country. If I do, there's always someone ready to remind me. That's why I've spent the last couple of days locked up in a cell in the Revenue building in Plymouth. Someone reported that I'd been given a keg of Cognac on which no duty had been paid. I'm quite sure Lieutenant Kennedy could have told you about that too.'

'What are you insinuating, Penn? That I had something to do with your arrest?'

'Are you telling me you didn't?'

Lieutenant Kennedy glared at Pilgrim for some moments, before his glance slipped away. When he spoke again, it was to Tacy.

'I think that for some reason Lieutenant Penn is determined to be offensive and provocative, Tacy. Rather than remain here and cause you embarrassment I will return to Princetown. No doubt he and I will meet elsewhere to discuss whatever is troubling him. In the meantime, I trust you will allow me to see you again?'

'Of course. I look forward to it.'

As the militiaman rode away, Tacy swung around to confront Pilgrim. There was nothing in her expression to suggest Joan Elford's assumption that her daughter was in love with him.

'Do you have any proof that Alan had you arrested by the Revenue men?'

'I know it was a militia officer. Had it been anyone else I feel sure Lieutenant Kennedy would have told you about it. He was quick enough to have you believe I was visiting the Sheepstor vicarage.'

'I'm not so certain he did. He might just have said that one of you from Tor Royal was spending a lot of time at Sheepstor. I probably assumed it was you.'

'Why should you do that?'

Tacy shrugged. 'Well, you haven't been here for some

time and we've heard nothing from you. I thought you must be going there instead. Anyway, you had no right to be rude to Alan the way you were. I want you to apologise to him the next time you meet him.'

'Apologise?' Pilgrim looked at her in angry disbelief. 'He had me arrested and has tried to poison your mind against me and you want *me* to apologise to *him*?'

'You don't know any of those things for certain. You just said so yourself. You have no right to be so rude to one of my friends.'

'Oh! So he's a friend now, is he?'

Pilgrim was confused and not a little hurt that she was taking Lieutenant Kennedy's side against him.

'He's not *my* friend. I like Pilgrim much better.' The support came from Johanna who had taken Pilgrim's hand once more.

'No one's asking your opinion,' said Tacy.

She was almost as confused as was Pilgrim. She did not really know why she was so angry with him. She had been delighted when she saw him coming across the moor to meet her just now. But it had all gone terribly wrong.

She was not even very fond of Lieutenant Kennedy herself. Yet somehow she had managed to back herself into a corner on his behalf and she could see no way out. Instead, she lashed out verbally at Pilgrim once more.

'Are you going to apologise to him?' she demanded to know.

Pilgrim was hurt by her attitude, but he could not back down now. 'No. I know I'm right about him. But, please . . . can't we forget all about him for a while. I came to meet you because I want to talk to you.'

Jerking the reins of the pony she was leading, she startled the animal into faster movement, the small cart jolting over the rough ground behind him.

'When you're ready to apologise to Alan for being rude to him you can come and tell me what it is you have to say. Until then we don't have anything to say to each other.'

Tacy began running and the pony ran with her. She left Pilgrim standing with Johanna, staring after her in dismay.

Yet, had she looked back, it was doubtful whether Tacy would have seen him clearly. She had missed Pilgrim very much indeed for more than a week and had been terribly hurt when she believed he was going to the Sheepstor vicarage to see Jemima Cotterell. Now, when he had returned with a very good reason for not coming to Roundtor she had driven him away. *Deliberately* driven him away.

Tacy stumbled on a tuft of coarse grass and angrily cuffed away the tears that had prevented her from seeing the obstacle.

At that moment she felt that the bottom had dropped out of her whole world.

From a window, Joan saw Tacy leading the pony and cart towards the farmhouse. Johanna was some distance behind, hurrying across the moor after her.

She reached the gate to the farmyard at the same time as her elder daughter and opened it for her. 'Haven't you seen Pilgrim? He was here earlier but left to go and meet you.'

'Yes, we saw him.'

'Then . . . why isn't he with you now? There was something he wanted to talk about with you. I've been looking out for you to return so you and he could talk without having Johanna listening to everything that was being said.'

Johanna reached them in time to hear the last part of

what her mother said. As Tacy backed the pony and cart inside the cart shed, the younger girl said, 'You're too late. Pilgrim spoke to Tacy, but she sent him packing.'

'It wasn't me he was talking to,' retorted Tacy. 'It was Alan. Pilgrim accused him of all sorts of things but didn't have any proof for any of them.'

'You mean the business of him being arrested by the Revenue men? I don't think there can be any doubt about Alan Kennedy's involvement in that.'

'He told Lieutenant Kennedy off for telling Tacy he'd been seeing that girl over at the Sheepstor vicarage, when he hadn't,' said Johanna.

'He was very rude to Alan,' persisted Tacy. 'And he wouldn't apologise. I said I didn't want to talk to him until he did. Anyway, I don't want to talk about it.'

'I like Pilgrim better than that militia officer,' said Johanna positively. 'He gives me the creeps.'

'You should at least have listened to what Pilgrim had to say,' said her mother. 'You and he have been good friends for a long time.'

'I've said I don't want to talk about him, haven't I?' said Tacy. 'If you two want to, then you can do it while you're putting the pony away. I'm going into the house.'

With this, she turned about and hurried away.

'Aren't you going to make her come back and finish what she's supposed to be doing?' asked Johanna spitefully.

'No, you can do it,' said her mother. 'I think it'll be best if we leave her alone to think her own thoughts for a while.'

'That's not fair,' complained Johanna as her mother walked thoughtfully towards the farmhouse. 'I suppose if she starts crying again she'll be let off doing any more work today.'

'Crying *again*?' Joan turned back towards Johanna.

'That's why she was hurrying home in front of me after Lieutenant Kennedy had gone off and she'd had words with Pilgrim. She thought I wouldn't see, but I did. I don't know which of 'em she was crying for, though.'

Walking slowly back to the house, Joan hoped Tacy had been shedding tears for Pilgrim. If so, there was hope for her. If the tears were for Lieutenant Kennedy . . . ?

It was a possibility she did not want to consider.

57

'What do you think we ought to do about Tacy's invitation?'

Sophie put the question to Virgil as they sat in Sir Thomas's study, writing out wedding invitations.

'We've sent it off to her, we'll just have to hope she'll come.'

'But Pilgrim hasn't been to see her for almost two weeks now. It seems that whatever there might have been between them is over.'

'I don't believe that,' said Virgil, as he carefully placed the page he had just written on the desk in front of him, to allow the ink to dry. 'They've had some sort of a falling-out, that's all. I believe Lieutenant Kennedy had something to do with it. It will blow over. Pilgrim is already more of a man than Kennedy will ever be. Tacy will see it for herself, if she hasn't already. She's a sensible girl. Anyway, the invitation is from us to one of our guests. She was the first person I knew here and she was very kind to Pilgrim and myself in those early days.'

'Do you think it will be all right, having Tacy, Pilgrim and Lieutenant Kennedy there together?'

'It's an excellent opportunity for Tacy to compare her suitors. I know who'll come out best from the comparison.'

'I hope you're right, Virgil. I don't want anything to happen that might mar the day for us.'

Rising from his seat at the desk, Virgil crossed the room and embraced his bride-to-be. 'Nothing's going to spoil the day. It will be the first of many happy and memorable days for both of us. You just wait and see.'

The threat to the wedding plans of Virgil and Sophie came not from the triangle of Pilgrim, Tacy and Lieutenant Kennedy – but from Winifrith, Sophie's mother.

The two Americans, Sophie and Sir Thomas were in the Tor Royal dining room, enjoying a pleasant dinner, when they heard the sound of a loud voice in the hall.

'I *thought* I heard a carriage a few moments ago,' said Sir Thomas. 'It would seem we have unexpected visitors.'

He dabbed the corners of his mouth with his napkin and had half-risen to his feet when the door was flung open and Winifrith swept into the room, the Tor Royal butler hesitating uncertainly in the doorway.

'Good God!' Sir Thomas sat down again, heavily. 'It's you!'

'That's right, it's *me*!' confirmed the knight's sister. 'And while I've been risking my life gallivanting half-way around the world, *you* . . .' She jabbed a forefinger in a sword-thrust at Sophie. '. . . You are sitting here as though butter wouldn't melt in your mouth. What sort of a daughter is it who makes her mother chase all over Europe looking for her?'

'I don't think I ever suggested you should chase

around Europe looking for me.' After a distressed glance at Virgil, Sophie regained much of her composure. She replied to her mother in a deceptively mild manner.

'You know exactly what I am talking about, young lady, so don't adopt that innocent attitude with me. I have suffered far too much already because of you. I'll take no more of your nonsense.'

Looking about the table, she glared at each of the Americans in turn before saying, 'I've no doubt you were encouraged in your wilfulness by those no one would expect to know any better. I've had a great deal of time to think about things on my way home in an absolutely disgusting ship. We'll return to London and not visit Tor Royal again until this war is over and those who have fought against us have gone home, where they belong.'

'*We* are going nowhere, Mother. At least, not together . . .'

'That's quite enough from you, Sophie! Your defiance comes as no surprise to me. No surprise at all, but we'll pursue it in the morning. I have had a dreadful time. All I want now is a drink, some food, then a good night's sleep.'

'Really, Winifrith, I find your whole attitude wholly incomprehensible.'

The usually mild-mannered owner of Tor Royal was as angry as the others had ever seen him as he rose to his feet and confronted his sister.

'After suffering the tragedy of having her husband killed on the battlefield, Sophie had to find her own way home to us. Yet all you are apparently concerned about is the slight to your authority. No words of affection for your daughter. No joy that she is safe. Dammit, Winifrith, you have always been selfish and overbearing, but I find your behaviour at this moment quite unbelievable!'

'You haven't had to suffer the indignities and discomforts I've known these past weeks . . . but we'll discuss this in the morning . . .'

'We'll discuss it now, Mrs Cudmore. There are a few things you should perhaps think about in the privacy of your room.'

Virgil's words were spoken quietly and politely, but for a moment Pilgrim thought Winifrith was about to suffer an attack of apoplexy.

'How *dare* you speak to me in such a manner! This is a family matter. Nothing at all to do with you . . .'

'It has a great deal to do with me,' said Virgil firmly. 'Sophie and I are to be married next Monday and we will be leaving for America at the end of the week.'

For a few moments, Winifrith stood with her mouth opening and closing soundlessly, reminding Pilgrim of a landed fish. Then she reached out, pulled a chair away from the table and sat upon it – but only for a few moments.

Leaping to her feet once again, she said, 'This is absolute nonsense. There will be no wedding. You do not have my permission.'

'That did not stop me before. It will certainly not stop me this time,' said Sophie. 'Besides, your permission is neither needed nor asked for. I am not an underage daughter, but a widow who has passed the age when parental consent is needed. You are welcome to attend the wedding, but it *will* go ahead, whether you are there or not.'

Winifrith sat down once more and this time she remained seated. 'I never thought I would live to see the day when my daughter would show such ingratitude to her mother – and after all I have suffered on your behalf! You have not heard the last of this, my girl. As for coming to America with you . . . !'

'No one has asked you to come to America, Mother – and no one will. In fact, were you to come to America I would persuade Virgil to take me to Africa, or Europe, or any place where you *weren't*.'

Sophie rose to her feet abruptly and inclined her head to her fellow diners. 'I'm sorry, Uncle, Virgil, Pilgrim, but I am no longer hungry. As Mother said, we should have saved this conversation for the morning. I am retiring now. Good night.'

Sophie left the room, followed immediately by Virgil.

Pouring a very large brandy from a decanter standing on a nearby sideboard, Sir Thomas carried it to his sister.

'You will be in need of this, Winifrith. You have just lost a very important battle. I fear that unless you have a radical change of attitude you may also lose your daughter. Think of what I have said, Winifrith. No! It is far more important that you think of what *Sophie* has said. Come, Pilgrim. We will go and arrange for Winifrith's luggage to be taken to her room.'

58

'Are you quite sure this frock looks all right, Ma? It's not cut too low at the front?'

'It looks absolutely beautiful, Tacy, and so do you, girl.'

Tom Elford answered his daughter's question in a voice that was as tired as the man, but he managed a wan smile for her.

It was the day of the wedding of Virgil and Sophie. The whole of the Elford family was assembled in the kitchen. Tacy was dressed in a brand-new gingham dress. It had been made especially for the occasion by one of the moorland's itinerant tailors. But now she seemed suddenly reluctant to leave the house.

In truth, she had not been enthusiastic about accepting the invitation to the ceremony and the reception which was to take place at Tor Royal afterwards. It was an afternoon wedding and meant she would be walking back across the moor in the dark. At least this was one excuse she put forward for suggesting she should decline the invitation.

Her mother used all her persuasive powers in order to make Tacy change her mind. She pointed out that it was a rare honour to be invited to a reception at Tor Royal; one that had never before come the way of anyone in the Elford family.

'I'm still not certain I want to go . . .'

'You must, Tacy. It's an experience that'll likely come only once in a lifetime.'

'All right, then I suppose I need to be on my way. I only hope it doesn't rain again, that's all.'

Tacy was to walk to Tor Royal. It had been arranged she would travel in a carriage from there to the church at Sheepstor. When the service was over she would return in the same carriage for the wedding reception which was being held at Sir Thomas Tyrwhitt's house.

As Tacy adjusted a shawl about her shoulders, Joan Elford said, 'Have a wonderful time, Tacy. You'll be the loveliest girl there, I'm certain of it.'

With a doubtful smile, Tacy left the farmhouse and struck out across the moor.

She looked back once and waved to the family who were standing in the doorway of the kitchen. Her father was with them, supported by the arm of her mother. His condition was a growing worry to the whole family.

But this was not a day for thinking of such things. She walked briskly, holding the hem of her dress clear of the wet ground. She had not gone very far before becoming aware that the wet from the grass was soaking through the satin shoes her mother had produced from a trunk in her bedroom.

They were beautiful shoes, but totally impractical for walking across the moor. After confirming she was out of sight of those in the farmhouse kitchen, Tacy paused and removed the shoes. She would go barefooted until she reached Tor Royal.

Tacy was proud of her new dress. It was the only item of clothing she had ever possessed that had been especially tailored for her. The pale blue of the patterned material suited her colouring and she thought it the most beautiful dress she had ever seen.

Until she reached Tor Royal.

Her wet shoes now back on her feet, Tacy was shown into a room occupied by men and women from Sir Thomas Tyrwhitt's circle of friends. These women were dressed in expensive gowns of satin, cut in the latest fashion. They also wore fur-trimmed coats and every one of them had on a hat.

Tacy had anguished over the only three hats owned by the Elford family, deciding eventually to go bare-headed. It was a mistake among this company.

She realised people were staring at her. The polite ones looked once and quickly looked away again. Others stared at her for longer.

Suddenly, she was confronted by Winifrith, who was as overdressed for the occasion as Tacy was under-dressed.

'Who are you, girl? What are you doing here?'

Before Tacy could reply, she was rescued by Sir Thomas Tyrwhitt.

'Tacy, how delightful to see you – and how wonderful you look. Winifrith, this is Tacy, the daughter of Tom Elford who farms Roundtor. She has been a very good friend to Virgil and Pilgrim.'

Leading Tacy skilfully away from his vitriolic sister, he said, 'Come and meet Doctor Dykar and his wife. You may have already met them at the prison. I'm sorry neither Virgil nor Pilgrim is here to greet you, but they have already left for the church. Pilgrim is acting as Virgil's groomsman. My duty is to give Sophie away – and I'm as nervous as a young boy! Here we are.

Mr Dykar, Mrs Dykar . . . this is young Tacy Elford, a member of one of the oldest moorland families. I'm quite certain she will be able to answer any question you might have about Dartmoor. Do enjoy yourself, my dear.'

For some twenty minutes Tacy remained in conversation with the Dykars. She found it somewhat hard going. It was a relief when a servant entered the room and announced that the carriages were ready to take them all to Sheepstor.

Tacy entered a carriage with the Dykars and a number of other guests but she was not expected to make conversation with them. The state of the moorland roads precluded normal conversation.

At the church, in the crowded pews, Tacy was more aware than ever that the dress she had thought to be so wonderful when she left Roundtor Farm did not stand comparison with those worn by the other women guests. Soon she came to believe that everyone who so much as glanced in her direction was thinking the same.

One of the congregation standing not very far from her was Lieutenant Alan Kennedy. She felt certain he must have seen her but he made no acknowledgement of the fact.

Once the bride entered the church on the arm of her uncle, Tacy forgot all else. Sophie wore an embroidered wedding dress of cream batiste and carried a posy of pink and cream roses.

Stepping out to join her from the front pew, Virgil wore the full dress uniform of a captain of the United States Marine Corps, as did Pilgrim, who stood beside him. Both uniforms had been made at Tor Royal by a tailor brought in from the garrison at Plymouth.

It was a brief but moving ceremony and as Tacy

watched Sophie walking along the aisle to the church door, on the arm of her new husband, she thought she had seldom seen a woman looking so happy.

When the guests left the church, the carriages were waiting. Rather than push herself forward, Tacy waited for everyone else to board first. As Winifrith seemed to be involved in a self-imposed task of seeing people safely on board, she too was one of the last left standing outside the church.

When it seemed too late to do anything else, Tacy realised she would be obliged to share a coach with Sophie's mother. The thought of it terrified her!

Suddenly a coach that was already moving off was brought to a halt. The door swung open and Pilgrim said, 'Here, Tacy. There's room for one more in here.'

Pilgrim had not been to Roundtor since he and Tacy had argued about the apology she felt was due to Alan Kennedy. For just a moment she hesitated. Then, behind her Winifrith shouted to the driver of the stationary coach to move off and allow the vehicles behind to get on their way.

She hesitated no longer. Putting one foot on the step, she allowed herself to be hauled by Pilgrim inside the carriage.

59

The return journey to Tor Royal in the carriage was no more comfortable than the outward one had been. Conversation was almost impossible and Pilgrim had not been telling the truth when he said there was room for her inside the carriage.

The passengers on the seat where she sat next to him were crammed uncomfortably close together and she was aware of his closeness to her.

Soon after the carriage got underway Pilgrim leaned towards her and she thought he was telling her that he liked her dress. She could not be certain because at that moment the coachman whipped up the horses until the coach was jolting along the uneven road at what felt like a breakneck speed.

Eventually they arrived at Sir Thomas's home and Tacy enjoyed a few moments' malicious pleasure when she looked at the two other girls who had been in the carriage with her. They were by no means as elegant as when they set out. Their ornate hats were askew, the feathers of one decidedly ruffled. Their hair, which had begun the journey pinned up in elaborate hairstyles, needed urgent attention.

Tacy's long hair, on the other hand, had been brushed back and tied behind her neck. It still looked almost as neat as when she had boarded the carriage.

Pilgrim handed Tacy down and as they walked together towards the house, he said, 'Tacy? Can we be friends again?'

The delight she felt should have provided him with the answer he wanted, but before she could speak, Sir Thomas hurried from the house. 'Ah, there you are, Pilgrim! You should have been on the first carriage. Pardon me for taking him off like this, Tacy, but, as Virgil's groomsman, there are one or two duties Pilgrim needs to perform.'

As he hurried Pilgrim away, he was saying, 'I trust you have a speech ready and that things go to plan now, Pilgrim. It seems Winifrith has taken a hand and suddenly order has become chaos . . . !'

From the moment Pilgrim left her side, things went from bad to worse for Tacy. Sophie greeted her warmly enough, but Winifrith displayed great rudeness by hurrying Tacy on in order to introduce some of the more influential guests.

When the guests sat down for a formal meal, Tacy's embarrassment became a nightmare. There were so many knives, forks, spoons and glasses she had no idea where to begin.

She tried following what others were doing, but even here she made mistakes. She managed to drop a knife on the floor and bump heads with one of the servants when she tried to retrieve it. Then she was shaking with nervousness to such an extent, she dropped a spoonful of soup on her dress.

'Oh, you poor dear!' said a lady seated on Tacy's left,

extremely loudly. 'But, of course, that's why we have table napkins.'

Removing the item in question from a silver ring beside Tacy's plate, she shook it out and dropped it on her lap. On the far side of the table a young girl wearing an expensive dress of dark green silk tittered, only to be elbowed into silence by a stern-faced woman beside her.

Tacy spent most of the meal with her eyes cast down upon her plate, only the high colour of her cheeks revealing her acute embarrassment.

The meal seemed to go on for ever, but finally port began to circulate around the table and the speeches began. It seemed everyone had something to say about either bride or groom. Pilgrim, Virgil and Sir Thomas all spoke.

Then Winifrith wanted to say something. She had been drinking heavily and her cheeks were as flushed as Tacy's. She was eventually persuaded by Sir Thomas to make her speech to the newly married couple in private, later in the evening.

The speeches over, everyone left the dining room and made their way to the candle-lit terrace. A canvas canopy had been set up here. With the adjacent drawing room, it would provide an area for socialising and dancing.

Twice on the way from the dining room Tacy had passed within touching distance of Alan Kennedy. On each occasion he had carefully averted his glance, pretending to be in deep conversation with his companion of the moment.

Pilgrim had smiled in her direction once, but Sir Thomas was holding a deep conversation with him. Tacy thought that now would be a good opportunity for her to slip away unnoticed and return to Roundtor Farm.

She succeeded in finding a servant and asked her to locate her shawl. In order that she might leave quietly, she told the girl to bring it to her outside the main door of the house.

When she had it, Tacy slipped quietly away into the darkness. She looked back only once, when the small orchestra struck up a tune for the dancers.

The house was bathed in light, and lanterns shone out from every window. In any other circumstances it was a sight she would have viewed with delight. But she had just spent a miserable couple of hours during which she had become increasingly aware she did not belong among those who frequented houses like Tor Royal.

The knowledge carried much wider implications too. Pilgrim was at home in such company. That had been perfectly obvious to her. Perhaps it was this which hurt most of all. The confirmation that they belonged in different worlds.

As she left the grounds of Tor Royal behind, Tacy thought she heard sounds close behind her. At first she believed it must be her imagination. When she heard it again, she decided it must be a sheep, or perhaps one of the moorland ponies.

Walking steadily down the hill from Sir Thomas's house she reached a stream in the valley bottom. Here she paused for a moment and listened again. There was a sound as though someone or something had stumbled – then she heard a muffled curse.

'Who's that? Who's there?'

'It's all right, Tacy. It's me. Alan.'

The slurring of his words might have been because he was out of breath. Tacy thought it was more likely a result of the amount of drink she had seen him consuming at the dining table and afterwards.

'It's not all right. Why are you following me?'

Lieutenant Kennedy took shadowy form in front of her, breathing heavily. 'I saw you leave and as I hadn't had an opportunity to talk to you during the wedding reception, I came after you.'

'You had plenty of opportunity to talk to me, had you wanted to, but you didn't. Why, Alan? Was it because you didn't want your grand friends to see you talking to a farm girl? Is that why you wouldn't talk to me at Tor Royal?'

'It wasn't like that at all, Tacy. You and I are friends. I'll walk home with you.'

'No you won't. You've had so much to drink you'd end up hopelessly lost on the moor.'

'Then let's stay here for a while. This is the first time you and I have been able to meet without having someone else spying on us. Let's make the most of it.'

He moved closer to her and she could smell the brandy on his breath.

'Go back to Tor Royal, Alan. I'm going home.'

As she turned away, he reached out and grabbed her arm. 'Don't play hard to get with me, Tacy. You've enjoyed yourself these past few weeks haven't you, leading me on the way you have? Now it's my turn to enjoy myself – and it's no good playing the outraged little virgin with me. I know what you've been up to with that American – with many others too, I've no doubt. Come on, it's time to stop playing games with me.'

He had a painful grip on her arm and now he pulled her towards him, clumsily attempting to lift the skirt of her dress with his free hand.

'Let me go! You're hurting me.'

Tacy struggled to break free. She had been holding her soft shoes, now she dropped them and began pummelling the Irish militiaman. As she did so they both stumbled momentarily and one of her feet slipped into the brook.

'Stop struggling! Stop it, I tell you!'

Suddenly, he ceased fumbling with her skirt and swung his arm. The flat of his hand exploded against the side of her face and she was momentarily dazed. Her foot turned on a smooth stone and she slipped, to lie half in and half out of the stream.

Kennedy went with her. Kneeling in the water, he dragged her to the grass of the bank. His hand went inside the top of her dress and, struggling furiously once more, she screamed.

Suddenly, he was pulled bodily from her.

'What the . . . ?' The remainder of the question was lost as the militiaman's head was thrust into the water of the stream.

'Perhaps this will cool your ardour.'

It was Pilgrim! As Tacy sat on the bank, pulling her dress up about her shoulders, there was a desperate thrashing of limbs in the water and a spluttered, 'Help!' before the sound ended in a frightening gurgle.

As the sounds of the struggling grew feebler, Tacy cried out in alarm, 'Don't drown him.'

'Why? Do you still care for him, after what he tried to do?'

'I don't care what happens to *him*. I'm thinking of what they'll do to you if he dies.'

'In that case we'll let him up.'

Pilgrim released his hold on Kennedy's hair and rose to his feet. The militiaman's head rose above the surface of the water. Choking and retching, he dragged himself to the far bank of the stream. He lay here alternately choking and noisily sucking in great gulps of air.

'Are you all right?' Filled with concern, Pilgrim dropped down beside Tacy, who was on her hands and knees.

'I've lost my shoes. They belong to Ma.'

'She'll understand. You're more important than shoes. I'll come down here and find them in the morning. Right now I'll see you safely home.'

He lifted her to her feet and she said, 'You're soaking wet. You should go home and change or you'll catch a chill.'

'Not tonight, I won't. There are things I want to say to you, Tacy. Things that should have been said a long while ago.'

As they walked away, Lieutenant Alan Kennedy began coughing painfully. Turning her head, Tacy said, 'What about him?'

'He'll be all right. If he's got any sense he'll go straight back to Princetown. Then he won't have to explain his condition to any of the wedding guests. After that he'll spend the rest of his service on Dartmoor trying to avoid both of us. Now, forget him. We have some catching up to do. Give me your hand. I don't want you disappearing before I've said what needs saying.'

60

Holding Tacy's hand, Pilgrim waited to speak again until they could no longer hear Lieutenant Kennedy fighting for breath.

'Are you upset by what happened back there tonight, Tacy? Had you grown very fond of Lieutenant Kennedy?'

'The answer to both your questions is "No". I was too angry with him. Frightened, too, for a while. But I was never particularly fond of him. I was flattered by his attentions and . . . I suppose that was all, really.'

She had been about to say she thought that by allowing the militiaman to pay her attention it might provoke an appropriate response from Pilgrim. She decided it would be better left unsaid.

Suddenly, she shivered involuntarily and Pilgrim expressed immediate concern. 'You're cold. Here, borrow my coat.'

He began unbuttoning his uniform coat, but she stopped him. 'No, it's all right. My shawl never went in the stream. It's warm and dry – anyway, your coat's every bit as wet as my dress. It'll be muddy too.

It's such a pity, you looked so smart at the wedding.'

Finding her hand once more, Pilgrim said, 'At least the wedding went well. I was very pleased for Virgil and Sophie's sakes. She, in particular, has had her share of tragedy. Virgil's got a painful time ahead too, with that wounded leg of his, but I'm convinced they'll come through it together. The greatest thing in their favour is that Sophie's mother will remain in England when they set off for America. She's a very difficult woman.'

'She'd have turned me away from the wedding if she'd had her way. She wanted to know what I was doing there when I arrived at Tor Royal.'

'I can well believe it. I'd have been excluded too had she been able to think of some way of doing it. She was bitterly opposed to Sophie marrying Virgil. In fact, she's opposed to her doing anything unless she's approved of it first. I believe she's aggrieved most of all because the wedding had been organised before she returned to England. She's that sort of a woman.'

'So I've heard. But she was right you know – about me, I mean. She knew right away I didn't belong among all those people who were at Tor Royal. It didn't take *me* very long to realise *that*.'

'What are you talking about, Tacy? You looked wonderful.'

'No I didn't. I *thought* I did, before I got there. When I put on my new dress at home, I believed it must be the most beautiful dress in the whole world. It's the best one I've ever owned, but it was home-made, with gingham bought from a moorland pedlar. The dresses worn by all the women at the wedding showed it up for what it was – cheap and home-made. Everyone else knew it, too.'

'I think you're wrong, Tacy. If anyone looked at you it

was because they realised you were the most beautiful woman at Tor Royal.'

Tacy put momentary pressure on his hand and said, 'If you'd said something like that weeks ago there would have been none of the trouble we've had tonight with Alan.'

'I would have said it *months* ago had I known of an honourable way to do it. It's what I've always thought about you.'

'Then why *haven't* you told me so before now?'

'I was trying to do the right thing. I felt I couldn't say anything until I could see a way forward for us. I knew that once the way I felt was out in the open there would be no way that things between us could stand still.'

'There *is* no way forward for us, Pilgrim. Anything we do can only be enjoyed for today. You and I have no tomorrow together. If there ever was any doubt in my mind, it ended when I went to Tor Royal. As I said, when I arrived there, the most wonderful thing in my life was my new gingham dress. It didn't take me many minutes to realise that had it been given to any one of the women or girls at the wedding they would have passed it on to their servants to be torn up and used as dusters.'

'That's not true, Tacy – but even if it were, what has that to do with you and me?'

'Don't you see, Pilgrim? The people at Tor Royal today are those you're used to mixing with every day. It's a different world to the one I live in.'

Bringing Tacy to a sudden halt, Pilgrim pulled her around to face him. 'Now just you listen to me for a moment. Are you suggesting that men like Lieutenant Kennedy or women like Winifrith Cudmore are *better* than you?'

'No, but they're *rich*. They know how to dress and

how to eat, and what to do when they meet other people.'

'Anyone can learn about such things, if they want to. It doesn't make them better than someone else. I've already told you about the early days of my own family. We headed west carrying all we owned in a couple of wagons. Our first home was a log cabin that we built ourselves. The folk we travelled with were farmers, carpenters, blacksmiths – and all the other occupations that go to making up a community. Some of them worked hard and made it. Others worked equally hard, and didn't – but we all of us worked, men, women and children. What's more, most of us remained friends. Those who succeeded and those who didn't. Those who've become rich and those who haven't. I'm not saying America doesn't have social barriers, Tacy, I know it does. But that's mainly along the east coast, where the British influence was always strongest. They cling on to what's familiar to them.'

There was passion in Pilgrim's voice now as he continued, 'The country's expanding westwards now, Tacy. Out on the frontier men and women are judged by what they *are* and by what they can do, *not* by what their parents or grandparents did in the past. *They're* the sort of people I'm used to. Folk who are working hard and taking chances in order to carve out a good life for themselves and their children . . .'

Tacy shivered and Pilgrim was immediately solicitous. 'I'm sorry, there's me getting carried away with my "speechifying", as Ma calls it when Pa does it, while you're wet and cold. Let's get you home. We can talk about all this some other time.'

'Shouldn't you be getting back to Tor Royal? We don't want you getting into trouble.'

'Nobody's going to look for trouble tonight – not if

Lieutenant Kennedy goes straight back to his quarters, as I feel sure he will.'

Tacy shivered again, but this time it had nothing to do with the cold. She had thought of what would have happened to her had Pilgrim not come to her rescue.

'Come on, let's hurry.'

'All right, but there's no need to run. You were explaining to me about things in America. I'm impressed, but what difference does it make? We're in England.'

'We are now, but I won't always be a prisoner-of-war. One day I'll be returning to the United States. When I do I want you to be with me.'

'What do you mean, you want me with you? I can't just leave everything and go gadding off to a country I'd hardly heard of before I met you.'

'I'd like you to go to America with me the same way Sophie is with Virgil. Marrying me here first and travelling there as my wife.'

Tacy stopped suddenly, pulling him to a halt. 'Do you realise what you are saying? You've never given me so much as a hint of the way you feel about me, whether as a friend, or anything else. Yet here you are suddenly talking of marriage and of me going to America with you! How much have you had to drink today?'

'Quite a lot. I think that's what's given me the courage to tell you all the things I have tonight. I've tried *not* to say them before because I thought it wouldn't be fair until an end to this war was in sight. But when I thought I might lose you to Lieutenant Kennedy, I knew I had to say something. You didn't make it easy, Tacy. Telling me to apologise to him was more than I could stomach.'

'I'm sorry.' Tacy was silent for some moments, then she said, 'Do you realise that he's been the one who's brought us together like this?'

'Yes.'

'I'm glad he has, Pilgrim.'

'So am I.'

In the darkness he drew her to him to kiss her for the first time, but she suddenly pulled back.

'What is it?' For a moment he thought she might have had second thoughts about him.

'It's your coat. It's wet and *freezing*!'

He was at a loss about what to do for a moment, then Tacy was moving closer to him again. 'Here, I've pulled my shawl about me. Shall we try again . . . ?'

61

When Tacy and Pilgrim arrived at Roundtor Farm a lamp was alight in the kitchen and they could see the shadow of someone moving.

'Ma's still up,' said Tacy. 'I'd hoped I might be able to creep in without her seeing me. I'd have not told her what happened until the morning.'

'It would have been easier for you,' agreed Pilgrim, 'but I'll come in with you.'

When they reached the door, Tacy stopped for a moment and said quietly, 'I'm very glad we're friends again, Pilgrim.'

'Oh! Are we only friends now?'

'You know what I mean.' She kissed him quickly and then lifted the latch on the kitchen door.

Tacy was relieved to see that her father's high-backed chair was empty. It meant he was in bed. She did not want him becoming over-excited by her explanation of what had happened to her. Johanna would be in bed too.

Joan was making up the fire but she turned around

when she heard the door opening. Her expression became one of horrified disbelief as she saw Tacy in the light from the kitchen lamp.

Pilgrim grimaced; Tacy was in a worse state than he had realised.

'My dear soul! Look at the state of your nice new dress . . . and of you too!' She included Pilgrim in her critical assessment. 'What on earth has happened to you both?'

A hint of suspicion crept into her mind and she said, 'What have you both been up to?'

'Can we get some clothes for Pilgrim, Ma – and put his uniform round the fire to dry? He must get back to Tor Royal before too long.'

'You know where the working clothes are kept, Pilgrim. In the outhouse. Change there while I breathe some life back into this fire. The trouble is, I've only just made it up for the night. While you're changing, Tacy can make a start on telling me what you've both been up to. She left the house looking like a princess and now she's come back for all the world like one of those tinkers Emma used to travel with – and who were back here this afternoon . . .'

Pilgrim changed in the outhouse by the light of a candle, carried with him from the kitchen. It took him only a matter of minutes, but by the time he returned carrying a bundle of wet clothing with him, Tacy had given her mother an outline of what had happened to her when she left Tor Royal.

Her mother greeted Pilgrim with, 'It seems we were both right about that militia officer.'

'I'm afraid so,' said Pilgrim. 'He certainly showed his true colours tonight.'

'That isn't all he would have done had you not been

on hand to help her,' said Joan grimly. Her voice broke as she added shakily, 'He might well have murdered her. A dress can be replaced, but not a daughter. Thank you, Pilgrim.'

'I'm not at all sure you'll be wanting to thank me when you hear what I have to say, Mrs Elford. The chances are you'll be losing her anyway.'

'What do you mean?' She looked from Pilgrim to Tacy, not understanding. 'What else has happened?'

'I've asked Tacy to marry me once the end of this war is in sight. It means we'd be setting up home in Ohio, in America.'

Reaching behind her, Joan found her husband's chair and sat down heavily. Shaking her head as though dazed, she said, 'I know I shouldn't be surprised but everything's happened so quickly, and coming on top of everything else . . .' She looked thoroughly bemused.

'You don't disapprove, Ma? You and Pa aren't going to say I can't marry Pilgrim?'

'After what he's done tonight? Anyway, would it make any difference if we said "no"? You'd only do what Sir Thomas's niece did. Run off and marry him just the same. But we won't try to stop you, child. Just as long as you wait and try to behave yourselves until we can see an end to this foolish war between our countries. Your pa feels the same, I know. We've talked about it more than once.'

'Does that mean Tacy *will* be having a baby soon? Can I hold it?'

No one had noticed Johanna come down the boxed-in staircase that led from the bedrooms to a corner of the kitchen.

'Your ears are far too big for a young girl,' said her mother, rising from the chair. 'One of these days you'll take off in a high wind and we'll never see you again.

Tacy and Pilgrim are only talking of getting married. It won't happen for a long time yet.'

'Can I go up and tell Pa? He heard me come from the bedroom and said I was to ask how Tacy got on.' She frowned. 'How did she get so muddy – and why is Pilgrim wearing them old working clothes?'

'Tacy slipped as they were crossing a stream on the way home. Pilgrim pulled her out – and, no! Tacy will go up and tell Pa herself, once she's taken her muddy dress off. I'll soak it overnight and hope the mud comes out. But first I want to give them both a kiss and say that I'm very happy for them . . .'

Tom Elford shared his wife's pleasure at the news that Tacy and Pilgrim intended marrying as soon as there was an end in sight to the war.

After hugging his daughter and shaking Pilgrim by the hand, he lay back on his pillows and gave his future son-in-law a wan smile.

'You don't need me to tell you I'm not a well man, Pilgrim. It's good to have been able to see the man that at least one of my daughters is to marry. I'd thought that her future husband might one day take over Roundtor Farm, but Tacy will have a far better life in America with you. All there is here for a man and his wife is a constant battle to eke out a living. A tenant farmer on Dartmoor will never grow rich, or be able to give his wife and family the things he'd dearly love them to have.'

'Now, Tom, don't start talking of such things. Not tonight. Anyway, it's not true. Not as far as you're concerned. You've given me all I've ever asked from life. A loving husband and two of the finest daughters a woman could wish for. If Pilgrim and Tacy are blessed with as much in their life together they'll never want for happiness, at least.'

Tom Elford reached out and grasped his wife's hand, not trusting himself to speak.

'But if Tacy and Pilgrim go to live in America I'm not going to be able to take care of their babies, am I?'

'I shouldn't worry yourself about that, young lady. The time will come all too soon when you have babies of your own to look after.'

'That's not going to be for years and years,' Johanna pouted. 'I don't want to have to wait *that* long.'

Suddenly she brightened. 'Oh well, if Tacy isn't going to have a baby for me to look after, then I'm just going to have to help Emma look after her baby, aren't I?'

'What are you talking about, child? Emma's not going to have a baby. She isn't married – and has no thoughts of getting married, as far as I know.'

Johanna remained silent and would not meet her mother's eyes and Joan Elford looked at her speculatively. 'Is there something you know that I don't, Johanna? I think you'd better tell me.'

'I promised Emma I'd keep it a secret,' said Johanna, unhappily.

'So there *is* something? Come on, girl, what is it? Is Emma expecting a baby?'

Johanna nodded, her eyes downcast.

'Well, who'd have thought it! There's her dangling poor young Billy along on a piece of string and all the time she's carrying someone's baby. I wonder who the father is? I hope it's not that tinker man who was around here today. It'll break Billy's heart if he finds her and they go off together.'

'It's no tinker's baby,' declared Johanna. 'It's Billy's.'

Seeing the scornful expression on her mother's face, Johanna said heatedly, 'It *is* Billy's. Emma told me. Besides . . .' Johanna dropped her eyes from her mother's face once more.

'Go on, girl, what is it you were going to say?'

'I *know* it's Billy's. I caught them together up in our hayloft a few weeks ago. Emma said I shouldn't say anything because it might get Billy into trouble. She said it would be all right, because she and Billy were going to be married very soon, anyway.'

62

Emma was working hard in the garden of the Yates cottage. All around were the man-made hills of waste, extracted from an underground skein of tunnels, dug when this had been a working mine.

The vegetable garden had produced nothing for many years. Indeed, there was now only the faintest of outlines to show where it had once been. Emma was making a start on digging it over, determined it would one day provide all the vegetable needs of those in the cottage.

It also got her out of the way of Mrs Yates. Billy's mother was up and about once more, but still not well enough to be left alone.

Neither had she accepted Emma's presence in *her* cottage, although it was cleaner than it had ever been and Emma had proved herself an impressive cook. She had the knack of producing a palatable meal from the skimpiest of ingredients.

It was of Mrs Yates Emma was thinking as she worked. She would like to have been accepted by her, for Billy's sake. He was torn between loyalty to his mother and his love for Emma, and he found it difficult to cope with his feelings.

Because of Mrs Yates's improved health, Emma had sent Billy to Roundtor Farm, promising she would remain at home and take care of the convalescing woman. They were out of provisions and the work Billy did for the Elfords was the only way of obtaining more.

So busy was Emma with her thoughts and the task she had set herself, she did not see the ragged man making his way stealthily towards her from the cover of one of the spoil heaps. He was dirty from the top of his greasy and battered high-crowned hat to the filthy ankles exposed between sockless feet and trousers that did not reach to within a handsbreadth of his decrepit shoes. The clothes in between were threadbare and full of holes.

Not until he was almost within touching distance of her did the man speak. 'Hello, Emma, my dear. I hope you didn't think you'd seen the last of old Charlie?'

Emma swung around at the sound of the man's voice, an expression of stark fear on her face. Swinging up the spade she was holding so it was between them, she said, 'You keep away from me, Charlie. If you don't I'll slice your head off with this, I swear I will.'

'Now what sort of talk is that, Emma? You *belong* to me, you know that. Didn't I pay good money for you when you would have been turned out by your own mother? You was *indentured* to me, girl, that's the word them smart lawyers use, but it means the same. You came to me when you was too small to pay your way. I taught you how to earn a living and how did you thank me? By running away, that's how.'

'You taught me to lie and cheat and thieve for you,

Charlie. As for the rest, I only have your word for how
you came by me – and that's never counted for very
much, has it?'

'It'll count enough for a magistrate to order you back
to me, you see if it don't.'

'You wouldn't dare take me before a magistrate. What
I could tell him about you would have you dangling on
the end of a hangman's rope – you *and* Bella, if I'd a
mind to tell about her too.'

Casting a quick glance in the direction of the spoil
heap from whence Charlie had appeared, Emma said,
'Where *is* Bella?'

'She's standing right behind you.'

Without thinking, Emma turned her head to look
behind her. Before she had time to take it in that she
had been tricked, Charlie hit her on the side of the head,
knocking her to her knees.

Before she could recover, the tinker had snatched the
spade from her hand and flung it from him before taking
a cruel grip on her arm.

'That fooled you, didn't it? Bella's been dead these
past three weeks. That's why I've come looking for you.
You can take her place.'

'No! Let go! Let go of me,' Emma shrieked at him.

'Oh no. You've run away from me once. By the time
I've finished with you you'll never try it again.'

By twisting her arm, Charlie forced her to her knees
once more, then, one-handed, he loosened a piece of
thin rope coiled about his waist beneath his shirt, and
passed one end about her neck.

His intention was to secure the rope about her neck
and lead her away, but before he could accomplish his
purpose he was interrupted by Tillie Yates.

She emerged from the cottage like an avenging angel.
No one who saw her would have suspected she was

a sick woman. In her hands she wielded a heavy, long-handled brush.

She ran at Charlie. Before he could recover from his surprise she swung the broom and struck him on the side of the head.

Releasing Emma and the rope, he wrapped both arms about his battered head and staggered away, pursued by Billy's mother.

Unwinding the rope from about her neck, Emma darted to where the spade lay. Snatching it up, she too went after Charlie.

A swing from the spade struck him in almost the same place as had the broom, but the sharp-edged blade of the spade was a far more vicious weapon. It almost severed one of his ears.

Spurting blood and screaming in pain, the brutal tinker fled across the moor, pursued part of the way by a vengeful Emma.

When it was apparent the tinker would not stop running until he had put a considerable distance between himself and the two women, Emma turned and looked back towards the house.

Tillie Yates was crouching on the ground, close to where she had attacked Charlie. Mouth open, she seemed to be having great difficulty in breathing.

Emma ran back to her. Dropping the spade, she kneeled beside the woman, thoroughly alarmed by her pallor. 'You shouldn't have done that, Mrs Yates. You still aren't well.'

Putting an arm about her she tried to raise her to her feet, but received no assistance from the older woman.

'No . . . no good. Has . . . Has the tinker gone?'

'Yes. You were marvellous. But let's get you into the house.'

'It'll be . . . no good, girl. Take care . . . take care . . . Billy. He needs . . . someone . . .'

Suddenly, Tillie Yates sagged in Emma's arms and the breath escaped from her in a soft, lingering sigh.

'Mrs Yates! Mrs Yates . . .'

In her panic, Emma shook Billy's mother. The only effect it had was to cause her to fall sideways.

'Oh my God!'

Emma let the other woman slip to the ground and rose to her feet. She ran a few paces and then turned and ran back.

Kneeling down once more, she put her ear to Tillie's mouth, but could neither hear nor feel anything.

'What am I going to do? What *can* I do?'

Tillie Yates lay crumpled on the ground and suddenly Emma began running. She ran away from the house, running as she never had before.

63

Billy had spent the morning gathering sheep from the hills and valleys about Roundtor with the aid of the two dogs.

He was well pleased with his work. Rip was at last fulfilling his earlier promise. He was now a first-class sheepdog. Billy thought Sir Thomas would be proud of him one day.

It was good to be working for the Elfords once more. Billy had told Mrs Elford that his mother was much improved and that Emma had insisted he come back to work again. In his simple, honest manner, he had explained there was no food left in the pantry of the Yates cottage.

'I'll give you a basket of food to take back with you,' said Joan. 'Now, off you go and find Tacy. She'll tell you what needs to be done.'

She would have liked to tackle Billy about Johanna's revelation that Emma was carrying his baby, but she decided that could wait for an hour or two, at least.

Pilgrim was working at the farm today. He had gone

out with the pony and wagon to fetch in some of the peat that had been stacked on the moor by Billy. Winter was very close. The peat needed to be brought to the farmyard and stacked beside the kitchen door. Here it would be easily accessible in even the worst weather.

Tacy would be working in the dairy for most of the day and a somewhat rebellious Johanna had been detailed to clean out the buildings occupied by cows, pigs and chickens.

At noon, Billy made his way back to the farm. He and the dogs had rounded up more than fifty Elford sheep. He considered it to have been a good morning's work.

He was feeling pleased with himself. When Joan walked from the farm to meet him he was eager to tell her what he had done.

'Rip did really well,' he said. 'Mr Elford was right when he said he'd turn out to be a good dog. Sir Thomas is going to be pleased with him.'

'I haven't come out here to talk about Rip, Billy. I'd like to have a word with you about Emma – and the baby.'

Billy looked completely baffled. 'Baby? What baby are you talking about, Mrs Elford? I don't know no baby.'

Joan was about to tell him what she had heard, but she changed her mind. She realised that to say any more right now would be gross interference.

'I must be getting you confused with someone else, Billy. Don't take any notice of me. Come inside the house and have something to eat. You'll have worked up an appetite this morning.'

She decided she would speak to Emma when next she came to Roundtor.

Joan Elford met with Emma far earlier than she had

anticipated, but there was no opportunity to discuss the young woman's condition with her.

She and Billy had almost reached the farmyard gate when they heard a shout from some distance behind them. When they turned, they saw a figure running towards them.

'It's Emma,' said Billy, in alarm. 'What's she doing running like that?'

'She's likely to do herself a mischief if she's not careful,' replied Joan, half to herself.

Emma was running at breakneck speed when she suddenly stumbled and fell to the ground. She picked herself up immediately, but Billy was already running to meet her. Joan hurried after him.

In the farmyard, Tacy came from the dairy in time to see what was happening. She called to Pilgrim and they both hurried after her mother.

When Billy reached Emma, she burst into tears. Clinging to him, she cried, 'I'm sorry, Billy. It's all my fault. I'm so sorry.'

Billy was thoroughly bemused. It was left to Joan to ask her what it was she had done.

Gasping for breath, Emma directed her reply to Billy. 'It's your ma, Billy. I . . . I think she's dead – and it's all my fault.'

'How . . . ?' Billy looked at her in stunned disbelief.

'You'd better come back to the house and tell us what's happened,' said the farmer's wife, but Emma shook her head vigorously.

'We must go back to the cottage . . . Billy and me.'

'All right, but calm down for a few moments first.' Joan took charge once more, as Pilgrim and Tacy reached them. 'Sit down here and tell us exactly what's happened.'

Sitting down heavily on the grass, Emma tearfully

told them of the arrival of Charlie and of the events that ensued. When she spoke of Tillie Yates's last moments, she broke down once more and kept repeating, 'It was all my fault. If I hadn't been there it wouldn't have happened.'

'You can't blame yourself for what some bullying tinker does, Emma. Besides, poor Tillie's been ill with that heart of hers these last three or four years. She could have gone at any time. Billy knows that. I've often said that she's only been hanging on because if she went there'd be no one to take care of Billy.'

'Her last words were about him,' said a tearful Emma. 'She said I was to take care of him.'

'I've no doubt at all she knew full well you would,' said Joan, adding meaningfully, 'Mind, you're going to need to have someone looking after you before too long.'

When Emma gave her a startled look, she added, 'But we'll talk about that some other time.'

Turning to a confused and bereft Billy, she said, 'I'm very sorry about your ma, Billy. She might have kept herself a bit too much to herself for most folk's liking, but she brought you up knowing right from wrong. That couldn't always have been easy with no man about the place.'

Giving him a motherly hug, she said, 'Now, you get over to her cottage – all of you – and carry her inside. I'll go back and tell Tom and Johanna what's going on, then I'll come over there and do what needs to be done.'

She hurried away, murmuring about 'Not knowing what the moor is coming to with all these goings on. First a militiaman and Tacy, and now a tinker and poor Tillie Yates . . .'

64

The funeral of Tillie Yates took place on the day Virgil and Sophie departed from Tor Royal, leaving Pilgrim as the senior United States officer in charge of the American prisoners-of-war.

The two events were emotional for everyone concerned. For Pilgrim the day began soon after dawn, when the newly married couple departed for Portsmouth. The parting came as a great wrench for him. He and Virgil had served together for a number of years, sharing war, escape and captivity.

Before leaving, Virgil promised that he would use the influence of his family and friends to bring the plight of the United States prisoners-of-war in Dartmoor prison to the attention of their Government.

The parting was equally emotional for Sophie and her mother. Theirs had always been something of a love/hate relationship. Fully aware they might never see each other again they had reached a tacit agreement not to quarrel during their final days.

However, Winifrith had felt unable to extend the

armistice to include Virgil. She continued to ignore him. Even on this, the day of his departure with her daughter. She did no more than give him a perfunctory shake of the hand, with a grudgingly expressed hope that American surgeons would be able to cure his wounded leg.

Sir Thomas, Winifrith and Pilgrim, together with all the house servants, stood outside the main entrance to Tor Royal. They continued to wave to the departing couple until the carriage taking them to Portsmouth passed from view, with Virgil and Sophie still fluttering handkerchiefs from the open windows.

Hurrying back inside the house ahead of the others, Winifrith retired to her room. She would not be seen for the remainder of the day.

'I'm going to miss that girl,' said Sir Thomas, in apparent surprise. He and Pilgrim were entering the house together. 'I've grown used to having her about the place. Still, she could not be in better hands. Virgil is a good man. He has sound commonsense and I understand he comes from a good family too.'

'Among the best in America,' agreed Pilgrim. 'Sophie will find herself at the very centre of east coast society.'

'Good!' Sir Thomas nodded his satisfaction. 'She'll fit in well, I have no doubt at all.'

Glancing at his companion, he said, 'You are going to miss Virgil.'

'Very much, and not only as a friend. I've taken over many of his duties in recent weeks, but he's always been here for me to discuss any problems with. I'm on my own now.'

'Well, if you ever feel the need to talk things over with anyone, you have my ear – although I fear I must return to London very soon now.' Giving Pilgrim a mischievous smile, he added, 'I'll see if I can persuade

Winifrith to come with me. It should make life easier for you here.'

Pilgrim felt it would be best if he made no reply.

'What are you doing for the remainder of the day, Pilgrim?'

'I have Governor Cotgrave's permission to attend a funeral at Sheepstor.'

'Of course! The mother of that young lad who works for the Elfords is being buried. He's rather simple, is he not? He and his mother have been living in one of the old mine cottages down at the old Whiteworks mine. What will happen to the boy now? Will he move in with the Elfords, d'you think? If he does I'll have the old cottage pulled down. I don't want it attracting vagrants. There seem to have been a great many of them around the moor lately.'

'I think Billy would like to remain in his mother's cottage,' said Pilgrim. 'He *is* rather simple, but he's honest and hardworking. Tom Elford also says he's better than most of the shepherds on the moor. He's certainly bringing that dog of yours on. Billy's also been fortunate enough to find a girl with enough sound commonsense for both of them.'

Pilgrim paused to allow Sir Thomas to pass through the front door of the house ahead of him before continuing. 'She's been living in the cottage while Billy's mother's been ill and has put the place in good order. She's even made an impressive start on the garden.'

Sir Thomas frowned. 'Are you suggesting I should condone having them both living there although they're not married? I would come in for a great deal of justifiable criticism were I to allow that.'

'My understanding is that they intend marrying quite soon, Sir Thomas.'

After a few moments' thought, Sir Thomas said, 'Very well. Have a word with Billy and this girl. Tell them that if they marry before Christmas they can take a tenancy of the old mine cottage. What amount of rent do you think they'll be able to afford?'

The question took Pilgrim by surprise and he said hesitantly, 'Neither of them is earning money. Billy works for the Elfords in exchange for food and fuel. Until Mrs Yates became ill, Emma was working at Roundtor Farm for her board only.'

Sir Thomas gave Pilgrim a shrewd look. 'What you're telling me is that they are unable to pay any rent for the cottage?' He shrugged. 'Very well. Tell them if they continue to make improvements to the cottage I'll see to it they have the tenancy on a peppercorn rent. Now, I feel chilled through after standing outside seeing off the newlyweds. Let's go to my study and have something to warm us up. You'll certainly need something. A moorland funeral is a cold and solemn service at the best of times.'

65

The funeral of Tillie Yates was a brief, perfunctory affair. In a box in the bedroom of his late mother Billy had found money to pay for only the simplest of burials.

The coffin containing her body was carried across the four miles of moorland between the old mine cottage and Sheepstor in the Elfords' cart, pulled by their pony, led by Pilgrim.

Following behind for the long walk were Billy, Emma and Joan and Tacy Elford. Tom Elford was not fit enough to attend the funeral and Johanna had been told to remain behind with him.

At Sheepstor church the small party of mourners was joined by two members of a moorland family who had known Tillie when she was a young girl.

The weather was as depressing as the occasion. Menacing dark clouds had built up above the moor and a chill northerly wind was a sharp reminder that winter was in the offing.

After the coffin had been laid in the ground and the gravedigger had begun the sombre task of filling in the grave, the party climbed inside the cart and made its way back to Roundtor Farm.

In the kitchen, Joan Elford bustled about, preparing a hot meal for all of them. It was now that Pilgrim repeated what Sir Thomas had said to him about the tenancy of the Yates's lonely old mining cottage.

Tom Elford had come down to his usual seat to share the warmth of the kitchen with the others. Taking a faintly smoking pipe from between his teeth, he said, 'That, at least, is a bright spot for you in a very unhappy day, Billy.'

Instead of being pleased, Billy appeared thoroughly bemused, 'But . . . Emma hasn't said she wants to marry me!'

There was a wave of laughter in the kitchen that helped to release some of the unhappy tension that had built up in everyone.

'I think she'd better say "Yes" before too long,' said Joan. Her words prompted Emma to give Johanna an accusing glance.

'Have you asked her to marry you, Billy?' The question came from Tacy.

'No, he hasn't,' said Emma. 'But perhaps he doesn't want to marry me.'

'I *do*,' declared Billy unhappily. 'But . . . what do I have to do to get us married?'

There was not one person in the kitchen who did not feel overwhelming sympathy for Billy. He had never known a father. Brought up in a remote part of the moor, he had met very few people. The Elfords were the only *family* he knew. Marriage was as much of a mystery to him as mathematics.

'If you really want to marry me and for us to be with each other for always, I'll be happy to wed you, Billy. We'd make a good couple, I know it.'

Joan Elford clearly approved of her decision and it was to her that Emma turned now.

'I don't know any more about arranging a wedding than Billy does. Will you help us, Mrs Elford?'

'Of course I will – and I'm very happy for both of you. We really shouldn't even be thinking of weddings on a day when Billy's ma's been laid to rest, but Tillie herself was never one for doing what was expected of her. She'd not have minded.'

'Well, if you're going to arrange Billy's wedding for him, perhaps I'll be allowed to act as his groomsman, same as I did for Virgil,' said Pilgrim. 'I'd like that.'

'Well! Such talk has brightened up a sad day, and no mistake,' declared Joan. 'Tom, where did you hide that cider we keep for special occasions? I think this is as good a time as any for it to be brought out.'

Tacy accompanied Pilgrim for part of his walk back to Tor Royal later that evening. There was a light drizzle in the air but, although it was cold, neither of them noticed.

'What an eventful day it's been,' said Tacy. 'First we bury Billy's ma, then it's decided that he and Emma will get married!'

'It's also the day when Virgil and Sophie set off for America to begin their new life together,' Pilgrim reminded her.

'Of course! Theirs was yet another unexpected marriage.'

Giving Pilgrim a sidelong glance, Tacy added, 'They do say that things always happen in threes. I wonder who'll be the third couple to be married?'

'Perhaps it'll be Mary and Henri,' said Pilgrim, in apparent innocence. He had seen her glance and was aware of the reply she wanted him to make.

Smiling sadly at her expression of disappointment, he said, 'I'd like to be able to say it might be us, Tacy, but that isn't possible just yet. You know that as well as I do.'

'No one could possibly be starting married life with less than Billy and Emma,' she pointed out. 'Yet they're going to marry.'

'They don't have a lot,' Pilgrim admitted, 'but they do have a place to live and Billy doesn't live on parole with the threat of a recall to prison hanging over his head. If the British Government suddenly decided it was a good idea, I and all the other prisoners-of-war could be sent to Botany Bay, or anywhere else. No couple can be expected to begin married life with a threat like that hanging over their heads.'

'I sometimes wonder if you really *want* to marry me, Pilgrim Penn,' Tacy pouted.

Pilgrim stopped and turned Tacy to face him. 'You already know the answer to that. If you didn't, you wouldn't dare to even suggest it.'

The drizzle had become light rain now. There was every indication that the cloud over the moor would lower and the rain become heavier, but the young couple did not seem to care at all about the weather.

66

A few days later, Pilgrim was working at Roundtor Farm when Ephraim came to find him.

Johanna saw the marines sergeant entering the farmyard and called out to tell Pilgrim of his presence before eagerly running to meet him.

'You haven't been to see us for *ages*,' she complained, when she reached him. 'Why not?'

'It's not you I've come to see this time, either, young lady, beautiful though you are. I'm here to see Captain Penn.'

Ephraim grinned at her before picking her up easily and swinging her up to a seat on one of his broad shoulders.

'Here I am, Ephraim.' Pilgrim came from the dairy, wiping his hands on the smock he wore over his uniform shirt and trousers. He had been helping Tacy with some cheesemaking. 'Is there trouble at the prison?'

'Not exactly, Cap'n. I've come to tell you that Captain Cotgrave's gone. He left with no fuss or farewell speeches, as far as I can make out. The new governor arrived yesterday. He's another naval man, a Captain Thomas Shortland. He sent for me this morning to say he's calling a meeting this afternoon of all senior prisoner-of-war officers. He wants you there and says I'm welcome to attend too. I'd like to do that, if it's all right with you?'

'Of course it is. What time this afternoon is the meeting?'

Ephraim shrugged. 'He didn't say, but Governor Cotgrave always finished his midday meal at about two o'clock. I reckon that'll be the time Shortland will be expecting you to be there.'

'Fine! We'll walk to the prison together. In the meantime, I'm sure Mrs Elford will be able to put together some home cooking to make your walk here worthwhile.'

Pilgrim was not wrong. When Ephraim walked inside the kitchen with Johanna still on his shoulder, bending extravagantly low to go through the door, and setting the young girl giggling uncontrollably, Joan Elford told him he had arrived just in time to eat.

A meal was laid on the table that Ephraim declared was better than anything he could remember tasting.

'That's not much of a compliment,' retorted the farmer's wife. 'Pilgrim is always telling us how awful the food is inside the prison.'

'I can't argue with that, ma'am,' agreed Ephraim. 'But I seem to have spent a whole lifetime being given awful food. Eating like this is rare indeed. It's food a man would happily kill for. I thank you, ma'am.'

Whether or not it had been his intention, Ephraim's complimentary remarks meant that he would return to the prison with his pockets stuffed with samples of Joan Elford's cooking.

*   *   *

On the way to the prison with Ephraim, Pilgrim questioned him about the new governor.

'It's too soon to know him just yet,' said Ephraim cautiously. 'He smiles a whole lot more than Cotgrave, but my momma told me never to put too much trust in a master who seems happy to know you the first time you meet. She said you can usually make a solemn master smile, but with the one who's already smiled at you there's no way to go but down.'

'I'll remember that,' said Pilgrim. 'Did she give you any other words of wisdom?'

'Every day,' replied Ephraim. 'But it didn't stop her being passed on to a team of raftmen when the last "master" lost more money than he had on him during a card game in Baton Rouge. True, when he sobered up he rode hell-for-leather down to New Orleans to buy her back.'

Ephraim said no more and Pilgrim prompted, 'Did he? Buy her back, I mean?'

Ephraim shook his head, looking straight ahead. 'She wasn't with the raftmen when they arrived, and no one was saying what happened to her. Not that it would have mattered, she was only a slave.'

'Were you her only child, Ephraim?'

The big marines sergeant shook his head. 'No. I had an older brother, but he was what they called a "bad nigger". He was forever running away, making for the northern states. Trouble is he kept getting caught. After a couple of times they gelded him. Then, when that didn't stop him they whipped him so hard he died.'

Still looking ahead, Ephraim said, 'There was a sister too. She was about the same age as Johanna when she was sold on. I never did see her again, though I heard she had a couple of children by the overseer on the plantation where she went.'

'We've known each other a long time, Ephraim, yet that's the first time you've ever told me anything about your family.'

Ephraim gave Pilgrim a faint smile. 'What family, Cap'n? A plantation nigger ain't allowed to have any family. That's another thing momma told me. We don't have no say in making the rules, but it sure as hell don't pay to break any of 'em . . .'

Ephraim broke off his conversation abruptly. 'Talking of family . . . if that man ever knew his father I'd be very surprised.'

Pilgrim looked up to see a militia officer on a horse riding towards them. It was Lieutenant Alan Kennedy. He was accompanied by about a dozen militiamen.

'Let's step out and get within shouting distance of the prison, at least, before we meet up with him.'

'I don't think he'll cause us any trouble,' said Pilgrim, with more confidence than he felt. 'But why don't you like him?'

'He's caught three escapees in the last week. Two French and one American. He's claimed that every one of them assaulted his men. As a result they've been flogged before being locked up in the *cachot*. If we're not careful he'll find some reason for having *us* arrested. He dislikes prisoners-of-war – especially if they happen to be American.'

'I think I know the reason for that, Ephraim.' Pilgrim told the marines sergeant of his various meetings with the Irish militia officer.

'Is that so?' said Ephraim. 'If you don't mind, Cap'n, I'll pass on the word about Lieutenant Kennedy. I don't think he's going to enjoy a very easy time for the short time he's got left on Dartmoor.'

'Short time? Where's he going?'

'Word is the Irish militia are due to be relieved by

some Scots militiamen. No one knows when, but it could be any day.'

'That will be a great relief,' said Pilgrim. 'I worry on the days I don't go to Roundtor, in case Lieutenant Kennedy goes around there looking for Tacy again.'

As they talked, Lieutenant Kennedy and his militiamen turned off the road and headed across the moor. 'Well, it seems you sure scare him, Cap'n. Let's hope it stays that way.'

67

'Come in, Captain Penn. Come in with your sergeant and join the others.' The apparent bonhomie of Captain Thomas Shortland, the new governor of Dartmoor prison, was exactly as Ephraim had described it to Pilgrim. It bordered on the effusive.

'You probably know most of the others here?' Governor Shortland waved a hand and his smile now included the assembled officers in its warmth.

Pilgrim nodded to the French officers seated around the walls of the governor's office.

'Well, gentlemen, now we are all gathered here, I will introduce myself. I am Thomas Shortland, a captain in the Royal Navy. Having spent the whole of my career on fighting ships I can understand many of the frustrations you are suffering as the result of being taken prisoner and unable to serve your country further. I have also learned to respect you as gallant adversaries in battle.'

His glance moved to Pilgrim and he said, 'I am addressing the French officers, Captain Penn. I have not fought your countrymen, but I have no doubt they too serve your country well.'

Pilgrim was irritated by the condescending manner of Dartmoor's new governor. He merely nodded his head in acknowledgement of Shortland's words, saying nothing.

For the remainder of the meeting, Captain Shortland spoke of his impressions of the French prisoners-of-war and of the pleasure it gave him to observe the manner in which they had settled down to life in Dartmoor, their orderliness and cleanliness and realistic adaptation to prison life.

Ominously, he said nothing at all about the Americans in this part of his introductory speech. After expressing his opinion that the war would soon be over, thus enabling them all to return to their homes and loved ones, Shortland brought the meeting to an end. It came as no surprise to Pilgrim when the new governor asked him to remain behind as the others were leaving. It seemed there was a number of matters the governor wished to discuss with him.

When the Frenchmen and Ephraim had left, Governor Shortland invited Pilgrim to bring his chair to the opposite side of his desk.

When Pilgrim had moved to face him, Governor Shortland leaned back in his chair and brought his smile into play once more. 'You heard what I had to say to the Frenchmen, Captain Penn. They are model prisoners. Were all the inmates of Dartmoor prison equally well-behaved, my term of office here would be a very pleasant one.'

The smile faded and he said, 'Unfortunately, the behaviour of those of your countrymen interned here falls far short of the standards attained by the French.'

Governor Shortland then read out a long list of misde-meanours committed by the Americans, adding, 'There have also been no fewer than three escapes in the last week alone. Such conduct is totally unacceptable, Captain Penn. Why can your men not accept their lot, as the French do?'

'There are a great many reasons, Governor. First of all, many of the American prisoners-of-war are resentful because they feel they should not be imprisoned at all. They have nothing to do with the forces of our country. They are sailors, merchants and traders who were going about their lawful business when war was declared between our two countries. Some have lost everything they ever had, including their freedom. In return, the United States Government has given them little. It took a very long while before an allowance of a penny-halfpenny a day was made to them. It does not go far.'

Thomas Shortland nodded in apparent agreement and made a note on a piece of paper on the desk in front of him.

Encouraged by the new governor's apparent sympathy, Pilgrim continued, 'They are also comparatively new to captivity. The French have had years to become organised. They have sufficient funds, not only to provide for their needs but also to bring a little luxury into their lives.'

Warming to his subject, Pilgrim said, 'There are a great many petty restrictions applied to the United States prisoners-of-war – but not to the French. The majority of Americans are kept in a prison block walled off from the remainder of the prison and are not allowed to attend the market. In addition, they suffer from having to parade outside in the yard of their block every morning, whatever the weather.'

'The morning parade is not restricted to the American prisoners, Captain Penn. The French are paraded too.'

'Yes, but the majority of them have reasonable clothing to protect them against the cold. Most of my men have little warm clothing, and no money with which to purchase any.'

Captain Shortland made another note on the paper in front of him, but this time gave no indication of whether or not he agreed with what Pilgrim had said.

For the next fifteen minutes the discussion continued, with Pilgrim airing many of the grievances held by the American prisoners-of-war.

When he ended, Captain Shortland put down his pen, leaned back in his chair and the smile returned, although now Pilgrim thought it was a trifle more forced than it had been before.

'Thank you for your help, Captain Penn. I feel our meeting has been most fruitful. Such frankness can only be in the best interest of everyone. I have a difficult duty to perform here, but I intend to carry it out as I did the command of one of His Majesty's ships: with firm but fair discipline. I will look into the grievances you have aired here today and put right those I consider to be justified. In return I shall expect the attitude of your men to change accordingly. I will not tolerate indiscipline from them.'

'If their conditions improve you'll have no trouble from them, Governor. They are civilised men.'

'I doubt if Governor Cotgrave would agree with you, Captain – and they have yet to prove it to me. I am quite willing to give them a chance, but one only.'

'Thank you, sir.'

Pilgrim turned to leave the office, but he had hardly reached the door when Governor Shortland called to him.

'By the way, I do not consider it possible for the senior United States officer to carry out his duties efficiently from a distance. I would like you to forego your parole and move back to the prison. You will be billeted in the Petty Officers' Block, of course.'

Pilgrim swung back to face the new governor once more. 'But . . . Sir Thomas is away. I promised him I would exercise supervision over the servants in his absence. I have made other commitments too.'

'You are a prisoner-of-war, Captain Penn. You realise that. Making commitments in such a situation is irresponsible – and who is this "Sir Thomas" of whom you speak?'

'He is the man to whom I am paroled. Among other duties, he is secretary to the Prince Regent and Warden of the Stannaries.'

If Thomas Shortland was impressed by Sir Thomas's duties, he did not show it. 'Obviously a man who serves his country well. He will understand the need for a man to be where his duty lies. And these other "commitments" of which you speak?'

'I am helping at a moorland farm while the farmer is ill – and have promised to do duty as groomsman at the wedding of a young Dartmoor man.'

'No doubt the farmer has family to carry on his work until he is well again. As for the wedding . . . when is it due to take place?'

'In about three weeks' time.'

'As I have already said, I am a reasonable man, Captain. You may take leave from the prison on the day of the wedding. Is there anything else?'

Pilgrim realised it would be useless to argue further with Governor Shortland. He shook his head unhappily.

'Very well. You may have forty-eight hours to settle affairs outside the prison. On your return we will have another meeting. Goodbye, Captain Penn.'

68

'But *why*, Pilgrim? Why does this have to happen, just when we had things sorted out between us? It's . . . it's not *fair*.'

Pilgrim had reached Roundtor Farm a few minutes before. Making his way to the dairy, he had found Tacy working and broken the news of his impending return to Dartmoor prison.

'I'm a prisoner-of-war, Tacy. It's something that's always easy to forget when I'm with you and we're so happy together. It brings home what I was telling you the other day. The reason I hadn't declared the way I feel about you before then. I'm not my own man, Tacy. I won't be until this war is over.'

Turning a stricken face in his direction, Tacy suddenly flung herself at him. Clinging to him, she said, 'I'm so sorry, Pilgrim. I'm only thinking of how unhappy *I'm* going to be without you. It's *you* who has to go back to live in that horrible prison. I wish Captain Cotgrave had never left.'

'I felt the same way when I left his office. But on

the way here I started thinking. Most of the Americans locked up in the prison will never be given an opportunity to take parole. They're living in appalling conditions and have nothing to look forward to, from one day to another.'

Reaching up a hand to stroke her hair, he said, 'They certainly don't have anyone like you. At least Shortland was prepared to listen to what I had to say about them. If he does something to improve the unhappy life they're leading, my loss of freedom will have been worthwhile – for them, at least. Besides, I'm going to the Petty Officers' Block, so I'll be able to see you when you bring goods to the prison market.'

'It won't be the same. We'll need to behave almost as though we're strangers.'

Looking up at him, she said, 'If things become too awful for you in there, I'll help you to escape, the same as Mary helped Henri. You could hide here, at the farm, and no one would ever find you.'

'Aren't you forgetting Lieutenant Kennedy?'

'He wouldn't dare come to Roundtor after what he tried to do to me.'

'He'd dare a whole lot more than that to have me thrown in the *cachot* and you arrested as an accomplice.'

'If he did we'd tell what he did to me.'

'We couldn't. It would be said that we'd made it all up just because he'd arrested us. No, Tacy, we'll need to go along with what the governor wants – for now, at least. He may change his mind at some time in the future.'

Tacy's face expressed the anguish she was feeling. Dropping her gaze, she said hesitantly, 'Would . . . would the governor let you stay out if . . . if I was having a baby?'

When he had recovered from his initial shock, Pilgrim

was aware that the suggestion had stirred feelings in him that were out of place in his present situation.

'I doubt it very much, Tacy. He might even take added delight in keeping me in prison.'

'If you thought it would help . . . you could.'

'No, Tacy, I wouldn't do that even if it *would* help. It isn't how I want things to be for us.'

Tacy clung to him once more and now she began to cry. 'I don't want you back in that prison, Pilgrim. I don't want you to go.'

'It will be all right, Tacy, I promise you. Things will work out for us in the end.'

He was still holding her close when her mother entered the dairy. She had seen Pilgrim's arrival at the farm and was disturbed when he had gone straight to the dairy without coming to the house first.

When he had not come out again after what she thought was a reasonable period of time, she had left the kitchen to find out what was happening.

She was startled when Tacy turned a tear-stained face towards her.

'What's going on here?'

Suddenly, with considerable alarm, she remembered Emma's condition. 'Is there something I should know about?'

'The new governor of Dartmoor had ordered Pilgrim to move back inside the prison,' Tacy wailed.

'Why? Have you done something wrong, Pilgrim?'

'No. It seems Governor Shortland has differing ideas to Captain Cotgrave on how the prison should be run. One of them is that senior officers responsible for their men should be living in the prison with them. He's given me forty-eight hours to settle my outside affairs, then I have to return.'

'What does Sir Thomas think about it?'

Pilgrim had released Tacy when Joan entered the dairy and now he gave a helpless gesture. 'He's not at Tor Royal. I don't think he's in London, either. He told me he was going to Scotland on the Prince Regent's business.'

'You must write to him. He'll have you out of there in no time.'

'Perhaps, but Sir Thomas has far more important matters to concern himself with than what's happening to an American prisoner-of-war.'

'Nonsense! You write to him. There's no reason at all why you should be locked up inside the prison. Things went along well enough with you on parole before this new governor came. There's no reason at all why you shouldn't enjoy parole, the same as all those French officers.'

Another thought came to her. 'What about young Billy's wedding? You promised him you'd be his groomsman.'

'I told the governor about that. He said I can leave the prison for the day to carry out my groomsman's duties.'

'Well, that's something, I suppose, but I still don't agree with the high-handed way he's behaving. It's the same with all these people who are put into important posts. They feel they've got to change things, to show they can do it better than the ones who were there before them.'

Looking at her distraught daughter, Joan showed her understanding. 'We're all going to miss you, Pilgrim. Tacy especially. You stay out here with her for a while. I'll go in and tell Tom what's happening. He'll feel as angry as I do about it, I've no doubt.'

69

Having enjoyed life outside the prison walls for so many months Pilgrim found difficulty adjusting to being locked up once more.

Although the regime in the Petty Officers' Block was much more relaxed than in the other blocks, he was unable to forget that the life of which he wanted to be a part was going on only a mile or two away.

Every few days he was able to meet with Tacy at the prison market but, as Tacy had pointed out, nothing was the same.

On the days when Tacy came to the prison, she was always accompanied. It was usually by Johanna, although on two occasions Emma came with her.

It was Emma who informed Pilgrim that Lieutenant Kennedy had been seen riding in the vicinity of Roundtor during recent days. She gave him the information while Tacy was busy serving a French officer at the back of the cart.

'Does Mrs Elford know about Kennedy?' Pilgrim asked anxiously.

Emma nodded.

'Good. Make sure Tacy doesn't go anywhere on her own – you need to be on your guard too. Fortunately, it won't be for too long. The Irish militia are overdue for relief from prison duty. Kennedy will be gone then and we can all breathe more easily.'

'What are you two whispering about?' Tacy finished serving the Frenchman and came to join them. 'If Emma wasn't marrying Billy next week I could easily be jealous.'

'Emma was telling me Lieutenant Kennedy has been seen about Roundtor lately. I don't like it. He knows I'm not there and might try to take advantage of the fact there's no man about the place.'

'There's Billy!' Emma sounded offended. 'He wouldn't let anything happen to Tacy.'

'I realise that,' said Pilgrim hastily. 'But you know yourself that he's not at Roundtor the whole time. There must be a whole lot of work to be done at the cottage.'

'Don't worry,' said Emma, only slightly placated. 'I won't let Tacy go out on the moor on her own.'

'Perhaps Mr Elford will be well soon?' said Pilgrim hopefully. 'That would make things a whole lot easier for everyone.'

Tacy shook her head sadly. 'Ma and I were talking about Pa only last night. I'm afraid we've all got to accept that he's never going to get any better. He seems to be a little bit weaker every day, but he's determined to go to Sheepstor for Billy and Emma's wedding.'

'Is that wise this weather?' Pilgrim glanced up at the dark sky.

'He'll be all right if it doesn't get any worse. Besides, it might be the last chance he'll ever have to leave the farm.'

Pilgrim murmured his sympathy, but at that moment

Ephraim was seen approaching with another inmate of Number Four Block. They were buying supplies for all their companions who were still not allowed direct access to the market.

The purchasing of the Americans was brought to a premature halt today. They had hardly begun when militiamen began moving among the market vendors, telling them to pack up their goods and move out of the prison.

Captain Shortland had tightened prison security in a number of ways. He now insisted that all market traders must be clear of the prison before dark.

Today, the traders were moved off earlier than usual. Dark clouds were building up ominously in the west and a bitterly cold wind had sprung up. Tacy had said it was likely winter would come early to Dartmoor this year.

Pilgrim watched with a heavy heart as Tacy and Emma drove the pony and cart from the prison yard. He and Tacy had been able to spend little time together after settling the misunderstanding between them. He felt there was still far too much that remained unsaid.

He had sent a letter to Sir Thomas, addressed to his London office, explaining all that had happened. He had not asked directly for his help and knew he had no reason to expect it. Yet there remained a hope at the back of his mind that the owner of Tor Royal might take it upon himself to seek to have Pilgrim's parole renewed.

'You thinking you ought to be going out with them, Cap'n?'

'That's about it, Ephraim,' said Pilgrim wistfully. 'It's a selfish thought, I suppose. I have at least spent some months enjoying life outside these prison walls. That's more than most have done.'

'True,' agreed Ephraim. 'But I don't suppose a man stops wishing for something or other until the day he dies.' He pointed up to the sky. 'Even then he's probably sitting up there somewhere, wishing he wasn't dead.'

Pilgrim smiled. 'How about you? What sort of things do you wish for?'

'Well now, that's not easy to answer, Cap'n. I've wished for many different things in my life. When I was small I wished I'd been born a white man. I wished very hard for that. When my ma was taken away from me, I wished she'd come back. Then one day I realised that wishing wasn't going to get me anywhere at all. I decided I'd have to do things for myself. The first was to get myself off the plantation. When that was done, I set out to make something of myself. Now I'm a sergeant of marines. All right, so I'm stuck in this prison, but so are a great many more Americans. I'll just take one day at a time now, Cap'n – how about you?'

'Perhaps I should do the same, Ephraim, but, unlike you, I'm still wishing. I'm wishing I was out of here and able to spend most of my days at Roundtor Farm.'

'Then you just wish away, Cap'n. That Tacy Elford is a girl worth wishing after. Take her back to America with you. If you need someone you can trust to work for you there, just call on Ephraim. Whatever needs doing I'm your man.'

'Thanks, Ephraim, I'll remember that. In the meantime, we're both stuck here, in Dartmoor prison. Keep me posted on what's happening in Block Four and we'll try to hold things down until this war is over. According to Governor Shortland we don't have very long to go.'

'I hope you're right, Cap'n. Of course, when you get back to the United States you know exactly what you're going to do. When we get shipped back we need to make sure the ship carrying us puts in to a northern port. If it takes us anywhere down south we're likely to find ourselves lined up on the jetty, being auctioned off to the highest bidder. That ain't going to go down very well with those of us who've served time in prison on behalf of America.'

Ephraim shrugged apologetically. 'You've got enough to worry you right now, Cap'n, but if you're really concerned about those of us in Block Four, I hope you'll give some consideration to what I've just said, when the time comes for our release.'

70

There had been a sprinkling of snow during the night preceding the wedding of Billy and Emma. The reluctant arrival of morning gave a promise of more. A heavy blanket of sombre grey cloud hung low over Dartmoor.

As Pilgrim walked to Princetown to meet with the others, large, soft snowflakes drifted down to earth and settled upon his uniform coat.

He waited for some twenty minutes for them to arrive. The time was spent stamping up and down and slapping his arms in a vain attempt to keep warm.

When the others eventually arrived they were travelling in the Roundtor Farm cart, pulled by their patient moorland pony.

Tom Elford was not with them.

'I didn't want him to run the risk of catching a chill,' explained his anxious wife, taking Pilgrim to one side. 'To tell you the truth, I was in two minds about leaving him at all. If it wasn't for the fact that we're all the family Billy and Emma have, I would have stayed home with him. I've still half a mind to go back. I can't run the risk of us all getting snowed in at Sheepstor, with Tom at home on his own.'

Billy and Emma stood nearby uncertainly, aware of what Joan was talking about, but not able to hear her words. Both looked ill-at-ease and unnaturally formal in the new clothes which had been yet another present from the Elford family.

'You of all people *must* be at the wedding,' declared Pilgrim. 'Look, you all go on ahead. I'll walk to Tor Royal and borrow one of Sir Thomas's horses. I have to be back at the prison tonight or I'll be in serious trouble. If the snow becomes too bad I can always bring Tacy back on the horse behind me, even if the rest of you are forced to remain behind.'

Joan's expression showed the doubt she felt about the idea. 'Will Sir Thomas loan you a horse at a moment's notice?'

'He's not at home, but the groom will let me have one. Go on to Sheepstor, I'll catch up with you before you get there.'

Joan agreed reluctantly, but when the small farm cart passed from view she was still looking back at him uncertainly.

Sir Thomas's groom was reluctant to saddle a horse for Pilgrim, until he was reminded that Sir Thomas had left instructions that Pilgrim could take out a horse whenever he wished. It had been before Pilgrim's return to the prison, but he did not remind the man of this.

When the groom finally agreed to saddle a horse for him, Pilgrim told him that if the snow became particularly bad he would have the animal housed in the prison governor's stable and see that it was returned to Tor Royal when the weather improved.

Once the decision had been made, the groom became

more helpful. He even found a waterproof riding coat
for Pilgrim to wear.

As he rode the horse out of the Tor Royal drive, Pilgrim
thought he was likely to be glad of the coat. Snow was
beginning to fall quite heavily now. It was settling too. It
felt somehow ghostly riding a horse whose hooves were
making no sound on the snow-covered ground.

There were no other travellers on the road and he saw
no sign of the party from Roundtor Farm. He had not
travelled far before it became difficult making out the
road beneath the crisp white blanket of snow. He was
greatly relieved when suddenly he saw the outline of
houses ahead of him. He had reached Sheepstor.

The Elfords with Billy and Emma were already at the
church but there was still an hour to wait before the
service was due to begin.

Fortunately, Reverend Cotterell came to the church
soon after Pilgrim arrived and invited the whole party
to the vicarage for a hot drink.

'I am most relieved you were able to reach Sheepstor
safely,' he said, as they walked from the church. 'I feared
you might not be able to make your way through the
snow. It has arrived early this year. All the portents point
to a harsh winter ahead of us.'

'I'm beginning to doubt the wisdom of coming,' said
a worried Joan Elford. 'I've left a sick husband at home
alone. No one will call in to see to him if we can't get
home after the wedding.'

'Then we'll bring the service forward,' said the
Sheepstor vicar immediately. 'While you are enjoying
your drink I'll be getting ready.'

Snow was still falling as the party made its way to the
church from the vicarage but, despite the bad weather,
there were far more villagers attending the wedding than

had been at the funeral of Tillie Yates.

It was a moving ceremony even though Billy was more nervous than anyone had ever seen him. The usually supremely confident Emma was equally nervous. It was a whispered and tremulous 'I do' that sealed the union of the young couple.

The ceremony over, Sheepstor villagers crowded around the newlyweds to offer their congratulations. Somehow, word of the marriage of the young moorland man to the tinkers' girl had spread around the area and moved the hearts of the Dartmoor villagers.

A number of small gifts had been collected and brought to the church for them: pots and dishes, a home-made leather-seated stool and a number of other small items.

A gift that particularly delighted Emma was a quantity of vegetable seeds that included onion, cabbage, carrots and turnips.

It was a happy party that filed from the church, but joy turned quickly to dismay. There must have been close to a foot of snow on the ground in front of the church – and it was still falling heavily!

As if this was not sufficient disaster in itself, Joan turned to say something to Pilgrim and slipped. He tried to grab her, but she fell heavily to the ground, twisting her ankle.

A couple of village men hurried to help Pilgrim lift her to her feet, but when she tried to put her right foot to the ground, she cried out in pain.

Helped back inside the church porch, Joan was close to tears. It was partly as a result of the pain of her injury, but mainly the culmination of a day spent worrying about her husband.

'Tacy, bring the pony and cart to the lychgate. Pilgrim can help me to get in it and we'll set off for Roundtor right away.'

'My dear woman!' Reverend Cotterell voiced his alarm. 'You must not even *consider* travelling home with such an injury. What if the cart went off the road – as is highly likely? You couldn't possibly walk. Oh no! You'll stay at the vicarage until the weather has improved sufficiently for you to leave.'

'I've only turned my ankle – and I *must* get home,' declared the distraught woman. 'Poor Tom . . . !'

'Don't you worry about Mr Elford,' said Pilgrim. 'I'll take Tacy back to Roundtor with me on Sir Thomas's horse.'

'Emma, Johanna and me'll take the pony and cart,' declared Billy importantly. 'You just stay here and get that ankle better, Mrs Elford. Leave everything to me. I'm a married man now, remember?'

Billy's statement forced a smile from Joan, in spite of her predicament. 'Bless you, Billy, but . . .'

'No buts, Mrs Elford,' said Reverend Cotterell positively. 'You'll stay at the vicarage until I think you are fit to travel. Off you go, Pilgrim. You and the others too, Billy. You'll be slower than Captain Penn, so let him go on ahead and explain things to Mr Elford. Now, where's Sadie Herrick? I saw her in the church just now. She'll put something on that ankle that'll have it mended more quickly than any doctor.'

'Here I am, Reverend.'

A small, toothless woman pushed her way through the crowd around Joan Elford. 'You just get her up to the vicarage. I've some opodeldoc, turpentine and some of me secrets already mixed up at home. I'll put it on that there ankle today and she'll be fit for dancing round a maypole in no time.'

The woman went on her way, cackling happily, and Pilgrim said to Tacy, 'We'd better make a move. I won't be happy until I've delivered you safely to Roundtor Farm, but I fear it's going to be a very unpleasant ride.'

71

Pilgrim's forecast that the ride from Sheepstor to Roundtor Farm would be 'unpleasant' was a gross understatement. It was a nightmare.

It snowed for the whole of the journey. For much of the time Pilgrim was hunched forward in the saddle, shielding his face from the driving snow. More than once the horse strayed from the now indefinable road. It was only Tacy's almost uncanny knowledge of the moor that brought them back again.

Arms gripped tightly about Pilgrim's waist, she would frequently peer around him, directing him to 'Go to the left of that tree', or advising him, 'You'll see rising ground on your left, soon. The road curves around the bottom of it.' Again, 'You should see a fast-running stream on your right in a minute. Tell me when you catch sight of it and I'll give you new directions.'

Almost unbelievably, it seemed to Pilgrim, just when he felt he would be unable to travel much farther, he recognised the snow-draped houses of Princetown. Now he too knew where they were.

When they finally reached Roundtor, he declared,
'That was little short of a miracle. Tacy, you're the
cleverest, as well as the most beautiful navigator I've
ever come across!'

Helping Tacy to slide to the ground he swung off the
tired horse to stand on the ground beside her.

He looked up at the sky and was forced to close his
eyes against the falling snow. 'I'd feel happier if the
others had remained behind at Sheepstor with your
ma.'

Tacy nodded her agreement. 'So would I, but Billy
could find his way here blindfold. He knows the moor
better than anyone I know. Let's go in and tell Pa what's
happening. I've no doubt he's been watching the snow
fall and worrying about us. You'll have something hot
to drink too? You needn't set off for the prison for a
couple of hours.'

'I'll put the horse in the stable and rub it down first.
I mustn't leave it too late getting back. Once darkness
falls I'll never find my way back – and it will come early
tonight.'

When Pilgrim entered the kitchen after stamping snow
off his boots on the doorstep, he was shocked to see
how frail Tom Elford was looking. His condition had
deteriorated in the few weeks since Pilgrim had left Tor
Royal and returned to Dartmoor prison.

After shaking hands with him, the sick farmer echoed
the words Pilgrim had spoken earlier to Tacy. 'I'd have
felt a whole lot easier in my mind had you and the
others arrived here together. Still, at least Joan will be
in the warm, even though she's turned her ankle. Is it
a bad injury?'

'It's painful, but Reverend Cotterell is confident a
Sheepstor woman can fix it for her. As for the others,

Billy should be here with Emma and Johanna by the time I leave.'

Tom Elford nodded. 'But what am I thinking of? Pull a chair up to the fire while Tacy pours you some tea. I've kept the kettle boiling for more than an hour. Now, while we wait for the others tell me all that's been happening up at the prison. There'll be little comfort for any of you up there, I don't doubt . . .'

Two hours later, when Pilgrim declared reluctantly that he would have to make his way back to the prison, Billy had still not arrived with Emma and Johanna.

'They should have been back by now,' said Tacy when she and Pilgrim left the farmhouse and were out of the hearing of her father. 'I'm worried, Pilgrim. We should all have travelled back together.'

The snow had eased off a little but the wind had increased. Pilgrim knew there would be drifting on the higher ground over which Billy and the others would have to travel.

'Perhaps they'll be here by the time I saddle up the horse,' said Pilgrim optimistically. 'You said yourself that Billy knows the moor better than anyone.'

They had not arrived by the time Pilgrim had left the farmhouse. He hated leaving them with such uncertainty hanging over their heads about the others, but if he did not he would never make it back to the prison before it was too dark to see his way.

He was on the outskirts of Princetown when he heard a sound on the road ahead of him. He was about to call out, to enquire whether it was the party bound for Roundtor, when it came into view.

It was not a pony and cart, but two figures, leading a pony. In the near-darkness he would have passed them by, had not a voice he recognised called, 'Pilgrim?

It *is* you?'

'Emma . . . and Billy! Where's the cart . . . and where's Johanna?'

In a voice choked with emotion, Emma said, 'She's gone, Pilgrim.'

'Gone? What do you mean, she's gone? Gone where?' Pilgrim stared at them through the gloom, not understanding, not *wanting* to understand what he believed Emma to be saying.

'We've lost her . . . in the snow.' Suddenly the words came pouring from her. 'The cart went off the road. We couldn't get it back on, so Billy took the pony out of the shafts. Johanna was riding it because she found walking hard going in the deep snow on the high ground. Then the pony fell – twice. So Johanna said she'd walk behind it. I walked with her for a while, then I went up front with Billy, telling Johanna to hold on to the pony's tail and not let go. I looked back a couple of times, to make sure she was all right. Then, when we reached some high ground, we ran into a blizzard. It was hard going for a while. When it eased off a bit I looked back – and Johanna wasn't there any more.'

'Where was this?'

Emma looked at Billy who had said nothing until now.

'Below Black Tor,' he said in a barely audible voice. 'About a mile back.'

'Didn't you go back to look for her?'

'Of course we did,' said Emma. 'We went back to where we'd last seen her and searched all around from there to where we found she'd gone. Billy floundered around in the snow like a mad thing and we both shouted for all we was worth, but . . . there wasn't a thing.'

Suddenly, Billy broke down and began to cry. 'It's all

my fault,' he said. 'They shouldn't have let her come with me. They shouldn't have trusted me to bring her home. I'm too simple to take care of myself, let alone anyone else. That's what my ma always used to say. They shouldn't have let Johanna come with me.'

Still holding the reins attached to the pony, Billy crouched down in the snow, rocking backwards and forwards in abject misery.

'Such talk will help no one,' said Pilgrim sharply. 'Emma, it's not far to Roundtor now, do you think you can find your way there alone?'

She nodded. 'What you going to do? It's too dark for you and Billy to go back there now. Even he couldn't find his way in the dark on a night like this.'

'I need him to give us an idea of where Johanna was last seen. We'll go to the barracks and get some militiamen with lanterns. Off you go now. Another thing . . . no matter how desperately upset they are, you're not to let Tom Elford or Tacy come out to try to help us. We don't want to have to start searching for anyone else. Take the pony with you. If you *do* lose your way, let the pony guide you. He knows his way to Roundtor.'

Taking the pony's reins from Billy, he passed them to her, then reached down and rested a hand on Billy's shoulder. 'Come on, Billy, there's no time to lose. Tacy has said many times that no one knows the moor as you do. Now's your chance to prove it. Johanna's life is in your hands.'

72

'But . . . this is a matter of life or death for a young girl. If we don't find her very soon she has no chance of survival in this weather.'

'I'm sorry, I can't risk the lives of my men. Besides, I have only a few men left in the barracks.'

Arriving at the militia barracks in Princetown, Pilgrim had learned with dismay that the duty officer was the one man he had hoped he would never again have dealings with.

Lieutenant Alan Kennedy was as unhelpful as Pilgrim had anticipated he would be.

'We're talking of the life of Johanna, for God's sake. You *know* her. Speak to your men. Call for volunteers.'

'I've told you, Captain Penn, I cannot allow my men to risk their lives on a night like this.'

Trying hard to control his rising anger, Pilgrim said, 'Then let me speak to your commanding officer. He'll probably lead the men himself – as any man worth his salt would.'

'The commanding officer is in Plymouth with the bulk

of our men. As it happens, they are there to escort another batch of Americans to Dartmoor.' Smugly, he said, 'Were your countrymen not so notoriously unruly, it would not have been necessary to send so many men on a simple escort duty. Then we might have had men to spare here.'

Pilgrim had an overwhelming urge to hit the militia officer but it would achieve nothing.

'Thank you, Lieutenant Kennedy. I hope your conscience allows you a good night's sleep tonight. Come, Billy, I know where we'll find some real men.'

As they walked away, Billy said, 'Where we going, Pilgrim? Where will we find the men you spoke of?'

'At the prison, Billy . . . God and Governor Shortland willing.'

Governor Shortland listened with growing concern as Pilgrim told him of the missing girl. During the brief period he had been in charge of the prison he had proved himself to be a more humane man than his predecessor. He also had a daughter who was about the same age as Johanna.

Pilgrim had gone directly to the governor's house with his request and also to ask him to take care of Sir Thomas's horse until the weather improved.

'What do you expect me to do, Captain Penn? The militia lieutenant was telling you the truth. Most of the militiamen are at Plymouth waiting for the weather to break in order to bring more prisoners-of-war here. I cannot spare more than a few of the militiamen who are on duty at the moment.'

'I'm not asking for militiamen, Governor. I'm asking you to allow prisoners-of-war to search for Johanna. American prisoners-of-war.'

Before Shortland could voice a refusal, Pilgrim added,

'I'll stand as guarantor for their conduct and return to the prison, Governor. I'll take only marines and soldiers. Disciplined men. *Please*, Governor. A young girl's life depends upon your decision.'

Pilgrim thought the prison governor was about to refuse the request, despite his pleas. But just then Shortland's daughter came to the front door. She slipped her hand inside her father's and smiled up at Pilgrim.

'Very well, Captain Penn. Go to the main gate. Tell the duty officer I will be joining you there in a few minutes.'

No more than ten minutes later, Pilgrim was standing in the ground floor of Block Four, occupied by the United States prisoners-of-war.

He outlined the problem, warned of the atrocious conditions they would be facing on the moor, then called for volunteers. Every man in the room stepped forward.

'Thank you, but I'll take only soldiers and marines. That should give us rather more than a hundred men.'

'Some of the prison guards and militiamen on duty have expressed a wish to help,' said Governor Shortland. 'I can let you have a dozen of them. The men may also draw lanterns from the store. You will no doubt have need of them.'

'Thank you, Governor. Right, shall we go . . . ?'

It was virtually impossible to distinguish the road that linked Princetown with Sheepstor. Even Billy was forced to stop on a number of occasions and retrace his steps.

Eventually, he stopped and said, 'This is where I last saw Johanna. I looked back and she was still there, clinging to the pony's tail.'

'Right, we'll go back along the road for a quarter of a mile, or so, just in case she headed back that way. Spread out in a line on either side of the road and we'll work our way back towards Princetown. Every man has a lantern, but we'll have only every other one lit. We'll keep the others in reserve. All right, Billy, lead us back along the road a way.'

It had begun to snow once more and when the men fanned out to begin their search, problems were encountered immediately. There were many hollows and gullies on the moor itself. More than once men disappeared and needed to be hauled out of deep snow by their companions.

It was a desperate feat of endurance to make any progress at all. During the course of a couple of hours they only managed to cover about half a mile. By this time the snow had closed in on them in a ferocious blizzard. Billy warned Pilgrim that there was a dangerous bog to one side of the road, even though it was now hidden beneath a two feet deep covering of snow.

Still nothing had been found of Johanna. Pilgrim wanted desperately to continue with the search, but prison life and rations had not enabled the men to maintain the standard of fitness soldiers and marines had once enjoyed. A number were close to exhaustion.

It was with a heavy heart that Pilgrim passed the order along the line of men on either side of him to call off the search and muster on the road.

Billy too was in a state of near-collapse. Even so, he pleaded with Pilgrim to allow the men to continue the search for 'just a while longer'.

'We can't, Billy,' replied Pilgrim through lips that were numb with cold. 'The men are exhausted; you're exhausted – and so am I. The weather's worse than it was when we began the search. If we go on as we are we'll begin to lose men. I'm sorry, we must call it off.'

'Then I'll stay out here on my own,' said Billy, in desperation. 'Leave me a lamp. I'll carry on searching.'

404 E. V. Thompson

'You're closer to collapse than anyone. I've watched you staggering for the past half an hour or more. You'll come back to Princetown with us, then make your way to Roundtor Farm to be with Emma.'

Billy sank down in the snow at Pilgrim's feet and began to sob. 'Poor Johanna. She's out there somewhere, Pilgrim. Lying in the snow, probably dead already! I can't go back to Roundtor, Pilgrim. I can't face Tacy and Mr Elford and tell them I let Johanna get lost in the snow. After all they've done for me, I've let this happen. It's all my fault.'

'It's nobody's fault, Billy. Nobody could have cared more for Johanna than you. It's just a terrible, tragic accident, that's all.'

Pilgrim hoped he sounded convincing. In truth, he believed the Elfords would feel as he did, that Billy had behaved irresponsibly by allowing Johanna to walk behind the pony by herself. But perhaps he too was to blame, for not insisting that Billy, Emma and Johanna remained at Sheepstor with Mrs Elford.

'Come on, Billy, let's get back to Princetown. You make your way to Roundtor while I get the men back to Dartmoor. I wish I could come to the farm with you, but that won't be possible.'

It took more than an hour to reach Princetown, so thick had the snow become and so fierce the blizzard.

They entered the town in single file, each man holding the coat of the man in front of him and the lead changing every few minutes.

The militiamen among them organised some hot soup for the searchers before they floundered their way back to the prison.

It was here too that a muster was carried out and it was discovered one of the marines was missing.

The missing man was Ephraim.

73

For Johanna, the journey in the snow from Sheepstor had become excruciating long before the pony fell over for the first time.

Chilled to the bone, she was so cold that her fingers throbbed painfully if she breathed on them for too long. Her legs and feet too felt frozen. As a final humiliating misery, she had failed to realise the uncomplaining pony's back had been soaked by the snow while it was pulling the cart. Soon after she settled astride the patient animal she realised her drawers were soaked through, adding to the freezing cold of her legs and bottom.

When the pony slipped and fell for the first time, Johanna was caught off guard. Falling with it, she was fortunate not to become trapped beneath its body as it struggled to rise.

When it happened again she was more alert and jumped clear in time. The animal was helped up and stood shivering from a combination of fear and cold.

Billy suggested she walk at the pony's head with him and Emma, but the snow was too deep for her short, thin legs. It was now she hit upon the idea of walking behind the pony. Clinging to its tail she could tread in the footsteps of the others. Emma walked with her for a while, but then went up ahead, to join Billy.

This worked for much of the time. However, if Johanna did not concentrate on where she was walking, she found herself struggling through the deeper snow on either side of the tracks made by the others.

Occasionally the party strayed from the road when they reached higher ground and the blizzard increased in ferocity.

She was tiring too. Twice in quick succession she lost her footing and fell in the snow. On the first occasion she maintained her hold on the pony's tail, struggling to regain her footing as her light body was dragged along behind the pony.

When it happened again her cold fingers lost their grip on the pony's tail. Picking herself up she floundered frantically through the deep snow until she was able to reach out and grasp the tail once more.

It was at this point that Billy looked around to check that she was still with them. He tried to smile, but the concerned expression on his face seemed to have been frozen there.

Only moments later, it seemed to Johanna, they walked into a blinding swirl of driving snow. She ducked her head quickly, but it was too late. She had snow up her nose, in her eyes and in her half-open mouth.

Unable to see, she made the mistake of releasing her grip on the pony's tail in order to brush the snow from her face.

It was a foolhardy thing to do, but the hand holding the tail was the one she always used for such things.

Unfortunately, they had strayed off the road yet

again. Her foot caught in something and she fell into the snow.

When she picked herself up she could not see the others.

Johanna panicked momentarily. Floundering after the pony, she fell again. Struggling to her feet once more she put up an arm in an attempt to ward off the driving snow. At the same time, she found herself in snow almost to her waist.

She fought her way forward for some minutes before making a terrifying discovery. There were no tracks of man or beast in front of her!

Turning ninety degrees to her left, she struggled forward once more, but found nothing. She turned back and tried another direction, stumbling blindly ahead.

Belatedly, she began shouting, but realised almost immediately it was a futile waste of her energy. It was as though she had put several blankets over her head before calling out. Her voice went nowhere.

She tried to control her panic and think logically. Surprisingly, she did not resort to tears. She remembered that when she had been following the pony the snow had been blowing in her face.

That was it! The snow had been driving at her from dead ahead. Turning her head slowly, she discovered that the snow was now blowing in from her left. Moving in that direction, she set off once more.

She continued on this course until she encountered a drift of snow so deep she was forced to make a cautious detour around it until she once again had the wind in her face.

But she was going downhill now. She knew this was not right. She turned to retrace her footsteps once more, but quickly lost her way again.

Suddenly, she felt thoroughly frightened. Her bottom lip was pushed out and it began to tremble.

Yet again, Johanna paused to take a grip of herself. She had to get back to the road somehow. When Billy and Emma realised she was no longer with them they would surely come back and search for her.

She forced her way through the snow, travelling tortuously in the direction in which she believed she should be moving, until she began to walk downhill yet again.

She turned. As she did so, she lost her footing – suddenly it seemed the whole ground was collapsing beneath her and she was falling through space.

She landed with a jolt, but the snow that had fallen with her helped to break her fall.

Above her was the hole she had made in the snow, with dark sky showing through it and flakes drifting down to where she lay.

There was a noise behind her and Johanna looked around in alarm. It was a startled sound, as though her sudden arrival had frightened something – or someone!

At this moment Johanna was more fearful than when she had been lost in the snow. Then she heard another sound. To her great relief she recognised the bleating of a sheep. Now she realised what had happened to her.

She had fallen into a gully occupied by a number of sheep. Snow must have drifted over them, but their movement and the heat of their bodies had created a cavern in the snow.

Johanna was greatly relieved. She was not afraid of sheep – but they were of her. They began milling about and the movement brought a fall of snow from the artificial roof of the cave.

She moved back from them and before long their panic subsided. Squatting down some distance away, she was forced to move after a few minutes because a flurry of snow blew down through the hole she had made in the snow roof of the gully.

Now she began to feel really cold and could not control her shivering. Not wanting to dwell on the hopelessness of her situation, she wished the sheep would allow her to creep among them and share their warmth . . .

74

Johanna started up in a sudden fright and realised she must have slept. An exhausted sleep.

Her unexpected movement caused another momentary panic among the sheep which had gradually moved closer while she was asleep.

Now they fled from her again. For a few minutes they milled around in the darkness, bleating and jostling. Johanna feared that at any minute their movements would bring the snow roof down upon them.

'It's all right . . . I won't hurt you.'

Johanna spoke soothingly, but with some difficulty because her teeth were chattering so wildly.

Desperately cold, she looked upwards, but could see nothing. For a moment she feared the hole had become covered over.

The thought struck terror into her. If snow had blocked the hole, she was trapped underground with the sheep and they would never be found.

Then she felt snowflakes drifting down upon her upturned face and she realised darkness had fallen.

Far from feeling relief at the discovery, she became thoroughly frightened. In the darkness, no one would come looking for her. They would not know *where* to look!

Now, for the first time, tears came, unwanted. There were not many but she felt them in her eyes.

She sank down to the ground and covered her face with her hands. It was while she squatted like this that she thought she heard a sound. At first she thought it must be the sheep again. Then she heard it once more.

It sounded like someone shouting, far away.

Johanna stood up and realised how cold and stiff she was. She began shouting as loud as she could in a thin, shrill voice. The sound startled the sheep and they began milling about again, bleating their alarm.

She shouted until her throat hurt and she started to cough. When she stopped, the sheep were still making a noise and she could hear nothing.

Then she thought she saw the outline of the hole above her and realised someone must be nearby, with a lamp.

She began shouting again, even more loudly this time.

Just when she was beginning to feel she had been mistaken, the snow roof suddenly collapsed, about halfway between herself and the sheep. At the same time she heard someone cry out in pain.

'Billy . . . ? Is that you?'

'Johanna? It's me . . . Ephraim! Are you all right?'

'Oh, Ephraim, I'm so glad you've found me. I was getting awful frightened . . .'

Johanna scrambled over the heap of newly fallen snow and found Ephraim. He was sitting up on the floor and made no attempt to rise, but he did pull her to him and give her a huge hug.

'You're *freezing*, child – and soaking wet too. Here, help me off with my greatcoat – and shout while you're doing it. There are men up top. They're quite a way away, but we've got to make them hear us.'

As he struggled to remove his coat in the darkness, they both shouted as loudly as they could, driving the sheep to distraction.

When they paused, they could hear nothing above the bleating of the sheep. Ephraim said, 'Try again. The sheep are helping. It was them I heard just before I found you.'

Three times they called, but could hear nothing outside of the snow-roofed gully. During all this time, Ephraim had remained seated and now Johanna asked, 'Are you all right, Ephraim?'

'No. I landed awkwardly when I fell. I seem to have done something to my knee. I can't move my leg.'

'I'm sorry! Can I do anything?'

'Yes, you can wrap that coat around you and try to put some warmth back in your body. It's got pockets. Put your hands in them. Then get to shouting again.'

They both shouted for another ten or twelve minutes before Ephraim said, 'I don't think they heard us, Johanna. I was afraid they wouldn't. I seemed to have strayed from the others in the line when I heard the sheep bleating. Then, when I got close enough to see the hole in the snow, I heard you. Before I could call out to the others I'd fallen down here.'

'That's what happened to me,' said Johanna. 'After I lost Billy and Emma I just wandered around in the snow until I fell down here.'

'Billy was up there with us. He and Captain Pilgrim. We've all been very worried about you, Johanna.'

'Poor Billy. I expect he's blaming himself for losing

me. He always lays the blame on himself when anything happens, even if he's had nothing to do with it at all.'

'Tell me about Billy, Johanna. Tell me all you know about him.'

Ephraim wanted to keep Johanna talking, to take her mind off the cold. It also gave him something other than his injured knee to think about. He wanted to put off thinking about the cold and the situation they were both in.

It had been all right while he was wearing the greatcoat. Without it his limbs were beginning to go numb. The temperature was dropping rapidly on the moor. The men had commented upon it as the search progressed.

He would like to have been able to stand up and beat his body with his hands to keep the circulation moving, but standing was out of the question. His leg injury was worse than he had admitted to Johanna, but he did not want her worrying about him.

'Your teeth are chattering!' Johanna said suddenly, while she was telling him about the days when Billy had first come to Roundtor Farm seeking work.

'Are they? Your story about Billy was so interesting I didn't even notice.'

'Your coat's *much* too big for me. We can share it. You can have one of your arms in a sleeve and put your hand in a pocket. I can put *both* my arms in the other sleeve. That way we'll both stay a bit warmer.'

'That's a very good idea, Johanna. Why didn't I think of that? I've got something else here we can share.'

He unwrapped a large piece of cloth from around his body and put it around both of them. As he moved, he had to bite his lip to prevent himself crying out with pain as he moved the injured leg. He hoped help would reach them by early the next morning. He did not believe he would be able to last any longer.

But ensuring that Johanna survived was more important at the moment.

'Here! I've just found a couple of prison biscuits in my pocket. I bet you've never had anything like these before?'

'No . . .' said Johanna doubtfully, taking them from him.

'Well, save them until the morning. Then you can see what you're eating. Now, you were telling me about Billy coming to your farm . . .'

75

'I'd like permission to take my men out on the moor again, Governor.' Pilgrim stood in front of Governor Shortland's desk and made his request.

It was the morning after the abortive search for Johanna. Despite his exhaustion, he had lain awake for much of the night, thinking about the missing young girl and Ephraim. Wondering what might have happened to them.

'One of your men escaped when you took them out last night, Captain Penn. How many might I expect to lose today?'

'Ephraim didn't make an escape, Governor. I'm convinced of that. He's out there somewhere. Perhaps he found Johanna and for some reason couldn't leave her. She might be hurt . . .'

'I am not prepared to take the risk of having more prisoners escape, Captain. Your request is not granted.'

'Governor, I know Sergeant Ephraim as well as though he were my own brother. I *know* he wouldn't have run off, certainly not while we were searching for Johanna.

He knows the girl and is very fond of her. He'd move heaven and earth to find her.'

'I am sorry, the answer is still "no".'

'Then let me go alone. I'll return Sir Thomas's horse and call at Roundtor Farm, just in case Johanna or Ephraim have turned up there. If not, I'll take Billy Yates out with me and have another look around the area where both Johanna and Ephraim were lost.'

Pilgrim pleaded with the prison governor. 'I know the snow is still deep out there, but it isn't snowing right now. I might find something we missed last night.'

Captain Shortland's inclination was to refuse this request too. However, during the couple of weeks he had been in charge of the prison he had heard a great deal about Sir Thomas Tyrwhitt and the power he wielded. It had become apparent that his influence extended far beyond Dartmoor. He was a power in London too and had brought about Captain Penn's parole against the wishes of Captain Cotgrave.

If called upon to justify his own decision to withdraw Pilgrim's parole, Governor Shortland felt he could satisfy the Admiralty, at least. But he did not want to be accused of being particularly biased against the American prisoners-of-war.

'Very well, *you* may go. I am told there is likely to be a partial thaw today. That might make your task easier. I wish you luck in your search, Captain Penn, but I fear that after a night on the moor in such weather, any chance of finding the girl alive must be remote.'

As Pilgrim rode away from the prison, he thought of the governor's words. He did not want to dwell upon the likelihood that the governor would be proven right, yet commonsense told him there must be little chance that Johanna had survived the night.

There was constant traffic between the militia barracks and the prison and an early morning attempt had been made to clear the road through Princetown. However, once outside the small settlement, the snow was still deep.

Fortunately, Pilgrim was familiar with the track to Roundtor Farm. He was able to choose a route that included sheltered spots where the snow was thinnest, avoiding places where there was likely to be drifting.

Paths had been cleared criss-crossing the Roundtor farmyard and as Pilgrim entered the yard both Emma and Tacy ran from the house to greet him.

Both girls spoke at the same time.

'Have you found Johanna?'

'Where's Billy?'

Startled, Pilgrim said, 'We found nothing last night, but I'm going out to look once more. I intended to take Billy with me. He left us at Princetown last night to come on here. Has he gone out again already?'

The colour drained from Emma's face and she replied, 'Billy hasn't been seen since he went off with you yesterday afternoon.'

'Then where can he be now? It was dark when we parted, but he'd been loaned a lantern and it had stopped snowing. I can't believe he'd lose himself on the way here from Princetown.'

'I don't think he intended coming to Roundtor,' said Emma shakily. 'He blamed himself for losing Johanna. He wouldn't have been able to cope with the thought of facing Tacy.'

'Then where do you think he would have gone?'

'Back to the cottage at Whiteworks, perhaps?'

'What's going on? Has Johanna been found . . . ?'

Tom Elford called from the kitchen doorway. Looking frail and ill, he leaned against the doorframe for support.

'Pa! You shouldn't be out of bed, let alone standing out here in the cold.'

Tacy hurried across the farmyard to him.

'We've found nothing yet, Mr Elford, but I'm going out searching again now.'

'On your own? You don't know the moor . . .' Breathing in the cold, winter air as he talked he began coughing uncontrollably.

'I'm on my way to find Billy. He'll come with me.'

'You can tell him I want words with him. If it wasn't for his stupidity . . .'

Another bout of coughing cut off whatever he intended saying. Moments later, still chiding him for coming out into the cold air, Tacy took him inside.

'I'll make my way to the cottage and see if Billy's there,' said Pilgrim. 'Mr Elford's right. Without Billy I'll be no good out there on the moor alone. We've already lost Ephraim. He went missing during the search last night.'

Pilgrim was not certain that Emma even heard him. Her thoughts were still with Billy.

'I'll come with you to the cottage,' she said suddenly. 'I . . . I don't know what I'll do if he's not there.'

'Come on then. The sooner we get started, the better.'

With Emma riding behind him on the horse, Pilgrim was passing out through the farmyard gateway when Tacy came running after them from the house.

'Wait! Where are you going?'

'To the cottage first of all, to look for Billy. Then back out on the moor to find Johanna. I hope we might find Ephraim with her.' He repeated the circumstances of Ephraim's disappearance. 'I don't think he got himself lost,' he added. 'Ephraim's far too sensible to do a thing like that.'

'I hope you're right,' said Tacy fervently. 'Just thinking that Ephraim might possibly be with her gives me new hope.'

She turned to Emma. 'Don't be too upset by what Pa just said. He's frantic with worry about Johanna – we both are, but at heart he knows that Billy would never knowingly have done anything to put her in danger. The only good thing about all this is that Ma isn't here to upset herself about what's going on.'

'I'm worried for Billy too now,' said Emma unhappily. 'He *does* feel he's to blame. I'm frightened of what he might do if he believes something's happened to her.'

'We won't talk about that,' said Pilgrim firmly. 'We're going out to find Billy, Johanna and Ephraim – and we're going to succeed.'

As they were talking, there was the sound from one of the farm's outbuildings of a dog barking, no doubt excited by the sound of voices. It gave Pilgrim an idea.

'I'd like to take one of the dogs along with us. Could I have Rip?'

Tacy looked doubtful. 'He doesn't know you very well – and the snow's awfully deep out there. We'd be in trouble from Sir Thomas if anything happened to him.'

'I'll tell Sir Thomas that I insisted,' said Pilgrim. 'He'd be a great help. He's got sharper hearing than we have. If he heard Johanna, he'd lead us to her.'

After only a moment more of hesitation, Tacy nodded. 'Take him. I'll pray that you find her safely. Pray that you'll find everyone.'

76

Rip thought snow was great fun. He gambolled excitedly in the wake of the horse ridden by Pilgrim and Emma as they retraced the path made by the horse on Pilgrim's way to Roundtor earlier that morning.

However, when Pilgrim turned off and headed for Whiteworks cottage through deep snow, the dog found the going more difficult. He leaped through the snow for a while before sitting down and barking until Pilgrim turned the horse around and rode back to him.

Dismounting, he passed Rip up to Emma before mounting the horse once more. They rode on with the dog between them, the animal apparently thoroughly enjoying the new experience.

It took much longer than was usual, but eventually they reached the cottage and Emma slipped from the horse's back.

With Rip leaping after her, frog-like, through the snow, she made her way to the back door of the cottage.

As Pilgrim tied the reins of the horse to the gate, Emma opened the kitchen door and let out a horrified scream.

When Pilgrim reached the doorway she was kneeling on the floor beside a sluggishly moving Billy. Hanging from a hook in a beam, once used for curing bacon, was a piece of rope with a broken end.

On the floor, beside Billy, was a noose which also had a broken end. A chair lay on its side, nearby.

Leaning over her husband of less than twenty-four hours, Emma lifted him to a sitting position and kneeled beside him, hugging him to her.

'Billy . . . ! Billy . . . ! What did you think you were doing? Why . . . ?'

Billy looked up at her, bleary-eyed, his face screwed up in anguish. 'I'm sorry, Emma. I couldn't face Tacy and Mr Elford. It was all my fault, letting Johanna get herself lost.'

He glanced up at the piece of rope dangling from the hook and looked away again quickly. 'I . . . I just didn't want to live any more, Emma . . . but the rope broke.'

When Billy raised his head, Pilgrim saw a rope burn encircling his neck.

'There was no cause to do anything like that, Billy. We're going out now, you and I, to find Johanna. Tacy said I was to tell you she knows it wasn't your fault that Johanna got herself lost. She doesn't blame you. No one does. Anyway, we're going to find her, you'll see.'

Emma hugged Billy close, her face screwed up in an expression of anguish. 'You mustn't ever do anything like this again, Billy. We're married now, you and I. We're man and wife and will share everything – both the good and the bad things. Being married means we help each other. You must never run off and do things by yourself when something's wrong. You have me now. Before very long there'll be a baby too. We need you – and I want to keep you.'

It became impossible to say more because Rip thought

it was time he joined in. Pushing between the couple he attempted to lick Billy's face.

Suddenly, Billy gave Emma a grateful and unexpected hug. Standing up, he said, 'I'm ready now, Pilgrim. I . . . I'm sorry I've caused everyone so much trouble.'

'Friends don't look upon the things they do for each other as trouble, Billy. I'm thankful we've found you safe and sound. Now, let's go and find the others.'

Unexpectedly, Emma turned and hugged Pilgrim too. 'I'm glad Billy and I have you for a friend, Pilgrim. I only hope things work out for you and Tacy. Now, off you go, both of you, and find Johanna and Ephraim.'

There had been a surprising amount of traffic on the road between Sheepstor and Princetown that morning. As they rode along, Pilgrim and Billy passed a couple of heavy wagons, more than one horse and rider, and a number of men on foot.

Travelling proved to be much easier today. There still seemed to be as much snow covering the moor as there had been the night before, but Billy assured Pilgrim it was beginning to thaw.

'There's lots of it, so it will take some time,' he explained. 'But in a couple of days' time there'll only be snow left in the gullies on the higher ground. Mind you, it still won't be easy to travel around the moor because the rivers and streams will be running very high.'

When they eventually reached the area where Billy believed Tacy had disappeared, they found a gnarled moorland farmer here with a cart laden with hay.

When Pilgrim explained the reason he and Billy were here, the farmer shook his head pessimistically. 'You're not going to find anyone alive on the moor after such a night. I'm out looking for my sheep, but I expect to find more than half of 'em dead, for all they're wearing a coat made for 'em by the Good Lord Himself.'

'I'm surprised you expect to find *any* of them alive in snow such as this,' said Pilgrim.

'That's because you don't know much about the moor, or about sheep,' said the farmer with blunt honesty. 'They'll find themselves a hollow in the ground, or a space between some big rocks and stay there. When the snow drifts and covers 'em, they'll move around to make themselves some breathing space. Leastways, those with a farthing's worth of sense will. Others will just stand out in the snow and die. Sheep aren't the brightest of animals.'

Pilgrim had been listening to the philosophical farmer with increasing excitement. 'These "hollows". Are there any around here?'

The farmer nodded. 'A few. Some of the old tinners dug out one or two tunnels that have collapsed over the years too. That's where I'm going to look now.'

'Can we come with you?'

The farmer shrugged. 'You can please yourself, but if you're coming along with me one of you can carry some hay. The other one can bring along this shovel. Might as well be useful as not.'

The first spot the farmer led them to with impressive accuracy was little more than a faint dip in the ground. Here they found three sheep. Two were dead. The third was hauled out of the hollow unceremoniously and left with a bundle of hay in the tracks they had made.

The farmer explained he would pick up the ewe on the way back and take her to his farm in the wagon. 'There's a much deeper place over here a ways,' he said, leading them through snow that came above their knees.

Rip was making his way through the snow with them, walking between the farmer, who was leading the way, and the others. Suddenly, he pricked up his ears and made a strange sound in his throat.

'Rip's heard something,' said Billy.

'Likely it's more of my sheep,' said the farmer. 'We're getting close now. But if the dog can hear them it means there's something alive in there.'

A few paces farther on, Rip raised his head and began barking excitedly.

The farmer immediately rounded on the others. 'I don't want him barking. If he frightens the sheep he'll bring down the snow on them and it'll be hard work to get them out . . .'

'Shh! Listen!'

Pilgrim had been only half concentrating on what the farmer was saying. Rip had stopped barking without being told and Pilgrim had heard something else.

The farmer stopped talking, his lips narrowing indignantly.

Immediately, they heard the bleating of sheep – and then they heard something else. It was a shrill, young voice calling for help.

'It's Johanna!' Billy was suddenly beside himself with excitement and now Rip began barking furiously.

The young dog became quiet when Billy gave him an order, but the farmer had an expression of disbelief on his face. 'Well I never did!' he exclaimed. 'It is a young girl and it sounds as though she's in with my sheep.'

A few minutes later, Pilgrim spied a hole in the snow and said, 'There! It looks as though someone's fallen through . . .'

'Don't go too close!' warned the farmer. That's one of the diggings I was telling you about. It's pretty deep. You'll hurt yourself if you fall through the snow.'

'Then how are we going to get in?'

'From down there.' The farmer pointed down the

slope. 'We'll dig into it gradually and make a tunnel, same as the sheep have.'

'You and Billy go and make a start. I'll be with you in a moment. I want to call down to Johanna. To let her know what we're doing.'

As the others made their way through the snow to the point where they would begin digging, Pilgrim cautiously edged his way closer to the hole in the snow.

Both the sheep and Johanna were silent now. When he felt he was as close as he could safely advance, he called, 'Johanna, are you there? Can you hear me?'

'Yes . . . Yes, I can hear you,' said Johanna excitedly. 'Who is it?'

'It's Pilgrim. Billy and a farmer are with me. We're going to start digging through the snow towards you. Are you all right?'

'I'm very cold. Ephraim's here with me, but he hurt himself when he fell and he's not moving. I think he's hurt bad.'

'So he *did* find you! We won't be long getting through to you. Stand beneath the hole, in case the snow collapses while we're digging – and don't worry. We'll have you out of there very soon.'

Retracing his steps, Pilgrim hurried after Billy and the farmer. He joined them in their task, digging through the snow with his bare hands.

Their activity excited Rip. He alternated between barking and digging, his tail wagging furiously.

It was half an hour before the spade wielded by Billy suddenly broke through into the snow tunnel, causing the sheep to bolt to the far end of their sanctuary.

Billy was the first to reach Johanna. Still wrapped in Ephraim's overcoat, she hugged him fiercely, before treating Pilgrim in the same manner.

When he had extricated himself from her embrace,

Pilgrim made his way farther inside the tunnel, causing consternation among the sheep.

They eventually fled past him and broke out of the newly made opening.

On the dirty snow of the cave floor, curled up as though asleep, lay Ephraim.

Johanna had followed Pilgrim and now she said, 'I was shivering during the night and I couldn't stop. Ephraim wrapped something around me, then he gave me his overcoat and cuddled me until I went to sleep. When I woke up this morning, Ephraim wouldn't answer when I spoke to him and he hasn't moved. He's awfully cold.' Looking up at him, wide-eyed, she asked, 'Is he dead?'

Pilgrim crouched down beside his sergeant and felt for a pulse, but it was unnecessary. As soon as he touched the ice-cold body, he knew the answer to Johanna's question.

Standing up, he found his vision too blurred to see anything about him.

'Yes, Johanna, I'm afraid he is. But he saved you. Had he known that, he would have died a happy man. Come along, Billy will take you home to Roundtor. The farmer can help me carry Ephraim out to his wagon. It's a poor enough carriage for a brave man, but Ephraim wouldn't have minded.'

'All right.' Johanna looked at the dead man, tearfully. 'I'm sorry Ephraim died. Would you like to wrap this around him?'

From beneath the overcoat she unwrapped the 'piece of cloth' Ephraim had wrapped about her during the long, bitterly cold night.

It was the United States flag that had once fluttered defiantly over Dartmoor prison's Block Four.

77

With the home-made United States flag wrapped around him as a shroud, Ephraim was the first man to be buried in the, as yet, unconsecrated burial ground of the unfinished Princetown church.

The church had been built by French prisoners-of-war. Although most of the exterior was completed, there was still much to be done inside.

All the United States marines from Dartmoor prison attended the funeral, as did the soldiers, many of the merchant seamen and Governor Shortland, with members of his staff. Among the Americans, only a hard-core of men from the southern states were not present.

The service was conducted by Reverend Cotterell from Sheepstor. Not unnaturally, he chose to base his eulogy on 'Greater love hath no man than this, that a man lay down his life for his friends'.

It was a very moving service. Pilgrim thought it was one of which Ephraim would have approved.

Pilgrim would have liked to spend some time with Tacy afterwards, but on such an occasion as this, he felt it important that he march his men back inside the prison as a single unit.

He had time only for a brief conversation with her, but was relieved to hear that Billy had been forgiven by the Elford family. They agreed it should never be mentioned again.

After marching his countrymen into the prison and dismissing them, Pilgrim was told Captain Shortland wished to speak to him.

When Pilgrim entered the governor's office, Captain Shortland seemed somewhat uncomfortable. Pilgrim wondered what might have gone wrong.

There was a letter on the desk. Picking it up, Shortland said, 'I have just received this from the Admiralty. It seems they have heard from Sir Thomas Tyrwhitt. He points out that your parole was the direct result of the Prince Regent's intervention. Sir Thomas has also said His Royal Highness is not used to having his wishes countermanded. I am ordered to release you on parole immediately. I regard this whole business as being highly irregular, but it is an order I dare not disregard.'

Standing up from his desk, the prison governor turned his back on Pilgrim and stared out of the window.

'I find myself in a difficult situation, Captain Penn. As I have just said, I cannot refuse to grant your parole. Indeed, I have no wish to do so. However, in the short time we have known each other, I have come to rely upon you. Having someone I know and can trust in my dealings with your countrymen is of great importance to me right now. There are more American prisoners-of-war on the road to Dartmoor at this very moment. It will bring the total to nine hundred.'

The figure came as a surprise to Pilgrim. It would

almost double the number of Americans in Dartmoor prison. However, it should make no difference to his parole and he said so.

'That is quite true, Captain, but among these men are a few known troublemakers. One in particular. Like the sergeant you have just lost, this man is an ex-slave, as are many of his companions. The number also includes the entire crew of a ship from one of your southern ports. There has already been a serious fight on their way here in which two men have died.'

Captain Shortland turned to face Pilgrim once more. 'If you take parole there will be no American officer left who possesses your experience of prison problems. You are respected by both sides, Captain, and trusted by the black Americans. I fear the chief troublemaker among the newcomers is likely to bring new problems with him. He has been in shackles for much of his time as a prisoner-of-war. He will arrive here in chains and is unlikely to have them removed unless he undergoes a dramatic change in his attitude towards his imprisonment.'

Remembering his own introduction to Dartmoor prison, Pilgrim said, 'I must protest, Governor! No man should be kept in chains for so long, whatever he's done.'

'I agree with you. However, unless he can be persuaded to accept prison discipline, he cannot be allowed to disrupt the routine here. I have more than nine thousand men in my charge, Captain Penn. It is difficult enough keeping order without the added tensions caused by the differences among Americans.'

'My understanding is that the American authorities have similar difficulties to cope with in our prisoner-of-war camps, when English, Irish and Scots prisoners are thrown together,' Pilgrim retorted. 'I doubt whether any prison governor expects his task to be an easy one. You've said nothing to persuade me I should forego parole and remain here surrounded by problems that are not of my making, and about which I can do nothing. I have no intention of providing you with a scapegoat, should something go seriously wrong. It's hardly an attractive proposition – except for you, perhaps.'

For a few moments Pilgrim thought Governor Shortland was about to make an angry reply to such outspoken remarks. Much to his surprise, the governor agreed with him.

'You are quite right, of course, Captain Penn. The presence of a responsible prisoner-of-war officer does ease my burden here considerably. What would make prison life more palatable for *you*?'

Pilgrim thought of Tacy and the pleasant life he had led for a while, shared between Tor Royal and Roundtor Farm. Nothing could compensate for the rupture of his relationship with Tacy.

But he stood before the governor now as the senior officer representing the interests of the United States prisoners-of-war.

'I could make a number of recommendations that might help to relieve some of the tensions and grievances that exist at the moment.'

'That's what I thought. Sit down and tell me about them, Captain Penn. We'll see whether anything can be done to put them right.'

Pilgrim left Governor Shortland's office despondent because he had agreed to forego parole, at least for the foreseeable future, although he had succeeded in gaining a number of concessions for the American prisoners-of-war – and for himself too.

The most important one was perhaps the one involving the accommodation of his countrymen.

The living quarters of black and white prisoners had been partitioned off to keep them apart, the exercise yard too being divided, but this solution had not been a total success. Their close proximity provided a constant reminder of the deep differences between many of those in the two groups of men.

The black Americans still gathered in the evenings to sing some of their plaintive and moving music from the plantations of America's southern states. But now some of the more extreme of the white southerners had formed their own choir to perform at the same time as their black countrymen. Their repertoire included a number of crude songs deriding those with whom they shared Block Four.

Missiles had begun to fly in both directions over the dividing wall, causing injuries among the two opposing groups of music makers. Feelings were beginning to run high once more. If ever men from the opposing groups were allowed to meet, fights were inevitable.

The influx of another four hundred and fifty men would greatly exacerbate the situation.

At Pilgrim's suggestion, the governor agreed that when the newcomers arrived all the white Americans would be moved to accomodation in another building.

Pilgrim had also tried to have the market thrown open to all United States prisoners-of-war, but Shortland insisted this must be put off until the tension between black and white Americans had eased. All he would agree to was that twice the present number of men from each racial group would be allowed to attend the market to buy goods for the others.

Pilgrim gained other concessions. One of the most important was that the French troublemakers were to be forcibly removed from the attic floor they shared with the Americans in Block Four. They would be transferred to the prison hulks in Plymouth harbour. The black Americans would have the whole attic floor to themselves.

Another concession was that the morning parade outside the prison blocks in all weathers was to cease. The men would also have a daily surgery.

Governor Shortland then informed Pilgrim he had been advised by American Agent Beasley that the United States Government intended raising the daily allowance of the prisoners-of-war by a penny.

It seemed little enough, but Pilgrim knew it would work wonders for the morale of the men.

On a personal level, Captain Shortland gave Pilgrim permission to leave the prison one day a week to pay a visit to either Tor Royal or Roundtor.

It was not the same as enjoying his former freedom, but it would suffice for now. The governor had promised Pilgrim he would be granted full parole once more should a more senior American officer be sent to the prison.

The governor also passed on a piece of news that came as a great relief to Pilgrim. Lieutenant Kennedy and the Irish militiamen were being relieved that very day. Their place was being taken by Scots militiamen.

Pilgrim would no longer need to worry about Tacy meeting up with Kennedy on the moor when she went about her daily work.

78

Pilgrim and Tacy were able to enjoy only one day of his weekly freedom before snow enveloped the moor once again.

This fall of snow was even more severe than the one which caused Ephraim's death. Those who lived on the moor declared it was the worst weather in living memory.

So deep was the snow that supplies were unable to reach the prison from Plymouth. It was necessary to fall back on the prison's emergency stocks of food. Even these were not readily available. Working parties needed to dig paths through waist-high snow to reach the storehouse from the various cell blocks.

In places the snow had drifted against the prison walls to a height of ten foot. The weather was so cold that the militiamen were withdrawn from their stations on the walls.

This was sufficient to tempt eight American seamen from the last batch to arrive at the prison to make an ill-planned break for freedom over the prison wall.

For most, their freedom was short-lived. The escape was made at night and dawn found six of them clamouring at the prison gate to be taken back inside.

A seventh ploughed through the snow until he reached a hut within sight of the prison. He was found here two days later by a hardy moorland farmer. Hungry and cold, the escapee was only too pleased to give himself up.

The last of the escapers suffered the fate of Ephraim, but his body was not found until the snow disappeared from the moor, three weeks later.

With the thaw, the inmates of the prison looked for something else about which to grumble. The black and white Americans were now far enough apart for the heat to have been taken out of their mutual antipathy and each side sought another target.

A natural and mutual choice was Reuben G. Beasley, the United States Government Agent – until the extra penny a day promised to each man was received at the prison. Suddenly, the agent found an unfamiliar popularity among his imprisoned countrymen.

At the same time, Governor Shortland announced that he was throwing open the prison market to the Americans.

There was method in this unexpected relaxation of the rules concerning the Americans. Shortland had received a letter from the Admiralty. In it, their Lordships pointed out that when peace came, the French prisoners would be returned to their homes. Dartmoor prison would be virtually empty unless new occupants could be found.

The letter confirmed that all the United States prisoners-of-war held throughout the country would be transferred to the Dartmoor prison. At present there were more than seven thousand of them, occupying prisons and hulks scattered about Britain.

*   *   *

The news of the entry of the Allied armies into Paris and the abdication of Napoleon Bonaparte reached the prison blocks before it was given to those who occupied the Petty Officers' Block.

Pilgrim heard the cheering as he stood with Tacy and Mary Gurney in the prison market square. It was cheering such as had never before been heard inside the prison walls. He guessed the reason even before an excited French inmate ran into the market square, shouting the news in his own language.

'What is it?' asked Tacy who had been startled by the outburst of sound.

'The war with France is over,' explained Pilgrim. 'The Frenchmen are cheering because they know they will be home in a matter of weeks. Some will be leaving within days probably.'

'Does that mean the war with America will end now too?' asked Tacy, suddenly concerned. 'Will you be going home just as quickly?'

Pilgrim shook his head. 'I doubt it very much. A separate peace will have to be negotiated with our Government. That could take many months.'

Mary had been listening with growing excitement. Now she said, 'Does this mean that Henri will be allowed to come back to England to see me?'

Pilgrim could see from Mary's uncertain expression that she was both excited and fearful at such a prospect.

'It does, Mary, although it might take some time for travel between the two countries to get back to normality.'

'It didn't stop Henri while we were at war, I doubt if it will now.' Grinning suddenly, she said, 'I doubt whether he'll be riding such a fine horse as when I last saw him.'

'The best thing you can do is forget all about that,' said Pilgrim hurriedly. 'If a whisper of what happened ever reached the ear of Sir Thomas I could say goodbye to any hope I have of getting parole again.'

'I'd never tell him,' said Mary, 'nor anyone else neither.' Fingering the locket she wore about her neck, she added wistfully, 'But it would be lovely to see Henri again.'

When Pilgrim said farewell to Tacy and Mary and returned to the Petty Officers' Block, he was surprised to find an air of silent gloom about the place. He had expected the French officers to be overjoyed at the prospect of returning to their homes.

He said as much to one of the officers who had been a friend of Henri.

'To go home will be a great joy, Captain, but think about it. Would you want to return to America as an officer in a defeated army? Would you not imagine that when your friends and your loved ones looked at you they were thinking that perhaps if you had fought a little more boldly your country might have been victors and not the vanquished?'

'I doubt very much whether anyone in France will think that,' said Pilgrim, at the same time fully understanding the feelings of the French officer.

'Probably not,' agreed the Frenchman, 'but we are proud men, Captain. There will be many times when we *think* that is what is in their minds.'

Another French officer had been listening to the conversation. Now he joined in.

'There is yet another reason why we are not celebrating, Captain Penn. Many of us who fought for France did so under the personal command of Emperor Bonaparte. We believe he is the finest general there has ever been. A masterly leader. Should we be happy that such a man has been defeated and stripped of office? No, Captain Penn, today is not a day for celebration for officers who fought for France. It is a day of sadness. I would willingly have spent the remainder of my life locked up in Block Four had it helped France to win the war.'

Looking as despondent as he sounded, the officer turned away, only to swing about suddenly to face Pilgrim once more.

'There is another matter you should ponder, Captain. It took vast armies to defeat France. Those armies have not yet been disbanded. What will happen if they are turned against America? It is my fervent hope that it will never happen, Captain, but one day you may come to know how we are feeling today.'

79

French prisoners-of-war began leaving Dartmoor prison only a few days after the war between France and Britain came to an end.

With such great numbers to deal with, the process took a great deal of time. It was two months before the final batch of prisoners was ready for repatriation. Their departure resulted in an unforeseen tragedy.

Before passing out through the gate, each prisoner had to present his bedding, no matter how tattered and dirty. The rule was 'no bedding, no discharge'.

One French prisoner discovered his bedding had been stolen and handed in by one of his fellow prisoners. Frantically he sought to explain this to the guard at the gate, but the militiaman was adamant. Unless he produced his bedding, the prisoner would not be allowed to pass through to freedom and repatriation.

Desperately, the man fled back to the prison block. Unable to locate his bedding, he tried to find something that would be acceptable in place of the missing items, but to no avail.

One final agitated plea to the guard went unheeded. The Frenchman was told he would have to remain behind. In a final act of near-insane desperation the unfortunate Frenchman, proclaiming to all and sundry that he had been a prisoner-of-war for eleven years and could endure no more, pulled a knife from his clothing. In front of the man who had so cruelly denied him his freedom, he slit his own throat, dying in minutes.

The last to leave the prison were some of the most senior French officers who had been on parole in neighbouring villages and houses.

One was a high-ranking general who had been housed in the home of a titled landowner. He returned to Dartmoor prison briefly while the final arrangements for his departure were made.

Here he was paid farewell visits by many of the gentry who had entertained him in their homes. In return they had been entertained by the Frenchman, who received a very generous allowance from his family, in the home of his host.

Among the visitors was Sir Thomas Tyrwhitt, newly returned from an extended overseas journey, made on behalf of the Prince Regent.

After paying his respects to the departing French general, Sir Thomas asked to speak to Pilgrim.

The two men met in the presence of the governor in that official's office and Sir Thomas greeted Pilgrim with all the warmth of an old friend.

'I had hoped we would never have to meet inside these walls again, Pilgrim. I wrote a letter demanding your release as soon as I heard your parole had been terminated. Then I heard you had agreed to Captain Shortland's request that you reside in the prison once more.'

Captain Shortland had been in charge of the prison

for some months now. Long enough to acknowledge the importance of the man seated before him.

'That is correct, Sir Thomas. When I first came here as a very inexperienced prison governor, Captain Penn very kindly agreed to set aside his parole and return, in order that I might better understand the problems of his countrymen. The arrangement has proved extremely satisfactory for myself and for the Americans. The problems I had were very quickly resolved. I am happy to say that Captain Penn will soon be able to take his parole once more. We agreed he would only remain in prison while he is the senior United States officer in my jurisdiction. As soon as the last French prisoner-of-war has gone, all American prisoners-of-war held in England will be brought here. There are at least two colonels among them. When they arrive, Captain Penn may return to Tor Royal, if you so wish.'

'Of course I wish it,' said Sir Thomas. Giving Pilgrim a mischievous look, he added, 'That is of course if you will wish to return to Tor Royal when you learn that Winifrith accompanied me from London. She tells me it is her intention to stay for a while.'

The last Frenchmen left Dartmoor prison in June 1814. Only then was it discovered that more than two hundred Americans had left with them.

They had used a simple enough ruse.

During their years of internment, some twelve hundred French prisoners-of-war had died, most through the various outbreaks of disease that frequently ravaged the inmates of the moorland prison.

Their deaths were recorded in a haphazard fashion, the bodies buried in unmarked graves on the moor beyond the prison perimeter wall.

As a result, it was a comparatively simple matter

for an American with a rudimentary knowledge of the French language to assume the identity of one of the deceased men and so be repatriated to France with his French allies.

Governor Shortland was furious about such a lapse of security. Angry accusations of complicity were thrown at Pilgrim in the privacy of his office, but the governor took no measures to punish the remaining Americans.

With the departure of the French prisoners-of-war, prison life improved beyond measure for the Americans. The governor was anxious to keep them happy.

They were allowed to move into the recently vacated blocks at will. In addition, they took on many of the tasks for which the Frenchmen had been paid. Carpenters, builders and artisans of all types came into their own, receiving an extra sixpence a day for their work.

Among many other tasks, they were employed fitting out the inside of the church, built but not completed by the French. In order to ensure they never took advantage of their new status, the prisoners were employed in teams. If any man escaped, the pay of his companions was confiscated – and it was paid some three months in arrears.

The result was that the prisoners now had a very good reason for preventing their fellow countrymen from escaping.

This was the situation in the prison when United States prisoners from all over the country began to arrive at Dartmoor.

Included among the first arrivals were the two colonels of whom Governor Shortland had spoken earlier. Both were regular army men – and neither had any time for a brevet captain of marines who had been used to commanding his fellow Americans inside the prison.

The two officers were of similar seniority. Each was

determined to become the man responsible to Governor Shortland for his fellow prisoners-of-war.

There was, and would continue to be, bitter rivalry between them, but one thing they were both agreed upon. Captain Pilgrim Penn of the United States Marine Corps had no place in their intended chain of command.

Within a fortnight of their arrival, Pilgrim found himself outside the prison gate, setting off to resume his parole at Tor Royal once more.

80

Pilgrim had told Tacy the time of his release on parole from Dartmoor prison. He had expected her to be waiting for him, either on the road to Princetown or, as on the occasion of his release with Virgil, at the entrance lane to Tor Royal.

To his disappointment, she was in neither place.

However, he could find nothing to complain about in his welcome at Tor Royal. The servants made him feel as though he was a member of the family returning home.

Sir Thomas, too, greeted him with equal warmth.

'I am very relieved you are out of that place once more, dear boy,' he said, shaking Pilgrim's hand vigorously. 'I had hoped the sad differences between our two countries would end with victory over the French. Unfortunately, there has been some bitter fighting on both sides of the Canadian border this year. I fear our generals are not ready for peace just yet . . .'

Breaking off, he led Pilgrim from the hallway. 'But we can discuss this foolish war later. You will want to clean up and remove the stench of that place from your nostrils. The servants have been told to heat lots of water and prepare a bath for you. I have also taken the liberty of having a new uniform made for you.'

When Pilgrim exhibited surprise, Sir Thomas said, 'A travelling tailor visited Tor Royal last week. His skill is well above the average. I have employed him on many occasions. I had nothing for him to do this time, then I remembered there was an old uniform of yours hanging in the wardrobe of your room. I had him copy it. I am quite certain you are going to be well pleased with the result.'

After thanking his generous and thoughtful host, Pilgrim was about to make his way upstairs when Sir Thomas called to him.

'By the way, a package arrived for you from London. It's from that agent employed by your Government to look after their prisoners-of-war.'

Believing the package contained documents about official business, Pilgrim did not bother to open it immediately. He would need to have it sent to the two colonels at the prison. They were responsible for official business now.

Not until he had enjoyed the unaccustomed luxury of a hot bath and put on the splendid new uniform did he open Beasley's package.

As he had thought, it contained a number of letters about prisoners, their numbers and the amount to be paid to them. But, to Pilgrim's delight, the package also contained two letters from America for him. One was from Virgil, the other from his mother.

He read Virgil's letter first. It told him how things were in the United States at the time of writing and informed him that the operation on his leg had been a complete success. He would always walk with a slight limp, but at no stage had the American surgeon contemplated amputation.

He went on to give Pilgrim the exciting news that he and Sophie would be parents by the end of the year. Sophie had written a conciliatory letter to her mother, giving her the news that she was to be a grandparent. The letter had been sent to her London address, so if she was not there it might take a while to reach her.

The letter went on to say that Virgil and Sophie were currently living in a very nice house in Washington, given to them by Virgil's parents who had taken to Sophie immediately.

Virgil further reported that in spite of the surgeon's skill, the United States Marine Corps had decided he would be unable to carry out the full duties of a marines officer. He had been promoted to major and pensioned off on half pay.

However, Virgil informed Pilgrim that he had no intention of leading the life of a retired man. He had been asked by Pilgrim's uncle to join the United States Diplomatic Service. This was the man who had been ambassador to London and a friend of Sir Thomas. It seemed he was now head of the Diplomatic Service!

It was the letter of a very happy man. Virgil managed to convey the fact that Sophie too was thoroughly delighted with her new life in America.

Such tidings did not prepare Pilgrim for the news given to him in his mother's letter. It concerned his father who had always prided himself on being an active man; a man of action. It seemed he had not been content merely to take care of Ohio's interests in Congress in Washington.

A strong band of Shawnee Indians had been carrying out some horrific attacks on settlements in the west of the state and the settlers had called for help from their Government. It was not immediately forthcoming and Pilgrim's father had organised a small army of volunteers and set off in pursuit of the Indians.

They located the Indians quickly. In a fierce battle the Shawnees had been comprehensively defeated. However, during the fight Pilgrim's father had been wounded in the head. As a result, he had lost his sight. Surgeons were unable to say with any certainty whether the loss was temporary or permanent.

Pilgrim's mother had contacted the same uncle mentioned by Virgil in his letter and asked him to bring his influence to bear in order to have Pilgrim returned to America.

It was disturbing news and threw Pilgrim's immediate plans into disarray. He was convinced his uncle would succeed in having him returned. There was a number of senior British officers in American custody. Their Government would be quite happy to have one of them returned in exchange for a junior American officer.

Before such an exchange was put into operation there was much that Pilgrim was determined to do.

When Pilgrim went downstairs, resplendent in his new uniform, he met Winifrith in the hall. After a quick, malevolent glance in his direction, she would have passed him by without a word had he not spoken to her.

'Mrs Cudmore, would I be right in thinking you've not yet received Sophie's letter?'

'What letter?' she asked sharply.

'I've just received one from Virgil. He says Sophie's written to you. As it hasn't reached you yet I think you should read the letter he's sent to me.'

'I don't care to read other people's letters, young man,' said Winifrith haughtily.

Pilgrim grinned. 'I think you might change your mind on this occasion. I certainly won't be able to keep the news to myself. I feel you ought to know about it before I tell Sir Thomas.'

Pilgrim watched as curiosity fought a duel with Winifrith's determination to remain aloof from him.

Eventually, as he had thought, curiosity won the day.

'Thank you, it's most kind. Perhaps you will be good enough to tell me which portions I may read and those I may not.'

Pilgrim pulled the letter from his pocket and handed it to her. 'You can read it all. It's a letter from a very happy man who has an equally happy wife. I'll leave you to tell Sir Thomas of the news it contains.'

81

Pilgrim set off to visit Roundtor Farm late that same afternoon. He left behind him a household buzzing with excitement. Everyone in the house was aware that 'Miss Sophie' was expecting a baby in far-off America.

All agreed it was a wonderful happening and were delighted that she appeared to have found happiness after the tragic loss of her first husband and the misery of life with her domineering mother.

Yet, for today at least, there was little of the domineering woman evident in Winifrith.

Sir Thomas told Pilgrim that after reading Virgil's letter she had hurried off to find him and tell him the news.

'I have never known her to be so excited about anything,' he said. 'She even *kissed* me! I cannot remember the last time she kissed *anyone*! Then she told every servant she met up with, before rushing off, declaring she was so overcome with emotion she needed to go to her room and lie down.'

Beaming at Pilgrim, he had added, 'You have made

Winifrith a very happy woman by allowing her to read your letter, Pilgrim, and when she is content life is easier for all of us!'

Sir Thomas had announced his intention of opening some vintage champagne before dinner that evening, to celebrate the news.

Pilgrim promised to be back to share in the celebration, but informed Sir Thomas he wanted to go to Roundtor first. He was concerned that all might not be well there.

Sir Thomas had suggested he should take a horse, but Pilgrim had preferred to walk. It meant he would have more thinking time, and he felt it was needed.

He had said nothing to Sir Thomas about the other letter he had received. Today was not an appropriate time to pass on such news. Nevertheless, the implications of it were immense. The Ohio lands owned by his father were extensive, to say the least. It would be impossible for a blind man to maintain control over them.

Pilgrim winced at the thought of such an active man as his father being blinded. He had a few minutes of very deep pity for the man he both loved and admired. The man to whom nothing had ever been accepted as impossible. It was a cruel blow.

As he walked across Dartmoor in the warm sunshine, Pilgrim's thoughts returned to the decisions that had to be taken – and with some urgency now. He had told Tacy often enough that he could not offer her marriage until the end of his internment was in sight.

That moment had seemed so far away even a few hours ago. But now it had arrived. Pilgrim knew that his uncle was not a man who put off things that needed urgent attention – and Pilgrim's father was his only brother.

Pilgrim had no doubt at all that arrangements for

a cartel with himself at the centre of it were already underway. He needed to set his plans and convince Tacy of the need to carry them into effect as quickly as was possible.

Roundtor Farm had always given Pilgrim an impression of being permanently busy. He could not remember an occasion when there was not someone working in the yard, or when they had not seen him approaching and hurried out to meet him: Tom or Joan Elford, Tacy or Johanna, or perhaps Billy or Emma. They were usually working and chatting, or calling across the yard to one another.

Today there seemed to be no one at the farm. Pilgrim felt uneasy. Then, as he went in through the gate to the farmyard, he heard a sound from the cowshed and headed in that direction.

Tacy was here, milking one of the cows, her cheek resting against the warm body of the animal as she worked.

She turned her face towards him as he stood in the doorway blocking out much of the light, and he saw the tears on her cheeks.

'Pilgrim . . . I'm sorry . . . I forgot all about coming to meet you this morning . . .' Suddenly she abandoned her task. Rising to her feet she threw herself at him and as he held her close she clung to him and began sobbing.

'What is it, Tacy? What's happened? Is it . . . your father?'

She nodded, but it was a few minutes before she felt able to talk. 'He collapsed in the kitchen early yesterday afternoon. I had to go to Tavistock for a doctor. He arrived late last evening. He said it's Pa's heart. There's . . . there's nothing he can do for him. He's dying.'

Pilgrim held her more tightly. 'I'm very, very sorry, Tacy. Is he conscious?'

Tacy nodded vigorously against his chest. 'Yes, but he can only talk with difficulty and can't move more than half his body.'

'Can I see him?'

'Of course. Ma's been with him for most of the day. We've decided that one of us should stay with him all the time. The doctor said . . . he said he doesn't know when it will be but . . . Pa can't last very long.'

Pilgrim knew this was not the right time to talk of any of the plans he had been making on his walk to the farmhouse. They must wait for another day – even though there might not be many days left.

He came downstairs after seeing Tom Elford feeling even more depressed about what the future held for Tacy and himself. The poor man was quite obviously deteriorating fast. He had been unable to say anything to Pilgrim that made any sense.

While Tacy went upstairs to keep her father company for a few minutes, Pilgrim sat in the kitchen while Joan made him some tea.

'It's a very sad business,' said the farmer's wife. 'It's something I should have seen coming a long time ago, but you tend to shut such things out of your mind in the hope it will never happen. There could never be a good time for such a thing to happen, but this is a particularly bad one. Young Emma will be having her baby any day now and I'll be needed over there. In the meantime, Billy can't leave the poor girl on her own, so we don't have him to help us out and one of us needs to be with Tom all the time. Johanna's over at Billy's too at the moment. I sent her there with a pie and some cakes I made.'

'I'll be able to help out now I'm out on parole once

more,' said Pilgrim. Aware of what was likely to happen, he added, 'At least, for a while. But it probably won't be very long before the Americans have left Dartmoor too.'

'When the end comes for poor Tom we'll need to leave Dartmoor as well,' said Joan unhappily.

'You leave . . . ? Why?'

'Because the tenancy of the farm is in Tom's name. The Duchy won't allow me to take over the tenancy. We'll have to go.'

'But . . . *where* will you go – and what will happen to the farm?'

'The Duchy steward will find a new tenant, but he won't find it easy. There aren't many these days prepared to take over such a farm. There's not enough profit in it. But it's a happy enough life for those prepared to work at it. Now, I'll leave you with your tea and go back up to Tom. You and Tacy haven't had much opportunity to sit and chat in recent months. She's had to take a lot on her young shoulders just lately. It'll be nice for her just to sit and be with you. She might not say too much about it to you, but she's missed you, Pilgrim.'

'I've missed her too, Mrs Elford. I don't think I realised quite how much until today.'

82

'You are very quiet this morning, Pilgrim. Did you drink too much champagne last night?'

Sir Thomas put the question to him the following morning, at breakfast. The previous evening had been one of celebration at Tor Royal. All the servants had been invited to drink a glass of champagne with their employer and his sister, to toast the news of Sophie's impending motherhood.

Later, a few of Sir Thomas's close friends had dropped by too.

'I seem to recall he was not saying very much last night either,' remarked Winifrith.

Her manner towards Pilgrim had undergone a remarkable change since reading Virgil's letter. It was not only because of the news that she was to become a grandmother – although this seemed to delight her. It was as much the manner in which Virgil had written about Sophie, and the life she was leading in America.

The letter had never been intended for her eyes, yet it made it very clear that Virgil was deeply in love with

Sophie, and that she was happy and had been made welcome by her husband's family.

The letter had also mentioned that Sophie had written to her. It meant that despite all the differences they may have had in the past – and Winifrith conceded to herself there had been many – Sophie had not broken all ties with her. This knowledge had delighted Winifrith more than she would ever confess to anyone.

'Do you not share everyone else's pleasure that Sophie and Virgil are having a child?'

'I'm *very* happy for them both,' said Pilgrim. 'It's not that. It's . . . I had another letter at the same time. From my mother . . .'

After some hesitation, Pilgrim told them the contents of the second letter.

Sir Thomas was immediately sympathetic, and asked why he had said nothing about it the previous day.

'Yesterday was not a day for such news, Sir Thomas,' said Pilgrim. 'There was far too much happiness at Tor Royal. I would never have forgiven myself had I allowed it to be marred in any way.'

'I have no doubt you were given all the sympathy you needed from that young girl at the farm you visited yesterday evening,' said Winifrith shrewdly. 'The one you invited to Sophie's wedding.'

'I couldn't tell her either,' Pilgrim said unhappily. He explained about Tacy's father.

'That is very sad,' said Sir Thomas. 'Very sad indeed. I knew Tom was ill, but I never realised it was quite so serious. He is a comparatively young man too. The family must be absolutely devastated.'

'They are,' agreed Pilgrim. 'And it isn't just the state of Tom's health they have to worry about now. His wife was telling me that if anything happens to him they will have to leave the farm.'

Sir Thomas nodded. 'That is so. The tenancy dies with Tom Elford. The Duchy land steward will need to find another tenant.'

'It seems very hard on the Elford family,' protested Pilgrim.

'Perhaps,' agreed Sir Thomas. 'But I doubt very much whether the tenancy laws are very different in your country, Pilgrim.'

'I don't think you need concern yourself too much with their troubles,' said Winifrith. 'You'll probably be on your way home before anything happens to this farmer.'

'It already concerns me very much,' said Pilgrim. 'You see, I went to Roundtor yesterday to ask Tacy to marry me and return with me to America when I go.'

'Good Lord!' Sir Thomas looked at Pilgrim in utter astonishment. 'I knew you had become very friendly with the Elford family – and Tacy is a splendid girl, of course,' he added hastily, 'but I never realised you were contemplating marriage.'

'The girl accepted you, of course?' The way Winifrith put it was as much a statement as a question.

'I never asked her,' admitted Pilgrim. 'She was far too upset about her father to discuss marriage and the possibility of leaving her family.'

'Yes, of course. If you go there today please offer Mrs Elford my deepest sympathy and say I will call on them at the earliest opportunity,' said Sir Thomas.

'You had all this on your mind last night, while we were celebrating Sophie and Virgil's good fortune?' The question came from Winifrith.

'As I said before, it would have been quite inappropriate to say anything about it yesterday.'

'There's rather more to you than is immediately apparent,' said Winifrith bluntly. 'If I am not very careful I will have to reassess my opinion of Americans. But . . . this girl? She is the daughter of a Dartmoor farmer. A tenant farmer. From all I have heard of your family, you should be looking for a girl of a much better class. One of the girls you met at Sophie's wedding, for instance . . .'

When Sir Thomas tried to protest at her outspoken criticism of Tacy, she impatiently waved him to silence and carried on talking to Pilgrim.

'I know you are not British,' she said, arrogantly, 'but your family is obviously wealthy, and considerable landowners, I believe. You need to be careful this girl is not marrying you for your money. You must also think of your own family in America. They will no doubt expect you to marry someone of whom they will approve?'

Managing with some difficulty to control the anger he felt at her words, Pilgrim said, 'Tacy has not yet said she'll marry me.'

Winifrith snorted. 'That is because you have not yet asked her. Of course she'll marry you. No girl in her position would refuse such an offer.'

'I sincerely hope you're right,' said Pilgrim. 'Because it's my intention to ask her to marry me before I'm sent back home. As for my family . . . my mother is from good farming stock – Quaker farming stock – and no one has ever said she wasn't good enough for my father – least of all my father himself. If I take Tacy home as my wife – and that's what I intend doing – she will be welcomed in my home as the daughter my parents always hoped they might have one day. She'll fit in very well with their ways because she shares the same standards they've always lived by: hard work, honesty and loyalty. Such qualities are things that are not restricted to any particular social class, Mrs Cudmore – any more than are prejudice and rudeness.'

Still fighting hard to control his anger, Pilgrim rose from the table. Turning to his host, he said, 'I will leave now, Sir Thomas, before I say something to abuse your hospitality. I will pass on your sympathy to the Elford family – and thank you.'

When Pilgrim had left the room, carrying his anger stiffly, Sir Thomas rounded on his sister. 'You deserved all he said to you, Winifrith – and a great deal more. Your behaviour was quite inexcusable.'

'I agree with you, Thomas,' said Winifrith enigmatically. 'I thought he behaved rather splendidly. Now we need to find out whether this farmer's daughter is worthy of him, do we not?'

Winifrith swept from the room with her brother's protests ringing unheeded in her ears.

83

As Pilgrim walked from Tor Royal to Roundtor Farm he was still angry with Winifrith, but the exchange with her had served to sharpen his perception of the situation as it affected Tacy and himself.

He wanted her to marry him. The sooner a wedding could be arranged, the better it would be for all of them, or so he reasoned.

The thought of marrying Tacy occupied his mind during the mile-long walk and he determined that today he would broach the subject with her.

His first question when he entered the Roundtor Farm kitchen was about Tom Elford. He was told the farmer's condition was unchanged. He was conscious, but finding great difficulty in communicating with his family.

Tacy was with her father and Pilgrim went upstairs to see them both. After greeting Tacy, he said 'Hello' to her father. There was a more positive response from the sick man today, but it was quite unintelligible.

Pilgrim remained in the room for some ten minutes,

before leaving father and daughter together and returning downstaris, to the kitchen.

Johanna sat in a corner of the kitchen, pale-faced and
close to tears. Speaking to her, Pilgrim said, 'It must
be time to start work. What's been done this morning
so far?'

Johanna shook her head. 'Nothing.'

'Nothing at all? Then I suppose you and I will need
to get out there and make a start, Johanna. We'll work
together this morning. First of all we ought to clean out
the cowshed, then give food to the cows and pigs. After
that you and I will collect the eggs. Come on, it's a long
time since I did any farmwork. Let's see how much I've
forgotten.'

Johanna was a reluctant starter, but once they began
she was able to put some of her unhappiness behind
her.

They had been working together for more than an
hour before Tacy came from the house to join them. By
then they were at work cleaning out the pigs.

When Tacy said she intended milking the cows, Pilgrim said he would come and help her in the cowshed.
To Johanna he said, 'You carry on and finish here, then
you and I will find something else to do together.'

Tacy protested that it would not take two of them to
milk the cows, but Pilgrim bundled her outside and
propelled her very firmly towards the cowshed.

'What are you doing?' Tacy protested, finally pulling
away from him. 'There's only work for one here . . .'

'I know all about that,' replied Pilgrim, 'but I need to
talk to you. I can't do it in front of your sister.'

'What's so important that can't be said in front of
Johanna?'

They were in the cowshed now, but instead of releasing her arm, Pilgrim turned her to face him. 'Tacy, I have

something very important to say to you, but first I want to ask you something. Do you love me?'

The blunt question took Tacy completely by surprise. 'What? What did you say . . . ?'

'I asked if you loved me.'

Tacy opened and closed her mouth a number of times before she finally said, 'I think you know the answer to that question, Pilgrim.'

'Tacy, this is too important for me to guess your answer. Do you love me? *Truly* love me?'

Tacy searched his face, seeking a reason for his question, but his expression told her nothing.

'Yes . . . Yes, I love you very much, Pilgrim. But . . .'

'There can be no "buts", Tacy. I love you very much too – and I want you to marry me. As quickly as possible.'

Tacy was in a virtual state of shock now and she stuttered, 'I . . . but . . . what are you saying? Why now? You have always said you could say nothing to me about the future until you were a free man! Why are you saying this now?'

'Because I'm likely to be a free man very soon . . .'

There, in the cowshed, with only the cow as a witness, Pilgrim told her of his mother's letter and of Sir Thomas's promise that he would have Pilgrim's return to the United States expedited as quickly as possible, once the request for his release was received.

Her thoughts in turmoil, Tacy said, 'But . . . I couldn't consider leaving the family right now.'

'I realise that, Tacy. But I want you to marry me as quickly as possible. Then, whatever else happened, you and I would be man and wife. Nothing that happened in the future would be able to change that.'

Suddenly, tears welled up in Tacy's eyes. 'Pilgrim, you'll never know how much I've wanted to have you ask me to marry you, but . . . but to ask me now . . . ! It's cruel! I can't leave the family the way things are right now – and if I were married to you then I would have to . . .'

At that moment, Joan shouted from the house, 'Tacy . . . Johanna . . . come here. Quickly!'

There was an urgency in her voice that caused both girls to run for the house. Pilgrim hurried after them.

When he reached the house, mother and daughters were upstairs in the bedroom where Tom Elford lay. By the time he reached the top of the stairs the farmer had taken his last breath and Pilgrim was greeted with a wail of despair from Tom Elford's family.

At the very moment that Tom Elford died at Roundtor Farm, Emma Yates gave birth to a lusty son at the Whiteworks cottage.

When she went into labour, Billy had wanted to run to fetch Joan Elford right away, but Emma realised the baby was in a hurry to arrive. Even as she was giving birth, she directed Billy to do all that needed to be done to bring their son into the world before he set off for Roundtor.

By the time Billy reached Roundtor Farm there was nothing more that could be done to help Tom Elford. His grieving wife set off across the moor to see what she could do to help the child that had been born into the harshness of Dartmoor life.

Behind her, Tacy told Pilgrim that although she wanted to marry him more than anything else she would ever want, she could not consider leaving her mother and Johanna now.

It was useless for Pilgrim to try to reason with her. Much as she wanted to marry Pilgrim, she believed it was her duty to remain to face the uncertain future with her family.

84

Tom Elford was laid to rest in the little churchyard at Sheepstor, on a day that Pilgrim believed God had surely intended for happier pursuits.

As the sombre party gathered about the graveside, the Reverend Cotterell's oratory was disturbed by the raucous sounds from a nearby rookery.

High above the tiny graveyard, the liquid notes of a high fluttering skylark rose and fell in a melodic requiem. Farther away, soaring over the tor that had given its name to the village, a young buzzard practised a broken-voiced imitation of the plaintive call of its wheeling parents.

In the churchyard itself, the cries of Emma and Billy's baby son reminded the mourners that, like the moor itself, there was a constant resurgence of new life, waiting to replace the old.

In addition to those members of Tom Elford's family who lived on and about the moor, there were many other mourners present. Among them were Sir Thomas Tyrwhitt and a number of moorland farmers.

Many had met Tom Elford on perhaps no more than a half-dozen occasions during his lifetime, but he was a respected man, a moorland farmer like themselves. One day they would hope for just such a gathering as this for their own funeral rites.

On the return journey to Roundtor, Emma and the baby rode on the farm cart with Joan, Tacy and Johanna. All the members of Tom's family had needed to leave immediately after the ceremony in order to reach their homes before dark.

Billy walked at the pony's head and Pilgrim rode one of the Tor Royal horses. The two dogs, left dutifully on the cart during the funeral service, now gambolled around them, enjoying the day, but there was very little cheer among the small Roundtor party as they reached the farmhouse.

Here, Joan had prepared a meal for everyone. While they were eating, Pilgrim posed the question that nobody seemed to want to ask.

The question of what the future held for them all.

'I'm sure I don't know,' said Joan unhappily. 'Tom's brother John said we can go to stay with them, but it's on the far side of the moor. I have a sister who lives over that way too. I haven't seen her for some years, but if her own family hasn't grown too much she might put us up for a while. Until we can find somewhere of our own, at least. Wherever we go, I don't want to leave the moor.'

'How long do you have before you need to move out?' asked Pilgrim.

'A month is usual. It depends whether they have anyone else waiting to move in.'

'I don't want to go,' said Johanna tearfully, her bottom lip trembling.

'There's no need for you to go until you're good and

ready.' Emma spoke so quietly that it almost passed unnoticed.

But Joan heard. 'What do you mean by that, Emma? How can we stay?'

Emma, breast-feeding the baby, looked up at Pilgrim uncertainly and he answered for her.

'First of all, let me say that this is *my* idea. It somehow didn't seem right that strangers should move into Roundtor Farm, after all the years of work you've put into it. Last night I had a talk with Sir Thomas. This morning, immediately before the service, I put my idea to Emma. I don't think she's even had a chance to discuss it with Billy yet . . . but the idea is this. Sir Thomas says that if Billy is agreeable, he'll speak to the Land Steward and see to it that Billy is offered the tenancy of Roundtor Farm.'

'Billy . . . ? At Roundtor?' Joan stared at Billy for long moments before shifting her gaze to Emma. Incredulity was gradually replaced by acceptance. After a while she said, almost as softly as Emma had spoken, 'Yes . . . Yes, you could do it, Billy. You and Emma. I'd like that. Tom would have been happy with it too.'

'You can stay here with us until you have something sorted out,' said Emma eagerly. 'You can stay for as long as you like, can't they, Billy?'

Billy had been listening in disbelief and still seemed unable to accept what he had heard. He could only look from one to the other, speechless.

'We couldn't do that,' said Joan. 'But what will happen about the stock? We'll need to sell it to get some money together for our new start.'

'Can I make another suggestion here?' asked Pilgrim. 'Once again, I've not discussed it with anyone because there hasn't been time. Tacy already knows that arrangements are being made to return me to the United

States as soon as possible. I've also asked her to marry me – but that was before her father died. She wouldn't agree to marry me then because she felt she couldn't leave the family while he was so ill. I could understand that, but I have no intention of losing Tacy. What I'm suggesting now is that you leave all the livestock and furniture – everything – for Billy and Emma. If Tacy and I can be married, you and Johanna can come to America with us. Once there you can decide what you want to do. If, as I'm hoping, you'll come to Ohio with us, I'll have a house built for you there. If that doesn't suit then *you* can choose where you want to live. I'll give you the value of all your stock and everything you've left behind here. You could open a store – or an eating-house, whatever you wanted. The standard of your cooking is a guarantee that you'll succeed. But you can do anything you want and I'll back you. What do you say?'

Pilgrim put the question eagerly, but Joan seemed to be finding it difficult to comprehend what he was offering her.

'But . . . why should you do all this for us?'

'Because I love Tacy. When I marry her, I'll be your son-in-law. I'll consider it my duty to make you happy in your new land and it will repay you in a small way for all you've done for me here.'

Joan tried to take it all in, but she failed. 'I couldn't do it, Pilgrim. It's frightening enough to think of moving to a new house on the moor. But to travel to America . . . ! No, I couldn't.'

'Yes you could, Ma.' This time the plea came from Tacy. 'It will be a wonderful new start for you – and for Johanna especially. You'll be able to put all the unhappiness you've known here behind you. Please . . . *please* say you will.'

'It hasn't been all unhappiness, Tacy. Your pa and I –
you girls too – have had some very happy times here, on
the moor. In fact, most years have been happy ones. It's
only recently, when your father's been so ill, that things
haven't gone well. That doesn't mean you can't marry
Pilgrim and go to America. You'll have my blessing.
You would have your father's too. We spoke about it
often before he died.'

'I couldn't do that, Ma. I couldn't go off and leave
you both with things the way they are right now.'

'And I couldn't leave your pa, newly laid in his grave.
It wouldn't be right . . .'

The discussion waged back and forth for more than
an hour, but Joan Elford remained adamant. She did
not feel able to leave England now, or in the foreseeable
future.

Tacy, although tearful, was equally convinced she
could not leave her mother and Johanna while their
future was so uncertain.

Eventually, bitterly disappointed, Pilgrim announced
he would need to leave in order to be back at Tor Royal
at the time decreed in his parole.

Tacy put on her coat to walk with him, not looking at
her mother as she followed him out through the door.

85

'I'm sorry, Pilgrim. Truly I am.' Looking as grief-stricken as she sounded, Tacy reached out and took Pilgrim's hand. They were walking from Roundtor Farm, Pilgrim leading the Tor Royal horse. 'But you must see that I can't leave Ma and Johanna, the way things are right now. I just can't.'

'There's no need for anyone to be left here. Your ma and Johanna would have a wonderful life in America, Tacy. You all would.'

'I know, Pilgrim. I want to marry you and live with you in America more than I've ever wanted anything. But I can't leave Ma and Johanna right now. Pa has been her whole life for so long. Now she's lost him. She's feeling afraid and alone. She also believes she'd be deserting him if she went away from Dartmoor. She won't always feel like this, I'm certain of it.'

'I know that, Tacy, but I have a duty to my father too. I can't wait for this war to end before I return to America. I must go when a cartel is arranged for me.'

He pulled her to a sudden halt. 'Of course, we *could* get married right away. Then you could come to join me in America as soon as you felt able to leave your ma.'

'That wouldn't work – for very many reasons,' she said unhappily. 'I'll certainly come to you in America, if you still want me to, when things are settled here, but that might take a year, or even more. I don't want to tie you to a wife who's going to be thousands of miles away for as long as we can look ahead. If you still want me when things are different, I'll come to you. We can be married there.'

'I'll still want you, Tacy, but it will be so difficult with us being so far apart – and our countries are still at war. That's going to make it doubly difficult for letters to go backwards and forwards between us.'

'I know.' Tacy felt every bit as unhappy as did Pilgrim. 'And I do love you – but there's nothing else I can do. Please, say you understand . . .'

Suddenly, the events of the day caught up with her and she began to cry. When Pilgrim held her to him she sobbed as though her heart was breaking – and to Tacy it felt as though it was.

Winifrith watched from her bedroom window as Pilgrim trudged to the stables to hand over the horse before walking up to the house. He looked thoroughly dejected.

She was in the hallway when he entered Tor Royal and she greeted him with, 'Well . . . when is the wedding to be?'

Pilgrim would have liked to ignore her, but it was not easy to disregard the presence of Winifrith Cudmore.

'There isn't going to be a wedding.'

'The girl turned you down?' Winifrith's surprise was not feigned.

'Not exactly . . .' In spite of the antipathy he felt towards this woman, Pilgrim found himself repeating the conversation he had held with Joan Elford and Tacy.

'It's refreshing to find a daughter who puts her duty

to her mother before her own happiness. Nevertheless, both she and her mother are wrong. But you look as though you have need of a drink, young man. Come along to the study . . .'

'No, thank you. I couldn't stomach either food or drink right now. If you'll excuse me, I'll go to my room.'

The Tor Royal grooms were locking the stables when Winifrith arrived in riding kit demanding that a horse be prepared for her to ride. 'Side-saddle, if you please!'

When the head groom protested it was not safe for Winifrith to be out riding alone after dark, she retorted, 'I have no intention of riding alone. You will come with me. I need someone to guide me to Roundtor Farm . . . and take me the easy way. My days of jumping horses over obstacles ended many years ago. As for it being dark . . . there is a wonderful moon tonight. Only a fool could lose his way. Come along now, I have no intention of spending the whole night wandering about the moor.'

Joan Elford was making up the kitchen fire when she heard sounds in the farmyard. She would have been in bed long before this had she not spent the last couple of hours affirming to Tacy that she would not change her mind and go to America. Tacy had just gone to bed in tears.

Feeling the loss of her husband more than at any time since his death, Joan was about to go up to the empty bedroom she had shared with him for so many years.

Wondering who would be about at this time of the night, Joan went to the kitchen door. When she opened it, she was brushed to one side as a large woman, dressed in stout riding clothes, swept into the kitchen.

'You'll be Joan Elford,' said Winifrith, turning to face the newly widowed woman.

'Yes. I . . . I don't think I know you . . . ?'

'Winifrith Cudmore, Sir Thomas Tyrwhitt's sister. Please accept my condolences on the loss of your husband. I lost mine many years ago, so I am aware of how you will be feeling at this moment. However, it isn't the dead I have come to talk about, but the living. I am here to prevent you making the same mistakes I have made during my years as a widow.'

'I'm sorry . . . I don't understand . . .'

At that moment, Tacy appeared on the stairs. Her eyes puffy as the result of too much crying, she looked at Winifrith in amazement. 'Mrs Cudmore! What are you doing here? Has something gone wrong at Tor Royal? Is it Pilgrim . . . ?'

'Nothing has gone wrong that can't be put right,' said Winifrith brusquely. 'I admire your principles, young lady. Putting duty before personal happiness is admirable in a young girl. However, I hope your sacrifice will not be necessary. Now, go upstairs again, if you please. I have come to speak to your mother. I would appreciate a little privacy.'

One did not argue with Winifrith. Tacy retreated upstairs once more, but she could be heard whispering an explanation of the voices to Johanna.

'Do you have another room, Mrs Elford? I would rather our conversation was not overheard.'

'Of course . . . We use it so seldom I'd almost forgotten it.'

Joan was flustered by this woman and her positive attitude to everything and everyone. Hurriedly she led the way to the only other ground-floor room in the farmhouse. It smelled somewhat musty but, asking Winifrith to be seated, she opened the window to let in some of the night air.

'Now,' said Winifrith, when the other woman had also

taken a seat on the edge of a wooden chair. 'You know why I am here?'

'I . . . I think so. But if you have come on behalf of Pilgrim, I must tell you I have no intention of changing my mind.'

'Only a fool would take such a stand before hearing what needs to be said, and I doubt very much whether you are one, Mrs Elford. Captain Penn told me of the proposition he put to you – and which you have apparently turned down. It is both generous and practical.'

'I realise that . . .'

Winifrith held up her hand and silenced the other woman before she could complete a sentence.

'Let me finish, please. When I lost my husband, I felt much as you do now, I suspect. I determined to take on the duties of both father and mother to my daughter. I believed it was what my husband would have wished. I was wrong.'

'I'm not trying to keep control of Tacy. I've told her she can marry Pilgrim and go to America, if that's what she wants.'

'So Captain Penn told me. I have no doubt you knew what her answer would be before you suggested it to her. She is a dutiful daughter, Mrs Elford, a girl who would not leave you at such a tragic time. Yet, knowing this, you have deprived your daughter of an opportunity to make a good – no, an *excellent* marriage. It would be a happy one too, I have no doubt. Take my very sincere advice, Mrs Elford, and change your mind. Unless you do, she will come to hate you for what you will have done, as my daughter learned to hate me. I can assure you, it will cause you more grief than you have for your husband at this very moment.'

Winifrith reached out and touched the other woman's hand for just a moment. 'If you put your own wishes

before those of your daughter, you will have lost more
than a husband, Mrs Elford.'

'But . . . I couldn't go away and leave him . . .'

'Your husband is in his grave. He is dead,' said
Winifrith, being deliberately callous. 'He can feel nothing.
You must think now of the future of your daughter – of
both your daughters. Where would they be better off?
What would your husband tell you? I suspect he would
not hesitate to advise you to look to the future. It does
not mean you need forget the past. But it must be kept
where it belongs. In the past.'

Joan was in tears as she said, 'But . . . who will tend
his grave? There will be no one who cares.'

'The vicar of Sheepstor is a caring man. He will care
for your husband's grave and pray for his soul too. You
do the best you can for his children, Mrs Elford. I don't
think you need me to repeat what is best for both of them.
In your heart you already know.'

Winifrith stood up. 'I must return to Tor Royal now.
Captain Penn is in his room, prevented from sleep by
his unhappiness. Do you have anything I can tell him to
ease his pain?'

The two women walked back to the kitchen before
anything more was said. Here, Joan Elford looked down
at the floor by her feet for a long time. When she looked
up, the tears had gone.

'Tell him he and Tacy can marry as soon as it can
be arranged. Tell him . . . Johanna and I will come to
America. Tell him . . .'

She had heard the stifled squeal of delight from the
landing at the top of the stairs and she said, 'No, Mrs
Cudmore. Perhaps you will allow Tacy to accompany
you home to Tor Royal. I think she might like to tell him
herself . . .'

Epilogue

Pilgrim and Tacy were married within the month. Three weeks later they, with Joan Elford and Johanna, were on their way to America. They settled in Ohio, where Pilgrim took over the running of the Penn estates and also followed his father into Congress. He was assisted in all he did by his English wife, who became one of the best-known and best-loved women in the young State of Ohio.

Meanwhile, in Europe, Napoleon Bonaparte escaped from his island exile and returned to France to raise an army and challenge the Allied armies once more. His return to power was short-lived, but it meant that Dartmoor prison once more rang to the sound of French voices.

The Americans in Dartmoor prison, numbering some six thousand men, had to wait for almost a full year before the prison was thrown open and they marched to freedom. Before this, they would experience great frustration and tragedy.

An attempt at a mass escape was foiled when the

tunnels they had intended should pass beneath the prison walls were discovered and blocked up by Captain Shortland.

Then, in December 1814, a peace document was drawn up between America and Britain. Due to the distance between the two countries, its ratification was not received in London until March 14th, 1815.

In April, the American prisoners-of-war were still locked up in Dartmoor prison – and their frustration boiled over into a riot.

It was in reality a very minor disorder, but it had disastrous consequences. The rioters confronted soldiers of the Somerset and Derbyshire militia and in an atmosphere of confusion and panic, the militiamen opened fire on the unarmed prisoners.

When the one-sided battle ended, seven Americans were killed and sixty wounded, two of these dying later.

This orgy of violence galvanised the authorities into action. Later that same month, many weeks after a ceasefire between the two nations had been agreed, the Americans began to leave for their native land.

For thirty-four years the brooding, granite prison lay empty on the great moorland of Dartmoor. Then it once again heard the clank of chains as it was brought into use as a convict prison.

It still serves the same purpose today. Men passing beneath the same archway as did Pilgrim, Virgil and Ephraim in 1813, still look up and see carved in the stonework, the words, *Parcere Subjectis* – 'Spare the Vanquished'.

Once inside, they tread the paths of long-forgotten men, many of whom would never again cast a shadow in the world outside the walls of Dartmoor prison.